THE ROMAN

Also by Barbara Gowdy

THROUGH THE GREEN VALLEY

FALLING ANGELS

WE SO SELDOM LOOK ON LOVE

MISTER SANDMAN

THE WHITE BONE

THE ROMANTIC

Barbara Gowdy

Flamingo

An Imprint of HarperCollins*Publishers*

Flamingo
An imprint of HarperCollins*Publishers*
77–85 Fulham Palace Road,
Hammersmith, London W6 8JB

Flamingo is a registered trade mark of HarperCollins*Publishers* Limited

www.**fire**and**water**.com

Published by Flamingo 2003
1 3 5 7 9 8 6 4 2

First published in Canada by
HarperCollins Canada 2003

This novel is entirely a work of fiction.
The names, characters and incidents portrayed in it are
the work of the author's imagination. Any resemblance to
actual persons, living or dead, events or localities is
entirely coincidental.

Biographical quotations about JS Bach are from a 1972 McGraw-Hill
paperback edition of Eva and Sydney Grew's book *Bach*,
copyright © 1947 by JM Dent and Sons Ltd.

The English versions of Rimbaud's poems are from *Arthur Rimbaud,
Collected Poems*, translated by Oliver Bernard (Penguin Classics 1962,
revised edition 1997) copyright © Oliver Bernard, 1962, 1997, and
are used by permission.

A catalogue record for this book
is available from the British Library

ISBN 0 00 715627 8

Printed and bound in Great Britain by
Clays Ltd, St Ives plc

For S.B.
and in memory of M.L.

The Romantic

CHAPTER ONE

The past isn't fixed if it isn't dead. How are we supposed to preserve it? If it lives—lives on in our memories, as we're always saying—then it can spoil.

Right after Abel died, every memory of him was so fresh that it seemed part of an ongoing story, like the smell of somebody's cigarette smoke or perfume lingering in an empty room. I kept expecting to hear his voice. Whenever the phone rang, my heart would race, as if it might be him.

But within a few days, these kinds of feelings were already fading, and then the older memories started to arrive. You hear about a flood; mine washed up at odd moments and in pieces, like debris from a plane crash. I'd be brushing my teeth and see his hands on the piano keys twenty years ago, his boy's hands with their blunt fingers and chipped nails, and for a moment I'd know, as purely as such a thing *can* be known, what his mother had meant when she'd phoned and said, "He's gone."

By Christmas, everything I thought about him seemed, in hindsight, to be a warning. I remembered how he had found desolate landscapes inviting and how reluctant he'd always been to defend himself. His soft voice, his sympathies, his damaged friends, his bursts of extravagant generosity all struck me as proof of his self-destructiveness.

He'd had a death wish, maybe he'd had it from birth. Perversely, it was why he could be so optimistic.

And then came months of memories connected to nothing and telling me nothing, and in this ambiguous atmosphere I stopped thinking of him as doomed. The memories themselves were generally pleasant. For at least a week I kept reliving the time he removed a splinter from my foot using surgical tweezers. Strangely, during this same week, a black Labrador retriever was accompanying me around town, appearing out of nowhere and trotting alongside me to the subway or the grocery store. As with the splinter memory, I had a sense of information being conveyed but through a medium too opaque to be grasped.

Now, three years since he died, I've gone over my memories so many times I hardly trust them. I can't imagine that every retrieval doesn't make for an infinitesimal alteration, an effect similar to photocopying the copy, and then photocopying the copy of the copy, and so on. Either that or all the handling turns to stone what were only questionable impressions to begin with, just one person's version of events. I hear myself talking about Abel, or about my mother, and I can't believe how confident I sound. I think, "Is that what really happened?"

I'm sure that my mother, at least, would say I'd got it all wrong. Abel might think I'd got it all wrong, too, except he wouldn't care. Looking back over his life never came easily to him, and for the sake of avoiding that ordeal—but also because, ultimately, he attached himself to nothing—he'd surrender to anyone's memories of him.

Even mine, these pawed-over resurrections. Even

though he knew I loved him too desperately ever to be a reliable witness.

The Richters move into our neighbourhood on December eighth, 1960. The reason I remember the exact day is that it is also the anniversary of my conception. While my mother still lived in our house, no December eighth went by without her mentioning the province-wide power failure and the bottle of French wine that conspired in the making of me. Early on I formed the impression that this event, which I knew centred on my father giving her a seed—shaken from a paper packet, I imagined, placed on her tongue— involved government interference and my father's lecherous French-speaking boss, Mr. LaPierre, and it is still true by the time the Richters show up, when I am ten, that I think of myself as having exotic origins and therefore something in common with these new, foreign neighbours.

I fall in love with Mrs. Richter immediately, Abel the following summer. I know how unlikely that sounds, a tenyear-old girl falling in love at all, let alone with a middle-aged woman. But to say I become infatuated doesn't describe the gravity and voluptuousness of my feelings. I trail after her to the grocery store and touch the grapefruits she has fondled. I gaze at her flannel nightgown billowing on the clothesline and am uplifted, as if by music. Under the pretext of welcoming her to the subdivision or asking if she gives piano lessons, asking if she heard about the white-elephant sale at the church—any excuse—I write letters advertising my availability and qualifications as a daughter. "Lend a Helping Hand!" I write on the back of the envelopes, as if this were my motto. Down the margins of the letters I draw pictures of a girl doing the dishes, scrubbing the floor, dusting. I draw the girl in bed, eyes closed under a quarter moon to illustrate that, unlike Abel, I would never leave the house in the middle of the night.

He goes out at least twice a week. We all know because she traipses around the neighbourhood calling his name in a wavering soprano that sounds unnaturally loud, as if she carried a microphone.

On the nights she wakes me, I sit at my bedroom window and wait for her to appear under our streetlight. I am always unprepared for how invincible she looks, so dramatic, wearing hardly anything against the cold, only a white lambswool wrap over her nightgown, boots but no hat, dark hair rolling to her waist, and when she calls "Abelard!" the Dingwalls' dog starts howling.

There are never any shouts for her to be quiet. Abel is adopted, and the only other child—a baby girl Mrs. Richter gave birth to years ago—had a hole in its heart and didn't live long. Among our neighbours it goes without saying that Abel's wanderings and her pursuits are connected to these events, not to mention the murky war history it is presumed must congest their household and from which a boy his age would understandably feel the need to escape.

Still, what I wouldn't give to hear my name called so indulgently, with such love. I attribute to her the highest qualities: kindness, wisdom, bravery. Somehow I've gotten it into my head that during the war she concealed Jewish children under her skirt and walked them to safety. Not true, although, as I will eventually learn, she did save a rabbi from being crushed to death when his jack gave out while he was changing a tire. This happened after the war, on a highway outside of Halifax. She lifted the car's entire front end. It isn't hard to believe. She is a muscular woman, and tall, a head taller than Mr. Richter and some fifteen years younger, making her ten years older than any other mother in our neighbourhood. Her clothes are from another place, as are Mr. Richter's, but whereas he comes across as dignified, she, in her laced-up boots and long, loud skirts, with her hair either hanging to her waist or roped around her head, could be a Spanish dancer. She has dark, heavy eyebrows and a big complicated nose flaring down to nostrils shaped like keyholes.

Obviously no beauty queen. But then beauty in mothers appeals to me not at all.

My former-beauty-queen mother left about a year before the Richters' arrival. Think of Grace Kelly and you have her, at least in appearance. In name, too. Her birth certificate says Helen Grace, but she always went by Grace.

Why she left and whether or not she is coming back we don't agree on, my father and I. He says, "She always loved and cherished *you*," the emphasis suggesting that I have the power to lure her home. It is possible she loved and cherished me; she never said. She *liked* me, I'm fairly sure of that. When she was doing the housecleaning, she wanted me there, not to help (her standards were such that they could be met only by herself) but for the company. "Louise knows when to keep her mouth shut," I heard her tell my father once. Another time: "Louise is good for a laugh."

She had a squawkish laugh I never got used to, and yet I courted it. For her amusement I committed to memory several hundred jokes taken from a book called *A Thousand and One Side-Splitters* that I'd found in my father's study. Rather than tell the jokes at random, I blended them into the conversation and thus skirted the risk of blurting out what I really thought. If she wondered, as she often did, why our neighbour Mr. Dingwall had married Mrs. Dingwall, I'd say, "For Mr. Dingwall, marriage isn't a word, it's a life sentence." Or, "Beauty is in the eye of the *beer* holder." Not that she and I talked much. As she pointed out, I knew when to keep my mouth shut. With me, she tended to go on about the world in general, and for some reason these pessimistic but dispassionate observations turned into rants if she happened to be washing the kitchen floor. She'd start wringing the cloth like a neck, slap it onto the linoleum and grind it around. What was she stewing about? It could be anything: women who sewed their own clothes, bottle blonds, slobs, the royal family. Babies.

Babies drove her mad. Well, not babies so much as other women's craving for them. She'd say that any cow could get herself pregnant, that the world was overpopulated thanks to people like "the grim weeper" (Mrs. Dingwall, who, after bearing two sets of twins, suffered a miscarriage and years later still burst into tears whenever she talked about it). She'd pull on her cigarette and glare at me sitting on the kitchen counter. Her pale blue eyes, admired by everybody, struck me as dangerously drained and therefore incapable of apprehending certain things essential to my well-being.

"Did you hear the one about the dumb mother?" I'd say.

(To give an example; I had a dozen baby jokes at my disposal.)

She'd wait. It was at the very height of a harangue, when her indignation was so great she could hardly speak, that she was most willing to be entertained.

"This mother was so dumb," I'd say, "she had to stop breastfeeding because it hurt too much when she boiled the nipples."

And my mother would squawk and throw triumphant glances around the room as if I had slayed not only her but a whole company of cynics.

During my season of pining after Mrs. Richter, I am haunted by two related facts: that her baby girl died, leaving the position of daughter open, and that she *chose* Abel, and not as a lumpen newborn, either, but, according to my father, as a fully formed three-year-old. "That one," she must have said. "The tall one with the curly brown hair. He is perfect."

Perfect for a boy, yes. For a girl, I count on her wanting somebody small and wispy, Abel's physical opposite. Otherwise, I imagine her wanting Abel and the girl to be alike, and there, too, I am ideal, since he and I have a lot in common. We both collect stones, we are only children, neither of us has any friends. I wish Mrs. Richter would walk past the school one day, during recess, and then she'd find out that Abel isn't the only one who migrates to the fringes of the yard and shakes the chain-link fence like a convict.

I am in grade five and he's in grade four, so I see him outside of class, at recess, going to and from school. Sometimes

I spot him in the ravine where, aside from collecting stones, I search for the Indian artifacts that a camp counsellor named Big Bear said could be found by the eagle-eyed and pure of heart. (In the summer months a children's day camp, Camp Wanawingo, establishes itself at the south end of the ravine across the river from the sludge factory, and the year that my mother disappears I spend two rainy weeks there pretending to be an Indian, that is to say, gathering twigs for the sputtering campfire and weeding a mostly dead vegetable garden planted by the campers from the first session.)

Abel snatches stones up fast, on the move. The steep wooded hillsides I can climb only if I grip roots and branches, he races up and down like an Indian, or as I have been led by Big Bear to believe Indians race: with stealth, scanning to the left and right. I wave at him, sometimes call "Hi!" In the ravine I have the courage to try to establish contact. He glances at me with the same alert indifference he confers on a squirrel. If he is nothing to me but a potential go-between, I am even less to him. I am that human over there. Skinny, female, no threat.

But one day, a Sunday afternoon in May, he approaches within a few yards of where I'm digging for artifacts down by the river.

"Hi," he murmurs. His eyes are on a pile of stones behind me, near the shore.

"Hi," I say, coming to my feet. "You're Abel Richter, aren't you."

He nods.

"I live on your street."

Another nod. The stones are what interest him. He

begins turning over certain ones, replacing each exactly as it was.

"What are you looking for?"

He keeps turning over stones, and then he finds something that he lifts so delicately I think it must be an artifact.

But it's only a toad. He holds it out to me. I step back.

"It won't hurt you," he says. He has a soft, oddly husky voice. An orphan's voice, I conclude, obscurely envisioning the beatings and damp living quarters that must have produced it. "I'll show you something," he says.

The toad's eyes are closed. In the palm of his hand it sits perfectly still except for the pulsing of its throat. "What?" I say finally.

"Just wait."

I can't bear to keep looking at it, so I look at Abel's forearm, which is slightly sunburned. I imagine Mrs. Richter examining his arms at the orphanage, and despite the ordeal he is forcing upon me, I have a pang of tenderness for him, as if in her stead.

"Come on," he says, giving the toad a little shake. Its eyes fall open. They shine gold, like sequins.

I am rudely startled. That something so glamorous could be contained in something so loathsome offends both my sense of fair play and my nervous grasp of cause and effect.

"Pretty spectacular," he says, "don't you think?"

Spectacular. A grown-up word. I remember what's at stake (my getting to meet his mother) and take hold of myself and say, "Is it ever."

He puts the toad back in its cavity and replaces the stone. "It's like a Martian toad," he says, straightening.

We look at each other.

His eyes, gold themselves but darker, the colour of maple syrup, hold nothing I perceive as cunning or sophistication, and yet I have a sense of being appraised by an intelligence superior to my own. A Martian intelligence. I look at the freckles on his nose, the dimple in his chin, his beautiful hair. I have a doll with hair like that . . . that heap of dark brown curls. His lips are plump and chapped. When he starts chewing the lower one I realize I'm staring and I shift my gaze to the patch on the knee of his blue jeans. "*She* sewed that," I think mournfully. I think of how Mrs. Richter toils away: mending his jeans, cooking from scratch (or so I imagine), hanging her laundry on the line instead of using an automatic dryer, draping her carpet over the porch wall and beating it with a broom, beating it again after her dog pulls it by the fringe onto the driveway.

Remembering that dog, I say, "You have a dalmatian, don't you?" my idea being to say that I love dalmatians and ask to see his.

"A dalmatian-hound cross," he says.

"Oh." I'm thrown off course. "Well, I love dalmatians."

"It's more hound than dalmatian."

"What's its name?"

"Cane. Short for Canine."

"I never heard that name before."

"Dogs are canines. Like people are humans."

"Like birds are a flock?"

He looks up as a crow comes flapping low over our heads. "Birds are avians."

"We had a budgie once."

It's true, we did, but I'd almost forgotten. It had a lime-green body and a lemon-yellow head. When my mother gripped it in one hand so that she could trim its claws, it opened and closed its beak without making a sound.

"We called it Bird," I say, as if this were in the same clever league as Canine. All it was, though, was that my mother never got around to settling on a name.

"Well," Abel says, still looking up. "I'd better get going."

"It died mysteriously," I say.

But he is already moving away.

After only two weeks, it died. After plucking out all its feathers, a few of which I kept for years in a pink plastic purse.

CHAPTER TWO

Abel died on my twenty-sixth birthday. Drank himself to death, everyone says, and so do I sometimes, it's just simpler. People know what you're telling them: he killed himself but he did it slowly and indirectly, maybe even unintentionally. They understand that there's probably a lot more to the story than you want to get into.

From the first crisis until the end took a little over a year, and during that time I saw him almost every morning, dropping by his apartment on my way to work. Usually he was still in bed, but he'd get up and I'd light him a cigarette while he stood swaying in his navy-and-white-striped pyjamas that made him look like a prisoner of war. They were clean, though, no buttons missing, a tear at the shoulder neatly repaired by his own hands, which, as he took the cigarette, trembled so badly I had to steer it toward his mouth.

I couldn't watch him smoke. I'd wander around and be heart-stricken by the vacuum-cleaner tracks in the carpet, the emptied-out ashtrays. He'd always been fastidious but this was different, this was him not wanting us—his parents and me—to worry any more than we already were.

He was so frail, so thin. Not gaunt, just sharper boned, his face suddenly sculpted, as if offering a preview of the handsome older man he would never become.

Why couldn't I save him? And if I couldn't, why couldn't

Bach or astronomy, why couldn't trees? "I'm not important," he'd say, and it didn't help, my saying that he was, or,
"All right, *I'm* important, what about me?" He'd give me a
look that made me feel as though I were begging him not to
run off with another woman. He loved me, he pitied me, I
could see he did, but there was a wash of absence over him
like nostalgia for a future he was already living in.

CHAPTER THREE

A hot windy night in late June of 1968 and I am on my way
to a party where I'll get pregnant.

Not that I know this or intend it.

My date is Tim Todd, son of Big Ben Todd, who used to
drink all the rye at my parents' annual charades tournament
and then invite the other husbands to punch him in the
stomach. Since he was their boss, a partner in the law firm,
they were all obliged to take a turn. Of course, they pulled
their punches, which only made Big Ben more belligerent.
"Come on!" he'd bellow. "Put some muscle behind it!"

Tim is small boned and careful, more like his mother. He
is my age, seventeen, almost eighteen, but with his drawn
face and hollow eyes he could pass for twenty-five. He drives slouched in his seat, brooding. Whenever I'm turned
away from him, as I am now (leaning out my opened window to imagine I'm in a convertible), he thinks my mind is
on Abel. Usually he's right. I can ignore his sullen spells.
What I dread are the apologies: long, pained speeches,
ambiguously tied to the writings of Ayn Rand or General
Ulysses S. Grant, about why, in fact, he actually respects my
attachment to a boy I haven't seen or heard from in years. It
drives me crazy.

The truth is, very little about him *doesn't* drive me crazy. I
have developed the habit of punching his arm, a persecu-

tion he takes unflinchingly, in the tradition of his father. When we arrive at the party and he rings the bell, I go to punch him just as he turns toward me, and somehow I end up socking him in the jaw.

"Oh, sorry," I say. "Are you okay?"

"What was that for?"

"The door's open. We're supposed to go right in."

Poor Tim Todd with his nursery-rhyme name and bad-tempered date. He is wondering what the two of us are doing here when we could be playing backgammon in the light of his tropical fish tanks. He's aggressively unsocial, but then so am I, or was, until yesterday on the Victoria Park bus when I sat beside a spectacularly beautiful girl who was inviting everybody around her, including the driver, to a party at her house in one of the wealthiest sections of the city. "Bring some cool guys," she said, addressing me specifically.

By which I knew she meant guys with long hair. Not Tim Todd, in other words, but as I thought I'd have nobody to talk to, I dragged him along.

I wish I hadn't. "Mafia money," he says when we enter the white marble foyer. He's still rubbing his jaw. When we enter the crowded living room and I say, "I wonder where Gena is," he snorts and says, "Not greeting her guests at the door."

The music, Grace Slick singing "White Rabbit," blows in from somewhere else, another room or from outside. "Oh," I say, "I love this song."

"Since when?" Tim says.

"Since right now." I start swaying to the beat.

"It's like an oven in here," he mutters. He lifts his chin and sniffs. "Is that marijuana?"

"I don't smell anything."

"I think it is," he says tightly. "I think it's marijuana."

"So what?"

He blinks at me, surprised.

"Why don't you get something to drink," I say.

"I'm not thirsty."

"Well, then go look around." I start squeezing through the group of people in front of us. "Try and find the aquarium."

"They have an *aquarium?*"

"Rich people always have aquariums." I give him a wave. "See you later."

I make for the marijuana smokers, a circle of them passing each other a pipe the size of a clarinet. One of the smokers (it's hard to tell from the back if it's a girl or guy) has hair like an explosion, bursting out in coils. The guy relighting the pipe wears a Che Guevara bandanna. A rush of desire goes through me, not just for him, for all of them, they're so shocking and nonchalant. I stand closer and inhale the smoke drifting my way. Maybe in a little while I'll work up the nerve to join the circle. I'm in a strange, reckless mood tonight. I have a tremendous feeling of anticipation. A girl cradling purple lilac blossoms taps me on the shoulder, and because she looks at me in a haunted, searching way, I think she has something important to tell me, *me* personally. But she only hands me a blossom and strolls off.

I bring the blossom to my nose. It smells like mystery, glamour. I glance back at Tim, who is standing with three other short-haired guys and cocking his head at an earnest listening angle. I turn before he can catch my eye. Holding the lilac like a cigarette, I walk toward a pair of open French doors and through them onto a veranda.

The music has switched to something bluesy featuring a flute, and down on the lawn about twenty people, Gena among them, do solitary dances around a fountain in which naked female statues pour water from jugs. The water shoots sideways into sashes, I can feel the spray all the way to where I'm standing. I go to the railing, and there is the whole golf-course-sized lawn, perfectly round bushes ranged across it like planets, causeways of white lights streaming overhead from the eaves of the house all the way to the aristocratic old willows that thrash at the back of the property. In order to get down the stairs I have to step over the legs of girls sprawled against boys and wearing dresses so short you can see their underpants in the veranda lights. They're friendly, these girls. "Sorry," they say, shifting sideways. "Can you get by?"

I go to the fountain and sit on the edge. Gena's dance is more like the dance of her long hair, which is really remarkable, jet black and sleek, like tar. While she slowly sways, it whips around in the wind. At one point she opens her eyes and looks in my direction and I lift a hand but I don't think she notices. I get up then, and make my way along the edge of the property. When I reach the willows I see water farther along, behind a stone wall, so I keep going. A gate is in the wall, and I pass through it and walk over to a wooden bench that is next to a wrought-iron replica of an old streetlamp. I sit and kick off my shoes. You can feel the coolness of the water gusting off the pond. There are water-lily buds like candle flames. Ducks, stationary as decoys, rock on the waves.

But they're not ducks, as I realize after a moment. They're geese. And the pond . . . the pond is a wide place in a creek.

"Nothing is what it seems," I think. I find this to be a deeply exciting idea. I sense a faint flash of light to my left, and I hold my breath, wondering if it's angels. For as long as I can remember I've been prone to seeing scarves of white light out of the corners of my eyes, especially when I'm keyed up, and I call them angels because the air around me seems to get somehow purer and emptier, a really spooky feeling. I have this feeling now. I turn.

Nothing. There's nothing.

No. There's a boy, tightrope walking along the peaked stones that form the top of the wall. Shoulder-length dark hair, bare muscled chest shining like tin. A tall, lean boy with a white cloth in one hand and a beer bottle in the other. When he gets to where I am he jumps, and that's how I know him, by the graceful landing.

"So it *was* you," he says. The same soft, hoarse voice, only deeper. He comes and stands in front of me. The cloth is a T-shirt. At my eye level a silver belt buckle catches the light.

I swoon.

He grabs my shoulder. "Are you all right?"

I nod.

"Are you sure?"

"I just got a bit dizzy."

He must think I'm drunk or stoned.

"Can you stand?"

"Why?"

"I want to show you something."

I come to my feet, dropping the lilac, and he tucks the T-shirt into his belt and takes my hand.

We go over to the wall. "There," he says, releasing me to point.

Up and down the stones, in the chinks, are dozens of green embers.

"What are they?"

"Glow worms. Look at them all."

"Glow worms," I say, remembering that they are the larvae of fireflies and that he showed them to me once before, down in the ravine. I say, "They're like little Christmas lights."

He twists around, his expression young and happy, and in his eyes I see him. There he is. He blinks and seems suddenly shy.

"I spotted you on the lawn," he says. "The back of you. I wasn't certain. But the walk. I thought, 'I know that walk.'"

I can't look at him. I look at his cowboy boots, his bell-bottomed blue jeans, the long slice of his thigh. In my mind, I'd kept him boyish, or at least not so tall. Handsome, of course, but not this handsome. I feel shaky, on the verge of tears. I move back to the bench and sit. "What are you doing here?" I say.

"The hostess is a friend of a friend's."

He has friends.

"How about you?" he asks.

"What are you doing *in Toronto?*"

"Oh." He sits beside me. "My dad flew out on business. I tagged along."

His dad. I imagine him bent over and feeble by now. When they left Greenwoods, Mrs. Richter said it was because the Vancouver climate would be better for Mr. Richter's rheumatism.

"How is he?" I ask.

"Fine. Working too hard."

Tears start streaming down my face.

"Hey." He touches my shoulder. "Are you crying?"

"I guess."

"What's the matter?"

"It's just that . . ."

"What?"

He offers me his T-shirt and I take it and wipe my eyes. "It's just that I never thought I'd see you again."

He glances at me and then down. He grips the bottle in his lap.

"I can't believe it," I say.

"It's been a long time," he says.

"Four years."

He takes a sip of his beer.

"Why didn't you ever write? I wrote you all those letters and you never once wrote back."

"I know. I'm sorry."

"But why didn't you?"

"I'm not . . ." He sighs.

"What?"

"I'm not good at writing letters."

He looks so tormented that I soften and say, "Oh, well, you're here now. Out of thin air." I take his hand and lift it. "Abel Richter. In the flesh."

He sets his beer on the grass and brings both of our hands closer to the lamp. His hands are big, his long fingers cool from the bottle. My fingers are thin and bony but I know he likes them because he said so once, he said I had the hands of a tarsier, which is a small monkey. Another time, in the same fascinated voice, he said my hair was like milkweed tuft.

Frowning, very intent, he runs a finger over the scar on my thumb. All the nerves in my body are flocked there.

"How'd you get that?" he says.

"Slicing onions." Without even thinking, I say, "I still love you."

The finger halts. We look at each other. And then we're kissing.

It's a long, unfrenzied kiss. I never knew you could kiss like this, holding each other so lightly, nothing moving except for your mouths. When it's over, I say, "We love each other. We never stopped."

He nods.

"We never stopped." I stroke his hair, feeling an immense tenderness.

He reaches for the bottle. "Want some?"

"No, thanks."

I nestle against his chest. Behind us, at the party, people sing along to "All You Need Is Love." Down here, the ringing of crickets rises like an electric mist I can hardly distinguish from the quivering of my own body. I feel as if I have been lifted out of my life. Only a few hours ago I was sad and unlucky; now I'm one of the lucky ones. The miracle of him being here washes over me like a spell, like voices murmuring into an anxious dream, "You're all right, you're all right." In a kind of trance, feeling immune now to anything but happiness, I start unbuttoning my blouse.

"What are you doing?" he says quietly.

"Taking off my clothes."

I stand and remove the blouse and drape it over the back of the bench. "I want us to be together," I say. I reach around and unhook my bra and let it fall on the grass. I am very serene, but excited, too. I know what he sees. Me fearlessly undressing. How white I am, the breeze off the water raising goosebumps on my skin.

He stands and faces me. He looks almost frightened. Hasn't he done this before either? "You're so pretty," he says, as if he wishes I weren't.

Nearer the creek, away from the light, we lie on the grass. Just before he enters me I am seized by a bursting feeling and I cry out, startled, then lose myself as the feeling branches down my legs in delicious, subsiding jolts. The pain of penetration is like a hundred tiny bones snapping, but it lasts only seconds.

"Are you all right?" he gasps. "Is this okay?"

Afterwards, after we have our clothes on, we smoke a joint. Holding our shoes, we walk across the creek and climb the bank onto a neighbouring lawn where we lie down and watch the sky, our old occupation. There it all is: the Milky Way, the North Star, the Little Dipper. He says Polaris, Cassiopeia, Ursa Major and Minor, Hercules, names he'd taught me and I'd forgotten.

What I see, though, isn't constellations, but a code, like Braille, all the stars positioned so as to tell us something. I ask him what he thinks it is and he says it's "Look. Look up." Only that. He rests a hand on my belly. I pull him toward me.

And then Tim Todd is hovering over us with his white spaceship face. He's the one who, driving me home, says, "How do you know you're not knocked up?"

CHAPTER FOUR

Greenwoods takes its name from the oak and maple forests that the developers have bulldozed, and like any other Canadian subdivision, it has the bungalows, the wide looping streets, the young housewives with their herds of children. As an only child I am regarded as strange and spoiled, and while I can't argue with strange, the presumption that I get whatever I want couldn't be more wrong. All I get are clothes. Which I *never* wanted.

Clothes is my word. My mother rarely uses it, she's more specific—she says "your tunic," "your organdie," "your pink cotton empire." Speaking of my clothes all together she says "wardrobe"—"Let's consult your wardrobe." Which we do, daily. We fret over it, tend to it, expand it, weed it out.

It contains at least twenty outfits, one for every school day in a month. Certain outfits are the child's version of the lady's. I have the leopard-patterned skirt and jacket, my mother has the leopard-patterned coat and Juliette hat. How do we afford this? My father isn't a full-fledged lawyer, he's only a law clerk, and yet he doesn't seem to worry about money. Where we get the clothes I know well enough. From the Eaton's catalogue, which guarantees our satisfaction. If something fails in the tiniest detail, such as a slight swerve in a line of stitches, back the outfit goes. The ease of these transactions strikes my mother as hilarious and unsound. She'll wear a dress for an entire day and then return it the next day to "those suckers."

My heart sags when the Eaton's truck pulls up and the driver climbs out and starts unloading. To spend an entire morning or afternoon watching my mother pose before her full-length mirror while she leans against the door frame or cha-chas with one hand on her stomach would be entertaining if I didn't know that my turn would come next. Never do I feel more like a scrawny genetic aberration than when I slowly twirl before my raving beauty of a mother while she laughs at how awful I look. "Like a pinhead!" Or, "Like Zazu Pitts!" Whoever *she* is.

Some of the girls at school get their clothes from Eaton's as well, which I realize when Julie MacVicker shows up in a reversible tartan kilt exactly like mine, but their mothers never go so far as to buy the matching blouse and jacket, the beret, the gloves. And nobody owns the volume of outfits I do. In my class, girls tend to wear the same dress at least twice a week. Girls with older sisters wear hand-me-downs. Small wonder I gall them.

Well, *I* don't, I am too unremarkable; it's my wardrobe that gets them worked up. And as soon as they hear about my mother's disappearance it's my wardrobe they seek to comfort. They pat my angora bolero sweater, my rabbit-fur coat, they beg me to wear my sailor dress and my umbrella-patterned flare skirt. A big bossy redhead named Maureen Hellier tells me a vote has been taken and I am now allowed to join a club she formed called the Smart Set Club, whose members do nothing except leaf through catalogues and magazines, cut out pictures of the models and paste the pictures into scrapbooks. At the Thursday-afternoon meetings, I pretend to gush over the child models my mother must have wished I looked like, the woman models she *does* look like. In the most recent Eaton's catalogue some of the models have on clothes I own, as Maureen never fails to notice. The captions, which she reads out loud, are especially excruciating for how they include descriptions of the outfit's ideal wearer: "Swirl-skirted charmer to suit *a pert little miss*." "Glamour cardigan for *the young sophisticate*."

"Oh, Louise!" she cries. "Cut her out!"

While I still have a mother, my clothes mark me for a show-off and imposter. "Miss La-di-da," Maureen says when I come to school wearing something new. The day I turn up in a lime-green cardigan that has a pompom drawstring collar and she says everybody knows only redheads are supposed to wear lime green, I take the cardigan off and hand it to her. "Go ahead," I say. "It's too big for me anyway."

She considers, then accepts, holding it by one pompom. "It's drenched in her germs," she informs the other girls. She carries it to a puddle and lets it drop.

I may as well leave it there. I know I'll never wear it again. My mother sends all our clothes, aside from underwear, socks and pyjamas, to the cleaners; anything too soiled for the cleaners she tears into rags or throws out. Easy come, easy go, and lucky me I'm not slapped when I spill grape juice on a white dress, but I am unsettled by how smoothly she slides from worship to indifference. A nice new sweater, that's what you live for. The same sweater with a stain on it never existed.

When I show her the muddied lime-green sweater, she stuffs it in the metal wastepaper basket and sets a match to it. "See how it burns?" she says. "Sizzling like hair? There's nylon in the weave, I knew there was. I knew that pure-virgin-wool label was crap."

The next day, in front of Maureen, I deliberately smear my pink chenille jacket with grease from a bicycle chain.

"You're a mental case!" Maureen cries, but at least I have graduated from contemptible to alarming.

After that I occasionally poke a pencil through a skirt, pour finger paint on velvet. My mother is irritated only by what seems to be the onset of a clumsiness from which I, the daughter of a woman whose many beauty-queen trophies include two for comportment, should be exempt. The carnage to my wardrobe she almost welcomes, since it necessitates buying the replacements. Here, of course, is the catch. Every time I ruin something (and if you ruin a blouse, you might as well throw out the matching skirt) I have to try on a half-dozen new outfits before she decides on the one that doesn't make me look like a pinhead.

What are these clothes for? My mother's, I mean. She leaves the house only when she has to, to shop for groceries, get her hair done, occasionally to take me to the dentist's or doctor's. Unlike everybody else's mother she doesn't attend church, she isn't a member of any committee or club. Her friend, Phyllis Bently, always comes to *our* house for coffee.

My mother is a woman who goes nowhere, both in the sense of being a homebody and then, when she packs her bags and leaves, of heading off to a place so undiscoverable it may as well not exist.

But the clothes don't accompany her. Even the police detective is flabbergasted by what she abandons—"Is that real mink?" She takes her jewellery, her beauty-queen crowns and trophies (which, alone, must fill one suitcase), a framed picture of her father as a young man in his soldier's uniform (chosen over the photograph of me as a baby that hung next to it) and the white satin bedsheets. It's my father's conviction that she has been enticed away by a "smooth talker," "a fancy Dan lady's man." And yet how can this be? When I am grilled for possible candidates, I can only come up with the Eaton's delivery man and Mr. LaPierre, whose first name is Daniel and who kisses her neck at our charades parties.

Every year up until the year my mother disappears, on the Saturday night nearest to January eighteenth, we invite people to our house to play charades. These people aren't neighbours or friends (my mother hates our neighbours, and she has only the one friend), they are the men my father works with and their wives, and January eighteenth is no monumental date unless you're my father and then you celebrate the birthday of Peter Mark Roget, the compiler of the first thesaurus. My father loves synonyms. He himself can hardly ever say "love" without adding "cherish" or "adore" but his delivery tends to be self-mocking and theatrical, he makes people laugh. My mother laughs when the words lean toward the racy or ridiculous. Now and then she surprises us with her own string of synonyms, a sarcastic burst. I remember her cooking eggs one morning, and my father asking, "Are they scrambled?" and her slapping his portion onto a plate and saying, "No, as a matter of fact, they're mixed up, confused, rattled," and so on, all the way to "stark raving mad," by which time my father looked petrified.

Ordinarily, though, her forays into his territory delight him, as does word play of any kind, from challenging verse forms (at nine years old I am acquainted with Spenserian stanzas and enjambments) to crossword puzzles, anagrams, clever song lyrics, horrible puns and his own name—Sawyer—shortened, when he entered professional life, to Saw so that he could introduce himself as Saw Kirk the law clerk. Scrabble he is addicted to, and he would prefer a Scrabble party, but my mother says the wives are too stupid.

On the morning of the party she goes to the beauty parlour as she does every Saturday morning, but instead of her normal pageboy she gets her hair pulled back into a French sweep, which shows off her tiny ears and her white neck, precariously long it seems to me, in danger of drooping. Back home, she washes and pin-curls my hair, then sets about doing her normal daily chores: scrubbing the floors and sinks, the toilet, vacuuming the carpets and venetian blinds, waving the vacuum nozzle through the air to suck up dust before it settles, but dusting anyway, her mood sour at the thought of the wives, with their dyed hair and girdles, tramping through her house. After lunch, while my father hides in his study, she gets down to the deep cleaning that charades night demands. With a paring knife she gouges out dirt from between the floorboards. She shines a flashlight on all the walls to reveal fingerprints, and here, because my eyesight is sharper than hers, I can be of assistance. We are a good team—zealous, aghast. "There!" I point, and she pounces.

Once the walls are immaculate, I am idle until it is time to pour pretzels and peanuts into bowls and dab Cheez Whiz into celery sticks. Late in the afternoon, while my mother tries on a half-dozen outfits before deciding what to wear, her spirits elevate to wry and I can make her laugh by telling some of my memorized jokes as if they feature the two wives she despises most: Mrs. LaPierre and Mrs. Todd. "If ignorance is bliss, Mrs. LaPierre should be one happy gal." "Mrs. Todd is so ugly that when she makes tea she can't even get the kettle to whistle." To me the jokes are either inscrutable or not very funny, and yet I know the humour is cruel and I know what a traitor is and when the wives arrive and compliment my dress and already sagging ringlets, shame makes me sullen and my mother flourishes her cigarette and says they should ignore me.

At the last party, less than two weeks before she disappears, she says to Mrs. LaPierre, "Miss Congeniality, Louise is not."

Provided I keep quiet, I am allowed to stay up and watch the game. There are five couples, including my parents, and whatever team my mother is on always wins. It's uncanny how quickly she can translate someone's smallest gesture into the title of a book or movie. You see one of the wives or husbands all geared up for a pantomime, grinning, preening, circling a fist at one ear ("Movie!"), holding up four fingers ("Four words!"), holding up three fingers ("Third word!"), then opening their hands and eyes to convey pleasurable surprise.

"*It's a Wonderful Life,*" says my mother, sounding a little bored, a little contemptuous.

"Right," the stunned person says.

"Objection!" one of the husbands quips. "Sustained!" from one of the others. "Request for an adjournment!"—that sort of talk.

The husbands joke and drink hard liquor, and the looks they sling my mother are empty and frequent. Mr. LaPierre, once he starts slurring, paws at her when she passes too close to his chair, follows her into the kitchen and slobbers into her neck while she absently swats his jowls. Mr. Todd invites her to punch his stomach; she is the only wife he extends that honour to. She gives him a soft sock in the mouth, and he kisses her knuckles. If such behaviour makes my father jealous, he doesn't show it. He's too happy on charades night, he wants everyone to have a great time. And of the husbands, he's the most handsome with his black hair slicked to his head like paint, a square-jawed man, tall and gangly, thick leaping eyebrows, long-lashed brown eyes capable only of drastic expression—exhilaration, terror, anguish—and pleasantly loose boned in his blue gabardine suit as he careens through a charade or strides around the room, which he does constantly, there not being enough chairs.

When the husbands play against the wives, my mother, who I notice never places herself too close to any of the other women, perches on the kitchen stool while the wives cram together on the chesterfield. The wives are all attractive enough, but next to my mother, with her delicate head, champagne hair and slim white limbs, they are swarthy and dwarfish and know themselves to be, you can tell by the looks they give her, which are uneasy or too bright or, in Mrs. LaPierre's case, when she believes herself to be unobserved, purely miserable.

As for my mother, she tends to look around the room. I imagine she is judging the effect of having rearranged the furniture and hidden her beauty-queen trophies in the broom closet. (One day I will decide that, at the final party, anyway, those looks were her debating whether or not our house made living with my father and me worth the tedium.) Why put the trophies in a closet, though, why not broadcast the official proof of her physical supremacy? Because she worries about the drunken husbands knocking them off our rickety end tables? Probably. Partly. And partly because she's shy.

Yes, shy. I say this not as a child watching the party from the floor, squeezed between the dining-room wall and the stereo cabinet, but as a woman only four years younger than my mother was when she disappeared. I know more about her life now; my father has finally told me. I'd always known about her being an only child, but I'd thought she had grown up in luxury and that her father had died after she'd left home. It turns out he died when she was only six months old and that the white house she'd once described to me—white walls inside and out, white tile floors— wasn't something she could have remembered because a year after the funeral Grandma Hahn sold it to pay off the creditors. She and my mother then moved into an apartment, a good-sized place in a respectable downtown Montreal neighbourhood, only by that time Grandma Hahn had given up on life. "Abandoned ship," as my father put it. All she cared about was going to seances so that she could conjure up Grandpa Hahn and yell at him for reading the books of French poetry she believed had brought on his brain cancer. Around the apartment nothing got done: unwashed dishes sat in the sink, a pile of dirty laundry sat next to Grandma Hahn's bed for so long that she started using it to hold her ashtray and bottles of pills. More than once the superintendent had to order a fumigation.

How all that would have humiliated my mother. But it's what gave her the gumption to make something of herself, or so my father believes. And yet she never bragged about her years as a beauty queen and then as a top professional model in Montreal. And it's not as if she showed herself off outside the house or even ordered clothes from exclusive shops. Compliments annoyed her so much that my father found it more profitable to be insulting. "*That's* a dress? I thought it was a gunny sack, a feed bag...." This being ridicule, she squawked. She knew what she looked like, and who in Greenwoods had enough taste to influence her own opinion of herself? Oh, she was arrogant, all right. But shy, too, I think. How to make friends was probably nothing she'd ever learned, and so with the exception of Mrs. Bently (another misfit) she steered clear of people and the possibility of their prying into her life, gossiping about her, judging.

But what *about* her squawk? Can somebody with a laugh like that be called shy? I suppose it depends on whether or not she hears herself. I don't think my mother did. She was tone deaf, which didn't stop her from singing along to blues songs on the radio (all those songs about women crying and carrying on—behaviour she would certainly have ridiculed had she encountered it in real life).

The effect of her laugh at the charades party, her first laugh of the night provoked by a particularly foolish guess or off-colour remark, was dramatic. The wives touched their throats, the men's heads snapped back. They'd heard that laugh on other occasions, they must have been expecting it. Still. From then on the atmosphere loosened, so it seemed to me. A laugh that can shatter glass tends to break the ice.

A couple of months after she disappeared, my father said—to my amazement—"I miss her laugh."

Disappear is the verb my father uses, for months the only one. To him, her defection is so sudden and unforeseeable that anybody who says she "left" or "ran off" gets a long-winded correction. Leaving and running off are not, he points out, the sort of actions that occur instantaneously. What my mother did—defrost the refrigerator freezer one day and put a goodbye note on it the next (in fact, there was no goodbye, only: "I have gone. I am not coming back. Louise knows how to work the washing machine")—he equates with the snap of a finger and the great mysteries.

He doesn't doubt that a man, fancy Dan, more or less hypnotized her. This man he quickly broods into complexity. "A towhead," he says, "a blond." He says that my mother has a soft spot for blonds like herself, and for moustaches, so Dan sports a weaselly pencil moustache. He's a "two-bit wheeler-dealer," he peels hundred-dollar bills from a fat wad, he files his nails, his ties are pure silk, his hats cashmere, Dan knows his fabrics, nothing but a "flim-flam man," and the worst of it is, my mother isn't the first happily married woman he has made disappear.

Or vamoose, or fly the coop, high-tail it. By summer, the sacred verb has spawned synonyms.

But even then, when his shock has slackened to gloom, my father sticks to his theory that she left in a thrall, on a whim: "You don't defrost the freezer one day, and the very next day . . ."

Yes, you do. Just as you buy a dress one morning and send it back the next. Not that I voice my opinion. I know as soon as I see her goodbye note that on charades night she was counting the days. After the last husband and wife were out the door, I said, "Mommy, you were the best player," and she waved away her cigarette smoke to get a good look at me, then stroked my face with the back of her fingers and said, "Honey" (she had never before called me honey), "nobody would believe you were my daughter."

If she took me with her, she meant.

CHAPTER FIVE

In the car, on the way home from the party, I don't defend myself except to say, "I had no idea he'd be there." Tim snorts, then falls silent, leaving me free to look out my window and think about Abel.

I'm meeting him tomorrow morning at nine o'clock on the Bloor-Yonge subway platform, but we have only an hour because at two o'clock he and his father are flying back to Vancouver. How will I bear to let him go again? "Oh, God," I murmur, and Tim, taking this for remorse, says, "It's a little late to be having second thoughts."

I glance over.

"I mean, Jesus Christ—" He punches the steering wheel. "How do you know you're not knocked up?"

We are parked outside my house. I'm still so stoned that I don't remember the car even coming to a stop let alone turning into the subdivision. I open my door. "Don't worry," I say.

"*I'm* not worried," he mutters.

Neither am I. Or at least not *very* worried. Off and on throughout the night his throttled "knocked up" slithers into my ecstasy, but then I reassure myself that I've just finished my period, I'm not in the fertile part of my cycle. I thrash around in bed, kicking off the sheets, amazed at myself, my womanliness. I'm not a virgin any more. I'm Abel's lover. Abel and I have made love.

Near dawn I get up and begin taking in the legs of my baggy, out-of-style blue jeans, and as we don't own a sewing machine, I stitch them by hand. After that there's no time to wash my hair, so I coil it on top of my head and hold it in place with two of my mother's teak combs. I find a charcoal pencil among her cosmetics and outline my eyes, then eat a handful of Corn Flakes straight from the box and race out of the house to catch the seven-thirty bus.

An hour and a half later, only a few minutes past nine, I arrive at the Bloor-Yonge subway stop. Abel is already there, leaning against a pillar and reading a newspaper. From a distance he looked like a twenty-five-year-old rock musician, but when I get closer and he glances up he looks his age, not nearly as self-assured as somebody that hand-some has a right to be.

"Hi," he says, dropping the newspaper into a garbage pail.

"Hi."

We smile at each other. I touch the jagged scar above his right eye from when a boy named Jerry Kochonowski threw a brick at him. He touches the combs in my hair. I take his hand and kiss it and he puts his arm around me and we walk out of the station into the torrid morning, the pave-ment already warm under my sandals. He's wearing the same clothes as the night before: the cowboy boots and bell-bottomed blue jeans, the white T-shirt, which smells of marijuana. When I tell him this he says it's a different shirt but that he had a joint for breakfast. A joint and a couple of bottles of beer.

"Really? What did your father say?"

"He was still sleeping, but he wouldn't have cared. Not about the beer, anyway. In Germany, even little kids drink beer. A watered-down version."

"For breakfast, though!"

"It's an old family tradition."

I laugh. "Yeah, sure."

"I meant my real mother."

"Oh." I let out a breath.

"She died. Just last month."

I come to a stop. "How do you know?"

"Somebody from the church phoned my parents."

"What church?"

"Where I lived. Before I was adopted."

When he was eighteen months old, his mother left him at an orphanage that operated out of the basement of a downtown Toronto church. Mrs. Richter was the one who told me this. She spoke of the place with a kind of reverent amazement, how clean and quiet it was, the high polish on the tile floors and the whiteness of the bed linen. "You could hear a pin!" she said, and, of course, she meant you could hear a pin *drop*, but for many years I imagined such a divine hush that the pins in ladies' hats and orphans' clothing hummed like tuning forks.

"I guess she still went there sometimes," Abel says. He reaches down and picks up a twig and begins rapidly threading it through his fingers—from forefinger to baby finger, back to forefinger.

"Did they tell you *how* she died?"

"No." Dropping the twig.

"But you think she drank a lot."

He shakes his head. "I don't know why I said that."

"Well, at least they told you she *died*. At least you know."

He nods.

My heart is bursting. I slip my hand around his waist. "There's a park near here."

He perks up. "Where?"

"In the next block."

Not a park so much as a lawn from when there were houses on this side of the street. A huge tree is growing in the middle, and we go over to it. "Oak," I say to impress him. I'm sure it's an oak.

"Beech," he says. He is gazing up at it, a passionate look on his face, and it occurs to me that out of all the millions of kids who are acting like nature-loving pacifists, he is one of the few with credentials. After the stitches came out of his forehead, when I was plotting revenge against Jerry Kochonowski, he kept making excuses for him, saying that Jerry's older brothers must have put him up to it, that Jerry hadn't meant to throw the brick so hard, and finally—a revolutionary admission for a boy back then—that he didn't like to fight.

He runs his hand along the tree's smooth bark. "Doesn't it remind you of those silvery living-room drapes from when we were kids?"

I embrace him from behind, pressing my face against his back.

There are some overgrown forsythia bushes in one corner

of the park and we hide among them to smoke a joint, then lie on the grass. He kisses the corners of my mouth, which feels lovely but seems too sophisticated somehow, too practised, and although I dread sounding possessive, I draw back and say, as casually as I can, "Are you going to tell your girlfriend about me?"

"What girlfriend?"

"In Vancouver."

"I don't have a girlfriend."

"You don't?"

He comes up on his elbow. "What about your boyfriend? What did you tell him?"

"Tim?" As I say his name, I can't even picture his face. "Oh, don't worry, that's over."

"He seemed pretty upset."

"We weren't even really going out together. Just dating sometimes. I never slept with him or anything."

Abel takes this in. "Last night was your first time?"

"You deflowered me," I say dramatically, with a little laugh. "You robbed me of my maidenhood."

He flinches slightly. Had he really thought I wasn't a virgin? Or is it just that I'm being too flippant? I used to think I could read his mind. "You love me," I told him years ago, before he even realized. "You love me very, very much."

Now, although I'm not as certain as I was last night, I say, "It was your first time, too."

He nods.

"Then we're even."

"So." He plucks at the grass. "So, are you on the pill?"

"No, but it's okay. It's the wrong time of the month."

He glances up.

"I can't be pregnant. It's impossible." I tug on his arm. "Come on—" pulling him back down.

We kiss. With the chance of somebody walking by, that's all we can do. We kiss and talk.

Or, from my end, it's more like an interrogation. Has he *ever* had a girlfriend? (He has gone out with a few girls, nothing serious.) Did they look like me? (One of them did, a little.) Was she thin? (Not *as* thin.) Does he still play the piano? (Every day. He teaches it now, too, gives lessons after school.) Does he still paint? (Not as much as he used to. He's doing a lot of pen-and-ink drawings, though.) Did he ever think of me? (All the time.) Why didn't he write to me, then? (We went through that last night.) What'll we do now? (He doesn't know.) What if, every Sunday night, seven o'clock his time, ten o'clock mine, when the long-distance rates go down, we phone each other, taking turns, he phones me one Sunday, I phone him the next? (Sounds like a good idea.) What if I visit him at Christmas? (Could I do that?) I have a part-time job at a women's clothing store in the Greenwoods Shopping Plaza. I could save for the plane fare.

He says, "You'd love Vancouver. It's so beautiful."

"In that case," I say, "maybe I'll stay on. I'll live with you and your parents. We'll tell people I'm your sister."

His face goes blank. I'm being too pushy, I think, and then I hear a clock chiming somewhere and realize he's reacting to that.

He looks at his watch. "I'd better get going."

"I love you," I say.

He runs his finger along each of my eyebrows. In the intolerable silence.

"Do you love me?" I say finally.

The finger moves down my jawline. "Can't you tell?"

"I need you to say it."

He taps my bottom lip.

"Say it. Say you love me very, very much."

"I love you *too* much."

I stare at him. "You can't." I grab his hand and start kissing it. "You can't. You can't."

"Louise, I've got to go."

"You can't love me too much. I'm a bottomless pit."

He smiles. "There's no such thing."

We walk to the subway. Every blade of grass, every red brick in the Victorian slums on the other side of the road is distinct and worthy. I know I'm stoned, but I feel as if I'm looking out through his eyes. He always saw the world as a lit-up place, a spectacle, and when he was with me, I did, too. But when he moved out West everything turned drab. Without him, I had nothing, whereas he had insects, lizards, cloud formations, music, whatever he turned his attention to. Still, if he loves me *too* much, then he has suffered more than I could have hoped for, and that makes his going back to Vancouver a romantic parting. Bearable.

CHAPTER SIX

When I dream about opening a box, and inside is nothing but another box, and that box contains another box, which contains another, and so on, I am more relieved than disappointed. In the same vein, when I see rows of vacant benches in abandoned sports stadiums and choir lofts, I don't try to picture them filled. Empty seats in empty rooms startle me with a feeling almost like love. It's not a sight I long for or am comforted by, it's a sight I seem to know. Deeply know.

I suspect this has something to do with how sparsely furnished our house in Greenwoods was. We had chairs and tables and lamps, just enough, and there were a few framed pictures and the beauty-queen trophies, but while my mother lived with us, all available surfaces were free of what she called crap and other people call vases, souvenirs, plants, knick-knacks. Her cluttering the refrigerator door with a goodbye note surprised me nearly as much as the note itself did. A few years earlier I'd taped a drawing of a farmer there, done in crayons at school and praised by my teacher for including eyebrows and a piece of straw sticking out of the farmer's mouth. My mother immediately took it down. "This isn't an art gallery," she said, dulling the wound with indirect praise (as she often dulled praise with an indirect wound).

If her disappearance is also behind my affinity for empty chairs and rooms, then the fact of my being an only child might be, too. For a couple of years I fantasized about having a sister, a younger one, but I found it hard to hold on to any clear idea of what she'd be like. Not like me. Not too beautiful, though, either. I couldn't even settle on a name. Kitty? Nadine? Laura? Kittys were clever and daring, and sometimes that's what I wanted her to be. But when I thought about combing her hair, I wanted her to be Laura, a name I'd got from a song I heard on the radio: "Laura! But she's only a dream . . ." I'm not sure where I got Nadine from. I liked the "ine" part of it; I thought it sounded glamorous.

I didn't need to ask my mother why she'd never had another baby. For as long as I could remember she'd been going on about women like Mrs. Dingwall overpopulating the world. But then one day I learned that there *had* been another baby. Almost. I found out only because my mother told Mrs. Bently, she just casually mentioned it as if it were something I already knew.

On Thursday afternoons Mrs. Bently and my mother would sit at our kitchen table and drink coffee, whisky-spiked in Mrs. Bently's case (she brought her own flask), and go through a large jar of Planters peanuts. My sitting with them, as I occasionally did if Mrs. Bently was still there when I returned from school, appeared to affect the conversation not in the slightest. Mrs. Bently went on using foul language and complaining about Mr. Bently, who was twice her age, bad-tempered and confined to a wheelchair. Why had she married him in the first place, I'd wonder. Except for her skin (she had a pock-marked complexion) she was beautiful in a dark, sharp-boned way, almost as beautiful as my mother.

About my father, my mother's habitual and sole complaint was that he let people walk all over him. "He's a doormat," she said. "He's the nice guy who finishes last." Mostly, however, she and Mrs. Bently tore to shreds other women and imagined their sex lives. When it came to their own sex lives they were cagey, although once Mrs. Bently said, "Hell, I'd rather eat an apple."

The closest my mother got to mentioning sex with my father was the time she told Mrs. Bently about this other baby. She said that right after she brought me home from the hospital, my father couldn't keep his hands off her, and when I was six months old she thought she was pregnant again. It turned out to be a false alarm, but in the days before she went to the doctor she lived in terror.

"I swear I could feel it growing," she said. "I knew it would be a girl. I could even picture it. Sawyer's bulging eyes and sallow skin. What a nightmare. I remember standing at the sink, washing the dishes and crying my heart out."

"I can't imagine you crying," Mrs. Bently said, "let alone your heart out."

"Well, I did," my mother said, sounding amazed herself. "I remember the tears falling into the dishwater."

As soon as Mrs. Bently was gone, I asked my mother what she would have called that baby if it had been born.

She shrugged. "Who knows?"

"Grace?"

"I hate people who name their kids after themselves."

"Phyllis?" After Mrs. Bently.

"Are you kidding? She'd grow up to be an alcoholic with a face like a can of worms."

"How about Laura?"

"What's with the third degree?"

But I couldn't stop now. "Okay," I said, "what if I die? *Then* you might have another baby. What will you call her?"

She gave me a long, empty look. "Louise," she said at last. "I'll call her Louise."

"Who?" I was confused.

"Who do you think? The baby."

"But that's *my* name."

"It's the only name I like. Why waste it?" She stabbed her cigarette in the ashtray. "Anyway," she said sternly, "you're not going to die."

The idea of my dying disturbed her! This was such unexpected, heart-swelling information (oh, I knew she didn't want me dead, I'd just never imagined her having much stake in my being alive) that the little-sister fantasy dropped from my mind completely. It never returned.

CHAPTER SEVEN

On Valentine's Day, my father's older sister, Aunt Verna, comes up from Houston to take over the housekeeping and to help find my mother. As a young woman, Aunt Verna quit her well-paying secretarial job to go to Houston and look after her parents (my father's parents, too, of course), who, in the belief that extreme heat thins the blood, had retired there six months earlier. They both died of heart attacks anyway, within weeks of Aunt Verna's arrival and only three days of each other. Grandma and Grandpa Kirk. Mutt and Jeff, my father says when we look at the black-and-white photograph of them on their wedding day, Grandpa being at least a foot taller than tiny Grandma. They were well matched in attractiveness, however, he with his dark hair and high cheekbones and she with her plump little face under a heap of blond hair stacked up like a temple. In the wedding photo they each hold a hand over their own heart, to seal the marriage pledge, so my father says, but to me that gesture, in combination with their severe expressions, has always been them warning the future, "Our hearts will kill us. You'll see."

After the funeral, Aunt Verna stayed on in Houston and got a job working as a secretary for a private investigator named Mr. Crimp. It was her idea to trim his business cards with pinking shears, and this so delighted my father that he took to keeping one in his wallet, along with a colour snap-shot of her being kissed on the cheek by the actress Sophie Tucker, whose kidnapped Siamese cat Aunt Verna single-handedly located, bound and gagged but alive, in a hotel laundry hamper.

People he shows the picture to invariably say, "Your *twin* sister?" and who can blame them? If he had hair the colour of concrete, short kinky hair identical to poodle fur, he would be her. I can't quite believe she isn't a man. Over six feet tall, spindly, no bosom, no make-up, not even lipstick, knuckles as big as grapes. Her three skirts, one beige, one brown, one dark green, are all made of some heavy, bristly material I've only seen before on chesterfields. Her luggage is the steamer trunk my grandfather brought as a young immigrant from Cheltenham, England, and when we first spot her at the airport she's carrying it on her back, people twisting around to gawk at the strong woman.

On the way to the parking lot she and my father each take one of the trunk's side handles. "What's in it?" I ask.

"Makeshift office!" she shouts. She shouts all the time and has a southern drawl, although she lived in Toronto until she was twenty-five. She calls me Lou-Lou and honey. It turns out I have met her once before, when I was three years old. "You were crazy about my varicose veins," she shouts. "Kept wanting to touch them." She holds out one pole-thin, stubbled calf entwined with what look like purple worms. "Well, honey, there's more to love now."

I step back.

She sleeps on the bed-chesterfield in my father's study. Her feet overhang the end, her snores travel the air vents

and wake me from nightmares of heavy machinery operated by men trying to break into the house. She works in the
kitchen, zooming from the phone to the table to the sink in
a wheeled wooden chair she brought with her because the
slatted back bows inwards and supports her creaking hips.
To fit it into the steamer trunk she took off the legs, which
she re-attached using her own screwdriver. My father has a
typewriter, a Remington, but there was room in the trunk
for her Underwood, so that's here, too. She says, "I've been
banging on this bunch of keys so long they know what I'm
going to write before I do. Like the old horse that always
knows its way back home."

I ask (thinking of Texas), "Do you have a horse where
you live?"

She guffaws. "*I'm* the horse where I live!"

I now remember my mother saying, "Verna's a card." So
she is, but of a kind I'm not used to in that the jokes are on
her. She's goofy, she crashes into the furniture, she buttons
up her blouse wrong and wears different-coloured socks on
each foot, and when I draw these mistakes to her attention
she slaps her own face and bellows, "What a lamebrain
dame!" She burns our suppers. Grease splatters the walls,
the ceiling, pots boil over, the spaghetti clumps into one
sticky ball "resembling a brain," as she herself points out. "I
could scorch ice!" she roars. When she laughs, her lips ride
up her long teeth and show a span of gum I look away from
with a shuddering feeling of having glimpsed nakedness.

But I'm glad she's here. She is so obviously devoted to
keeping our spirits up, although I'm hardly the pining
orphan she thinks I am. She clamps her big Texan's hands

on my shoulders and blares, "I'm on the case!" At least once a day she says, "Don't be glum, chum."

"I'm not glum," I say.

I ask, what if she finds my mother, and my mother tells her to get lost? "Some people don't want to be found," I say, quoting the police detective.

"Depends whether or not she left of her own volition," Aunt Verna says crisply, professionally.

"Whether she got lured away, you mean?"

"Somebody or something might have balled up her good sense."

"Fancy Dan," I offer.

"Maybe some snake in the grass, maybe not. Maybe a blackmailer. Maybe narcotics."

"What are narcotics?"

Her face slams shut. She didn't mean to let that slip.

Whereas I am careful never to let anything slip. *I* believe, even if nobody else does, that my mother left simply because she hated Greenwoods. She was always saying she did. One day, off she went, with a man or without, what does it matter, nobody ever bossed *her* around. Why should she have to come back? We're doing fine without her. We play Scrabble every night after supper, we watch television, and nobody ridicules the actors or the way the women in the commercials are dressed. When I wake up with a migraine headache, instead of forcing aspirins down my throat, Aunt Verna rubs my temples until I fall back to sleep. The possibility of my mother returning sickens me in the same way that the brewing end of the summer holidays always does, and to postpone and even extinguish the possibility, I am not above planting the odd false lead. When Aunt Verna asks, "Did Grace ever mention a place she had her heart set on going to?" I answer, "Australia."

"Australia?" my father says, dazed.

"Also Japan," I say.

The investigation is uproarious. Aunt Verna flips over the mattresses and seat cushions. She empties out all the drawers, closets and cupboards, paws through the contents, then just tosses everything back in. At first I am horrified, and I refold sweaters, neatly arrange cans on shelves.

"You take after your mother," Aunt Verna observes, and it's such a perplexing statement—I am *nothing* like my mother—that I let drop to the floor the opened box of white sugar I happen to be holding.

So the house is a mess, and I don't care, and my father doesn't seem to notice. Specifically, Aunt Verna is looking for a diary, a note, a map, a letter, a private keepsake, a suspicious doctor's prescription. We find none of these. But inside the white leather-bound Bible my mother was given as a child and claimed not to have opened in twenty years, we find her birth certificate. It's a break, of sorts. Aunt Verna maintains that if you run off and don't take your birth certificate, nine times out of ten you intend to create a new identity.

And that, she says, is "easy as muck." She tells us how you do it. You go to a city library and ask for the obituary pages from a newspaper published in the year you were born. You look for the death notice of a baby who is the same sex as you and who lived only a few hours or days. When you find such a baby, you record its name, parents' names, the exact date and place of birth. You take the information to a government office and pass it off as your own history. If anybody double checks, and usually nobody does, all they'll discover is that there really was a baby born when and where you say. You get your birth certificate. You soak it in coffee and bask it in the sun to give it an aged appearance.

"Grace wouldn't know to do all that," my father says, rasping his hand over his unshaven jaw.

Like the house and Aunt Verna, my father is a mess. Hair spiking out, nobody ironing his shirts. Nevertheless, he goes to work every morning, cleans his plate at supper, wins at Scrabble. He's more than coping, it seems to me. In the middle of the night when I wake from Aunt Verna's snores and hear the floorboards creaking down the hall, I don't picture him pacing in heartbroken torment (since I don't yet know that he misses my mother's laugh). He is a man who has flung himself around his study plenty of weekends simply out of frustration that one word in the cryptic crossword continues to elude him. He is pacing, yes, I picture that. He is punching his fist. Wanting answers.

"She might know," Aunt Verna says, regarding the fake birth certificate, "might not. All we can be sure of is that she had her secrets and kept them tucked under her hat. Anyways, her accessory might know plenty along those lines."

My father nods. "Small-time hoodlum." Because he adopts this slangy tone only when talking about fancy Dan, I immediately grasp who "accessory" refers to. "Fraud artist," he says, his eyes taking on a crazy gleam.

"Crook," I say. "Pickpocket." To me, this is no longer the true story it is to my father. And yet I somehow know that the more lost my mother becomes, the more substantial Dan must be, and so I tend to nudge the biography along.

As does Aunt Verna. "Never did an honest day's work in his life!" she bellows.

"Freeloader," my father mutters.

My father and I aren't much help. It's during the day, while we're out of the house, that Aunt Verna does her real work. She badgers the police, hospitals, modelling agencies, beauty salons, clothing stores, tracks down many of my mother's old Montreal connections, gets copies of her medical and dental records. She keeps notes and every morning types them up and sticks them in a copper-coloured accordion file labelled "Case Report: Helen Grace Kirk, née Hahn." For a couple of hours most afternoons, in her drab skirt, mismatched socks, paddle-sized penny loafers and man's tweed topcoat, she stalks up and down the streets of Greenwoods, banging on doors and interrogating housewives. On my way home from school I sometimes hear her booming voice—"I won't take but a minute of your time. . . . Sawyer Kirk's sister, Verna," and I hide behind bushes in terror of her spotting me and shouting, "Lou-Lou!"

Back at our house she lies flat-out on the living-room floor to ease her aching hips. I lie beside her. She has explained to me that an investigation is not so much a gathering of evidence as an elimination of the universe of possibilities. Little by little the universe contracts. She demonstrates by bringing her hands together in a strangling motion. She keeps me posted as to what can be ruled out: My mother is not an inmate of any Canadian jail or mental hospital. She is not wanted by the Mounties. Under her real name she has not taken out a library card or contacted the Canadian office of any Swiss bank. Since she is striking enough that, even if she were wearing a wig, people would remember her, it's a safe bet she has not personally picked up an airplane, train or bus ticket at any Toronto travel agency. She has not checked into any southern Ontario hotel or motel. She has not pawned her jewellery. Her accessory, her fancy Dan, is no local husband. Nor is he an Eaton's delivery man.

Over supper she repeats her day's findings to my father, and his reaction veers from anxious attention to brooding cynicism (aimed at Dan) to dumb astonishment. He says, finally, invariably, "I can't believe it." He can't believe she disappeared without a trace. Without a word, not even to Mrs. Bently.

He has phoned Mrs. Bently, of course. "That sneaky bitch," Mrs. Bently snarled venomously enough to convince him she knew nothing. She then came up with a couple of suggestions as to who should be tracked down: some heavy-drinking model from Flin-Flon, Manitoba. Jane or Anne or Joanne. And my mother's high-school sweetheart, a guy with webbed feet and the incredible name of Duck. Tom or John or Ron or Rob Duck. "Dead ends," Aunt Verna predicted, but she phoned every Duck in the provinces of Quebec and Ontario. She also phoned everybody my father phoned, including my mother's mother, Grandma Hahn, who for a decade has lived in a mobile home outside of St. Petersburg, Florida, and whose annual Christmas gift of three red-and-green crocheted place-mats—the exact same gift year in and year out—my mother always threw in the garbage but not before calling attention to the flaws and stains and saying, "That woman is out of her mind."

Coincidentally, Grandma Hahn said the same of my mother when my father told her the news. "Must be," she reasoned, "to throw away a steady meal ticket." She said my mother always did have a reckless streak. "Miss Anything Goes," she said. "Miss Free and Easy. Miss Devil May Care. Well, she's Miss Devil Take Her, as far as I'm concerned. Miss Don't Come Crying to Me When You Get Thrown in the Gutter," and the escalating pseudonyms did not go unappreciated by my father, who reported them with a kind of wonder.

Weeks later, in reference to that phone call, Aunt Verna says, "I, for one, don't think your mother is crazy or unhinged or anything like that."

She and I are lying next to each other on the living-room floor. After weeks of going unvacuumed, the carpet is opulent with colourful specks whose source I cannot imagine, also threads, hairs and dead flies kindled within the rungs of light that come through the venetian blinds.

"She's nothing but high-strung," Aunt Verna says. "Beautiful, skinny creatures often are, you know. Wound up so tight they snap."

"She never screamed or yelled," I say. "She never hit me."

This is simply information. It hasn't yet occurred to me either to defend her or to blame her or even to wonder very strenuously where she might be.

"Well, who said she hit you?" Aunt Verna shouts, all agonized. "My lord, I would hope she never did!"

Usually I lie on my side facing Aunt Verna, arms pressed against my ears to protect myself from her blare. Sometimes she'll give my leg a pat, clutch my knee. In my every utterance she detects either an orphan's sorrow or a daughter's loyalty. I say, purely speculating as to my mother's activities, "I wonder if she's curling her own hair," and Aunt Verna cries, "Oh, honey, I'd curl your hair but I'm all thumbs!"

One afternoon in early March she says, "Lou-Lou, we're at the end of our rope."

"What do you mean?"

"We're out of leads."

"We are?"

"It doesn't mean we close the file, though." She squeezes my knee. "The file stays open. UFO. Unsolved, Fully Open."

"So," I say, "she got away." I can't believe it. She's really gone.

"For the time being, yes, ma'am, she got away."

We lie there looking at each other. It takes me a moment to sense that her failure to find my mother is only her most recent disappointment. The sorrows of the homely spinster whose paramount achievement is that she remains hopeful, I perceive with the gauzy, unimpeachable understanding of my nine years. I say, a pain in my throat, "Don't worry" (because while I may not fully understand everything I am just then seeing, I *have* learned to recognize the glint in the eye that signals a person's imminent departure), "I know how to cook."

CHAPTER EIGHT

In my father's brain are an infinity of analogies attaching everything to everything else. Provided he is his normal, expansive self. After my mother leaves, in those first weeks, "everything" narrows to thieves and smooth-talkers, and "everything else" to sharks, snakes, leeches, rats, cockroaches, nuclear rain, hot-air balloons, silver tongues.

But as his attention shifts from the culprit to the loss, so the world cracks open to show all its pathos. Anything that goes missing, and in our overturned house much does, anything that falls to the floor, that runs out, such as cereal, he sighs and waxes over. Eating his meals, long back hunched in woe, he stares at the stool my mother used to perch on to fix supper. There it is, awaiting her. A pillar of faith. A bastion of trust. Or Time, all of it: the present because it is empty, the past because it hasn't changed, the future because it is unknowable.

And yet, like his sister, he remains ever hopeful, convinced that one day my mother will return to her sweaters and shoes, her blue Noxema skin-cream jar. None of these does he view as remnants. Even while they bring tears to his eyes he flaunts them as evidence of an absence merely temporary. Each little thing of hers is so incontestably *there* (if not exactly where she left it), so imperturbably itself that, apart from its siren call to her, the simple fact of its existence seems to sustain him. He will open the door of the hall closet and take one of her hats out of its box, any hat, it doesn't matter which. He'll turn it in his hands, study it. If it's her matador he'll remove the pin and say, "A cultured pearl." Enchanted, holding the pin to the light. "A real cultured pearl."

Around the time that Aunt Verna announces her intention to leave, he begins to retreat from this kind of idolatry. He stops speaking of my mother at all except to say "She'll be back" when Aunt Verna suggests her clothes be stored in the basement or donated to charity. Our two family photo albums, formerly kept on a shelf in the linen closet and filled mostly with studio shots from my mother's modelling days, he transfers to the locked bottom drawer of his desk. Out of fear that Aunt Verna will confiscate them for investigative purposes, or so I presume. Not for years will I imagine him looking at the pictures, immersing himself in memory, fury, lust. Blame. I'll be twenty-six and Abel will be dead before I'll understand that even blame can be a memento.

Before going away, Aunt Verna commits herself to one more search. For a housekeeper, a temporary one, naturally, since the file remains Unsolved, Fully Open.

"*I* can burn a meal," I argue and am told that, grown up as I am, there is a law against children my age being left by themselves. But I mustn't worry, I won't be overly supervised. The housekeeper will arrive midmorning, she'll clean, shop, make my lunch, wash our clothes, do the ironing and fix supper. As soon as my father gets home at six o'clock, she'll be on her way.

"No reason for her to lollygag here all evening," Aunt Verna says. "And you won't have to put up with her on weekends, either." She sounds annoyed, as if her successor is already throwing her weight around.

There are many applicants. On three different afternoons I meet the three finalists, who are like the three bears: one hefty and blond, one tiny and dark, one medium-sized, brown-haired and pretty. Or to put it another way: one a cheerful chatterbox, one a nervous near-mute (who lost the lining of her throat in a botched adenoid operation), one who says, calmly, about as much as you'd expect. I don't like the hefty, blond, cheerful chatterbox. She reminds me of Maureen from school, a covert persecutor; she talks a little too zealously of fattening me up. The medium-sized, calm, pretty one seems the obvious choice, until she is about to leave and I catch her glancing at herself in the hall-way mirror and see a momentary absorption, a receding from everything but herself, and a chill goes through me.

So it's the tiny, dark, nervous near-mute. Mrs. Carver. She may well be the best cook anyway. At her second interview (the interview that included me) she arrived with a cold meat loaf wrapped in aluminum foil, a potato salad in a Mason jar and a paper bag containing homemade short-bread cookies. Each of these offerings she excavated from an enormous navy purse and slipped to Aunt Verna in the manner of somebody passing smuggled goods. That evening Aunt Verna, my father and I wolfed the food down and pronounced it delicious (which it may or may not have been; as Aunt Verna pointed out, compared to *her* cooking, a dog biscuit tasted like a gourmet meal), but we still felt that Mrs. Carver's difficulty with speech, pitiable though it was, counted against her. Then, the next day, the pretty candidate fell out of the running and we came around to the view that a tiny, silent woman might be just what we wanted: not apt to be much of a disruption, not apt to bore us with her life story.

"You'll hardly know she's here!" Aunt Verna yelled. "You'll have to watch you don't step on her!"

April first, April Fools Day. My father takes Aunt Verna to the airport at dawn, Mrs. Carver arrives some time later, after I've gone to school. I come home at noon and don't have to shove the front door against a mound of boots and shoes. The landing is empty. The tiles gleam. Since these are unmistakeable signs of my mother, my knees buckle in the moment before I notice Mrs. Carver standing at the top of the stairs.

"Oh, hi," I say. I kick off my boots. My jacket I throw over the bannister, as I've got into the habit of doing.

Mrs. Carver starts wringing her hands. Her eyes, magnified by thick glasses into great brown puddles, circle wildly.

"What?" I say, frightened.

She jabs her finger in the direction of the closet. I think she's trying to tell me that somebody is in there. An intruder!

"Hang it up," she whispers.

"Oh." Breath returns to my chest. "Okay. Sorry." I open the closet door to another surprise. Coats on hangers. Hangers on the rod. Shoes on the floor, all lined up.

The kitchen is still in the throes of reclamation. The oven door sprawls open, racks lean against the wall. There are cups and plates all over the counter because she's laying down new shelf paper. But the table (where only yesterday you had to push aside unpaid bills, pencil stubs, dirty dishes and who knows what else to clear a spot for yourself) has nothing on it except for my lunch: a glass of milk, an egg-salad sandwich quartered on the diagonals, a few sliced carrot sticks, two small pieces of chocolate cake and an apple that has been cored and sectioned.

"Everything's cut into pieces," I observe, making the curious association between this fact and her name.

She motions me to sit.

"What about *your* lunch?" I ask.

She gestures at an empty plate and glass near the sink.

"You've already eaten," I say.

She nods. I feel an ember of satisfaction leap between us. I am beginning to decipher her.

I take my seat and she abruptly climbs on a chair and gets back to scrubbing the cupboard shelves. She is so small and jerky, like a little kid, but she's not young, she's forty-five years old. I know this from Aunt Verna's interview notes. I know that she was born in Kingston, that she is the widow of a bankrupt inventor (whose best ideas—the electric typewriter and the electric curling iron—were stolen out from under him) and that she has a twenty-two-year-old daughter who got married last June and is now living in Port Hope.

I await her signal: a questioning glance, or maybe she'll come right out and ask. I am accustomed, during lunch, to describing my day so far, either a fairly honest account, which is what Aunt Verna demanded, or—what my mother liked—a joking, exaggerated version. But Mrs. Carver just goes on cleaning, and by the time I have finished two sandwich quarters I understand that there will be no conversation. I slump in my chair, relieved. I take a good look at her.

From the back you can see that her short black hair is thinning, alarmingly so at the crown. And that it's dyed. In the pink terrain of her balding spot the white roots blaze. She wears the same short-sleeved yellow blouse she wore to her second interview. Stained under the arms, nylon. Her black skirt is a thin flannel. "Cheap fabrics," I think but without my mother's derision. Poor Mrs. Carver, with her dead failure of a husband and her unlined throat. Driving a beat-up sedan, forced to clean other people's cupboards in order to pay the rent on her downtown apartment. Several weeks ago, when Aunt Verna and my father were discussing the need for a housekeeper, I heard Aunt Verna say, "A girl Louise's age needs a woman around the place."

Now, here she is, the woman I needed. Better than a slob, I tell myself. Or a chatterbox. Better than that bossy chatterbox lady. I think of who else I might have ended up with. Mrs. Bently! Well, better than *her*. Better than an alcoholic with a face like a can of worms.

Within three days Mrs. Carver has the house in order, if not up to my mother's standards. For all her incessant cleaning, Mrs. Carver lacks the perfectionism of the scouring angel who appreciates that dirt floats before it settles and that it settles even on vertical surfaces. Thus you vacuum the air and walls. As far as possible you banish landing pads: picture frames, knick-knacks. The last thing you would ever do is transfer, from the back of a kitchen cupboard to the centre of the coffee table, an intricate china basket holding three china cats. The day this basket appears I pick it up and say provocatively, "A magnet for dirt."

Mrs. Carver rapidly wipes her hands on her apron, which I take for a rattled "Yes, I realize that and I'm not happy about it but I'm only trying to cheer the place up." Then she dashes back into the kitchen.

During my mother's reign I was tidy so as not to trigger a sarcastic remark. Now my fear is that I will be adding to Mrs. Carver's seemingly countless worries. Which isn't a very prohibitive fear. As I never did before, I leave things out on my dresser—a deck of cards, a pack of crayons. When I play with my dolls, I don't just dress them, comb their hair and put them back in the toy box, I carry them around, sit them in front of the television. I eat my lunch in front of the television and Mrs. Carver frets only if I neglect to use a plate, and even then I am given an opportunity to *perceive* that she frets (by her sharp intake of breath or her hands rubbing together) and to go and get the plate myself before she scurries into the kitchen to get it for me.

My father, who sees her for no more than a few minutes a day, keeps trying to engage her in conversation. I berate him afterwards and he looks stricken and says he's just being civil, for pete's sake. But he is touched by her, it's hard not to be. He helps her on with her threadbare twill coat. From the front door he watches her drive off in her hulking old Ford and wonders how she can see over the steering wheel.

And then, the very next afternoon, he greets her with,

"What's for supper, Mrs. Carver?" and she rolls her eyes behind her glasses and whispers: "Pork chops, peas, potatoes" (for instance), and he says, "How's that?" and she tries again: "Pork chops, peas, potatoes," which he still doesn't hear. Or he does and blithely goes on to ask what kind of potatoes, and I am driven to intervene.

"Scalloped potatoes," I hurl at him, "grilled pork chops, boiled frozen peas, okay?"

"Fine," he says sheepishly. "Sounds delicious."

I translate her gestures as well. In no time, I have figured out how to read her twitches and flutters. I attribute my success to the investigative techniques I picked up from Aunt Verna, who told me such things as: liars rub their noses and blink either too much or too little; people who aren't lying outright, but nevertheless have something to hide, rub their chins and look to the left. Watch the eyes, the mouth and the hands, Aunt Verna advised. I do, and it is clear to me that Mrs. Carver is both honest and full of secrets.

I have also concluded that she is afraid of dying of a heart attack from the shock of a loud noise, which is how her husband died. If I drop a spoon or slam a drawer, she clutches her chest, and she is constantly on high alert for a knock at the front door, even though knocks are rare and—on the odd occasion that they do materialize—brief, because in her canine way she has already heard the footsteps and has dashed down to the landing, whipped open the door and startled somebody into a silence *she* won't be the one to break. Other kinds of sharp sounds have her dashing to a window. If what she sees excites her, she'll hiss and wave me over, and we peer out like captives or spies.

Often the exciting thing is only a dog, or one of the Dingwall boys. "Only" to the uninformed observer. To Mrs. Carver, who knows about omens, somebody's black dog on your property is bad luck. A yellow dog is good luck, as is anything yellow: a yellow bird, the sight of a person in a yellow coat or hat, a yellow car going by. A yellow car with a licence plate that has one or more threes in it is an especially good sign—three, not seven, being the lucky number. There are signs almost everywhere you look. At the good ones Mrs. Carver smiles—the only time she does smile—and you get a glimpse of the dimples and straight white teeth that must have attracted her husband.

CHAPTER NINE

Thanks to Mrs. Carver I know about the Richters from the day they arrive. One Thursday afternoon in early December, coming home from a meeting of the Smart Set Club, I find Mrs. Carver in her coat out on the front walk. She points, and I turn and see, parked down the street, a big yellow van into which three men in yellow overalls have just disappeared. "Holy cow," I say at so much good luck. A mirror-fronted cabinet emerges from the van and coasts above a hedge that hides the men from view. The mirror is like a fallen sheet of sky, just hanging there, just floating along on its own.

"The O'Hearns must have moved," I say. Immersed as I'd been in my current serial daydream (which has me as a beautiful Egyptian princess and the members of the Smart Set Club as my slaves), I'd failed to notice the van.

"Oh!" gasps Mrs. Carver. The setting sun is caught in the mirror.

"It's like an orange," I say. A moment later the orange bursts and then vanishes as the cabinet reaches the end of the hedge and the men beneath reappear.

I look at Mrs. Carver, who, as you'd expect, is smiling. "They'll be nice people," I say about the new neighbours as I try to imagine how the good luck will reveal itself.

Mrs. Carver nods deeply.

"*Very* nice," I say.

The next afternoon, I come home from school to an unprecedented event: neighbours inside the house, and one of them—Mrs. Dingwall—being somebody my mother swore would cross our threshold over her dead body. The other two are Mrs. Dingwall's four-year-old twins, Gord and Ward, whom I find lying on our living-room floor in front of the blaring television. I cross the room and turn the volume down and they gaze up without expression. Because they are prone to such wordless stares and because they have no eyebrows, I'm not convinced they're sane. "You don't want to go deaf," I say, but it's poor Mrs. Carver I'm thinking of.

Now I can hear Mrs. Dingwall's voice rolling out of the kitchen. "Oh," she sighs when I enter and say hello. "Here's Louise." She gives me a few slow blinks. Her eyes are the same watered-down gold as the twins', ginger-ale-coloured eyes, but unlike the boys' they reach out to you, her entire round face reaches out, sloshed in gloom and craving. She has on one of her husband's old shirts over those baggy red slacks of hers, which my mother used to call clown pants and said Mrs. Dingwall should be shot for even owning let alone wearing outside the house.

I go to the other side of the table, where Mrs. Carver sits very straight in her chair and furiously kneads the red food-colouring bud in a bag of margarine while ogling the disaster of crumbs, sugar and spilled milk surrounding Mrs. Dingwall's coffee cup. Two lemon cookies are left in the tin, which was full at lunch. I ask if I might have one.

"Help yourself," answers Mrs. Dingwall. "I just came over for a little visit with Mrs. Harver here."

"Carver," I say.

"Carver? Oh. Well, that's me for you, deaf as a post on account of the drops I used to take for my ear infections. If it isn't one darn thing it's another. With this cold weather, it's my lungs acting up." She produces a cough. "Anyways, I was just asking what your dad might have told you about the people who bought the O'Hearns' place."

"Why would he know anything?"

"According to Mr. Dingwall ..." She glances at Mrs. Carver. "That's my husband of going on nineteen years. Bill. Anyways, he says that where your dad works they drew up the whatchamacallits, the mortgage papers."

Mr. Dingwall is a clerk for the government, and the nature of his job occasionally brings him into my father's law office.

"He worked late last night," I say about my father. "I'd already gone to bed by the time he got home."

"They moved in yesterday. You must have seen the van. I was laid up all day with my bad chest, missed the whole thing. All's I know is what Dora O'Hearn told me, and she only met them the one time. They're German, you know. Came here after the war, so that's going on fifteen years, but they still have those heavy accents. Dora could hardly understand a word the woman said. Greta, that's her name. That's the woman's name. He's Karl. Greta and Karl Richter. I suppose that sounds German, although I know a Greta from Strathroy, where I grew up, and there's a Karl at church, Karl Stock, he's an elder, and neither of them are German. I never met a Richter that I can recall. I said to Bill, I said, how do we know they're not Nazis? and he says, how do we know they didn't fight in the Resistance? Bill always looks on the bright side. They've only got the one boy and he's adopted."

I perk up. "Adopted?"

"And around your age, Louise, which threw me for a loop when Bill told me, considering as how they're old enough to be the grandparents. I'd go over, welcome them to the neighbourhood and all, but if they say Heil Hitler I'll keel over dead."

"I've never met anybody who was adopted," I say.

"Probably couldn't have her own babies for one reason or another." She turns to Mrs. Carver. "I don't know if you heard, but I lost a baby, it'll be four years come Valentine's Day. The doctors said it was because I was run ragged. I'm lucky to be alive." She presses her palms into her eyes.

Before I understand that she is crying, Mrs. Carver is out of her chair. She hurries around the table and pats Mrs. Dingwall's bouncing shoulders. "Should I get a Kleenex?" I ask. No response. I look at the calendar—it's thumbtacked to the wall beside the phone—and realize that yesterday, December eighth, was the anniversary of my conception. Feeling entitled, I take the last cookie.

It is Mrs. Carver who moves me, with her twitching face and her fast pats that I doubt can be very comforting. For Mrs. Dingwall I feel only exasperation. I nibble the edges of the cookie and look at her chewed-to-the-quick fingernails, the dirt in the creases of her knuckles, and feel a pure, ruthless disgust for the tragedies of adults. The mess they make of things.

The following morning, instead of waking up anxious, as I almost always do, I wake up happy. I review the events of the previous day to come up with a reason, but there isn't one. It's a strange, hollow happiness, almost unbearable. Joy, I think. Maybe what this feeling is, is joy.

I look at my bedside clock. Eight-fifteen. That isn't my father shovelling, then, so early on a Saturday morning. I get up and draw back the curtains. The glass is frosted over. With my thumbnail I try to clear a spot, but the frost is too thick, so I undo the clasp and crank the window open.

Snow lies like a pelt over everything. Cars, shrubs, hedges. The only tracks—and they cut across our property a couple of yards from the window—were made by a person walking over everyone's lawn, straight through the drifts. Who? The shoveller is Mr. Parker, across the road. In all the whiteness his red cap is a gash. "Day is breaking," I think, equating this fracturing event with the rasping sound of his shovel.

Even happier now because of the snow, I go to the closet and get my bathrobe and mule slippers. The bathrobe is the same style and colour as the one hanging in my mother's closet, and whenever I put mine on I remember how my mother agonized over whether we should buy the champagne or the cornflower blue. We ended up with the champagne because it matched her hair. "The blue matches your eyes," I pointed out and was told, coldly, that her eyes are delft.

I open the bedroom door, tiptoe down the hall. In front of my father's door I listen. His quiet snores remind me of men on television breathing through skin-diving nozzles or gas masks. I would like to burst in and tell him about the snowfall but I have never entered my parents' room when the door was shut, and now that my mother has left and I know my father misses her laugh, I'm afraid of finding him in some unimaginable grief-ridden condition.

I keep going, down to the bathroom where, after using the toilet and washing my hands and face, I brush my hair with my mother's glass-handled brush. I then apply a drop of her baby oil under each of my eyes and rub Jergens lotion into my elbows. I tell myself I am fighting wrinkles (according to my mother, I have the kind of thin skin that is prone to premature aging), but my mind is on the transgression, which I would never commit if I thought my mother might catch me and so, because I do commit it, I feel that there can be no possibility of her coming back. I am closing the lid on her coffin. Bang. (Although I don't think of her as dead.) I sometimes consider wearing her perfume and her scarves, except there is still my father to contend with, his incurable hopes.

A few minutes later I go down to the front hall and manage to shove the door open against a bank of snow. Just as I'd thought, there's no newspaper or milk bottle; I'd have seen the footprints of anybody who had walked up the drive. But it has become my morning routine to fetch the milk and paper and then to pour out two glasses of orange juice. On weekday mornings I percolate a pot of coffee for my father, but on Saturdays and Sundays, because he sleeps late, I don't bother.

I drink my juice, standing at the kitchen window. All the junk on the Dingwalls' lawn is buried, the broken tricycles and chairs. You can't even see the picket fence between our yards. There is no private property today, there are no eyesores. Under parcels of snow our four cedar trees bow down in postures reminiscent of Aunt Verna carrying her steamer trunk. When she said goodbye to me, the night before she went back to Texas, I drew away from kissing her, but only because I wasn't used to kissing people, and she said, "Oh, I know you're cross with me for leaving!" and her eyes reddened. I think of Mrs. Dingwall crying and of the German family—the Richters. I decide to walk by their place after breakfast.

By the time I am getting ready to go out, my father is up and stalking from window to window, flourishing a putty knife. "How will the fire trucks get through?" he exclaims. "The ambulances?" With the knife he takes swipes at the frost. "Don't have a brain seizure, Louise! Don't burst your appendix!"

"I won't," I say, getting into my snowsuit. He hasn't been this chipper since before my mother left.

"If you do, I'll be forced to operate!" Bathrobe billowing, hair on end, he flies down to the landing and scrapes at the long window next to the door.

"Could you?" I ask, surprised.

He considers. "I'd have to consult my atlas of human anatomy. Sharpen the paring knife." He presses his forehead against the pane. "Virgin snow," he says. "Pristine."

"Somebody walked on our lawn."

He scrapes a bigger clearing.

I say, "It was the German boy, I'll bet."

We discussed the Richters last evening. Mrs. Dingwall was right about their lawyer being somebody my father knows, a man from his office. Six years ago, my father himself was involved in drawing up the papers for the adoption of the boy, whose name he couldn't remember. What he did remember was how the Richters had wanted a baby girl, having lost their own baby girl ten years earlier, but at a church orphanage they found themselves taken with a boy, and not a baby either, a three-year-old. Which was better all around, my father felt. He said it would have been hard for people the Richters' age to get a healthy newborn.

"Abelard," he says now. "That's his name. Abelard."

I leave the house and plough my way to the trail of footprints. Once I'm in them, walking is easy enough. Everywhere, people have started shovelling. The older set of Dingwall twins, Larry and Jerry, are on the roof of their carport, heaving off shovelfuls of snow from each side and in time with each other so that what I see are white wings opening as the snow is thrown, folding as it drops. Behind them the sky is such a clear blue I feel drawn upwards, as a blue lake can draw you.

Sure enough, the footprints lead me to the O'Hearns' house. The Richters' house now. And there they are, Mr. Richter and the boy. Abelard. I own an old book, which was my father's when he was my age, called *Peoples of the World,* and consequently I am surprised that the two of them aren't wearing the short leather pants, suspenders and little Robin Hood hats that the father and son in the book have on. Abelard is dressed like any boy: blue jeans, brown jacket, brown cap. Mr. Richter, in a long black coat and black fedora, looks like a judge.

I move along to the Gorys' property, directly across the road, where I hope I'll be anonymous among a gang of little girls tobogganing down a drift. Abelard does the shovelling, strong, fast throws. Mr. Richter sweeps what is left behind. The thought enters my mind that the Richters adopted a boy so he could do the hard labour around the house, and it is just then, as I'm feeling sorry for him, that Mrs. Richter comes out the front door.

Although she is dressed nothing like the German wife in my book, she is nevertheless very foreign looking, very dramatic. Big for a woman, much bigger than her husband, and wearing a red-and-orange skirt and red shawl. No coat or gloves. It takes me a moment to realize that her hair, braided and twined several times around her head, isn't a brown hat. She carries a tray holding two steaming glasses, and Mr. Richter and Abelard stop work and each take one. She sets the tray on the porch wall. Abelard removes his cap, he's hot, and she ruffles his hair, which is the same dark brown as hers. While he and his father drink, she does a little dance step and swirls her skirt. She points to the pattern her feet have made in a dusting of snow, and there is a discussion, in German supposedly (over the screaming of the little girls I can't catch any words) regarding these patterns. Abelard puts his glass on the tray and stamps out his own pattern. Mrs. Richter wraps him in her shawl and they embrace before she unspools him. At what he says next she claps her hands and throws back her head, and then she breaks into song: "La, la, la, la, la, la, la." This I clearly hear. So do the little girls, who go silent. She sounds like a lady on the radio. She sings the same phrase again, no words, only, "La, la, la, la, la, la, la." Abelard glances in my direction. He puts his cap back on and picks up the shovel. Behind me the children resume screaming and clambering up the drift.

Mrs. Richter turns. She opens her arms at all the snow, and then she turns again and seems to be including in her delight the little girls, and me as well. In a burst of feeling, a kind of anguish, I smile back.

CHAPTER TEN

Was Abel always saying "curiously enough"? Mrs. Richter thinks so. A couple of months after he died, she told me that she found herself using this expression all the time, "the way Abel used to." She said, "You remember."

No, I don't, although I pretended to.

What I *have* noticed is how she and I and Mr. Richter seem to be acting like him in small ways, taking on his mannerisms and even his passions. He loved tree frogs and now so do I; I love their slim waists and gawky legs, I make special trips down to the ravine just to look for them. When he was nervous he'd pull on his earlobe. When he was listening to you, he'd cock his head to the right. Mrs. Richter now cocks her head. Mr. Richter pulls on his earlobe.

The examples go on and on. How he shelved his books: the tallest top left, the shortest bottom right, an eccentric arrangement I have been driven to adopt. And his smoking! None of us smoked, but within a week of the funeral his father and I were puffing on Player's plain, Abel's brand, and I observed that Mr. Richter held his cigarette the way Abel used to, between rigidly straight fingers.

As if his spirit flew piecemeal into the ether, and we gathered up whatever parts drifted back down. Despite ourselves, even against our wills.

CHAPTER ELEVEN

We never went to church, we never said grace or bedtime prayers, not in my family. To my mother's way of thinking, religion was the crutch of superstitious weaklings. God, Jesus, heaven and hell, that was all "a load of bull."

My father, who is the grandson of an Anglican bishop, once gave me a lesson in the layout of a church (the pulpit, the altar and so on) as well as in the elementary tenets of the Protestant religion, the idea being that I'd then have some understanding of what most of the people in our neighbourhood did on Sunday mornings, and why they would go to the trouble. Considering that I was seven at the time, I found the magical components—the birth of Jesus, the resurrection and angels—extremely compelling, and I asked my father how he could know that such things *weren't* true.

"I *don't*," he said.

I said, "Why don't you believe in them, then?"

"Because I believe in mankind" was his impenetrable answer.

As I would later learn, he also believes in the miracle of life. Life appearing out of nothing and returning to nothing. He has said that anybody who tries to explain this miracle (by way of a parable, for example) is engaged in a process of debasement tantamount to sacrilege, since the defining principle of a miracle is that there *is* no logical or even com-prehensible explanation.

Which, I suppose, amounts to a more civil expression of my mother's view.

But when I am seven, he tells me only that in our house-hold we are non-believers and that I should answer "secular humanist" if the teacher asks me my religion. I answer "Protestant." What's more, I pray, starting out with "Our Father, who art in Heaven" as I've learned to do in school, and then begging to be popular or invisible. From the day that I first see Mrs. Richter, I pray for her to want to adopt me.

I am sick with love. Sometimes, when I'm thinking about her, a white light wavers at the edge of my vision, an angel shape, a young woman angel. I call her the Angel of Love because she seems even more desperate than I am for Mrs. Richter to notice me. At her urging, I write letters:

"Dear Mrs. Richter. Welcome to Oaktree Terrace. I live at number 4. When we had the big snowstorm I heard you sing and I think you have a beautiful voice. . . ."

"Dear Mrs. Richter. When you go out in the middle of the night to call your son, don't think twice about waking people up. We don't care! We only wish you would dress more warmly. You don't want to catch cold. . . ."

"Dear Mrs. Richter. In case you're worried that other chil-dren will make fun of your son because he is adopted, I'll bet they won't. They don't make fun of me any more now that I am almost an orphan. My mother left and never came back. I don't think she will come back. Her last name when she was a girl was Hahn and that is a German name. . . ."

I walk past her house just before dinner, waiting until after dark so that I can see into the lighted living room. It is like no room I've ever laid eyes on, jammed with thrillingly romantic old-fashioned furniture: high-backed chairs, a ruby-red chesterfield, dark wooden tables, fringed lampshades of deep greens and blues. Also a piano, which Abelard—or Abel, as I've heard him called at school—always seems to be playing. ("Dear Mrs. Richter. I enjoy music very much. . . .") In the pocket of my jacket is the letter I promised myself I would stick through her mail slot—today would be the day—but I always balk. I don't even have enough nerve to step on her property.

I pray to run into her and then, when we pass on the street, I lower my eyes. Sometimes I turn and follow her, or "shadow" her as I have learned from Aunt Verna to think of such an activity. Unlike any other grown-up I know, she goes for walks. In her black lace-up boots and her calf-length purple cloth coat, she peers up at the sky and down into sewer grates, she stops and studies people's houses, and if the owners are out front, shovelling snow or carrying in their groceries, she smiles and waves as if they were her old friends. The owners wave back in a dazed fashion. I can hear their thoughts: "There goes that strange German lady who woke us up last night," and my heart stumbles after her protectively.

In March I learn that the Richters attend church. The news comes from Maureen Hellier, whom I overhear in the school washroom saying, "She drowns out the whole choir," and somehow I know that "she" is Mrs. Richter. A few casual questions get me the particulars. Nine a.m. service, St. Mark's Presbyterian.

I tell my father that I have to go to the Presbyterian church next Sunday because the school music teacher said I should hear the wonderful choir.

"Are you interested in choral music?" he asks with his sometimes frightening intensity.

I nod cautiously.

"Why didn't you tell me?" And I am forced to listen to excerpts from his record collection while he thrashes around, conducting. Then he says, regarding Sunday, "What the heck, I might even tag along, keep you company," but since my plan is to sit in Mrs. Richter's line of sight and look abandoned, I say that I've already arranged to go with a group of girls.

"Ah!" Nodding, plunging his hands into his pockets, and for the first time I realize that my living with Mrs. Richter might hurt his feelings and, just as upsetting, that he might fire Mrs. Carver.

Well, when the time comes I'll just have to figure something out. Visit him every day, I'll do that, I've always intended to do that. From the start, my vision of the future has placed him in the role of a friendly neighbour who is welcome to drop by. Mrs. Carver is his loyal housekeeper, and his Scrabble partner, once he teaches her to play.

As for Mr. Richter and Abel, they feature hardly at all. I picture them in other rooms or out of the house, except at meal times, and then I picture them eating quickly and in silence like hired hands. All my creative thought is consecrated to fantasies of Mrs. Richter and me. Together we bake cakes and pies, flour whitening our arms and identical frilly aprons. She teaches me how to play the piano. I braid her hair. She calls me Greta, after herself, "Little Greta." She lies beside me in my bed and tells me the story of her life, which (as I have imagined it) features her father being killed under the wheels of a cart, and her mother, sisters and brothers all dying of the plague, though she nursed them.

Choosing what to wear to the church absorbs me for several days. I must look well brought up but uncared-for. Shabby, but still clean and respectable. I finally settle on a yellow wool dress (yellow for luck) with pale green eyelet embroidery encircling the wrists and neck. I've grown out of it, as I have most of my clothes, and this alone suggests at least some neglect, although not enough to attract attention. On Saturday afternoon, while my father is at the hardware store, I let the hem down in several places and rip a few holes in the embroidery. I plan to vandalize the matching yellow coat as well, but lose heart when I remember the morning I wore it to the dentist's and my father said, "That colour suits you down to the ground."

My mother, that morning, wore her white fox-fur stole, and thinking of the stole, its repulsive head, I go down the hall to my parents' bedroom, open the cedar chest and pull it out from under a pile of blankets.

I try tearing the head off right there but it won't give. I drag it to my father's study, get a pair of scissors from his desk and start cutting. Not an easy job through such thick fur, and when at last the head falls, the pointed nose hitting my stockinged foot, I feel deliberately struck, and I loop a handful of fur around one of the scissor blades and push the blade through. I do it again, a third time, then I hurl the stole across the room. I snatch up the head and hurl that, too.

Bits of fur toss in the draft from the heat vents. The stole slouches against a bookcase. The head has landed on the filing cabinet and it lies face up, one black beady eye aimed my way. "Who cares?" I think furiously.

Not my mother, that's for sure. My father would, if he found out. Which he won't. He never paws through her things any more. I suspect he no longer even knows, as I do, to the hairpin, exactly what her things consist of.

I get a paper grocery bag and put the head and stray fur inside it and then stuff the bag in the outside garbage pail. Back in my bedroom, I try on the stole and conclude that it's just right: tattered, a wreck, really, and yet genuine fox fur, after all. I think that instead of a hat I should wear one of my mother's kerchiefs so that I'll look more German.

The next morning I am up at a quarter to seven. Without turning on a light, I use the bathroom and tiptoe down to the kitchen where I pour myself a bowl of cereal, but my stomach heaves at the prospect of eating. I sit at the table, chewing the sides of my thumbnail.

I haven't slept well. I kept waking up from bad dreams. Once, it was Mrs. Richter calling for Abel that woke me, and I went to the window and watched her swell out of the darkness. Another time I bolted upright at the thought of the collection plate, and I got out of bed and shook two quarters from my piggy bank and wrapped them in a handkerchief, which I tucked into the pocket of the yellow coat.

I pour my untouched cereal into the sink and return to

the bedroom. Although it's only seven-fifteen, I put on the yellow dress and a red kerchief, red to match Mrs. Richter's shawl. I sit on the edge of the bed. After a few minutes I feel cold and I wrap myself in the stole and lie down, just my upper body, with the stole under my cheek.

And in the fur, I smell my mother. The faintest whiff—a dead-roses blend of perfume and cigarette smoke—but startling for being so intimately and unambiguously her.

I push the stole onto the floor. "She's gone," I think, awed. Oh, I know she has left and is never coming back. What has just struck me is the corollary: I will never see her again.

I say it out loud: "I will never see her again," and the room seems to dilate, and I smell the bleach Mrs. Carver uses to whiten the sheets, and it's as if I'm being offered an atmosphere open and antiseptic enough that I might dwell on her without conjuring her back into our lives. Almost nostalgically, I remember the silver satin scooped-back dress she wore one New Year's Eve. I picture something I never witnessed: her smiling and waving goodbye. I let that image glide away until all I see is a tiny white-gloved hand fluttering, until the hand is a speck, and outside my window the streetlamp goes off.

It's seven-thirty. Still far too early, but down the hall my father is coughing, so I retrieve the stole and slip out of the room. In the front hall, as I'm putting on my boots, there is a moment in which I know how preposterous it is to imagine that Mrs. Richter will want to adopt me. Well, I haven't any provision for reconsidering let alone calling a halt to the plan. All I *have* is the plan, and it's under way.

A cold, windless, grey dawn. From the street I can see a light on in the Richters' bathroom, and as I am under the impression (no doubt because of something my mother said) that European women never take baths or showers, a picture enters my mind of Mrs. Richter standing at the sink in a corset, sponging her bare arms. It's a disturbing image: her large bosom (my mother's was small), the dark rift between her breasts, and the breasts themselves, bulging like bread loaves. I throw clothes into the picture . . . anything, a bathrobe. All the way to the church I drape Mrs. Richter in assorted voluminous dresses. By the time I arrive I have her resplendent in an ermine-trimmed hooded cape over a floor-length burgundy gown, the kind of outfit I imagine the queen might wear on Sundays.

But never into this church.

I stand there looking at it. Not for the first time I wonder if God even knows what it is. Except for the peaked roof and the plain plank cross on top, it could be a factory. Two cars are in the parking lot. The door is probably open, I could go in. But I resist. Considering how I look (suddenly I'm not nearly as confident as I was in my bedroom) I decide I'd better stick to my plan of slipping in at the last minute with the stragglers, not drawing too much attention to myself beforehand. I cross the street to a low-rise apartment building. On its front steps I sit and tuck my hands in my armpits, nestle the lower half of my face into the stole. Nobody else is around, no cars are on the road. I start to sing, quietly, the songs my father belts out in the shower, or used to belt out when my mother lived with us: "Way down among Brazilians, coffee beans grow by the millions . . ."

and "I want to win some winsome miss, can't go on like this . . ." At the edge of my vision the Angel of Love flickers weakly.

About a half-hour passes before I see another soul. It's a woman, coming out of the apartment building. Rough-looking, a motorcycle-gang type in a brown leather jacket and tight red slacks. I shift sideways to let her pass. She squints at me over her shoulder. "That's bad luck," I think, that mean squint, and I cast around for lucky signs: a black squirrel, a Royal Mail truck, anything yellow.

My extremities are now losing sensation. I am on the verge of getting up and trying the door of the apartment building when people begin materializing across the road. A family of five teeters on the icy lawn, and at the same time two cars pull into the lot. Another car arrives, another. Pretty soon there's a stream of people . . . in which no very tall lady appears. The church has a back entrance, though; it's possible the Richters have gone in that way.

When the stream begins to thin out, I stand. "Please God," I say. I go down the steps. I feel as if I'm walking toward an open manhole, passersby screaming, "Stop!" but I can't hear them because I've drunk a potion, I'm hypnotized, I'm the living dead. At the church door, as I reach out my hand, a man's gloved hand grabs the handle. Where did *he* come from? There's a lady, too. "Oh my!" she says. The man pulls the door open, and I dash inside, stumbling into another lady, who snaps, "Watch out!"

With numb fingers I tug the kerchief over my brow.

At least twenty people still linger in the foyer. I thought they'd all have gone straight to their seats. I shuffle forward among a small crowd moving in the direction of a hall where an organ plays. I hear a lady say, *"Who?"* and another lady say, "The Kirk girl." Behind me, a voice I recognize cries, "Louise?"

Maureen Hellier, together with three other girls from my class. They block the top of a basement stairwell, boys and girls of all ages jostling to get by them, and it dawns on me that children go somewhere else, separate from their parents. "Sunday school," I think. I'd forgotten that there was such a place.

In my confusion I stare back at the girls, and after a moment they grab each other's arms and whisper, and then, in unison, present to me faces of great concern, great kindness. My mother's disappearance has driven me to create this spectacle, their faces announce. Well, *they* understand. The blame lies not with me but with my tragedy. (More to the point, with Mrs. Carver, as I will learn tomorrow when Maureen comes up to me and says, "That lady who looks after you should have told you what a person wears to church. Why didn't she mend your dress? Your father should fire her." And I will say, coward that I have become in the schoolyard, betrayer of all I hold dear, "She *made* me wear that stole. She's crazy.")

But here, in the foyer, I am at a loss. What's the point of going down to the basement? Mrs. Richter won't be there. Will I be allowed in with the adults, though? The third alternative—leaving—doesn't occur to me. I resume my shuffle. I pass through the doors.

I'm in.

I step to one side and scan the seated congregation. I

don't see her, or Mr. Richter, but with all the ladies wearing hats and with some people still standing and obstructing my view, it's hard to tell. Everyone seems to be staring at me, so I start moving up the aisle, peering from under my kerchief until I reach the second row, and there, because I haven't got what it takes to walk all the way to the back again, I sit.

She isn't here.

Only one other person occupies my pew. A hunched-over old woman. She twists my way and nods. I nod back, shrugging the stole off my shoulders. I fold up the hem of my dress where it droops. I would like to remove my screaming-red kerchief as well—I have a sense of every-body behind me being shocked—except I'm not sure that showing your hair isn't the greater sin.

I bow my head. It occurs to me that I should take the opportunity to pray. "Our Father, who art in Heaven," I think as a blast from the organ jars me upright again, and some people at the rear of the church start to sing. I look around. The singers are coming up the aisle, in pairs, in blue gowns. When they reach the front they climb the stairs and file into the pews on the stage, and now I see the man who limps behind them. Is he the minister? He can't be. He is. His ascent up the stairs is perilous and yet nobody jumps up to take his arm, supposedly because he *will* make it, God won't let him fall. Over to the pulpit he reels. Once there, he surveys the room, his glance resting briefly on me. I slink down in my seat. "Let us pray," he says.

I close my eyes and finally experience what I feel. A pounding in my head. Terrific pain in my thawing fingers and toes. Relief.

She isn't here.

If she had been! I picture her sitting dead centre, sticking out like a steeple but not embarrassed by that, not like I am. She'd be straight-backed, happy with herself in her purple coat, although, now that I think of it, she might not wear purple to church. Still, whether she knows it or not she is scorned (Maureen's mother saying that she drowns out the whole choir), and during the week people gape at her.

The choir is on its feet once more, the organ playing. Everyone around me is getting up as well, so I do the same.

"Pssst." From the old woman.

She has a little navy book opened in her hands, and when I catch her eye she nods at the pew in front of me. Another such book is there, in a pocket on the back of the seat. I take it out. "Number five hundred and forty-one," she whispers.

"Stand up, stand up for Jesus," the congregation sings, "ye soldiers of the cross."

I find the hymn and join in: "From victory unto victory, His army He shall lead." By the middle of the second verse I have caught the melody and sing more confidently. By the fourth verse I am in the throes of an exhilaration I think must be the Holy Spirit.

But it is Mrs. Richter, not Jesus, I imagine marching into the mighty conflict for. Against *her* unnumbered foes, so that *she* shall reign in glory, I scream along with the highest voices in the choir.

CHAPTER TWELVE

The day in the ravine that Abel shows me the gold-eyed toad is a breakthrough. From then on I feel entitled to say hi to him at school. He murmurs hi back, occasionally allows himself a nod. In that nod, which due to some aberration of timing or incline seems foreign, I distinguish courtliness, modesty, commiseration: qualities I can't name but sense the benevolent array of. Even so, there is no question—while we have witnesses—of going beyond our cautious greeting. A boy without friends is a leper. A boy without friends who talks to girls is a leper asking to be bullied. I wander around the schoolyard, keeping an eye on him, imagining events that would oblige him to take me to his house (I find a note with German writing on it; I overhear a plot to murder his father) while he leans against the chain-link fence and watches the boys in his class play marbles or cowboys and Indians. Now that the weather is warmer he has become absorbed in the weeds growing along the fence's base. Sometimes he'll pick a thing up and turn it over in his hands as if it were money.

I feel sorrier for him than I do for myself. I've grown accustomed to my unpopularity; it makes sense to me. I'm not pretty, I say the wrong thing so reliably that whenever I open my mouth a deathly silence falls, I can't dance the Highland fling, as can a perplexing number of girls at our school, although I do own the most authentic-looking kilt, the most expensive wardrobe, which, of course, is another offence, a less insufferable one than it was before my mother left, and yet still an ongoing irritant to Maureen Hellier, who, at the sight of me and as the months pass, takes longer and longer to twitch her face into a look of friendliness.

But Abel . . .

He's handsome. He's quiet. Everything that counts against him is the result of a circumstance beyond his control (whereas the circumstance beyond my control—my mother's disappearance—counts very much *for* me). It isn't his fault that his mother is nothing like other mothers and that a rumour is adrift about his father being a Russian spy and former Nazi. Never have I seen him with a baseball glove or hockey stick, and because I can't imagine Mrs. Richter refusing him anything, I assume, correctly as I'll learn, that nobody ever taught him how to hit a ball or puck. And yet to suppose he might be lonely doesn't occur to me until one afternoon in the ravine when I spot him tossing up a stone and trying to swat it with a length of metal pole he must have found at the sludge factory.

He is too preoccupied to notice me, and after watching for a few minutes I creep away, mulling over this hole in his self-reliance. Should I have offered to pitch the rock? No, too forward. As even "Hi" is now too forward, in the ravine anyway. From my increased surveillance I have come to appreciate how segregated his worlds are, the lurking, stationary boy of the chain-link fence contrasting so drastically with the Tarzan of the ravine as to make the latter seem like a secret identity. Maybe it is. If Mr. Richter really does spy for the Russians, then Abel might be his deputy, scouring the woods for . . . what? Buried maps? Buried bombs? I don't care. *I* won't give him away and I suspect that his nod at school is partly to acknowledge my complicity and discretion—qualities that, again, I have no vocabulary for, although, as an amateur spy myself, I instinctively value.

But even if he isn't working for the Russians, he would still appreciate my leaving him alone in a place so clearly his. Seeing him grab branches and leap over crevices reminds me of somebody racing through a house and flicking on lights without having to glance at the wall. The intruders—me, gangs of boys playing on the slopes—he tolerates out of no choice. At school when we recite the Lord's Prayer, the part where we say "Forgive us our trespasses," I think of him. He knows I monitor his whereabouts, he knows I'm there, and it's true that he has kept his distance ever since the incident with the gold-eyed toad (did my fake enthusiasm offend him?), but it is also true that he never hides from me. To escape boys I've seen him shimmy up the trunk of a wild-cherry tree as fast as those men in pole-climbing contests. I've seen him outrun a dog. He's like a signal: a flicker of him in one place, a few moments later a flicker in another, farther away than seems possible.

I have a feeling that the ravine is where he goes to at night, and I find it odd that Mrs. Richter hasn't figured this out. My father finds it odd that the Richters haven't taken to locking him in his bedroom. I say, hotly, "Mrs. Richter would never do such a thing! She's *nice!*" I tell myself that the morning after one of her nights of roaming the streets, when she asks him where he went, he keeps his answer vague.

"Just out," he says. "Wandering around."

In the ravine. Once school finishes for the summer, he spends every day there, no matter what the weather. Except for Saturday mornings, so do I.

Saturday mornings Mrs. Richter does her grocery shopping, and that's my opportunity to look at her for at least an hour.

I wait across the street behind the Gorys' cedar hedge. At about ten o'clock she leaves her house, pulling a bundle buggy. I follow her. At the Dominion store I stand close enough that I could reach out and touch her skirt if I had the nerve. I don't think she'd even notice. Everybody could be naked and she wouldn't notice, she is so caught up in trying to figure out what to buy. She taps a finger on her cheek, cocks her head. She makes me think of someone playing charades. I wish I could help her. I could push the cart, I could pull her bundle buggy, going home. As it is, I do what I can to mentally urge along her decisions. I think, "The Macintosh apples, pick them, the Delicious are too bitter." Nine times out of ten she does what I command.

So then I think, "Turn around and see the girl in the pink shorts, love her, want to adopt her," but this never works.

In the ravine, I enter a daydream that has me as an orphaned Indian princess called Little Feather and Mrs. Richter as a captured German settler whom the chief has renamed Nightingale and taken for his bride. Because Mrs. Richter is too old to bear children and I am like a daughter to her anyway, she and the chief have adopted me. I teach Mrs. Richter Indian songs, the ones I learned last year at Camp Wanawingo—"Indians are High-minded," "We Are the Red Men," "Pow-Wow, the Indian Boy." She teaches me the German language and customs. Everything is fine until Maureen Hellier waltzes by. Maureen is a sleazy half-breed named White Pig. When she starts throwing her weight around, the chief orders her to be tied to a tree and gagged. Sometimes she's not in the daydream at all, she has been banished to the wilderness. Sometimes I imagine everyone, including Mrs. Richter, gone. I am alone in my tee-pee. I am the sole survivor of a massacre by white men.

I have built myself a shelter on a wide ledge along the eastern slope, and though I call it a tee-pee, I know it's only a lean-to: a row of branches tilted against a pile of logs, the branches secured to the uppermost log using pieces of wool, forest-green for camouflage, that I unravelled from the cable-knit sweater my mother wore the last Christmas morning she lived in our house. To break the wool I burnt it with matches, these, too, once the property of my mother, rescued from pockets curiously overlooked by Aunt Verna, who might have come up with leads by tracking down the places on the matchbook covers: Satin Doll Lounge, Bart's Esso. Of the five full books from Bart's, most contain duds.

I now have a knife if I need to cut anything. My father's penknife, which I took from his desk drawer and which he has yet to report missing. In the tee-pee, among sticks of sunlight, I sort through my stone collection and feed Jell-O powder to black ants. Sometimes, overhead, I hear a faint whine I think must be the clouds gliding by. Then there are moments of silence so absolute I am convinced I hear the ants' footsteps; it is a tinkling sound, as if they wore bells on their ankles. When I lie with my ear to the dirt floor, the tunnelling of the worms is distant thunder. All around me pine trees cross out the view. I am at the heart of an impenetrable fortification. Safe.

The valley and its cool slopes are also Abel's preferred part of the ravine. The other part, where the valley ends, is open land, the trees shrinking to scrubby sumachs and crab apples, a few willows. A river is down there, and the boys who swim in it get rashes and smell like the sludge factory, and like Camp Wanawingo, too, when the wind blows from the south. It's a spookily quiet camp, I thought that even during my brief stay there. Now, from my tee-pee, the only sound I ever hear is the noon-time shouting of the camp motto, "Yip yap honika wonika! Tip tap eenika si!"—supposedly Huron for "Brave and true are we! First of all the tribes!"

(My father, after I'd told him about the lack of drinking water and how we were forced to weed the vegetable garden, changed the translation to "Slaves and blue are we! Thirsty, dull, deprived!")

My tee-pee is as far away as you can get from the camp, hidden among all the logs and branches that have landed on the ledge over the years. Boys walk above the ledge and beneath it, oblivious. Only Abel knows I'm here, and the reason I am pretty sure of this is that the ledge is the only place in the ravine he avoids. I'll see him on the other slope and wish I had something worth calling him over for. One of those gold-eyed toads would do, and it's not as if there's a rock within a hundred yards of my tee-pee I haven't upturned. An Indian artifact, or even a particularly good stone would do.

A body would do.

On a Thursday afternoon toward the end of July, I arrive to find a man lying face down in front of my tee-pee.

He's big and old, or at least not young. Grimy green overalls, no shirt underneath, the soles of his shoes worn through, but his white hair is thick and silky.

"Hello?" I say.

There's a tattoo on the flab of his upper right arm. It's a wreath of snakes encircling a word I can't see properly from where I am, so I tiptoe around to his other side. "Greta," I read. I step back, shocked. No, it can't be. Can it? But even if it's another Greta, the name is German. "A spy," I think, "a spy disguised as a hobo." Thoroughly frightened now, I look across the valley for Abel.

I look back at the man.

I can't tell whether or not he's breathing. His right hand is clenched. Keeping my eyes on that hand (he might have a grenade), I pick up a stick and touch it to his calf. "Wake up," I say. I touch it to the sole of his bare, blackened foot. "Wake up." My voice seems to profane an immense emptiness. I move to his head and bend down but am driven up again by his foul smell. "Mister," I call testily. Then, louder, "Mister! Wake up!"

A large black insect wriggles out of the hair by his ear.

I scream.

From him, not a twitch.

I run screaming to the end of the ledge, leap off and run down the hill.

Before I reach the bottom, Abel bursts through the trees. His terrorized face tells me how blood-curdling my screams must have been.

"There's a man." I point. "Up there. A dead man."

"Dead?"

"He isn't breathing. He's just lying there. He won't move."
Abel looks up at the ledge.

"I poked him with a stick."

"Is he bleeding?"

"No. Maybe. I don't know."

Abel continues to look up at the ledge. A strained composure overtakes his features. He seems to have a thought, an idea. Watching him, I calm down. "Should we go call the police?"

"Not yet." He scratches his arm. He's wearing a red-and-yellow-striped T-shirt and new blue jeans he's meant to grow into, the legs rolled up into wide cuffs. His belt is a piece of rope. Clipped to the belt loop by his right hand are a magnifying glass and a jackknife. "Okay," he says, hiking up his jeans. He starts climbing.

I scramble after him. "He's an old man. He's really filthy. He has a tattoo—" I stop myself. Abel will see the tattoo.

He gains the ledge. By the time I get there, he's standing over the body. I go and stand next to him. He's looking at the tattoo.

I say, "Greta's your mother's name, isn't it?"

He glances at me. Nods.

"But it wouldn't be her," I say quickly.

No response.

"I wonder who he is?" I say, as if I suspect nothing.

"A vagrant."

My heart starts jumping. "From another country?"

"Search me."

"What's a vagrant?" I ask then.

"Somebody with no place to live."

I sigh. "A hobo." Obviously, he's a hobo.

"I've seen him before."

"You have?"

"Down by the factory. One of the men who works there gives him cigarettes."

I am reluctant to abandon the spy angle. "I think he's holding something. A grenade, maybe."

Abel doesn't even consider it. He crouches and places his hand on the man's upper arm. "He's not cold." Politely, to the man, he says, "Sir? Sir?" He shakes the shoulder. When nothing happens, he presses two fingers under and at the side of the jaw.

"What are you doing?"

"Feeling for a pulse."

I look from the man to Abel, and automatically start assessing him. At such close range he becomes merchandise, the orphan among all the other orphans whom Mrs. Richter chose. The dimple in his chin . . . she'd have liked that, people like dimples. His hair would have been the clincher, though, the same dark brown as hers.

"He's alive," Abel says, straightening.

"Injured though, I'll bet." It's a pitiless conjecture. Now that the man is neither a spy nor dead I find him repulsive.

"He didn't fall, not from the top."

"How do you know?"

"There aren't any broken branches." He indicates the hill above us. "You'd see the slide he made."

"So he *climbed* up?"

"Probably looking for a place to sleep. Where nobody'd pester him."

"So he climbed all the way up and then threw himself flat on his face?"

"Not on purpose. He was drunk. That's what that smell is."

"He's a lush," I declare. It's a term my mother used to apply to Mrs. Bently.

"Well . . ." Abel hikes up his jeans. "I guess we should just leave him."

"Are you crazy?"

He looks at me.

"What am I supposed to do?" I cry. "Stand here and wait? What if he goes to the bathroom in his pants? What if he rolls over? He'll wreck my tee-pee!"

Abel blinks and folds his arms across his chest. I realize I've scared him. *I* have. There's a huge drunken man on the ground, but *I'm* the one he's scared of. It's insulting. It's flattering, too, though. "Why don't we set his pants on fire," I say recklessly. "We could use your magnifying glass."

He moves his hand to the glass, as if I might make a grab for it. This only provokes me. "We could *kick* him in the pants!" I say. I swagger closer. And then, surprising myself, I do kick him, not very hard, in the rear end.

"Hey!" Abel says.

I go to kick again.

"Don't," Abel says painfully.

I hesitate, affected by his tone. "Don't *what*?" But I kick my knapsack instead. "I hardly touched him."

Abel picks the knapsack up. "Do you have any water in here?"

"Why?"

"If we can get him to drink something, that might wake

him up. He's probably dehydrated, and that's a dangerous state."

"I only have grape Freshie."

"That'll do."

"No."

He waits.

"His germs," I say. "They'll get all over my cup."

"We don't have to touch it to his lips. But that's okay, I have water. I'll run and get it."

"No!" Horrified at being left alone. I sigh. "He can have my Freshie."

Abel opens the knapsack, removes the Thermos and sets it on the ground. "We're going to have to get him on his back. We'll roll him over, then I'll get his mouth open, and you can pour in the Freshie." He moves to the man's side. "I'll push his shoulder. You push there," nodding toward the man's legs.

I go down on my knees. The smell is overpowering. "I'm going to throw up," I mutter, resting my hands on the over-alls.

"No, Louise, like this."

He knows my name. Why wouldn't he? I'm a neighbour, or he might have heard it at school. Maybe they talk about me at his house. An intoxicating thought. "Who is that girl who's always out front?" "That's Louise." "There goes Louise!" "Louise doesn't have a mother."

"You need to get leverage," Abel says. His hands are bent back, palms shoved under the man's shoulder.

"Leverage," I say. I have no idea what the word means.

"Okay. One, two . . . three!"

We push. We grunt. We rotate him a few inches but my arms turn rubbery and I let go.

"Come on!" Abel gasps. "Keep pushing."

"I can't."

The man groans.

"Sir?" Abel says.

I scramble to my feet.

"Jesus Christ," the man mutters.

Abel stands and steps back.

The man comes up on his elbows, grunts and works himself onto his knees. "Fuckin' Jesus."

I move away, appalled.

"Where the fuck—?" He has seen Abel. "Hey!" he says.

"Are you thirsty?" Abel asks.

"What do ya got?"

"Grape Freshie."

The man mumbles something, slaps at his chest. "Ya got a smoke?" he barks.

"No, sorry."

Somehow the man senses me and he thrashes around and barks, "*You* got a smoke?"

I shake my head.

"Ha!" He sits there leaning on his arm and smiling at me sappily. "What's a matter?" he yells. "Don't ya love me any more?"

I look at Abel. He's looking at the man. "They'll have cigarettes at the factory," he says.

"What are we waitin' for?" the man yells. He tries to heave himself up but drops onto his hip.

"Here, I'll help you," Abel says. He takes hold of the

man's arm. The man grimaces. I'm afraid Abel is going to get slugged, but the man leans his weight on Abel's arm and shoulder. Abel staggers.

Weeks, months, years later I will think of his buttressing of the man. After he's dead, I'll think of it not as a feat of bravery or of strength, which, of course, it was (the man must have been four times his size), but as my first experience of Abel's uncalled-for heroics. He'd have stood there until his spine snapped. And for what? The man would have gotten himself up one way or another. It was Abel's misfortune—one of his misfortunes—that not-quite-helpless acquaintances, people he owed nothing to and who might safely have been left to their own devices, were the ones he could least resist.

Right now, however, I'm just glad he's here. I presume that, like me, all he cares about is getting the man to leave. "I've got you, I've got you," he says. The man says, "Fuckin', fuckin'," until at last he's standing and then he shakes Abel free and weaves around, inches from my tee-pee, knocking over the Thermos.

"There's a path down," Abel says. "I'll show you."

"Hold your horses!" He is looking at me, his face demolished again into that witless smile. He gropes between his legs, unzips his fly, pulls out what looks like a dirty pink sock, flops it a few times, then urinates.

I spin around.

"What's a matter? Never seen a dick before? Didn't your boyfriend show you his?" His laugh is a grinding, mechanical sound, like a motor that won't catch. I can smell the urine from here. I keep thinking he's done and then there's more. "I got a gal in Kalamazoo!" he sings, bellowing. "Don't wanna boast but I know she's the toast of Kalama-zoo-zoo-zoo-zoo!"

Finally I hear him zipping himself up.

"If you want a cigarette," Abel says, "we'd better get going."

He leads the way. The man stumbles and crashes after him. I don't move. Even when I can't hear them any more, I wait. Eventually birds begin crying out, like casualties. I go to where the urine is and kick earth over the spot, then I crawl inside my lean-to.

I figure that Abel won't come back, but he does. "Are you there?" he says from only a few yards away.

I start to crawl out. Just beyond the entrance, while I'm still on my knees, I place my hand on a wet spot. I scream and jump up. "I touched his pee! I touched his pee!" I drop to the ground and grind my palm in the dirt. "It won't come off!"

Abel snatches my hand and pours Freshie on it. "Now rub it with dirt again."

"He's wrecked everything," I whimper. "The whole place is wrecked."

"There are lots of good places."

"No, there aren't."

"There *are*." He screws the lid back on my Thermos. "Places he could never find."

"Where?"

"I'll show you."

He'll show me. I stop crying.

"There's even a cave. Have you been there?"

I shake my head.

"Do you want to see it?"

I nod.

"Do you want to see it *now?*"

"Maybe"—I bring the quaver back into my voice—"maybe tomorrow."

"Okay." He stands up.

"Right now," I say, "I want a glass of milk. Milk always makes me feel better. Except the milkman didn't come by our place today." This last part happens to be the truth.

"He missed us, too," Abel says. "But I think we still have a bottle. We can go see."

There it is: the invitation. Drums thunder in my head. Lights burst. "Really?"

"Sure, why not?" He blushes.

I jump up and gather my things—the box of Jell-O powder, my stone collection—and put them and the Thermos in my knapsack, which, without looking at me, he offers to carry.

We set off.

As an adult, whenever I move out of a flat or apartment (which will happen regularly enough that I'll never have to defrost a refrigerator) I'll feel exactly as I do now: that the place failed me in its promise of peace and impregnability. I'll see myself following Abel down this slope with its broken branches and skid marks like exposed muscle, entire bushes trampled as if the hobo commandeered a bulldozer. It made the descent easier, I'll remember that, too.

CHAPTER THIRTEEN

Throughout the summer and into the first weeks of September, Abel sticks to our deal—the one we made the morning after the party—of calling each other on alternate Sunday nights. When it's my turn to call, even if one of his parents answers, he's right there waiting.

If it's his mother who answers, her voice can still produce a small clutch in my heart. I love her conspiratorial-sounding "Hello?" Her enthralled and shouted "Louise, how *are* you?" I say that I'm fine, thank you, how is she? "Wonderful!" she cries. And then, like the host of a TV show, without further ado, she shouts, "So, here he is, he's right here. Abel!"

During our first two or three calls I do most of the talking. Unlike him, I have a hard time letting a pause stretch out. These calls remind me of my attempts to get to know him seven years ago, when I'd be chattering away while he stood looking at me politely and attentively, like somebody watching a performance.

A consequence of such attentiveness is that you're liable to reconsider what you're saying, even as it's coming out of your mouth. For instance, when I tell him about running into Tim Todd at a donut shop. This happened on the Labour Day weekend. Unfortunately, he saw me before I saw him, and he called me over and introduced me to the cashier and some other employee, then said he'd just been hired part-time to clear tables. He seemed like somebody else, all upbeat and friendly. "Well," I said, "congratulations," and I turned to go but he caught my arm and muttered he'd been meaning to phone me, he was coming very close to deciding I should be forgiven. "It wasn't really your fault," he said. "It was that hippy creep making you smoke marijuana. So"—back to his friendly voice—"I've got a new freshwater aquarium, you might want to drop by sometime and take a look at it." To which I said, "I'd rather spend ten years smoking marijuana with that hippy creep than two seconds looking at a stupid fish tank."

When I'm only at the part where Tim called me over, I know this story isn't as entertaining as I'd thought. "Where does he get the nerve?" I finish lamely. "We only went out for a couple of months."

In the long silence, distant voices from a crossed line flicker: ". . . A quarter cup of maple syrup . . . oh, hooey, you can just double up on the brown sugar."

"Are you still there?" I say.

"I'm here."

"I couldn't let him get away with calling you that. And you never *made* me do anything."

"It's just that it was in front of his friends."

"They weren't his *friends*."

But I am chastened.

I keep forgetting this about Abel: how kind he is. When he talks about *his* friends, the ones he likes best seem to be the outcasts and eccentrics. One guy, Lenny somebody or other, has left home and is living in the Richters' basement, where instead of going to school he spends all day drawing up charts of professional sports statistics. "Underneath," Abel says, "he's like a cosmologist, searching for the ultimate logic." In Abel's opinion, everybody is somebody else underneath, somebody finer or at least deserving of our sympathy. Regarding my lifelong enemy, Maureen Hellier, whom he remembers from public school, he says he always thought that underneath she was "a frightened little kid."

"Well," I blurt, "on top she's a big fat bitch."

Silence.

"But I know what you mean," I say quickly. "You can't really know who people are on the inside."

I try to believe this because I want to be like him. I look—as I stopped doing after he moved out to Vancouver—at the sky, slugs, dog dirt, old ladies' freckled hands, and no matter what I see I marvel at. He tells me he's studying Bach's *Goldberg Variations,* and as soon as I hang up the phone I search through my father's stack of albums and find a 1954 Glenn Gould recording, and I listen to it for the rest of the evening, but it's Abel I picture at the piano, his muscular shoulders working in tormented yearning for me. My father, who ever since the party has had to put up with me endlessly listening to my "White Rabbit" forty-five, says, "You've moved on."

"Progressed," I say. "Advanced."

"Made strides," he says, playing along. "Blossomed."

"Effloresced," I say.

"Ah ha!" he cries. Because the word is proof that I've actually read the field guides I've been stealing from his study. I've more than read them, I've memorized entire sections: insect orders, the names of Jupiter's satellites, the meaning of *ovoviviparous* and *pinnate*. And *effloresce*. On the borders of the letters I send to Abel I draw the plaid skin-patterns of snakes, the twelve variations of insect antennae.

It's in these letters that I pour out my feelings (*portion* them out is more like it, a minute-by-minute drip): "I woke up feeling carefree and sure. I knew in my heart that nothing could ever come between us again. Then, at breakfast, my father asked, How is Abel doing <u>these days</u>? and I could only tell him how you <u>had been</u> doing, last Sunday, five long days ago, and I realized there <u>is</u> something between us—two-thirds of a continent!!! And the loneliness came rushing back."

After mailing the first letter I tell him over the phone that it's on its way. I say, "You don't have to write back."

So when a letter arrives two weeks later, I'm almost afraid to open it. The envelope is small and robin's-egg blue, the single page inside a matching blue and venting an odour of cigarette smoke. Not a letter, after all, but a poem, copied out in calligraphic script. "Romance," it's called. By Arthur Rimbaud.

> When you are seventeen, you aren't really serious.
> —One fine evening, you've had enough of beer and
>   lemonade,
> And the rowdy cafés with their dazzling lights!
> —You go walking beneath the green lime trees of the
>   promenade.
>
> The lime trees smell good on fine evenings in June!
> The air is so soft sometimes, you close your eyelids;

The wind, full of sounds,—the town's not far away—
Carries odours of vines, and odours of beer . . .

—Then you see a very tiny rag
Of dark blue, framed by a small branch,
Pierced by an unlucky star, which is melting away
With soft little shivers, small, perfectly white . . .

Under this, in his own block-lettered writing, he writes: "You are not alone, so don't be lonely. You are the <u>lucky</u> star, framed by a small branch. Love Abel." And a little farther down: "Beauty is truth, truth beauty."

I cling to the title, to the "Love Abel" and to the suggestion that I'm *his* lucky star.

One other letter arrives that summer, at the end of August. Again on the blue paper, two sheets this time, and again featuring a poem by Rimbaud, whose writings I am now acquainted with, having found a volume of his collected works in a second-hand bookstore downtown and having therefore learned that, in the first letter, Abel wrote out only part of the poem. Why didn't he write out the last stanza, which goes on to tell how the boy falls in love with a young girl of "charming little airs"?

"I was getting to the end of the page" is his explanation.

This next poem, called "Eternity," is short enough that he includes the whole thing.

It has been found again.
What?—Eternity.

It is the sea fled away
With the sun.

Sentinel soul,
Let us whisper the confession
Of the night full of nothingness
And the day on fire.

From human approbation,
From common urges
You diverge here
And fly off as you may.

Since from you alone,
Satiny embers,
Duty breathes
Without anyone saying: at last.

Here is no hope,
No *orietur*.
Knowledge and fortitude,
No torture is certain.

It has been found again.
What?—Eternity.
It is the sea fled away
With the sun.

That's more like it. More romantic, more obviously having to do with us. Eternity found again, satiny embers. No

hope *here,* no hope out in Vancouver, away from me. The sea fleeing away is our forced parting. Flying off is getting stoned. *Orietur?* I don't know what that is, I can't find it in my French-English dictionary.

At the bottom of the page is a pen-and-ink drawing of "A Proliferating Sea Anemone," which resembles a bunch of worms spilling out of the top of a striped pouch. It's extremely meticulous, he must have worked on it for hours. But the drawing on the next page, although it couldn't have taken him more than a few minutes to do, is the one that thrills me. It's the two of us. There's my thin face and heavy-lidded eyes, his ringlets and thick eyelashes, and we're smiling and wearing monks' robes. We are, as he's written underneath, "Abelard and Hell-Louise," an old joke of my father's. Under this is "The truth shall make you free," and under that a brown blotch and an arrow pointing away from it to the words: "Beer Spilled by Lenny."

Beer Spilled by Lenny. As the day progresses, so does my resentment that the drawing should have even been *seen* by the slovenly Lenny. Who could just as easily have been an American draft dodger named Judd or a card sharp named Thumbs, or who knows who else? All the weird people Abel meets on buses and in parks and at a bar called the Parliament, where, even though he's underage, he gets served draft beer. On the phone, when he tells me about these characters, I try to act entertained despite not under-standing why he would prefer them to no one at all, or at least to his school friends, of whom he seems to have a staggering number. From being a loner here in Greenwoods he has gone to being Vancouver's pied piper. Strangers follow him home, they move right in.

For me to say that they sound like bad influences would come across as bourgeois. Still, I hint at it, releasing my disquiet in a parody of concern over his welfare. I can hardly admit to myself, much less to him, that the truth is I'm jealous. He seems abnormally interested in these people, far more so than he is in me. His having friends at all feels like a betrayal.

Sunday night. His turn to phone.

Three days ago I celebrated my eighteenth birthday. Mrs. Carver baked a mocha cake and gave me a pair of surprisingly fashionable patterned knee socks. My father gave me a biography of J. S. Bach and a double-record set of Glenn Gould playing Bach's partitas. From Abel, though I'd dropped several hints, there was nothing: no letter or telegram, no phone call. This evening I have expectations of a good excuse and an apology.

Ten o'clock arrives. Ten-fifteen. At ten-thirty, worried that something terrible must have happened, I call the operator and am put through.

It's Mrs. Richter who answers. "Louise!" she shouts. "How *are* you?"

"I'm—" I'm unprepared for her good humour.

"Hello?" she shouts.

"Hello. I'm here."

"How *are* you?"

"Well, I'm waiting for Abel to call. He should have called half an hour ago."

"He didn't call?"

"No."

She makes a guttural noise. "Oh, bad boy, he must have forgot!"

"Forgot?"

"Because, you know, he's not here. He's gone out."

My throat seizes.

"Hello? Louise?"

"Yes."

"We have a bad connection!"

I ask if Abel said where he was going.

"Where he was going? No, no. He could be anywhere! Just a minute and I will find out." Away from the mouthpiece she shouts, "Karl! Karl! Did Abel tell you where he was going?" A pause, then, "Louise, he just *vamoosed!* But I'm sure he'll be home soon, and he'll call you."

He doesn't. I stay up, waiting. In bed, I cry and endlessly review the possibilities: he was in a car accident; he was murdered by one of his weird friends; his friends got him drunk and he blacked out; he was caught smoking marijuana and has been thrown in jail; he ran into an old girlfriend, who seduced him; he got turned off by my telling him he was the only person on earth I could talk to, the only person I wanted to be with.

Better dead than turned off! No, no, I didn't mean that. Don't let him be dead!

Near dawn I sleep for about an hour. As soon as I open my eyes I am hit by a wave of nausea, and I get to my feet and stumble to the bathroom, where I throw up last night's chicken cacciatore.

"Louise?" my father calls. As I'm coming back down the hall he opens his door. His face startles me, it's so haggard, not yet hoisted into its cheerful daytime aspect.

"I think I have the flu."

This throws him into his physician's persona. He feels my forehead. "You're not running a fever. Do you have diarrhea, the runs? Stick out your tongue."

I push past him. "I just need to sleep."

"I'll get you a glass of ginger ale."

"I don't want one. I'll be okay. I'm going to stay home today, so could you call my school and leave a note for Mrs. Carver?"

Back in bed I lose consciousness until Mrs. Carver arrives. She brings me a warm red tea that tastes like worms. I spit it back into the cup. "What *is* this?"

"Drink it down," she whispers. "It'll settle your . . ." She rubs her stomach.

"I don't feel sick any more."

"It's also good for . . ." She makes a sharp shoving-away motion with both hands.

"Banishing my enemies," I finish.

She gives me a reproachful look that says I should know by now she doesn't think in terms of enemies or wicked people. If you act badly, it's because you've been goaded by harmful spirits, who themselves are only fulfilling the prophecies of harmful omens. In her school of thought, there is no will, no morality, only atmosphere.

I force down more of the tea. Over the years I have come to welcome her occult interventions as insurance against the faint possibility that she's actually on to something. She presses her child-sized, sandpaper-textured palm against my forehead. "I'm not hot," I tell her. She adjusts her glasses to peer at me, her frazzled eyes arrested for a moment in a look almost penetrating.

"What?" I say.

She pats my leg.

"What?"

She takes the cup and sets it on the bedside table.

When she's out of the room I sink into dread, convinced she has envisioned some catastrophe in my future. No, no, I'm imagining things. She can't see into the future! I hear her clattering around in the kitchen. "Mrs. Carver," I think fondly, and after a few minutes manage to shrivel her down to the sweet, harmless crackpot I've lately come to see her as.

Still, I finish the tea.

By now it's a quarter to eleven, a quarter to eight Vancouver time. If Abel is at home, and not dead or in jail, he likely won't have left for school yet.

I use the phone in my father's study. While the operator makes the connection I pray for Abel to answer, but it's Mr. Richter's sedate "Hello" that comes over the line. Obviously, no calamity has struck at that end.

"Is Abel there?"—altering my voice in case he isn't and then he'll never have to know it was me who called.

"Louise?"

I drop the disguise. "Yeah, hi. May I speak to Abel, please?"

"Of course. Yes, of course. Just one moment."

The dog barks. Mr. Richter calls, "Abel!" and, farther off,

Mrs. Richter sing-songs something I can't make out. A happy morning in the Richter household. Longing pours through me.

"Playing hooky?" It's Abel.

"I don't feel well."

"What's the matter?"

"I didn't sleep last night."

One of those eternal, excruciating pauses, and then, "I'm sorry I didn't phone. Mr. Earl, you remember that old black saxophonist I told you about, he was playing at the Bear Pit and I stayed for his set. It was after two by the time I got home."

"He was playing on a Sunday night?"

"Hey, this is the West Coast."

"And this is the East Coast."

Silence.

"Abel, I was really worried. I thought you'd been murdered or something."

More silence.

"I know it's crazy."

"Don't do this to yourself," he says quietly.

That does it, that mixture of detachment and pity. Tears start streaming down my face. "Don't do what?"

"Get yourself down."

"I don't get myself down. *You* get me down. You don't call when you're supposed to, and that gets me down."

"I'm sorry. I guess I just . . . forgot."

"Forgot!"

"I'm sorry."

"Everything's falling apart."

"No, it isn't. Don't say that. Everything's fine."

I sigh.

"I've got to go. My father's calling, he's giving me a ride."

"Can you phone me when you get home from school?"

No answer.

"Abel!"

"I'll try."

"Four o'clock your time. Is that too early?"

"It should be okay."

"I love you."

"I know." Barely audible.

"Do you love me?"

"Yep."

"Okay, I'm okay now."

Throughout the day I master the skill of multiplying by sixty, counting down not the hours, which feel like centuries, but the minutes. Five hundred and ninety. Four hundred and eight-five. I stay in bed and read Rimbaud's collected poems. "Your eye-teeth gleam. Your breast is like a cithara, plucked notes run in your pale arms." Why didn't he send me *that* one? Why doesn't he see me in everything, as I see him?

At suppertime I rouse myself to eat a bowl of beef broth in the kitchen. My father says I still look "a little pale, a little ashen, a little wan."

"Which?" I burst out. His inability to settle on a single adjective suddenly strikes me as a form of mental illness. "Pale? Ashen? Wan? Washed-out? Colourless?"

He blinks.

"Callow?" I yell.

"I believe you mean sallow," he says carefully.

"I'm fine," I mutter.

He fades to nothing. There is only the clock and the phone. When he pours his coffee, I become aware of him again and say, "You don't have to sit with me. I'll do the dishes." He escapes gladly. "If the phone rings," I call after him, "I'll get it."

Twenty-five after six.

At a quarter to seven, the dishes done, I sit on the chair under the phone.

Five to seven.

Seven.

Seven-fifteen. Seven-thirty.

I rest my head on the table, in the cradle of my arms. The seconds tick by. They fall, drop by drop, the smithereens of my life. Presently my father strolls in for a second cup of coffee, and I cover my ears with my hands but he speaks anyway.

"Wouldn't you be better off in bed?"

In bed I am not better off. All I can think about is Abel's "Yep" when I asked him if he loved me. "Yep." Like somebody who doesn't want to talk about it. Or—oh, God—like somebody who is only telling you what you want to hear. But he might have just been confirming the obvious: Yep, of course, goes without saying. In the park he told me he loved me *too* much. Too much for what? For who? Doesn't he *want* to love me?

I can't phone him, I won't. There's still time. It's only five o'clock in Vancouver. He could have got held up at school or at a piano lesson.

I reread his two letters, for clues, for hope. They just

upset me more. How can he say I'm not alone and shouldn't be lonely and then abandon me? The "Eternity" poem now seems to be a warning with all its flying off and fleeing and diverging. Why, though? Why would he want to flee? Or maybe it isn't that, maybe when we're so far apart he can't hold on to me somehow. Out of sight, out of mind.

I return the letters to the bedside table and get up and go to the window just as the streetlights come on. After a few minutes a moth appears beneath the light on our property. It circles, ascending. "Don't, don't," I think. But up it goes. When it hits the lamp it drops almost to the ground, recovers itself and starts another climb. I know, because Abel told me, that moths navigate by the Moon, and so big moonlike objects tend to throw them off course. On summer evenings we used to capture lost moths in his butterfly net and release them down in the ravine. Once, to rescue a luna moth that had been bashing itself against the lamp for at least a half-hour, we solicited the help of my father, his long arm. "Blind faith," my father observed as the three of us stood looking up and waiting for the moth to fall within reach.

Now, watching this moth, I think that maybe it isn't a matter of faith. Or of hope, or even guesswork. Maybe it's just that certain moths decide to smash themselves to death. Who knows why? Or maybe what's going on is that moths don't understand shades of resemblance. To them, if a thing looks enough like another thing, it *is* that other thing. All lights are the Moon. The moth is all other moths, and all other moths are the moth. There is one human, and he is everywhere.

There is one human, and he is nowhere.

Why doesn't he phone?

The next morning I throw up again. Quietly this time, into my bedside wastepaper basket. In the bathroom I rinse out the basket, then undress and step into the shower. I look down at my body. "Not *as* thin," Abel said about the girl he dated who looked like me. Was I wrong to take that as a compliment? I feel my breasts. They seem heavier, but maybe not, I can't tell. They're a bit sore, though. I move my hands down to my belly. Still flat. I can't be pregnant. Since Abel and I were together I've had two periods and, besides, I'm fairly certain that morning sickness starts earlier than this. I'm a nervous wreck, that's all. Nervous wrecks throw up.

But what if I *am?* The thought sends another wave of nausea through me, pure fear. I imagine quitting school, the scorn, my father wild eyed and helpless, Aunt Verna arriving to hammer together a crib and be the midwife. I imagine dropping the bombshell on Abel: "Sorry to bother you, it's just that I thought you should know . . ." Would I move out to Vancouver and marry him, then? Set up house in his basement, the two of us and the baby? And Lenny? No, we'd get rid of Lenny. Abel would keep going to school while I hung around with Mrs. Richter, chopping cabbage, planting tomatoes, as in my old fantasies. It wouldn't be so bad. Abel and I would be together, at least.

Whether he wanted me or not.

I start to cry. He doesn't want me. He'd pretend he did, out of decency, and pity. He might even *love* the damn baby.

CHAPTER FOURTEEN

I think of myself as having no friends at Greenwoods Collegiate, but that's probably not fair to Alice Keystone, the girl I walk to and from school with. On Tuesdays and Thursdays, because our lunch hours coincide, we eat together in the cafeteria.

Alice gives the impression of being a worrier until you discover that she isn't constantly wringing her hands, she's moisturizing them. The family-size jar of Jergens lotion she carries in her purse (along with the pickle jars of leftovers that hold her lunch) would weigh down a less robust girl. Not that she's big, she's sturdy: thick calves and wide hips, about my height. "I can't stand touching paper if my skin gets too dry," she told me shortly after we got to know each other. Before then I'd thought she was vain about her tapered fingers. It turns out she's far from vain; she seems to have no idea how pretty she is. You look at her—her round blue eyes, small white face—and see a doll. When a teacher asks her a question, a red circle the size of a silver dollar materializes on each of her cheeks and her resemblance to a doll becomes even more pronounced.

Our understanding, Alice's and mine, is that we have almost nothing in common aside from our unpopularity and that this glaring fact will go unmentioned between us. *I* wouldn't mind talking about it, gloating over it sometimes, but I'm fairly certain Alice would be crushed by even the most oblique suggestion, from me anyway, that she's an outcast. Of course, she must know that she is. I know *I* am, and why. People think I'm weird and sarcastic. Alice herself has said a few times, "Oh, you're so sarcastic!" Let it burst out after I've made a remark as self-evident and unscathing as "That girl sure is tall."

I try to be careful around her. Not only is she easily scandalized, she's also deeply religious, a junior Sunday-school teacher and a volunteer Bible reader at the old-folks' home. When I was dating Tim Todd (she referred to him as my fella: "There goes your fella") I would talk about what movie he and I had seen on Saturday night or what his tropical fish were up to, but I would no more have told her that he had touched my breasts than I would have told my father. Even to say "breasts" would have been going too far.

She lives only two blocks from me, in a newer part of the subdivision, and yet we rarely run into each other on weekends or holidays. This past summer I caught sight of her just once. I was waiting for a bus to go to my job, and her father's station wagon pulled up at the red light and there she was in the passenger seat, the baby in her lap, her three little sisters in the middle seat and, behind them, in the back, her little brothers. Alice was holding the baby's wrists to make it clap. She seemed to be singing to it. From what she has told me, she's her mother's right hand, she's the one who puts all those kids to bed and dresses them for church. "What drudgery," I thought as the car drove away. By then I'd had sex with Abel and could hardly imagine having had anything to do with somebody so straitlaced.

But when the first day of school came round and from my living-room window I saw her waiting at the bottom of the street, I didn't sneak out the back door, partly because I was working at being a nicer person, partly because I thought that my new look would come between us anyway. It occurred to me she must have figured we were of one mind concerning fashion in that, up until a few months ago, everything I wore used to belong to my mother and was therefore at least ten years out of date. But this hardly constituted an expression of taste. It was laziness, practicality, it was me saying to my father, "She's never coming back," and it was also, I suppose, a reluctant appreciation of the fine fabrics and designs. Alice's clothes were *deliberately* out of date, not to mention new, cheap, homemade and spinsterish: sack-like dresses, high-necked cotton blouses and full skirts past the knee, all plain pastel, or if there was a pattern, it was some wallpaper motif of horses or windmills. Her one concession to style, and even that looked old-fashioned, was her teased hair. Neither of us wore make-up.

Now here I was traipsing toward her in a tie-dyed tank top and a skirt that barely covered my rear end. Bare legs, no bra, and I wore leather sandals and a navel-long necklace of wooden beads I'd bought from a street vendor downtown. I had on lipstick, pale pink, almost white, and black eyeliner so thick that at breakfast my father, usually wary of provoking me, steeled himself into asking, "Don't you think you should tone that down a little for school?"

"I toned it *up* for school," I said with less annoyance than I felt, fantasizing that Abel could hear how tolerant I was being. But my father kept casting me alarmed looks, kept palming back his oiled, thinning hair, and I couldn't resist muttering, "Some people are so uptight."

"Talk about uptight," I thought now, as I watched Alice clutch her purse to her chest. "Hi!" I called. She lifted one hand.

When I reached her she said, "I hardly even recognized you."

"I've gone through some changes. I'm not going out with Tim any more, for one thing."

"Oh. I didn't know."

"It was never very serious."

"What happened? If you don't mind my asking."

I hadn't intended to go into detail, but the sight of her exasperated me, her matronly teacup-patterned dress, her bouffant hairdo (*she* hadn't changed), and I found myself wanting to give her a shock. "Oh," I said, "I ran into my old boyfriend at a party and we ended up smoking pot and making out on the neighbour's lawn, and then Tim came along, I was so stoned I forgot he was even there, and he caught us rolling around half naked."

I walked off, sure she'd stay put. But no, here she was, trotting up alongside me. "By rolling around," she said, not looking at me, cheeks aflame, "do you mean what I think you mean?"

"We went all the way."

She sucked in her breath.

"It's not like it was a one-night stand or anything," I said more gently. "Abel and I—that's his name, Abel, it's

German—we're in love. We've been in love ever since I was eleven." My voice thickened to be telling somebody this pure, true thing. "Seven years."

Alice's expression eased. "That's a long time."

We didn't speak the rest of the way to school. "Bye for now," I said once we were inside the front doors, adding "for now" only to be civil, as I had no doubt that our friendship really was finished. I felt her big, uneasy eyes on my back as I went down the hall to my home room. I felt other eyes as well. "Is *that* Louise Kirk?" Everybody thinking it so loudly I could hear.

Still, no one talked to me, other than to say hi, ask how I was doing, the mechanical acknowledgements I'd always gotten. But the pity, the condescension, that was gone. Maureen Hellier, passing me, turned right around to keep gaping. So did a couple of boys, sliding their eyes up and down my body. For the first time in my life I knew what it felt like to hold a little power in my hands. My mother used to say, "You are what you wear." She was right.

And I was wrong. About Alice, that is. After school she called "Wait up!" as I was crossing the parking lot, and when she was beside me she started right in with a report on who else she'd noticed dressed like a hippy: "Beverley Bowman was wearing, I guess you'd call it a psychedelic skirt, did you see her? Down to the floor, all sorts of swirling colours. Very eye-catching. And Steve Plath, his hair is longer than yours, I'll bet. It must have grown like crazy over the summer. He had on a kind of Indian bracelet, you know, those woven straps with the coloured beads. And then that fella who plays the drums . . . oh, gosh, what's his name? Brent something. Brent Coren, that's it. He was wearing one of those Beatles jackets with the collars that stand up."

"A Nehru jacket," I said, stunned. Who'd have guessed that not only would she completely absorb the shock of how I looked and what I'd told her but that a few hours later she'd be delivering a bulletin apparently meant to spur me on.

"It was really very smart," she said. "Gold buttons and red brocade trim."

We began walking.

"I bet you all end up chumming around together," she said.

"I'll bet we don't."

Funny she came out with that, though. Since the night of the party I'd occasionally fantasized being part of a group of like-minded people, but I accepted that there was something incurably offputting about my personality, and however agreeable I tried to be I'd still end up irritating everybody. Anyway, this outfit I had on, my make-up, they weren't intended to be lures. They were me saying, "I have Abel. Who needs *you?*"

"I just thought . . ." Alice said. "Birds of a feather . . ."

It dawned on me that she was seeking reassurance. "I don't want friends," I said. "I mean, I don't want *more* friends."

I wanted Abel. Even though we were together I still tended to think of my love for him and my loneliness as inextricable. He had always been the real difference between me and the rest of the world, the real tragic loss in my life next to which the *supposed* tragic loss, the one that garnered all the pity, counted for nothing.

"I've never been one for the social whirl myself," Alice said. She was going after her skin cream, slipping her hand in her purse, unscrewing the lid, scooping out a dab, screwing the lid back on, all without breaking stride. She cleared her throat. "Do you mind if I ask you a personal question?"

"What?"

"Well . . ." She briskly rubbed her hands. "It's about you and your fella, you know, Abel, about the two of you." Out popped the red circles.

"About us what?" I thought I knew where she was headed but I wanted to see if she'd actually say it.

"I'm sticking my nose in and I won't blame you if you tell me to mind my own beeswax. It's just that my mother has had seven kids and I know how darned easy it is. . . ."

She turned on me such a stricken face I decided to rescue her. "It's all right, Alice. He lives in Vancouver. We only had the one night together, and I have a feeling I'm not going to get pregnant over the phone."

"Vancouver? I didn't realize—"

"Anyway, I have no intention of being stuck with a baby."

She released a shaky laugh. "Oh, I love babies. But they're oodles of work, believe you me. Oh, gosh!"

CHAPTER FIFTEEN

A few months before he died, Abel told me he had never believed in God or heaven or any kind of metaphysical salvation, but I found that hard to believe considering what a fanatical optimist he'd always been. "Don't worry," he'd say, when panic was the only sane response. "Don't get yourself down," when you were scraping your soul off the pavement. Right up until the last days of his life he tried to assure me that we'd both be okay.

"*You* won't be," I said. "A dead person is not okay."

By then he was spending most of his days and nights swilling Canadian Club whisky and spitting up blood into a red towel (red makes the carnage less evident) and still he could say, in a sympathetic tone that seemed to suggest *I* was the self-destructive one: "Everything's fine."

Part of me, *parts* of me—the petrified core, the dumb heart, the tender extremities where arousal still flickered— let myself believe this. He was so smart, he must have a plan. His parents and even his doctors nursed the same delusion. We agreed among ourselves to try to refrain from hectoring him. "He has to reach rock bottom," we all said, as if rock bottom were one floor higher than death.

I have an essay he wrote when he was in university. It's called "Oblivion"—ironically enough, since it's the only one of his papers that he didn't burn over his neighbour's barbecue. ("This is what spies do," I said as he lit the pages. I asked him to at least let me keep the pen-and-ink drawings and was refused. "This is you afraid of being judged," I said then. A weak charge. Judged by whom? His parents and me? Still, because I knew that he revered the lowly and humble, I pushed it, I said, "This is vanity." He picked up a sheaf of poems. "*This*," he said, "is vanity.")

The essay turned up among the cats' vaccination papers. For a while his mother held on to it and then she gave it to me in a shoebox containing a few things she wanted me to have: his calligraphy pen, his fossil trilobite cufflinks she suggested I could have made into earrings, his roach clip, which she thought was a specimen collector.

She admitted to not having read the essay through to the end. "The sentences are hard going," she said, and my feeling, confirmed once I'd taken on those sentences myself, was that she meant more than difficult, she meant disheartening.

"Life," it starts out, "is oblivion erupting, for a brief moment, into non-oblivion in order that oblivion may proclaim: 'I am.' The assumption being, of course, that living things are aware enough to make such a proclamation. Let us suppose that they are. Let us suppose that they are, to a degree, *self*-aware. This makes for the possibility of life recognizing itself, yes, but not as oblivion, only as life. In order for life to recognize itself as a fleeting pulse of oblivion, self-awareness must be refined into pure awareness, which is observation unimpaired by either ego or preconceptions."

At least he allowed that life is an event, to the degree that it is a springing-out of nothingness. Except that he felt it was only another *form* of nothingness, nothingness taking a look at itself. Did he think that he himself was just some particle of oblivion, then, put on Earth for no other reason than to observe? But why would he drink, if that were the case? Unless he wanted to *deliberately* dull his senses . . . to reach a point where he could observe from a state of mind so close to oblivion itself that there'd be no risk of corruption by *either ego or preconception*.

Well, that's one way of looking at him, as fatally enlightened.

The other way—as just another gifted but damaged human being—I still tend to avoid, even though I suppose a pretty compelling case could be made when you think of what he had to contend with. The orphanage. His real mother and father, whoever they were. Me. What I did.

CHAPTER SIXTEEN

Two days since I phoned him.

It seems pointless putting on make-up let alone a mini-dress. I've been dishonourably discharged, the uniform no longer means anything. Anyway, the last thing I feel is sexy.

What'll I do, then? Go back to wearing my mother's skirts and dresses that I shortened using Scotch tape because my father, who's still convinced she'll waltz through our front door one day, refuses to let me "sabotage" her clothes with a needle and thread? Go back to my virginal look? I'll bet that would make Alice happy. Despite the cheerful interest she seems to have taken in my transformation, I can't believe she isn't praying for me to come to my senses: "Please, dear Lord, restore Louise to the path of decency and modesty."

With a fingernail I scrape the vomit crust from the corner of my mouth and get out my tube of lipstick and try to remember that I made the decision to become someone else *before* Abel and I reunited (only a few hours before, it's true . . . still, *before*). Except I wouldn't have acted on it. The belief that he loved me is what gave me the courage, and everything I did from then on I imagined he could see.

Up until now. I can't imagine him seeing *this,* the throwing up and sobbing. But I can't imagine him seeing me calm or sleeping either, if he has stopped loving me. If he has pushed me out of his mind, I don't even have the ghost of him. I have nobody worth being interesting for. I am nothing.

I choose my green-and-black-striped empire-line mini-dress owing to its relative looseness. Since getting out of the shower I have the feeling that the least pressure will shatter my torso. I feel hollow, the empty shell you hear about. Putting on my underwear and then the dress and my shoes is a cruel chore. As for breakfast, forget it. I have only a couple of mouthfuls of orange juice. My father looks at me piercingly over his coffee mug. "Are you sure you shouldn't stay home?"

"I'm dressed," I say. All that work!

"Your eyes are bloodshot." Because I almost never cry in front of him, he fails to diagnose grief. "I wonder if you've got conjunctivitis. Pink eye. It's highly contagious, you know. You could have got it from your mascara, especially if you share it around."

I tell him to leave me alone, I'm going to school. I forget why I'm so determined. Something to do with not wanting to cry in bed all day, not wanting to slit my wrists in the bathtub. He offers to drive me but I feel I need the walk to fortify myself.

Alice is waiting at the corner, of course. I apologize for not showing up yesterday. "I had the flu," I say.

"You still look a little green around the gills," she says.

"I do?" I touch my stomach. It feels rubbery and big, twice as big as an hour ago. A nauseating dread wallows through me.

"Whoops-a-daisy." She grabs my hand. She is as solid as a wrestler. "I'm taking you straight back home."

"No, no." I pull free. "I don't want to go home. I'll be okay."

She adjusts her books so that she's cradling them in one arm. "Come on, then," she says, linking her free arm through mine. "We'll try and keep you on your feet at least."

The walk is a little under a mile, not far compared to the distance some kids have to travel. Our route goes through the subdivision to a small plaza (barber shop, smoke shop, bank, milk store, beauty salon), around the plaza into Matas Parkette with its wooden benches and granite statue of Dr. Adolph T. Matas, 1812–1882, Physician, Surgeon and Linguist, Friend to All (which doesn't stop people from saying Doctor Fat Ass and Fat Ass Park), then along a sidewalk that runs adjacent to a main road.

As we're entering the park I feel sick again. "I've got to sit down," I say, yanking myself free and staggering over to a bench.

Alice bustles up behind me. "Put your head between your knees."

I obey.

She sits and snaps opens her purse. From my bent-over position I look at her calves under the thick nylons that crush her blond leg hair into a mat. I hear her unscrewing the lid of her hand-lotion jar. "Nobody's watching," she says. "You might feel better getting it out of your system."

I know what she means but I decide I am being urged in another direction, and so I say, "Can you be pregnant and still get your period?"

Silence, except for the faint sound of her hands rubbing together. "I'm not sure," she says at last.

"What about morning sickness? Do you know if that can suddenly start after two months?"

She clears her throat. "I remember when my mother was carrying Teddy she had the worst time that way right in the middle, the fourth and fifth months. Before and after she was fine." She screws the lid back on and closes her purse. "How are we feeling?"

"Okay." I sit up. Would Dr. Matas, Friend to All, have given me an abortion? "The thing is," I say, "they weren't my usual heavy periods."

Alice picks up her books and purse. "We should get a move on."

I let her take my arm again. "Oh, God," I say at the thought of the rest of my life.

"Have you seen that sign in the window of Parker's Drug Store?" she asks.

"What sign?"

"Pregnancy tests." Her cheeks flare up. "Confidential and quick."

Why would she, of all people, have noticed that? "No."

"I'll bet you any money you've only got a touch of the flu, but if you want to put your mind at rest . . ."

"You pee into a bottle, don't you?"

"Yes, they need a specimen. First thing in the morning is best, before you've eaten anything."

"Alice—" I force us to stop. She looks at me. Her burning little face. "You won't tell anybody."

"Tell? Good heavens, no! Who would I tell?" She gestures zipping her lips. "There. Tucked away all safe and sound."

CHAPTER SEVENTEEN

I sit on the piano bench. There used to be a chair, a good one, mahogany with green leather upholstery (Mr. and Mrs. Richter brought it over from Germany), but Abel gave it to the manicurist across the hall after her only chair collapsed under the weight of a hefty client. The gold velvet loveseat that he picked up a few weeks later at a thrift shop lasted only a day before the superintendent made some passing comment about how nice it would look in the lobby. So that's where it got moved to.

Why Abel stays on in this small, rundown basement apartment is a mystery to the Richters, especially as they're always offering to help pay the rent on a bigger apartment in a better part of town. They can't understand that he stays on precisely *because* it is small and rundown. But it's not a hovel—hardly that with all the cleaning he does—and it's not empty, either. His books are here, three floor-to-ceiling cases of them. Also his piano, his desk, his old four-poster bed and the tea trolley and Oriental carpet that used to be in his parents' dining room. I myself like the effect of all this. The suggestion of genteel poverty, of a scholarly indifference to comfort.

It's Saturday, late morning, and I've dropped by on my way to lunch with a friend. Abel sits across from me, on the bed, leaning one shoulder against the wall whose network of cracks he likes to speculate describes the river system on a distant planet. Nudging each other for space on his bony lap are his two stray cats: three-legged Peg and drooling Flo. The bed is made, the bottles hidden somewhere. I notice that since I was here last the tea trolley, where he keeps his pills and vitamins, plus the medical paraphernalia his father bought for him (thermometer, stethoscope, blood-pressure gauge), has had its shelves lined with white paper. Normally, at this time of day, he'd be in jeans and a clean shirt, but I got him out of the shower, so he's wearing his bathrobe. His nails have been cut, probably by the manicurist, what's her name, something helpless-sounding: Nell or Cindy. Absurdly, I am jealous of her. If Abel was still in any condition to have a type, a fading beauty with a flagging nail-cutting business would be it.

I cope with the jealousy by never bringing up her name. The sense I have in this apartment of sexy angels fluttering around the windows, I never talk about, either, I couldn't say why. It's certainly not being afraid he'd think I was crazy. Nobody is crazy in his books, and he'd be only too happy to talk about something other than the dried blood in the pleats of his lips, the flaking skin on his neck. He's dehydrated again, he must be. I won't ask, but when he brings a shuddering hand to his neck, I can't resist alluding to it, saying, "Whoever thought an alcoholic could end up dying of thirst?"

The hand moves to his chest. Is the skin there coming away as well? I haven't seen him naked in over six months, he won't let me. We still lie down together, and he touches me all over, but subtle flinches give me to understand I am to confine myself to his head. Everything up there, above the neck, still works perfectly. His teeth are white and straight, and despite a yellowish tinge to the whites of his eyes he can still see an ant across the room. All this vigour upsets me when I think of the waste. If he lets himself die, it all dies, his whole body.

He keeps glancing toward the bathroom. He probably has a bottle stashed in there and can't wait to get to it. Since signing himself out of the Marwood Clinic, he won't drink in front of me or his parents. Of course, we aren't fooled, or, at least, I'm not. His mother, finding him at home and sociable, will say that he's "off the wagon," by which she means "on." She tells him what she wants to hear. "You're getting better!" she announces, and take his silence for affirmation. (I do this, too, although not where his drinking is concerned. It's his feelings, specifically his feelings for me, that I decree.)

"So, do you need money?" I say, returning to the subject of why he had his phone disconnected, and why I raced over. When the operator said his number was no longer in service, I panicked.

"It isn't the money. The ringing . . ."

"What about the ringing?"

"It's loud."

I decide not to pursue that.

"I'm fine," he says. He takes a clean, folded handkerchief from his bathrobe pocket and dabs at the puddle of drool Flo has deposited on his leg. "Everything's fine."

"If you say so."

"Louise."

"What?"

"I think you should go now."

Two days later. I've brought groceries: cream of wheat, applesauce, Gerber baby food, ginger ale. As recommended by the doctor. He puts everything in the refrigerator rather than in the cupboard, which tells me that last night Mr. and Mrs. Richter came by with more or less the same things and he doesn't want me to see this and feel I wasted my time. Except I *have* wasted it, and so have they. We all know that most of what we give him ends up in the garbage.

He offers me a glass of the ginger ale. "That's for *you*," I say, exasperated. I sit, as before, on the piano bench, him across from me on the edge of the bed, the cats on his lap. He isn't agitated, he must have been drinking before I arrived. He is considering my question: does he ever pray? Through the ceiling we can hear the upstairs tenant screaming, "God almighty! Lord Jesus!" The first time I heard her carrying on like this I thought she was having sex. I say, "I don't believe in God but sometimes I catch myself begging Him, 'Please God, please God,' and I only went to church the one time."

Abel taps out a beat on the bedpost and then stops and looks at his hand as if startled by its dexterity. He has told me he still occasionally "fools around" on the piano, but whenever I'm here the lid is down and there are books and an ashtray on top. "Yeah," he says. "Every once in a while I pray."

"To God?"

"No. No, not God."

"To who, then?"

"To the ether, I guess."

"What do you say?"

"Give me faith."

"What else?"

"That's it. Give me faith."

"In what?"

"Faith in whatever is happening."

"Why don't you ask for strength?" In one form or another we've been having this argument for years. Me on the side of fighting, him on the side of surrendering.

"God would know you need strength," he says, "if His plan is for you to survive. If that's not His plan, it's faith you need. You need it anyway."

"Except you don't believe in God."

"No, I don't."

From upstairs comes a scream.

Abel looks at the ceiling. "Okay," he says, "I do." He smiles.

I won't smile back. "So what do you believe in, then? Other than giving up."

"Giving *in*."

"To weakness," I say miserably. I don't even have the satisfaction of offending him. You can't offend him with personal insults, other than in the roundabout way of signalling you're upset. "Just giving in to what comes easiest."

"Giving in to what is."

"Oh, come on. What is, is what you decide it should be."

"Did you decide to be born? To be a girl?"

"That's not what I'm talking about."

"But those are the facts of your life. They are what is. Did you decide you'd have a mother who'd walk out on you?

Did you decide you and I would live down the street from each other? Did you—?" He falters.

Did I decide I would get pregnant? Was that the next question?

Maybe not, but a list of the big events in my life is bound to invoke the ones we try not to talk about. As he must have just realized. "I decided I would *punish* you," I say. "I decided to act as badly as I felt."

He frowns. I can't offend him but I can hurt him.

He leans toward the desk, careful not to disturb the cats, opens the drawer and pulls out the cigar box in which he keeps his tobacco pouch and a few emergency joints. On the bed, using the surface of the box, he starts to roll a cigarette. He has the bowed back of an old man. The trembling of his hands, because it seems sure to defeat him, makes a performance of the activity.

"Did you decide to be an alcoholic?" I ask.

He smiles. "Was I born an alcoholic, did I achieve alcoholism or was alcoholism thrust upon me?"

"Why do you joke about it?"

"I don't know if I made any conscious decision. I don't think I did."

"You've decided to kill yourself, though."

"No."

"All right, you've decided to die." When he offers no response, I say, "You've decided not to live. By not saving yourself, you've decided not to live."

He gets the cigarette lit. "I haven't decided anything," he says, looking at the ceiling. The woman is moaning now, or singing.

"There's one thing you *have* decided," I say. "Which is to let the people who love you suffer."

He looks down and strokes Flo's head.

"It's true," I say.

"I don't want that."

"Are you happy?"

"It isn't a question of happiness or unhappiness."

"Then what *is* it a question of?"

He shrugs.

"Oh," I say. "Right. Giving in. We're back to that. You know what I think? I think it's a question of your wanting to drink no matter what. You don't want to stop, so you're not going to. It doesn't make any difference what I say, what your parents say, what the doctors say. You don't care. You *can't* care. You're an addict."

"Maybe." He sighs. "Maybe that's it."

"Okay," I say. "Good. Now we're getting somewhere."

No, we aren't. If he can agree with me so readily, then I don't agree with myself. This could just be him surrendering on another front: giving up trying to explain. Giving up, at least temporarily, his own complicated ideas of himself.

CHAPTER EIGHTEEN

"I'm going to do it," I tell Alice when we arrive at my locker.

She nods, tight-lipped. "When?"

"This morning, I guess. Now. Why not? I haven't eaten anything yet today."

"Are you sure you feel up to it?"

"I'm okay. I need a bottle." I glance around as if there might be one lying in the hall.

She opens her lunch bag and extracts a jam jar filled with mashed potatoes. "Here," she says in a low voice. "Empty it in the washroom. Clean it really well with soap and then rinse away every last smidgen of the soap with hot water and then dry it with a paper towel. It should be as sterile and dry as possible. If I were you, I'd wait until after the bell. You don't want anyone seeing."

I take the jar. Again, she has astonished me. I feel like a novice spy being briefed by the head of the agency.

"Oh, God," I say. "What if I'm pregnant?"

"Not so loud!"

"I'll have to have an abortion. I'll have to go to that Dr. Jekyll guy in Buffalo." According to Nola MacDougall, a girl in my home-room class whose cousin has been pregnant at least twice, there's a mad-scientist doctor in Buffalo who will give you an abortion for next to nothing because he needs fetuses for his experiments.

"You won't have to do any such thing," Alice says, close
to anger. "Don't think that way. All you have to think about
right now is scouring that jar, doing your business in it and
taking it to the drug store. Okay, how much money do you
have?"

I dig through my purse and find my wallet. Five dollars
and fifty-five cents.

"That might not be enough." She snaps open her purse,
removes her wallet, unzips a pocket behind the empty
credit-card section and withdraws a folded ten-dollar bill.
"Take it. No, take it. Just in case. You can pay me back later.
I'll go to the office and tell them you were feeling poorly
and went home."

Only now, at the prospect of deception, do her cheeks
redden.

"I'll tell them," I offer.

"No, no, no. They'll phone your house and ask Mrs.
Carver to come pick you up. Oh, gosh, I hope they believe
me and don't phone anyway. But it's true, isn't it? You *are*
feeling poorly." She squares her shoulders. "Well, I'll just
have to *make* them believe me, that's all there is to it."

Parker's Drug Store is in a plaza about a half mile north of
the school, behind a block of high-rise apartments. Walking
there, I start fretting about the jam jar tipping and leaking all
over my purse. I take it out, wrap it in Kleenex and hold it in
my hand. If I'm pregnant what will they find in the urine? I
imagine some kind of marine life, not sperm but a corrupt
offshoot. For my seventh birthday my mother bought me a
goldfish that I called Judy Garland and carried from the
store in a clear plastic bag. I am now reminded of this. We

had Judy Garland only a couple of weeks before she slipped down the drain while my mother was cleaning the bowl. "She'll be happier in the sewers," my mother said. "Who wants to live in a goldfish bowl anyway?"

"A goldfish," I sobbed.

"Judy Garland was going round the bend," my mother said.

My mother's name—Grace Hahn—is the one I give to the pharmacist.

"Telephone number?" he says.

"Oh, I'll wait."

The pharmacist (Mr. Parker?) looks like Liberace. It's hardly reassuring that the verdict should be left in the hands of a liver-spotted old man wearing a rust-coloured toupée and lipstick. Or am I hallucinating? He slaps a label on the jam jar. "Two hours."

"I'd like the quick service, if that's all right."

"Two hours *is* the quick service."

I wait in a donut shop across the road from the plaza. I order a Coke float but can't drink it because my stomach is still queasy. "Please God," I pray, although I'm no longer sure what it is I want. To be pregnant is an event, a crisis. It is either a trip to Buffalo or Abel and me living together. Not to be pregnant is going back to my empty life before the summer, emptier for containing no hope and no boy, not even Tim Todd.

The waitress has a sympathetic, motherly manner. She calls me Sweetie. Maybe she know's why I'm here, maybe this is where all the pregnancy-test girls wait out their two hours. There is a *Miss Chatelaine* magazine on the counter, and I leaf through it, page after page of beautiful, happy, unpregnant models. I try to read an article called "Looking Super on a Shoe String" but keep getting distracted by the architecture of the letters, the needless dots above the *i*'s and *j*'s, the gaping *c*'s and *u*'s, the alien, insolent *z*'s and all the words in this article that start with *z*: *zingy, zip, zest.* When the two hours are up I return to the drug store, certain that the worst is going to happen. Except I still don't know what the worst is.

The pharmacist says nothing, just hands me a receipt with "Positive" written across it.

I expel a relieved breath. So it must be that I don't want a baby after all. "Thank you," I say.

"Positive," he says, "means you're pregnant."

"Pardon?"

"You're pregnant."

For a moment, owing to his toupée and unnaturally red lips, I think he's toying with me. "But positive—"

"Means you're pregnant."

"Are you . . . Is it ever wrong?"

His hound-dog eyes look me up and down. "Not when it's positive."

A moment later, made weak in the knees by a boy at the cash register who, from the back anyway, could be Abel, I decide to go to Vancouver and tell him. Spring it on him, face to face. If I've somehow scared him away, then my belly—I push it out and already it seems enormous—then *this* should scare him back.

I leave the plaza almost happy. I'm going to see Abel. My earlier misgivings (he'll marry me only out of duty, I'll be stuck in his basement) I don't revive. I picture Mrs. Richter cooing at the bundle in her arms. I picture Abel playing Brahms' lullaby on the piano. I even picture giving birth, insofar as I envision thrashing my head on a white pillow while Abel paces in an adjoining room. I'll have to quit school, of course. The thought exhilarates me. Goodbye, Maureen Hellier and her cohorts. Adios, chemistry, geography.

Since it's too early to go home, I head for Matas Parkette. The back of the bench I sit on is so scored with initials and hearts it's like grille work. When Abel and I were kids I wanted him to carve our initials into the magnolia behind his house, but he wouldn't take a knife to a tree. I feel heartened, remembering this. Light funnels along the grass, and everywhere black squirrels—the lucky kind—leap like frogs, and this also gives me hope.

I devise my travel plans.

The money should be no problem. In my bank account I have over two thousand dollars, more than half of it deposited by my father for my university education. Provided I can reserve a seat on the Saturday-morning flight, which is the one Abel recommended back when we were talking about my visiting him at Christmas, I'll arrive around nine in the morning Vancouver time, before he has left the house. I'll phone from the airport and have him pick me up. No, I'd better take a taxi—Mr. Richter might already be out somewhere in the car. We'll spend Saturday together, and part of Sunday. What will I tell my father? Oh, anything. Some story about going to visit the Parliament Buildings in Ottawa with my civics class. Such an outing is, in fact, scheduled for the spring. He'll be all for it. I'll say I can save money on the chartered bus to the airport if he gives me a lift.

At the milk store in Matas Plaza I change a quarter for two dimes and a nickel and then use the pay phone outside the restaurant. A few quick calls and I've made my flight reservations. Next, I go to my bank, two doors down, and without raising an eyebrow the teller hands me, *me*—a strung-out-looking hippy girl—seven hundred and fifty dollars in ten- and twenty-dollar denominations. Mrs. Carver would say I have the black squirrels to thank. Maybe so. But I also feel that everything going so smoothly is a sign I'm on the right track. Less than four days from now I'll be with Abel. He'll put a hand on my belly.

"A little you in there," I'll say. I'm already sure it's a boy.

CHAPTER NINETEEN

I now know that most people have to drink hard for at least a couple of decades before they're in real danger of killing themselves. Of course, you can die at any time from blacking out at the wheel of your car. You can stumble around a ravine until you fall down a slope and break your neck.

Abel had been drinking for only nine years when an ulcer in his stomach ruptured and he hemorrhaged. He did try to stop drinking. It was his decision—nobody pushed him—to live at the treatment clinic, and he stayed there for two months. But as soon as he checked himself out, he headed for the liquor store, and six months later, while driving his taxi, he hemorrhaged again.

He would have gone into shock if his passenger hadn't taken over the wheel and raced through red lights getting him to the hospital. The Richters and I only heard about it once he was back in his apartment and then only because the passenger, who happened to be an eighty-year-old retired police chief, told his story to the *Toronto Star* as part of an article about heroic senior citizens. We had assumed Abel was off visiting some French-Canadian friend from the clinic. I'm not saying he lied to us. He took care never to lie outright.

Not even to himself. Better than we did, he knew his symptoms, and his odds. At the clinic he'd read all the pamphlets, attended all the sessions, and when he was still strong enough to drive a taxi, he spent part of every afternoon taking notes at the University of Toronto's medical library. You couldn't get him to talk about those notes, but one day I looked at some of them (he'd gone to the bathroom, and I pulled a few pages out from under a stack of musical scores) and what I read was "life-threatening complication of portal hypertension," "black tarry stools," "convulsions," "poor prognosis." On the second page was a list of words: "bewilderment, denial, fear, anger, grief, mistrust, aversion, apathy, alienation." When he returned to the room I held up the list and asked, "The range of your feelings?"

He checked his surprise. "Other people's feelings. Family and friends."

"Family and friends of *alcoholics*."

He tugged on his earlobe. Nodded.

"*My* feelings," I said, ignoring his discomfort.

He gave me a keen look. "Are they?"

I studied the page. "Not the last three."

I put the pages on the top of the piano and he came over and began to rearrange them. With his head lowered he looked only preoccupied, a bit prim, but when he glanced up I caught an expression of pleasure so private it was almost obscene. He blinked, startled. Had he forgotten I was there?

"You reduce your horizons," he said, "and all the little things, the slightest things, they suddenly . . ." He shook his head.

"Matter," I finished.

"Grow," he said. "Expand out into the world."

"They only seem to because you're ignoring all the big important things."

"That's the idea. You have to go right in close and concentrate on every detail and on every move you make and then you start realizing how it's all joined together. But so . . . so delicately. So delicately and eternally. It's like overtones in music, they go on forever, we just can't hear them. You put a pile of papers in order and the principle of order itself is solidified. You straighten a picture on the wall and a flock of birds corrects its flight path."

I said woodenly, "You don't have any pictures on the walls."

He smiled like a man deeply charmed.

"If you love me," I said, "why don't you just straighten *yourself* out?"

And then I was crying.

"Oh, God." I swiped at my tears. "Look at me. I suppose some plugged-up drain somewhere is starting to flow."

"A seed is germinating." He reached out and stroked my head. "A baby is being born."

I flinched from his hand. "Why did you say that? Why would you say a thing like that?"

CHAPTER TWENTY

According to plan, my father drives me to the airport. "Happy to, delighted to!" he said, excited at the prospect of my seeing Pierre Trudeau. He asked if any of my classmates needed a ride, and I told him no. Straight to his eager, honest face I said, "Most of the them have already paid to take the bus."

Now, sitting beside him in the car, I remember hearing Aunt Verna telling somebody over the phone that the real damage liars do is in forcing you to question your instincts. I think of how Alice blushes at even the idea of a lie. The news of my pregnancy, and my decision to confront Abel in person, Alice accepted with surprising composure, as if mentally ticking off items on a list of probabilities. It was when I got to the part about pretending to go to Ottawa on an outing funded by a school bake sale that her cheeks lit up, although she deflected the implied reproach by exclaiming, "Bake sale! I never would have come up with that!"

"It's all for a good cause," I reminded her . . . with a first quiver of doubt.

There is hardly any traffic so early on a Saturday. My father tunes the radio to classical music and conducts with his right hand. I press against the door, out of swatting range. A grey morning. Fog packed into the gullies and low-lying fields. I look for lucky birds: yellow finches or warblers. There are starlings. A flock the shape of a thumbprint moves diagonally up the sky. Are starlings lucky? I don't know. I am sobered by the wooden telephone poles, which I see as a pageant of crucifixes, one for every aborted baby.

At the airport my father offers to help check me in. "Mr. Kline will do it," I say, referring to the supposed chaperone. I am out of the car before my father can say that he'd like to meet Mr. Kline. I wear my mother's white leather jacket. I carry her white overnight case. Waving goodbye to my father and, as I do, feeling the hike of my short skirt, I am overcome by the unpleasant sensation that I *am* my mother: glamorous and running away. My father leans over, rolls down the passenger window and tells me to give his regards to Trudeau. I pretend to laugh. "See you Sunday," I say, another deceit. During the past several hours my plan has advanced to staying permanently at the Richters' and, as people do in novels, "sending for my things."

I've never been on an airplane before. I am amazed by how unspectacular it is—the smooth lift-off, the momentary view and then clouds. No UFOs, no angels. I soon fall asleep. The seat beside me is empty, and when I awaken with the serving of breakfast I find I have kicked off my new open-toed, too-small pumps (the right size made my feet look like canoes) and hoisted my legs over the armrest. I sit up straight, tugging at my skirt as the stewardess, whose blasé pantomime of the safety instructions I had admired, reaches across my legs, unfastens the little table on the seat back, bangs it down and then, still without a word, as if returning some repulsive thing I mislaid, hands me my breakfast tray.

I take it, although I have no appetite. I even eat the fruit cocktail and one piece of toast, my fear of vomiting not as strong as my fear of annoying the stewardess if I don't at least make a dent. Yesterday, when I got home from school, I ate half a dozen chocolate chip cookies and a minute later threw up into the kitchen sink. Mrs. Carver herded me to a chair and began brewing one of her awful stomach-settling teas. Over her shoulder she gave me that penetrating look again.

"What?" I challenged her.

She turned back to the stove.

"This flu is hanging on," I said. I didn't put it past her that by some voodoo indicator she had lit on the truth.

The stewardess reappears and snatches away my tray without offering me any coffee. To comfort myself I think of how I'll be seeing Abel in only a few hours. But the prospect, now that it is almost a certainty, unnerves me. "Are you on the pill?" he asked. Since getting the pregnancy test I haven't allowed myself to remember this, how solemn he sounded. More than solemn, frightened. "I can't be pregnant," I said, "it's impossible." By which I guess I meant impossible to imagine.

From the Prairies to Vancouver the sky is overcast. We land in rain. Because I haven't checked any luggage I keep walking, past the carousels and through the exit doors. Spotting a phone, I go over, fish a dime out of my change purse, put it in the slot.

Hang up.

Better to show up in person. That was the original plan.

A white-pages directory lies open on the ledge under the phone. Hardly aware of what I'm doing, I leaf through to

the *K*'s. There's half a column of Kirks, none of them pre-
ceded by the initial G., though. Or H. (my mother might be
going by Helen these days). Or S. (she might have listed
herself under my father's first name).

I leaf back to the *H*'s. Haggerty. Hague. Hahn, her maiden
name. No H. or S. Hahn, but—what do you know?—a G.

I check my watch. Nine-fifteen. I drop the dime back into
the slot and dial the number. One ring, two rings. The
blood booms in my head.

"Hello?" says a woman's voice. She sounds impatient,
interrupted. "Hello? Who is it?"

Noiselessly, as if I'd been eavesdropping on an extension,
I hang up.

I head for the taxi stand. Halfway there I stop in delayed
shock. I take a breath and keep walking. Was it her? I don't
know, I don't *know!* It might have been. An older, more
jagged voice than I remember, but she *is* older. Why would
she be living in Vancouver, though? And if she is, why
would she use her real name?

Why did I phone? That's the real question. What did I
expect? If she wanted to get in touch with me, she'd have
done so long ago. I should have at least said something. I
imagine the following exchange:

Me: "Is this Helen Grace Kirk? Formerly Hahn?"

Her (after a pause): "Who's calling?"

Me: "Your daughter, Louise. I thought you might be interested in knowing that you're going to be a grandmother."

Her (with a sarcastic snort): "Oh, great."

Me: "If it's a girl I'm calling her Millicent" (after my
grandmother, her mother and enemy). "But if she only lives

a few hours, that is to say, if she *fucks off,* I'm calling her Helen Grace."

Just as well that I hung up.

Me: "What did the mother cow say to the daughter cow?"

Her: "What?"

Me: "Any cow can get herself pregnant."

Her: "That's not funny."

The rain stops during the drive into the city. A few minutes later, the fog thins and I glimpse mountains, water. So I really am in Vancouver. I made it.

I wonder if my mother, when she first arrived at wherever she disappeared to, experienced this dull astonishment, this strange letdown.

I wonder if she was pregnant.

The thought hardly stirs me. It is as though I have alighted on the proper expression for something, an odd behaviour, say, or a circumstance, that I've been dimly conscious of for years. My mother pregnant by another man. By fancy Dan. The surprising part is that nobody ever suspected it. Or maybe everybody did, and it was just that nobody mentioned it in front of me.

Which would mean I'd have a half-sister or half-brother somewhere. Right here in Vancouver, it's possible. If it's a girl, she'd be Louise, given my mother's views on wasting a perfectly good name. "Let's hope for her sake she's ravishingly beautiful," I think with a tremor of resentment that dismantles the entire fantasy. If there *is* another Louise (or Louis), it's none of my concern. My mother did as she pleased. She minded her own business and wasn't very curious about anyone else's, except as it seemed to bear out what she already thought. I can't remember her ever once asking me how I felt about something, or even paying much attention to me, other than to be entertained by one of my jokes or to fuss over how I looked. "Louise knows how to work the washing machine," she wrote in her goodbye note. No, I didn't.

We have left the highway and are driving along a street lined with rundown furniture and hardware stores, a Chinese restaurant called O.K. Happy Food. After a couple of blocks the places begin to look and sound more respectable: Everton Flower Shop, Cedric's Antiques. Elegant Fashions—the same name as the store where I work, or *used to* work (I had to quit to get this weekend off). Behind the stores you can see wooden houses on wide lots, many of them surrounded by high, dense hedges like ramparts. We turn onto one of these residential roads, and almost immediately pull over in front of a ranch-style bungalow whose front lawn is a jungle of flowers.

"Are we here?" I say with a feeling of having just woken up.

"Twenty-four Saint Clarens," the driver says.

I pay him, get out. Why doesn't he stop me? Why doesn't somebody shout, "Wait!"

A German shepherd watches from the living-room window. Sirius, it would be, Cane's replacement. He sits in the gap between the drapes, his big patrician head cocked. Oh, and there's the station wagon! I hadn't noticed it under the carport. The same old station wagon with the wood-panelled sides. "It goes with the house," I think and drift for a moment, disoriented.

The sound of an approaching car rouses me. I step onto the sidewalk and look at my watch. Twenty to ten.

Abel might still be sleeping. In all my plans (they now seem insanely provisional) I never pictured anyone other than him answering the door. Well, if the station wagon can undo me, I'll be a wreck with Mrs. Richter. She'll only have to say my name and I'll start crying and confessing. I can't let that happen. Before I tell anyone else I have to tell Abel.

I look around. There aren't any houses on the other side of the street owing to a drop-off down to a ravine. Between the drop-off and the street is a strip of public lawn landscaped with cedar trees and shrubs, a few slabs of granite, a drinking fountain. I cross over and go behind the cedars. Several of the slabs are arranged like chairs, a tall one abutting a squat one. I choose the pair offering the best view, set my case beside them on the grass, remove my mother's leather jacket (a previously forbidden treasure—flarewaisted, soft as raw meat—that my father allowed me to wear for this "rare and important occasion"), fold it and lay it on top of the squat slab, which is still damp from the rain. I sit. Now I'm chilly. I open the case and get out my blue jeans. That's all I packed, except for a change of underpants and powder-blue baby-doll pyjamas I bought from Elegant Fashions on my salesgirl discount a few minutes before I quit. I should have put the jeans on the slab. But the jacket will be wet on the underside; I may as well leave it. I drape the jeans around my head and shoulders. It doesn't matter what I look like, I'm hidden from the street. I can see out, however. By moving a few branches I can see the Richters' garden, front door, driveway. Anybody leaving the place, I won't miss. I'll just wait. The sun is shining, it's warming up. Unless Abel is sick, he'll come outside sooner or later.

I'm good at waiting.

And I've done this before. Seven and a half years ago, day after day, I hid in shrubbery and waited for Mrs. Richter to walk past her windows. I have also (the Presbyterian church episode) sat on a cold surface in an odd headdress as I prepared to spring myself on my beloved. The coincidences strike me as portentous ... and unsettling, that my life should be repeating itself in this eccentric, hazardous way.

"He loves me too much, he loves me too much," I say to banish anxiety. I consider the lilies of the yard: white gaping flowers with petals like splayed limbs. I contemplate the house and hallucinate a fish from the sleek length, the shingled siding and a bathroom window whose partly opened venetian blind gives the impression of gills.

Abel's room is at the back, he told me once. Abel, asleep. The whole neighbourhood asleep, caught in an enchantment until he wakes up. So you'd think.

An hour elapses before a single person—a bald man carrying a rolled-up newspaper under his arm—strolls past. His silver hound noses into the park, stops, hunches, trembles all over, casts me a mournful, abject glance, then defecates. About fifteen minutes later, a boy flies down the middle of the road on a high-speed bicycle, which, before I see it, I hear as crickets.

I am, by this association, reminded of the five types of North American cricket: house, field, California tree, snowy tree and black-horned tree. I try to remember what insect family crickets belong to. Can't. I turn, then, to remembering jokes from *A Thousand and One Side-Splitters*. ("What did the mother cow say to the daughter cow? We owe all we have to udders.") I drift to song lyrics. "Baby, baby, where did our love go." No. "Be my, be my little baby." No, I don't want to think about babies, mine growing down there, bones brewing, fingernails forming, a fetal shape. See it? In that cloud of cells, see the big bean head? Well, no, I see a bomb. Make that a hand grenade.

I think about the Vietnam War and wonder, if Canada should ever get involved, where Abel would draft-dodge to. Germany? For long moments I fall under the street's enchantment and think nothing. It is during one of these spells that the Richters' front door opens.

I jump to my feet.

Mr. Richter steps out. He is thinner than I remember, but not bent over or feeble, as I had feared. Jingling keys, he goes down the steps and toward the car. Before he reaches it the front door opens again.

"Karl!"

Mrs. Richter! With white hair! Abel never told me. And she's fat, she's gotten fat! She's wearing a red bathrobe, not the same old one, surely, she wouldn't fit into it. She calls out something in German. Mr. Richter holds up a finger, gives a curt nod: *Ja, Danke schön* for the reminder, he won't forget. He climbs into the car and drives off. She descends the porch steps. Hands on hips, she surveys her yard. She squints my way and for a delirious moment I'm convinced she has spotted me. Then she bends at the waist. When she straightens she is clutching a bunch of carrots. She turns and goes back into the house.

It is all I can do not to run over there and pound on the door. It is all I can do.

The morning passes. Eleven-thirty. Noon. Mr. Richter doesn't return. Nobody enters the park. I am the street's witness, its prisoner. I drink from the fountain, pee among the shrubs, occasionally I stand on my slab to get a better view of the mountains bolting out of their laurels of cloud. Otherwise I stay put, sitting now on both the jeans *and* the jacket and using the overnight case as a footstool while I try to read the book I brought along, the J. S. Bach biography. I wonder if Abel knows that Bach, too, was orphaned. This, I learned on the plane. Here, in the park, I have skipped ahead to Bach's marriage to Anna Magdalena. The book describes her as "a flower or a star . . . so faithful was she, so unwearying, so simply useful and so courageous with the courage that only women have or by natural decree need to have."

Nothing much has happened across the road, not since Mrs. Richter went inside. Late morning she opened the curtains, then the window of the room nearest the garage. A little later she opened the living-room drapes with a flourish, standing in the gap and throwing them apart as if she were about to break into song.

Sirius, by that time, had abandoned his post. I figure they let him out into the back yard, which adjoins somebody else's back yard, the two properties separated by a chain-link fence that I can see part of where it extends past the Richters' house. So anyone leaving by a rear door would have to come around to the front. I presume. Maybe I should make certain, and get something to eat while I'm at it. Suppose I ran over, reconnoitred, pulled up a bunch of carrots, ran back?

I close the book and set it down beside me on the slab. If I get caught . . . If I get caught, I get caught. It's almost two o'clock, and I'm starving. I'm jet-lagged. I'm pregnant, for God's sake!

Just as I'm coming to my feet I see a skinny guy hurrying down the sidewalk across the road, about fifty yards to my left. His head is bent to one side and held there unnaturally. His hair is a burning bush, an orange Afro. He wears flapping beige trousers, not bell-bottoms, just trousers too big and belted high on his torso, and a short-sleeved sky-blue shirt with a navy collar. For all that he's speeding along, he doesn't swing his arms.

"A weirdo," I think. I can guess where he's headed. Sure enough, there he goes, turning onto the Richters' property.

On the back of his shirt, in large navy letters above an inverted pyramid of bowling pins, it says GARY. Did Abel ever mention a Gary? I'm sure he never mentioned a guy who wears an imaginary straitjacket and yet belongs to a bowling team.

Gary reaches up (so his arms *do* move) to bang the knocker. The door opens.

And out comes Abel.

He shuts the door and follows Gary down the porch steps. My heart punches at my ribs. No, it's not my heart, it's the baby leaping up, sensing proximity to its other genetic half. I step from behind the tree.

I step back.

I've lost my nerve. I forgot how good looking he was. Or

has he gotten even better looking? His hair has grown. His arms, too, they seem longer, more muscular. I move back onto the sidewalk and watch him and Gary disappear around the corner. I dash to the rock, stuff my jacket, jeans and book into the case, grab it and my purse and start running. When I reach the corner they are only half a block ahead of me, stopped at a fruit vendor's and getting yelled at.

I slip behind a telephone pole and step partway out of my shoes, which are already giving me blisters. The yelling woman wears a black kerchief; she waves her arms around. Gary stands there, hands stiff at his sides, head still cocked toward his left shoulder. Abel's head is also cocked, though less drastically. It is so familiar to me, the slow nod that means you have the enormousness of his attention. The woman can have no idea how passionately and sympathetically she is being listened to. I wish I were her. At that moment I would gladly recast my skulking self into a ranting foreign woman who, purely because she *is* ranting and foreign, has (I've no doubt) won Abel's heart.

She waves her hands, slaps her breasts. I can't make out what she's going on about—a diatribe against long-haired boys, I imagine. But then Abel says something and she bleats out a laugh and seizes an apple from a bushel basket and presses it on him. He takes it and bends down closer to her, and with both hands she brushes back his hair, as a lover would, to kiss his forehead. I am surprised, but only for a second. Of course! She adores him! She is one of his million best friends. She gives him another apple. He passes it to Gary, who flings out one stiff arm to snatch it.

They move on.

I step back into my sadistic shoes and follow, scuttling from mailbox to newspaper box to phone booth. As I pass the old lady she glares. I smile at her. Anyone who loves Abel, I have a soft spot for. Even Gary I am warming up to because of how he walks almost sideways so that he can direct his tipped-over head at Abel's face, and because his whole upper body bounces in sprees of nodding as though he savagely endorses everything Abel says.

I have no plan. If they're on their way to Gary's place, and they go inside, I guess I'll find some bushes to wait behind. Obscurely I feel as if I'm building up my courage by reacquainting myself with the way Abel looks: his hair, how he's dressed—bell-bottomed blue jeans, a silver belt of linked stars, like sheriff badges, a blue-and-purple tie-dyed T-shirt under which his shoulders move in the loose roll of a person far from the grip of heartache or regret.

Oh, Abel!

Has he stopped loving me? How is that possible? How do you love somebody one day, and the next day you don't? I *know* who he is. By letting me love him, he made a path to himself, and what I gathered up is mine. If he doesn't love me, how can he not love the perfect version of himself *in* me?

These thoughts start me crying. I am a spectacle, clumsy and darting, limping, crouching. Whimpering "Excuse me . . . Sorry" to Saturday shoppers I zip by and accidentally bash with my overnight case before we turn onto a desolate strip of auto-body shops and second-hand clothing emporiums. Here, however, with fewer people about, I'm more visible. I cross to the other side of the street, just in time. A few seconds later Abel glances over his shoulder, then he and Gary duck into an alley, where Abel draws something out of his pocket. A cigarette. No, a joint, I can tell by the way he inhales. He passes it to Gary. As soon as Gary inhales he has a coughing fit and spins around smacking his thighs. Abel thumps him on the back. When the coughing abates they re-enter the street and start crossing, but on a diagonal away from me, headed for the building on my right. They go inside.

It's an old theatre converted into a tavern or a coffee house. "EAR PIT" the mauve neon sign says. The brick is painted a washed-out pink, the door a purplish brown. I suppose you're meant to think along the lines of ear tunnel, pathway into the unconscious. Then I discern the unlit B. Oh, it's the Bear Pit, where Abel was on that Sunday night he didn't phone me.

Across the front are four vaulted windows clogged on the inside with potted plants. I press my face to the window farthest from the door and peer through the foliage. (Here I am again, peering through foliage.) I make out a big space, fluted pillars, small round tables, each bearing a little candle. There seem to be a lot of hippies sitting around and drinking from paper cups. Facing me at the table closest to the window, a girl with the word *Love* inked on her forehead and with daisies stuck to her hair inserts a cigarette between her lips and leans forward to light it at the candle. When she glances up I move to the next window and see, against the back wall, an orchestra pit, or the bear pit I guess it is. It houses an electric keyboard, a couple of microphones and an electric guitar leaning against a bar stool. A red footlight lends the tableau a private, inner-recess feel. An ear-tunnel feel.

From this window I can also see booths along the wall to my left. It's brighter there owing to the illuminated red paper lanterns that hang above each table. I spot Gary, his orange Afro. He is sliding into a seat.

And now I see Abel, standing a few feet away. A blond girl wearing a full-length red cape tries to steal his apple and he tosses it up for her to catch. She misses. Her laugh pierces the window glass. A petite brunette sinks against him in a theatrical swoon, and even though I can tell by the respectful way he eases her upright that there is nothing going on between them, a vein of jealousy opens in me and alerts me to my claim on him.

I decide to go inside. "I've got nothing to lose," I think. I don't know what I mean, it seems I have everything to lose. I put on some lipstick while continuing to peer through the window. An elderly black man wearing white trousers, a white dress shirt and a white homburg strolls up to Abel. Mr. Earl, I'm guessing, the old saxophonist Abel talked about a couple of times. He offers Abel a flask. Abel accepts, takes a long swig and then opens his mouth and shakes his head as if he'd just drunk gasoline. Mr. Earl nods like a physician witnessing the desired effect. Does he know that Abel is only seventeen? His hand alights, big as a raven, on Abel's shoulder, and the two of them head over to Gary's booth, Mr. Earl getting in first, Abel sliding in next to him.

Abel is now faced away from the door, and this calms me somewhat, as it means I can put off the showdown a little longer.

There is a cover charge of two dollars. I pay and slink over to the only empty table in sight. It's behind a pillar that blocks off most of the orchestra pit, but I can peek around it to see Abel, who, as I sit, is taking another drink from the flask. I blow out my candle. A moment later a waitress strolls by. "Oh," she says, "bummer," and extracts a lighter from the pocket of her jeans.

"It's okay," I say, placing my hand over the wick.

For drink there is either apple cider or grapefruit juice, for food only peanut-butter-and-banana sandwiches. I order two sandwiches and a large cider. Meanwhile, somebody is tuning the guitar and talking into a microphone, so I move my chair until I can see the orchestra pit without putting myself in full view of Abel. The guitarist is a delicate-looking Art Garfunkel type, frizzy blond hair transformed into a rosy vapour by the footlight. He starts off playing straight blues, then bursts into a wilder Jimi Hendrix sound. There aren't any lyrics, unless his off-key groaning counts. At every slide up to a high note he winces, and I am disturbed by what seems to be a spastic expression of my dread inflicted on his features without his even realizing.

In the middle of a climactic segment of repeated wails my order arrives. I begin devouring the sandwiches. The sense I have is not of eating or even filling a cavity but of stanching a hemorrhage, packing on the gauze, more gauze. I stare at Abel, who, when the piece ends, applauds by slapping the table, since his other hand is occupied with tipping the flask at his mouth. Why is he drinking so much? Nobody else seems to be, not even Mr. Earl.

"For my next tune," says the guitarist, "I'm going to be

joined by a cat who is no stranger to the Pit. Abel Richter, last heard . . ."

The rest is lost in whistling and cheers. I can't believe it. As a kid, Abel suffered almost paralyzing stage fright when he had to perform in front of an audience. Well, no wonder then, no wonder he's fortifying himself with liquor.

He gets to his feet and starts coming this way. I look down, now not being the moment I want him to spot me. When I look up again he is descending the pit stairs and I perceive the old shyness in his bowed head and then, once he is seated at the keyboard, in the studious hunch of his back. Immediately, as though the least deliberation will change his mind, he sets down a series of soft chords.

It's another lyric-less blues-rock piece. Abel remains in the background, submitting quiet responses to the flashy guitar licks. Every note the guitar fires off, he catches on a cushion of sound, and I am reminded of when we netted dazzled moths and set them free in the ravine; there is, in his playing, that same quality of a fragile transaction being intelligently and lovingly undertaken. I glance at Mr. Earl. He nods to the beat. Across from him, Gary also nods but at a higher frequency and one not obviously associated with the music.

I look back at Abel. His face is hidden behind his hair. Floodlit as he is, in red and from below, his arms appear sunburned and oddly, childishly tubular. I seem to unknot and fall toward him in a sheltering sprawl, the whole room banked his way. The piece ends and he comes to his feet. I come to my feet. People yell, "More!" The guitarist says, "He'll be back next set!" Abel leaves the pit and I walk around the tables and through applause like gunfire, whistling like rockets. I imagine myself to be blazingly conspicuous and wonder at his failing to notice me.

He appears to be headed for the toilets. I follow. When he gets to the corridor, however, he strides past the washrooms, past the kitchen, then out an exit door, which is ajar.

Light shrieks in through the gap. Over the noise of traffic and ventilation equipment I think I hear him talking. I strain to listen but the voice goes silent. I tiptoe forward and peek around the frame.

He is about ten feet away, across a narrow alley. His back is to me and he embraces a girl. The girl's arms dangle. She holds a half-eaten apple. Next to her head (which I can't see, only a plank of ash-blond hair at Abel's left shoulder), hooked on something protruding from the wall there, is a red cape. A siren howls nearby and I think she must have fainted or hurt herself and Abel is propping her up until help arrives.

I am puzzled by her managing to keep hold of the apple. No, there it goes, she drops it. Both her hands slip under Abel's shirt. He bends his head. "He's kissing her," I think, still without comprehension. He begins to stroke her hair and my own scalp tingles and it's as if from this sensation, as if from extrasensory signals, that I finally grasp what I'm looking at.

He's *kissing* her.

I step outside, onto the stoop. His hand moves down to her waist. How can he not feel how close I am? I could be anybody: an axe murderer, a heavenly host. I am dying behind his back and he has no idea.

There is then a moment like death, a pop in the atmosphere, and I believe that even if he looked around he wouldn't see me. I go back inside, down the corridor into the Babel and cigarette smoke, the struggling candles. I put a ten-dollar bill, more than five times what I owe, on my table. "Is that yours?" a girl says as I start to walk away. She is pointing at my overnight case. I pick it up and leave the building. Where should I go? Anywhere. Home. I start walking east.

CHAPTER TWENTY-ONE

I've always thought of them as angels because they're beautiful and young and delicate, although I say this without ever having seen them straight on, only glimpses at the edges of my vision. I say it, what's more, having suspected for years that they are auras brought on by my migraine headaches.

When they arrive—drifting down like scarves—I sense a purity and a kind of indifference, a strange emptiness as if they were moths drawn by the atmosphere surrounding me rather than by me specifically. Only the one I call the Angel of Love seems to have any stake in my affairs.

She is both brighter and wispier than the others. She first turned up about a month before the Richters moved to Greenwoods, by which time I'd been seeing angels for years and I took for granted, almost, that they were a hard-to-believe phenomenon akin to germs and the sound of dog whistles. I had a feeling I wasn't the only person they showed themselves to, and so for all that I hoped to attract Mrs. Richter by virtue of my negative charms—scrawniness, unkemptness, friendlessness, motherlessness—I appreciated that pity can't compete with enchantment and that if *she* could see the Angel of Love I would be lit up in the general irresistible glow. This would also help the angel, who required Mrs. Richter to love me in order to come fully alive. With only my love to draw on, she drifted and was flimsy.

Not that I ever thought about her too directly. I never spoke of her. She was unspeakable, a nearly imponderable subject, the frail nucleus of love. But *there,* in whatever lustrous or sorry or refurbished state. The moment my passion leapt from Mrs. Richter to Abel, she vanished (a folding of wings, a dissolving), to be instantly replaced by another, who, with the enhanced sensitivity of a newer version, smashed into houses or glided on air currents depending on how he and I treated each other.

That intricate scrap of grace fluttering between us. I'd like to think of her as incapable of feeling pain, but I can't.

CHAPTER TWENTY-TWO

I'm not so stupefied that I imagine I can walk all the way back to Toronto, though the idea has its epic, drastic appeal. I picture myself trudging up the Rockies, sleeping in caves, then slogging across the Prairies, through walls of wheat. I get lost in a corn row. I give birth in a barn, in the hay, the cattle are lowing and dipping their big slab heads over my stall.

To hold my course, this one in Vancouver, I rely on the sun and the occasional street sign with East in its name. I have a sense of going in and out of radio frequencies as the mood of one street gives way to the next and as certain houses and stores clamour with the possibility of a life that might have been mine. Might still be mine. I could live in that clapboard bungalow, put up with the canary-yellow trim and red mailbox that says "THE BINGLES" in cock-eyed yellow letters, be the wife of strapping Mr. Bingle over there with his brush cut and hedge clippers. That girl in the grocery store, the cashier spinning dreamily on her stool? I could be her.

When I finally stop walking, it isn't because I'm tired, it's because for some time I've been noticing blood oozing out of the open toes of my shoes, and the thought that this should concern me has become a distraction.

I look around. I'm in the middle of a block of shops that

are just now closing for the day. Behind me a woman turns a crank to roll in a green canvas awning. A man comes out of the neighbouring cigar store, tilts the wooden Indian back against his chest, lifts it off its pedestal and drags it inside like a hostage. I think of sitting on the vacated pedestal, then I spot the bench across the street, in front of Dory's Five and Dime, and go over there. Taking off my shoes releases more blood than seems right. My feet are a mess: at least five open blisters on each one, and deep cuts around the big toes. I dab at the blood with Kleenex and when I'm out of Kleenex, I twist around to see if Dory's is still open. The lights are off, but a lady in hair curlers is doing something behind the counter. I hobble to the door, knock on the glass. The lady squints in my direction.

"Do you sell Band-Aids?" I call.

"We're closed!"

"I just need some Band-Aids! I'm bleeding!"

She slams shut the cash register and hurries toward the rear of the store.

I return to the bench, feeling bolts of pain now. There's blood everywhere, a smeared trail to the door and back. What would Abel think? I wonder this casually, out of old, despondent habit. I imagine him walking by here a week from now, and even though the stains have darkened and almost worn away and everybody else passes them by, Abel, being Abel, takes an interest. "Human blood," he says to whomever he's with, that blond girl. The two of them try to figure out what happened: Somebody got stabbed or shot. A drunk fell and cracked open his skull.

I start to cry. I do it silently, although I'm making no

effort to be quiet. It's as if I've been scoured out, the breath pouring straight through because of no internal organs to get snagged on. No bones, nothing.

"What did you do? Step on glass?"

I look up. It's the lady from the store. Dory. Or maybe she's *Mrs.* Dory. A tall, auburn-haired, ledge-bosomed woman in a navy shirtwaist dress that would have been fashionable fifteen years ago. And I was wrong about the rollers—that's just how her hair is arranged, in Shirley Temple spools. She looks to be about fifty, maybe older.

"Those your shoes?" she says.

I wipe my nose on the back of my hand. "They don't fit. They've rubbed my skin off."

She shifts a paper bag to her other hand, the one holding her purse, and pulls a handkerchief out of her sleeve. "Here. Blow your nose." The edges are lace. It looks more like a doily than a handkerchief. "Go ahead," she says. "I've got a drawer of them at home."

Her voice is penetrating without being loud, the severe, slightly beaten voice I associate with farm women. She starts extracting things from the bag. "I got you your Band-Aids," she says. "And some iodine and cotton batting to clean yourself up with first."

I put everything in my lap and reach for my purse. "How much do I owe you?"

"Oh, forget it. It's all free samples."

"Thank you."

"I'd throw those shoes straight in the garbage if I were you."

I look at my shoes, the howling red mouths of the toe-holes. I fumble with the wrong end of the Band-Aid box.

"Here—" She moves my overnight case onto the sidewalk and sits herself down. "I'd better fix you up. If you do it wrong and get an infection, you could end up with gangrene. Give me that one," indicating the foot nearest her.

There's no question of objecting. I twist sideways and lift both feet onto the bench. She picks up my purse and hands it to me and says, "Tuck that in there," and I realize that with my knees bent she can see my underpants. I shove the purse against my crotch. She tears off a wad of cotton batting and opens the bottle of iodine. She has long red fingernails you'd think would interfere with pushing cash-register keys. No wedding ring. "Brace yourself," she says, then presses the wad to my big toe. "How's that?"

"Fine."

"Doesn't sting?"

"A little."

Only a little. I've gone dull and meek, and these sensations deepen as I watch her work. She seems to know what she's doing, which end of the Band-Aid you tear, how to pull off the tabs simultaneously. Maybe she used to be a nurse, a statuesque, unflappable army nurse. "Talk to me, Dory," the soldiers would beg, but she's no talker. Other than asking, "How in the world did you walk on these feet?"—a question I can't answer—she says nothing until she's done and then she says, "I take it you don't have another pair of shoes in that suitcase there."

I shake my head.

"You'd better have mine, then."

I look at her feet. Astonishingly, she has on the black

leather ballet-type slippers that are just now coming into style and that I would have bought instead of the pumps except I didn't think they were appropriate for out of doors. I say I can't take her shoes and she says sure I can, she has another pair just like them at home, and no—she sees me going for my purse—she doesn't want my money. She asks where I'm headed to.

"The airport." Eventually, I suppose, I am.

"I'll give you a lift. It's not so far from where I live." She then peels off the slippers and puts them on my feet, and I'm so swathed in Band-Aids they almost fit.

"They're nice," I say.

"My new discovery." She tightens the laces. "Easy on the bunions, and I'm lucky my arches don't need support. Unlike certain other parts." She laughs—a one-note squawk that jolts me like gunshot.

We go to a lane behind the store. She carries my overnight case and strides blithely over the gravel in her nylon-stockinged feet. I hobble behind her, carrying the bloody shoes and my purse. When we get to her car she tells me to put the shoes on the floor, not to ruin my skirt. During the drive she says very little, which is fine with me. I'm holding up shakily. Even if I weren't, I'd feel no obligation to make small talk. She is a familiar presence: a cross between Aunt Verna, Alice and even (the laugh and fingernails) my mother. Now and then she alerts me to her next move—"I think I'll take Marine Drive"—as if I know the city, but she doesn't ask me my name. Or where I'm flying to, until we arrive at the airport and then she asks only so that she can pull up in front of the right airline entrance.

"Are you sure about the shoes?" I say, opening my door.

"Oh, forget it."

"Well, thanks a lot. You've been so nice to me. I don't know what I'd have—" I swallow down a sob.

She pats my leg. "Whatever's the matter," she says, "whatever it is, it'll get better."

"Not necessarily," I think as I limp into the airport. "There's no guarantee." It's as if she were delivering a message from Abel, whose faith in my resilience has, it appears, erased any guilt he may have felt about not phoning me.

Where does faith like that come from? How do some people live their entire lives trusting everything to turn out for the best? "The darkest hour is always before the dawn," they like to point out. Even if that's true, so what? Nature isn't the same as human nature. They say, "Whatever doesn't kill you makes you stronger." Really? Tell that to a starving child.

Or at least clarify it, say, "Whatever doesn't kill you *might* make you stronger if it doesn't kill you."

And yet.

And yet, in the women's washroom, I shut myself in a stall and sit crying on the toilet, flushing to muffle the sound and telling myself, "It'll get better, it'll get better," and eventually a thin cloud of optimism falls over me. I leave the washroom and sit on a bench where I look at people with a tenderness I don't remember ever having felt before. "They were all babies once," I think. When the bleakness strikes (after seeing one too many couples kiss each other good-bye) I return to the stall and cry until another cloud of optimism falls, then I sit on the same bench and get back to watching people lovingly. At some point I search out the restaurant and buy a grilled-cheese sandwich and a glass of root beer. The shaggy hair of an elderly man seated several tables away makes me think of the mad-scientist doctor in Buffalo. I keep forgetting about him and the possibility of having an abortion. It's a lifeline, but a gory one, like being thrown somebody's intestines.

Around ten o'clock, with the airport almost empty, I lie on a bench and try to sleep. I can't get comfortable. I go outside to the taxi stand and ask a driver to take me to a nearby hotel. He takes me across town to a pink-stuccoed place called the Water's Edge. "Everywhere close is all booked up," he says.

I don't bother asking how he would know. I say, "Are we by the ocean?"

He waves his cigarette at the passenger window. "Ocean's that way."

The Water's Edge is all booked up, too. "Except for the ridiculously overpriced not to mention hideous honeymoon suite," says the effeminate clerk. "And I don't suppose you'd be wanting that."

"As it happens," I say, "I would."

He turns the register toward me and hands me the pen. "Don't say you weren't warned."

I write my mother's name. "Is it an ocean view?"

"Oh, brother. Here we go."

I wait.

"Oh, it's not you. It's the owner. His name is Waters, James Waters, so in his deranged mind he had every right to

give this dump its misleading name. Can you believe the gall
of the man? People who've booked from out of town, some
of them just blow up. At me, of course: 'What do you mean,
five miles from the ocean!' I could just shoot him in the
head. Many times." He hands me my key. "Top floor.
Room ten-fourteen. You can't miss it—the door's plas-
tered in little red hearts. I do *not* recommend the full-service
breakfast."

On a gigantic bed under a lumpy red satin coverlet, I cry
and thrash, but this time the cloud of optimism fails to
materialize. Something resembling its silver lining does
instead, a hard metallic feeling. I sit up and take off the ballet slippers. Here and there spots of blood have seeped
through the Band-Aids. "Bastard," I mutter, as if Abel were
directly responsible.

I look at myself in the mirror over the desk. I don't even
know who that person is: the smashed eyes, the swollen
mouth.

"I could just shoot him in the head," I say to her. "Many
times."

CHAPTER TWENTY-THREE

I keep stopping. I'll be fine for a couple of hundred yards, then I'll start worrying about my bangs being too short and whether or not I brushed my teeth this morning, and I can't go on.

Abel must think I'm still reeling from the hobo. When I stop, he doesn't ask why, he uses the opportunity to study tree bark with his magnifying glass or to turn over rocks, and even though his tactfulness is connected to the wrong event, it gets me moving again. This is what I dreamed of and schemed for, this invitation to his house, but I feel lured by invisible forces. I look around for signs of luck, good or bad. He thinks I'm looking for the hobo. "He's gone," he says. "He's miles away by now."

We leave the cool olive light of the ravine and emerge into the hot white glare of the subdivision. The streets are empty. Still, it's a risk for him to be seen with a girl. "You go on ahead," I say. "I'll meet you at your house."

He glances around. "Okay." He knows what I'm talking about.

When he's about half a block ahead of me, I resume walking. He reaches our street and cuts through the Fosters' lawn. I stay on the pavement, as I'm sure he means me to. I pass my house. In a kind of trance, nostalgic for a safer time, I give it a long look. By now he's under his carport and waving at me to make a run for it.

We go along the side of his house. Somebody—her?—is pounding out a military march on the piano as if to usher us onto the property. We enter the back yard. One half, the half where we are, is a vegetable garden. The other is like the moon, all baked mud and craters owing to the dog, who, at the sight of us, bounds to a corner and starts digging another hole. A wall of pink rose bushes separates the two halves. By the cabbages, breathless, I stop.

Abel has opened the screen door. "You can come in," he says.

"Who's playing the piano?"

"My mother."

Mother, not *mom.* It makes her sound so unapproachable. The playing breaks off.

"If you want to," he says uncertainly. Too late. She has flared up behind him, a pillar of fire in a long burnt-orange skirt and an orange-and-red-striped blouse. Covering her hair is a red kerchief knotted at the front, cleaning-lady style.

"A visitor!" she cries, opening the door wider. "Abel, who is your little friend?"

"Louise," he murmurs. He slides the straps of the knapsack off his shoulders, and at the verge of my own turmoil I am aware of his. She has embarrassed him by saying "little friend," or maybe just by her loud voice and clothes and her thick accent, which, with me there, must seem all the louder and thicker (in the same way that my mother's beauty never really struck me until I noticed somebody else looking at her).

"Louise who?" She is smiling, squinting, betraying no sign of having seen me before.

"Louise Kirk," Abel says. "From down the street. The house with the blue spruce out front."

"Oh, yes! Yes! Louise Kirk from the blue-spruce house! But this is wonderful! Well, Louise! Come in, come in! Before all the biting flies do!"

I walk past the tomatoes, the lettuces. I ascend the wooden steps, up the centre where the grey paint has worn off. My arm brushes her skirt. "No!" she screams, and my knees buckle.

And then what happens? I'm not sure. My memory of the next half-hour or so feels unreliable and scrappy, adulterated by later knowledge. I don't collapse at her feet or otherwise disgrace myself, I know that. (Even as I teeter on the threshold I realize that it's the dog she's screaming at.) I can see myself in the house, Abel and me sitting on one side of the kitchen table, her on the other, a small electric fan moving the tendrils of hair that escape her kerchief. There is milk in a cut-crystal pitcher, and something sweet on a china plate, there must be: homemade cherry strudel or her apple tarts; she never worried about us spoiling our supper. I do remember marvelling at the ornate wooden table and chairs, dining-room furniture in anyone else's house, and at the Oriental carpet underneath, except I wouldn't have thought "Oriental" but rather "old-fashioned." That kitchen's perpetual state of unwashed dishes, baking in progress, mud-caked vegetables tumbling from quart baskets, the wallpaper with its pattern of tiny bluebells, the stacks of yellowed newspapers, the framed needlepoint pictures of farm animals (sheep, cow, horse, goat) hanging one above another in a crooked line between the sideboard and the fridge . . . all this I'd have taken note of and been pleased by, drawn as I was—and still am in kitchens—to upheaval and congestion.

As for conversation, I remember that it's entirely between her and Abel at first, and that she touches his hair the whole time, running her fingers through it with an obvious pleasure I can't blame her for. He doesn't seem to mind this; he hardly seems aware of it. He's very interested in what's she's telling him, something to do with a piece of piano music she heard on the radio that morning. Watching her play with his hair, I drift away from their voices. It gives me a start when she suddenly sits up straight and declares, "Abel, you know, is a gifted pianist!" He blushes. But she is looking at me now, giving me her full attention.

What does she say? For some reason I've blanked it out. I suppose she asks do I like school, what's my favourite subject ("lesson" she'd have said, as she did in later conversations, and I'd have hesitated, unsure of what was meant until Abel supplied the right word). I remember what we *don't* talk about. We don't talk about the man, as I suspected and hoped would be the case, and we don't talk about my mother, although my circumstances are known because when I leave it's with a basket of carrots for my "house lady." Here I am, in a position to deliver one of my lonely-orphan speeches, but I falter, something I've never before considered having struck me, and that is the possibility of other mothers thinking my mother didn't *run* off, no mother would do that, she must have been *driven* off. By me!

I can just hear Mrs. Dingwall saying, "Louise *always* moped around. Louise was an awful disappointment to Grace."

If only my mother had been bitten by a rabid dog or murdered by fancy Dan. I remember this, all right, this yearning for my mother to be dead, and dead spectacularly.

I leave, as I said, with a basket of carrots. Also with Abel's instructions to meet him tomorrow morning at nine o'clock in the sumach grove. Nine o'clock, the sumach grove. Every morning for what remains of the summer, that's the time and place of our rendezvous.

Nothing keeps us away, not thunderstorms, not my migraines, not his mother's grocery shopping, which, now that I can go into her house, I no longer feel compelled to monitor. We are confederates, Abel and I, secret agents. We take care never to be seen together, developing ploys far more extravagant than the intelligence and antagonism of his enemies call for, but subterfuge is a habit with both of us and, besides, the threat of him getting beaten up is real enough, more so in my mind than in his.

I let him lead the way. I never thought we could be friends, but since we apparently are, I am determined to win him completely. I want him to more than like me, I want him to pine for me, to wish I could be his sister. His mother is already treating me like family, saying "Louise, sit down in *your* chair" when we go to his house for something to eat before supper. With her, I am still too shy to say much, and yet I love sitting in *my* chair at that table, it's my reward for being fearless and nice around Abel all day. She works on a needlepoint picture of a pig and tells us how she has been occupying herself since Abel left the house that morning: she ironed Mr. Richter's shirts, she tied back the rose bushes, and so on. She can talk for long stretches without demanding a response or even our attention, and since her thick accent causes me to miss some of what she says any-way, and since Abel is usually immersed in a book or a *National Geographic* magazine, I feel free to look around—at the pots and pans hanging from hooks above the stove, at the collection of beer steins on the sideboard, at her, her kind eyes and fascinating nose, her wide, naturally red lips and her broad, quick hand working the needle.

Every once in a while she'll stop, look up, smile with an expression of fresh pleasure and then, because Abel goes on reading, she'll fix on me and say, "Louise!"

"Yes," I say, heart racing.

"What did you have for lunch?" or, "Are the red-winged blackbirds still in the cattails?" Some friendly, easy-to-answer question restricted to the day's events.

I keep my responses short, out of real timidity but also in order to *appear* timid. I defer to Abel. Let her see that if she adopted me, I wouldn't try to hog all her attention.

Regardless of my ulterior motives, my big plans, it makes sense to defer to Abel, especially in the ravine. He knows where everything is down there, how it all works. It's as if the ravine were an old mansion I'd thought was empty, making do with bare floors and no furniture while he was sliding back panels onto rooms crammed with treasures, onto attics inhabited by ghosts . . . or bats. I'm thinking of the cave now. He takes me there that first morning. We get to it by climbing up to a ledge covered in stinging nettles except for a narrow path he cleared himself. Inside, there's a heavy, musty smell, not unpleasant. It's hard to see anything but I have a sense of walls soaring up.

"It's huge," I say.

"It doesn't go far back," he says. "It isn't even really a cave. There aren't any real caves in southern Ontario. But I call it a cave."

"*I* would call it a cave," I say loyally.

"Listen."

"What?"

"Hear that? That rustling?"

"What is it?"

"Bats."

My hands fly to my hair.

"A small colony." He turns away. "I've got a flashlight I keep in here."

"No!" Some of them are squeaking now. "It's okay," I whisper. "I can see." What I mean is, I don't want them to see *me*.

He notices where my hands have gone. "That's just an old wives' tale," he says. "They're spectacular flyers. They use sonar, which is sending out a pulse of sound and listening for the echo. It's better than eyes. And they don't drink your blood like everyone thinks. Only vampire bats do that. These are little brown bats. They eat insects."

"Do they mind us being here?"

"We probably make them a bit nervous."

"Maybe we should go, then." I start backing toward the entrance, something that feels like seed husks crunching under my feet. "If they're nervous."

"Okay. But isn't it neat?"

Is he crazy? Did he really think I'd want to turn this place into my new fort? "Yeah," I say. "Is it ever."

He's not a crazy, I know that. He's a boy. He's a *smart* boy, smarter than anyone I've ever met, including my father, whom my mother used to call an egghead, smarter than Mrs. Richter, who (in occasional unbesotted moments, I must admit) is a bit dense about certain things, such as where Abel sneaks off to in the middle of the night, and how to manoeuvre herself and her bundle buggy through the Dominion store turnstile. Abel has no such gaps in his intelligence, none that I can find, unless his overestimation of *my* intelligence is a gap, but I don't think it is, I think it's just that he doesn't know much about girls.

He's very polite with me, very serious. A couple of times a day I get a lecture about something I've noticed or, more often, something I've passed by without noticing. I don't mind. For one thing, he hardly talks otherwise. For another, most of what he says is useful and reassuring, such as that the juice from a jewelweed stem, if you rub it on a rash, takes away the itch, or that chicory root can be used to make a type of coffee that his mother prefers to normal coffee (so naturally I plunder the roots of every chicory plant we come across). He promises that there are no rattlesnakes in this part of the province. He says that if we ever ran out of food because of some catastrophe such as World War Three—an event he seems to take far more seriously than he does an attack by the school bullies—we could live on dandelion greens, fiddleheads, raspberries, mushrooms, boiled cattail roots and small game.

And yet the threat of the bullies is nothing he dismisses. Except he won't call them bullies, he shrinks from applying even mildly offensive names to anyone. He says "five boys approaching at four o'clock," some sort of neutral, military report. For him, the adversary is not the invading person, it is the invasion, and therefore by modifying my terms (calling a lone hiker "an advance guard" instead of "a crazy-looking guy with a beard") I can get him to fall in with my fantasy of our being surrounded on all sides by hostile forces.

Even the men who work at the sludge factory we steer clear of. From the way several of them hold their cigarettes between their thumbs and forefingers, and because they all spend a lot of time sitting outside at the picnic table, looking around, looking up at the sky, I've pegged them for a spy ring. Abel has his doubts but he goes along. (He also has his doubts about his father being a spy, although he considered the possibility when I came right out and asked if the rumours were true. "I don't think so," he said at last. "Nobody ever phones him, and he never has to go out all of a sudden after supper.")

We study the men through the big old binoculars Abel keeps wrapped in an oilcloth rag and stuffed in a hollow log across the river from the factory. He has about a half-dozen of these cubbyholes around the ravine, in other logs and abandoned fox burrows. They're where he stores things he doesn't want to carry around all day: food, water, stones, a trowel, gardening gloves (to wear while cutting back nettles) and a book called *The Tracker's Companion*. So now I do likewise, hiding my knapsack, Thermos and lunch box in the other end of his lunch log. At the rear of the bat cave, along with the flashlight, he keeps a collection of maple-sapling spears whittled to perfect points. The second time we visit the cave he brings the longest one out onto the ledge and lets me hold it.

"Wow," I say. "You could *kill* somebody with this!" I make a stabbing motion. "Take *that!*"

"It's more for hunting game," he murmurs.

"Hunting enemies," I say.

Since he's the leader, however, our strategy is entirely defensive. We constantly reconnoitre, ranging up and down the slopes about thirty feet apart and communicating with each other by means of caws and hoots. To cross the river we avoid the footbridge and swing over on a wild-grape vine. Under the vine, in the muck of the riverbank, we dig booby traps, not very deep ones (we only have the trowel), but a person chasing us might step in them and trip and be held up for a few seconds. Because it rains almost every afternoon, a short violent downpour, we re-dig and re-roof the traps every morning. We search the bank for footprints. We search everywhere for animal droppings, or scat, as Abel calls it—human, fox, raccoon, squirrel, skunk, rabbit—checking our findings against the turd-pile drawings in *The Tracker's Companion*. I find these drawings shocking, though I refrain from saying so. Nor do I act disgusted when he pokes a stick at raccoon turds to see if they contain dung beetles. Many of them do. I say what he wants to hear: that the beetles are beautiful. By August, having been obliged to study enough of them, having seen how some shine blue and others purple, I can almost say this honestly.

Our own tracks we cover. When we need to relieve ourselves (or "go," as we call it; "I have to go," one of us will say, and the other will turn and wander off a respectful distance) we use a stick or stone to scrape out a toilet cavity, which we afterwards cover up. Any footprints we make in soft ground we disguise by retracing our steps, or by just walking backwards in the first place. We move like Indians, at least he does. I can't get the knack of stepping silently over pine needles and twigs.

He says I should pretend that I'm hanging from strings: "Like a puppet. Your feet hardly touch the ground."

That doesn't work.

"Okay," he says then, "pretend there's a layer of anti-gravity surrounding the entire planet, and it's impossible for your feet to touch the ground unless you wear special gravity boots."

That doesn't work either.

Late afternoon we go to his house, taking separate routes. At the kitchen table we eat strudel or tarts, drink milk, sometimes iced tea. Abel reads. I spoil my supper and listen to the sound of Mrs. Richter's voice, although I am now bold enough to offer the occasional response, so it might be said that we have something close to a conversation. I praise her baking and needlepoint. One day I work up the nerve to say I wish somebody would teach me how to bake: "But not Mrs. Carver. Her pastry is chewy. Yours is so light and flaky."

She fails to take the hint. "Such compliments!" she cries. "I will have a swell head!"

"*Swelled*," Abel says, without looking up from his book.

"I will have a swelled head!" she cries.

I smile. I smile continuously, what I hope is a brave, sweet smile. I hunch to appear frail and motherless. I have begun to talk about my mother. It gets their attention, I've noticed that. Abel stops reading, Mrs. Richter sets down her needlepoint. I am anxious to explain *why* my mother left, to discredit the slander I'm convinced is being spread about me by Mrs. Dingwall. At the same time I am shy of broaching the matter. I need an invitation, a cue.

It comes one afternoon when Mrs. Richter says that the Fuller Brush man showed up on her doorstep and she bought two brushes she didn't need because he was such a "stealer-dealer."

"*Wheeler*-dealer," I say, sitting straighter.

"He was such a wheeler-dealer!"

"I know all about wheeler-dealers," I say.

"You do?"

"My mother ran away with one, that's why."

Mrs. Richter blinks. "Ah!"

"He lured her away."

Mrs. Richter clicks her tongue.

"She wrote a goodbye note, and she said she really didn't want to leave us."

There's no proving otherwise. As far as I know, the note is long gone, probably Aunt Verna took it. Anyway, I can't imagine my father divulging the contents to a neighbour.

I say, "She said she loved me very much."

"But of course she loved you very much!" Mrs. Richter cries. "What mother does not love her child very much?"

It's a sultry, stormy August, black clouds heaving up from the southwest almost every day just about the time we finish eating our lunch. At the first rumbles we head for the cave, where a few of the bats will already be flying around. I've stopped being frightened after all these weeks of not even getting brushed by a wing tip. They swoop within inches of us, though; you feel the small swipes of air, like somebody blowing out a match. Their squeaks perforate the darkness and give a sense that it's the cave itself squeaking, shifting under the force of the thunder.

There's no wind yet. It arrives just ahead of the first slaps of rain on the ledge. The downpour, coming seconds later, sounds like loud radio static and sometimes Abel pretends it is, he says, "Communications tower is down," or, "Headquarters is still trying to get through." Sometimes the rain gusts in, which creates a commotion among the bats that still cling to the roof. At especially loud thunderclaps a few fall away and join the flyers. "That was close," Abel says, fantasizing artillery fire. "Direct hit!" he calls when the lightning and thunder strike simultaneously. We duck down.

He looks dramatic in the lightning flashes, the bats arrested in mid-cyclone above his head, which is just inches from mine. As this happens only in the cave, this proximity, it is only here that I become conscious of him as a boy. What if he kisses me? What if I kiss him? It shocks me that I have such thoughts about somebody who is practically my brother. And yet it doesn't shock me at all that when I'm at home, by myself, I have thoughts about him getting hit by a car or shot by a burglar, and Mrs. Richter clinging to me for comfort. I am lovelorn when I'm by myself, full of yearning. When I'm with him, I go in and out of elevated states of expectation. Something is going to happen, it has to. The regular commotion of thunderstorms is a clamouring for this thing. Which is? I don't know, I don't know what it is, but crouched beside him in the cave I am ready. I wonder if he feels the same. I see, as I never will again, an almost offputting fragility in the curve of his back, or maybe it's his curly hair or his full lips, I can't hold the impression of it in one place. Otherwise, I see him as superior to every boy I know. I think, not caring in the least, that most of the girls at school must be secretly in love with him.

These are the days. The nights are warm and windy, thick with the whirring of crickets. When the streetlights come on, and children of less lenient parents get called inside, Abel and I rescue moths. Like ghosts of the bats, the pale moths flutter in a magical zone where a collision between them and us seems inevitable and yet we couldn't touch one if we tried. Hence the net, which requires skill in order not to cause injury.

I leave that part to Abel, also the transferring of a moth from the net to one of the jars. I stand there looking up, begging: "Don't! No!" Nothing is so frustrating as watching a moth's jerky, exhausted climb back up to the light.

"We only want to help you," I say. "We want to save your life."

CHAPTER TWENTY-FOUR

From Abel's essay "Oblivion," page 10:

"How can we know that every living thing is not aware? Perhaps the order and symmetry we perceive in Nature result less from genetic determinism than from an awareness, between one like thing and another, that they *are* alike and to exactly what degree this is so. The branches on trees grow to a length that results in the mature foliage having an overall bloom shape, with no single branch shooting out conspicuously, because each branch is so perfectly aware of its neighbour as to be in perfect agreement with it. Hair, fur, grass and petals grow only so long and no longer. Similarly, intelligence and aspiration, in all creatures, are constrained within consensual limits. If it were possible for a hair or a branch or any creature to live its entire existence from conception onward in a complete isolation of which it were completely unaware, who knows how far it might reach?"

This stymies me, this paragraph. On the one hand he seems to be praising observation and conformity. The more attention you pay to everything and everybody around you, the less risk there is that you'll go "shooting out conspicuously" and upsetting the natural balance.

On the other hand he calls this kind of diffuse appreciation a constraint. Not a constraint to a deeper appreciation, though, to the possibility of—for instance—finding just one person so remarkable you can't tear your eyes away. It's the stifling of individual potential he regrets. "Complete isolation"—I can never read those words without sighing. What is he suggesting if it isn't that attachment interferes with fulfillment?

I think of the emptiness of outer space, and men in their little pods going up there alone, wives and girlfriends left behind. I think of Abel and me lying on the grass, looking up at the stars, and how great that was, but, still, I was always waiting for him to turn his head. To look at me.

CHAPTER TWENTY-FIVE

The hard, metallic feeling persists. I lie face up on the barge-sized bed, arms rigid at my sides, eyelids heavy as coins, and immediately fall asleep. My dreams feature glass high-rise buildings and insidiously clean bathrooms. Nine hours later I haven't moved, except for unclenching my fists. I now notice that gold stars are stuck all over the ceiling, some clinging by a single point and some already fallen but commemorated by the glue mark. This sight is not disorienting. I have woken up knowing exactly where I am (the Water's Edge Hotel, room 1014, Honeymoon Suite) and why (Abel, that bastard).

I take a shower. While shampooing my hair I sense a plunge of dim light behind my left shoulder. "The Angel of Love," I think wearily, and let myself dwell on the prospect that I have some kind of eye disease that causes me to hallucinate light in my peripheral vision. Either that or I'm delusional. I believed Abel loved me, didn't I? I look at my belly and remember I was going to say, "A little you in there." Well, the mad-scientist abortion doctor in Buffalo can *have* the little him in there. Wrench out its tiny black heart.

I put on my blue jeans and T-shirt, tug the ballet slippers over the bloodied bandages that, despite the shower, hold fast, and limp down to the dining room, where I eat a stunningly bad breakfast of rancid orange juice, undercooked bacon, rubbery scrambled eggs and soggy toast. All the other guests are complaining and spitting mouthfuls back onto their plates. When a woman at the next table turns to me and says, "You must have a cast-iron stomach," I say, "I can't really taste anything," although I can. It's just that for the first time in days I'm not even slightly nauseated, and so taste is a negligible sensation compared with the relief of effortless swallowing. "Anyway," I say, touching my belly, "I've *got* to eat. I'm eating for two now."

Why do I tell her that? Because I want to shock her, I guess (and there it is—the blank expression, the eyes scanning me up and down, then zeroing in on my naked ring finger before she says, "Well, congratulations"). Also because I *am* eating for two, however reluctantly, however temporarily, and I'm in a mood for looking at things dead on. An hour later, in the taxi on my way back to the airport, I admire the scenery but I don't try to see the mountains as metaphors for some noble sentiment, and I don't worry about forgetting what geological era they belong to, either. I think, "This is how it feels to have Abel out of my life." Everything truer to my own experience of it. In his letters he was always going on about the truth—"The truth shall make you free," "Beauty is truth, truth beauty"—as if betrayal and pools of vomit were fabrications. Or, even more ridiculous, as if even these things, because they *aren't* fabrications, must be counted as beautiful.

I read the J. S. Bach biography. Flying out, the idea was to pick up interesting details for the sake of smartening up my end of the conversation. Going home, I find myself gripped by what now seems to be a cautionary tale about the perils of involving yourself with brilliant, artistic men. Passages such as "never would he use words to explain or justify anything he had done of a personal character" have me nodding and snorting, although I'm just as contemptuous of the saintly, obtuse Anna Magdalena and her serial childbirths (thirteen!) and then her weepy amazement at discovering, *after* Bach's death, that he'd made no will. Bach, it seems, "gave no thought to his wife's financial position." Had he done so, "she would possibly have escaped life in an almshouse and a pauper's grave."

As it was, and if you ask me, she got what she deserved.

We land at sunset. Since my wallet still bulges with money, and since my feet feel like burnt stumps, I treat myself to a taxi. My father is under the impression that a chartered bus is dropping everybody off at the Greenwoods plaza, but if he happens to be looking out the window when the taxi pulls into the driveway, he'll just assume that the bus must have broken down, some mishap. That I might have lied to him—about anything, ever—won't enter his mind.

He's in the kitchen. As soon as I open the front door, he springs out, face all alight. "How was it?" he asks. "How's our nation's capital?"

"Still standing." I pry off the slippers. "Which is more than I can say for myself."

"Good lord, what happened?"

"My new shoes rubbed the skin right down to the bone."

"Let's go into the kitchen." He takes my arm. "I'll have a look."

We sit at the table, and I lift my feet onto his lap. "Did *you* do this?" he asks of the bandaging.

"A lady did. A nice lady. She gave me the slippers, too."

He gingerly unpeels one of the Band-Aids that covers the big toe on my left foot. "Some swelling," he says. "But starting to heal over. She applied iodine, I see."

"Yeah."

"Who was she? A nurse?"

"No. She was just passing by when I noticed the blood gushing out. She took me to an infirmary but the nurse isn't there on Saturdays, so she did everything herself. We never found out her name but my teacher thought she might be Judy LaMarsh."

Judy LaMarsh is the only female politician I can think of, probably because I used to have a teacher named Miss LaMarsh. My father looks up. "No kidding?"

"She was ordering everyone around like she was a big wheel."

"Dark hair? Glasses?"

"That's right."

"Well, what do you know?" He smiles. "I thought she'd left Parliament Hill but it's possible she was back for some reason, visiting someone."

I hadn't intended to keep the lie going. On the plane, and even walking up our driveway, I was determined to tell the truth, right down to saying I wanted an abortion. And then I put my feet in his lap.

No, I broke before that: coming into the kitchen and seeing his Sunday dinner of warmed-up meat loaf, nothing else on the table except for *The Globe and Mail* cryptic crossword, a chewed pencil and his reading glasses, whose missing hinges he has replaced with twisted paperclips. That lonely little scene. Added to which he's wearing the ugly purple-and-green diamond-patterned sweater-vest I know he thinks my mother would approve of because he bought it out of the Eaton's catalogue.

How do you drop a brick onto that house of cards? Oh, he'd turn himself inside out trying to be understanding and helpful; there'd be no lectures or demands. He'd probably even drive me to Buffalo if I said my mind was set on going. Afterwards, he'd brood, but not for long. In spite of everything, he'd believe himself to be blessed.

He goes to the bathroom and returns with the first-aid kit. As I watch him dab my blisters with a cotton ball soaked in iodine I feel an almost painful surge of love. He's talking about Ottawa, a city I've never been to and can scarcely picture. He makes it easy, though, by phrasing his end of the conversation in such a way that all I have to do is agree: "Some people think it's too staid, even for a capital city, too institutional, too grey."

"They have a point."

"A shame you missed seeing parliament in session. I presume they at least let you in."

"Yeah, we got in."

When I'm cleaned up and rebandaged and my feet set back on the floor, he gives me a probing look that makes me wonder if, after all, he suspects something. Except I've had these looks from him before and never felt myself to be at their crux. Those other times I felt either that he was searching for my mother in me (a resemblance, a clue to her behaviour) or that my eyes, because they're so much like his, had ricocheted him back to himself and his thoughts. Being

pregnant, however, I may now be radiating a quality he rec-
ognizes but can't put his finger on. "What?" I say finally.

"Oh . . ." He shakes his head. "Nothing, nothing. Are
you hungry?"

I tell him I ate on the plane and just want to go to bed. "I
think I'm still fighting off the flu," I say. "No—" leaning
away as his hand reaches for my forehead, "I don't have a
temperature. I'm just a bit weak. I think I'd better play it
safe, though, and stay home from school tomorrow."

Near dawn I creep down to the kitchen, where he'll be
less likely to hear, and throw up in the sink. I then go back
to sleep until Mrs. Carver sits on the edge of my bed, sometime around ten o'clock. She, too, gives me a probing look,
her third in less than a week. But where my father seemed to
be trying to locate something, I sense that Mrs. Carver is
urging me to confess the thing she has already figured out.
So I say, "The father isn't Tim Todd. It's Abel."

She blinks.

"You thought it was Tim."

"What do you . . . ?" She touches the rim of her glasses.
"What are you . . . ?"

"You *know* I'm pregnant."

Her mouth opens and shuts, opens and shuts.

"I'm pregnant," I say. "I thought you knew."

She shakes her head.

I sit up. "Then why do you keep looking at me like that?"

She comes to her feet.

"Just now. I wake up, and there you are looking at me."

Her eyes circle. She clutches her chest. "I thought . . ."
She gasps.

"Are you okay?"

"I thought . . . you . . . were on . . . on . . ."

"On what?"

"Drugs."

"Drugs? *What* drugs?"

"Mrs. Sawchuk saw you."

"Mrs. Sawchuk?"—her friend, a middle-aged legal secretary who claims to have been covered in warts before rubbing herself with one of Mrs. Carver's concoctions.

"You were with a . . ." She twirls her fingers down each side of her head to describe long, curly hair.

"That must have been Abel. Where? Where did she see us?" But there could only have been the one place, and I answer for her. "At Bloor and Yonge."

"In a park. You were smoking."

"So?"

"A pipe."

I find this entire turn of events incredible. "What would Mrs. Sawchuk know about that?"

"It was last June."

"And she only just *told* you?"

"When I told her about the . . . the vomiting."

"Well, for *Mrs. Sawchuk's* information, smoking marijuana doesn't make you throw up. You can tell her everything's okay. I'm not a drug addict. I'm pregnant, that's all. And I'm going to have an abortion."

I start crying.

Mrs. Carver sits back on the bed and puts her arms around me. "Shh, shh, shh, shh," she whispers. She extracts a wad of Kleenex from her sleeve and I blow my nose.

"I don't know anything about babies," I say. "I never babysat one. I've never even held one."

She rubs my arm. "Are you sure?"

"I had a test. At the drug store."

"How far along?"

"Two months."

"Does Abel . . . ?"

"No. And I'm not telling him, either."

She points at the wall adjoining my father's study.

"No, no, he has no idea." I sink back against the headboard. "There's a doctor in Buffalo. He doesn't charge very much."

She waves her hands. She doesn't want to hear this.

"I'm getting rid of it," I say warningly.

"*I'll* do it!"

"Get rid of it?"

She nods. She looks alarmingly zealous.

"You'll *operate* on me?"

"No! No!" Waving her hands again.

"How?"

"There's a tea."

A tea, it turns out, that she gave to her daughter, Stella, eleven years ago when Stella was pregnant out of wedlock. This is stunning news. Happily married Stella, whose childish voice asking over the long-distance crackle, "May I please speak to Mrs. Carver?" has led me to picture an even tinier, more nervous version of her mother. "Is it painful?" I ask, thinking that Stella's nervousness may have begun *after* whatever the tea put her through.

Mrs. Carver shrugs. You get cramps (she digs her fists

into her stomach) but you can control them by swallowing a spoonful of cod-liver oil every morning and by taking hot baths.

"How often do I take it?"

She holds up four fingers.

"Every four days? Every four hours. At night, too? How long before it starts to work?"

"Until you bleed."

I sigh. "Okay, well, what does it taste like?"

"Bitter. Bad."

"What's in it?"

A disapproving look. She never tells anyone her ingredients.

So either I find my way to Buffalo and let a professional crackpot tug the baby out with tweezers (or whatever he does) but at least get the whole thing over with quickly, or I stay here and kill the baby slowly, with a secret potion that allows me to imagine I'm having a miscarriage and that, because of the cramps and the bitter, bad taste, offers a kind of penance.

Specifically, it tastes like horseradish and rotten eggs. And the cramps are constant, and she should have told me about the dizzy spells and sudden, clanging headaches. Walking, I fix my eyes on a spot in the middle distance so that I don't stagger. Alice tries to take my arm, but I shake her off, she's only drawing more attention to me, and I have the feeling that half the school must think I'm stoned. Alice thinks I miscarried on the flight out to Vancouver and am now in the throes of after-effects. (When it came down to it, I couldn't bring myself to tell her the truth.) "I hogged the washroom for at least an hour," I said. "The stewardess kept knocking on the door and asking if everything was all right."

"You poor thing," Alice says, "to have to go through it all by yourself."

"God was with me."

"I know you're being sarcastic. But He *was*. He *is*."

In the evenings, in the kitchen of her apartment, Mrs. Carver brews enough tea to see me through the next day. We use a duo-Thermos method. When I get home from school I give her my empty Thermos, she replaces it with a full one. I then soak in a scalding bath, which not only eases the cramps but also, apparently, irritates the baby, or "it" as Mrs. Carver counsels we should say so that I don't start forging a bond. Meanwhile, she prepares a douche meant to further irritate "it." By the time I've finished my bath, the douche is in a miniature turkey baster on my bedside table, and I lie back and squirt into myself the warm, coffee-coloured, tar-smelling liquid, then stay there awhile, keeping my legs raised. Afterwards, if I can muster the energy, I go down to the basement and skip rope. The whole point is to make "it" feel unwelcome. You can't kill it this way but you can drive it to suicide.

My father thinks I'm suffering from menstrual complications and heartbreak. Mrs. Carver, uneasy about my telling an outright lie, said I should just steer clear of him, but I knew he wouldn't be put off. He's always on the lookout for a burst appendix, and here I am reeling from room to room, obsessively kneading the heels of my hands down my stomach (because why can't I just *push* it out). Nothing other than the (for him) mortifying subject of my period could have curtailed his craving to take my temperature. The supposed Dear John letter from Abel had him retreating even further. No questions, no indirect prying, only his big commiserating eyes falling on me at supper, trailing after me when we pass in the hall so that at these times my thoughts, affected by his presumption, teeter toward Abel, and farther, to a baby in a crib. Just for a split second, though, and then the cramps call me back.

The cramps keep me from sleeping more than two or three hours a night. In my dreams I'm covered in fur, my teeth are falling out. I have a recurring dream that instead of miscarrying I give birth to dozens of tiny babies who already talk in complete sentences but they're no bigger than mice and they're shrinking by the hour. I lose them in the cracks of our hardwood floor. I bundle them in winter clothes, line them up in a toboggan and send them down a steep hill. Chattering, they all go flying off. I paw madly through the snow and peer at pieces of grit, wondering, "Is that one?" The love and terror I feel in this dream vanish the instant I wake up. "I'm shaking," I think with dull surprise. "I'm crying."

CHAPTER TWENTY-SIX

Toward the end of the Richters' first summer in Green-woods, I start to feel more relaxed at their house, enough so that if I need to use the bathroom I don't go directly there and hurry back to the kitchen. I take my time. With an eye to one day living here, I look at things.

Outside the kitchen door, on the far wall, are sixteen framed black-and-white photographs of Mr. and Mrs. Richter's relatives. Four rows, four photographs per row, every frame the same size and of the same dark wood, and the relatives more or less the same size as well, making for an impression of apartment-building windows and the residents all standing there looking out. Because they look so serious I assume, before being told otherwise, that they are from Mr. Richter's side of the family. But more than half are from hers. All of them, his and hers, were either femmes fatales or artists of some sort, and many died sensationally. From her chair in the kitchen Mrs. Richter can see the wall, and one of the times I lingered there, she called out names and biographies:

"That one. No, top row. There. That is my mother, Greta. The same name as me. She had eight proposals of marriage. And there is my aunt Freda, sitting. You should have heard her sing, like a flute, but so sad. My father, he was always saying, 'Freda could make a stone cry.' She married a Frenchman and went to live in Marseilles. He had all this money and these houses but he was a bad man and gave her a disease you are too young to know about. She died a lunatic. That one? That is Mr. Richter's great-uncle Otto. He wrote the story for an opera. What do I mean, Abel?"

"Libretto," Abel says. "It's the same in English."

"Libretto! You know. The words they sing. He wrote for fifteen years. Then the man he showed it to, the man who would make the show, he put his own name on it and took all the money. Poor Uncle Otto, he had no legs by this time, you can't tell in the picture. He lost them in the First War. Then one day in the Second War this furniture falls on him—"

"A dresser," Abel says.

"A big high dresser. The Allies were bombing the city, and crash, bang. So that is how he died."

Farther along the wall is an oil painting of a shepherd and his sheep on a dirt road bowered by two enormous trees. It's either dusk or dawn, the murky edges of the picture about to close in on the golden centre where the little group has halted. The shepherd, who is turned away, holds out his staff in a braced posture. Something down the road has startled him. What? Every time I look at the picture all my cravings and expectations and vague dreads blend into a hypnotic pining to find out what it is the shepherd has seen. If only he would turn around, I'd know. By the look on his face, I'd know.

When *I* turn around, I'm facing Abel's room. After tearing myself away from the painting I usually stand in the doorway for a few moments and let myself be depressed by this shrine to his superior talent, intelligence and tidiness. For a small room it has a lot of excess furniture—two bookshelves, an upholstered wingback chair, an easel. On the wall beside the bed is a map of the world, and on the ceiling a map of the stars. The rest of the walls are papered in tacked-up paintings and drawings. Of insects and reptiles mostly, a few ferns and airplanes. All done by him. I couldn't believe it when he told me that; I thought his father or some other adult must have been the artist.

I couldn't believe he had read all those books.

His father's study, next door, is about twice as big. Just as crowded though, just as tidy. On the wall are framed oil paintings of country scenes, similar to the shepherd picture only gloomier, and there's a glass case holding butterflies that have pins stuck through their middles. When I first saw this case and returned to the kitchen saying I'd glanced into the room and noticed it (not quite true; I'd taken a few steps past the threshold) and that the butterflies were, to use Mrs. Richter's favourite word, "wonderful," she shrugged and said, "Wonderful when they are flying. It is not good to kill a thing just so you can look at it."

Abel glanced up. "Father didn't kill them."

"No, no." She patted his arm. "He did not. Of course he did not."

The room that holds me longest is the master bedroom. Here's where she sleeps. Here's her dressing table, the burgundy skirt of which matches the velvet drapes. The furniture is all dark heavy wood, the large bedstead flaring out at the top corners like the hull of a Viking ship. The wallpaper has a pattern of what could be upside-down crowns, dark green, and the bedspread is the same dark green with gold brocade trim. All fittingly and stirringly regal, provided you ignore the crooked hems on the drapes and the top of the dressing table, the mess there: an almost toothless comb, a brush jammed with hair, several broken elastic bands hardened into rinds, a cracked hand mirror, a white garter and a bunch of empty, dusty perfume bottles, these at least redeemed by the romance of their spired, coloured-glass tops.

At the back of the table are two framed photographs. Twice now, I have tiptoed into the room to look at them. The bigger of the two is a black-and-white portrait of her and Mr. Richter on their wedding day. Strange to see a bride so much taller than the groom. Strange to see her, who always dresses in reds and purples and oranges, dressed in white, although, of course, it would be stranger if she weren't.

In front of this is a coloured picture of Abel at about four or five years old. Except for being smaller, he looks the same. He is wearing a short-sleeved white shirt under a green vest and is holding out his hand as if to catch a ball. You can tell from his eyes that his smile has been coaxed.

On Labour Day morning the weather turns. Since mid-July we've had nothing but tropical heat, almost every afternoon thunderclouds smoking out of the treetops and flexing into giant fists and hairdos before collapsing eastward. Then there's a brief, hard rain, then blue sky again.

Now the sky looks cemented over. And it's cold, too cold to leave the house without a jacket.

Still, we meet in the ravine as usual. We track raccoon

prints and search for fossils. Around noon a misty rain starts to fall, and we retrieve our Thermoses and lunch boxes and head for the cave.

We sit to one side of the entrance, where the light is best, and look out through the vines at what, to my mind anyway, is the dismal unravelling of the summer. There are piles of sticks here (whenever we find a long straight one, we bring it in) and after eating our sandwiches, we get out our knives and start whittling spears.

It's comfortable enough in this particular spot. Over the summer we've scraped away most of the dried dung from the floor and we've spread pine needles and ferns, and now the bats avoid flying directly overhead, even when we're not here, it would seem, because there are rarely any fresh droppings. Today the entire colony clusters at the back. Every time the wind gusts in, they make an echoing rustle; otherwise they're quiet.

I am miserable. For me, the last day of summer is always like the last day of life. I see myself tied to railway tracks, and the approaching train is being driven by Maureen Hellier. I say to Abel that I wish she would die: fall into a manhole or choke to death on a chicken bone. Finally Abel says, "Why don't you just ignore her? That's what I'd do."

"Who cares what *you'd* do?" I mutter.

He glances up.

"Okay," I say, "why don't you just *ignore* Jerry Kochonowski? Why don't you just waltz up to me tomorrow, and in front of everybody give me a big fat kiss!"

"Maybe nobody would care if we hung around together," he says.

I stab my knife into the floor. "Are you crazy? Jerry twisted Donny Morgan's arm and almost broke it that time all Donny did was give Brenda Slack an old India rubber ball. What do you think he'll do to somebody like you? He'll break your stupid neck, that's what!"

Abel turns the stick in his hands. Carefully, as if it were dynamite.

I grab my knife. "So," I say, "smarten up."

For at least a quarter of an hour we work without speaking, then, feeling the chill, I say I want to start a fire with our shavings.

"Better not," he says. "The smoke will upset the bats."

There is nothing of resentment or hurt in his tone. If I've offended him, he's over it, and this strikes me as so admirable, the mark of a nature so far above my own, that although I don't care about upsetting the bats I refrain from insisting on the fire. I say, looking up, "I think they're *already* upset."

He goes to get the flashlight and shines it at the colony. Some of the bats flutter but none drops away and starts flying around, which is what normally happens when they sense the beam.

"They're probably freezing to death," I say.

He steps closer to the wall. "One of them's hanging funny."

"What do you mean?"

"Oh, no!"

"What?"

"It fell!"

I race over. He crouches and fixes it in the light. It has

landed face down, a clump of sandy-coloured fur.

"Is it dead?" I ask.

He turns it over, and before I understand what that wrin-kled growth on its stomach is, he says, "She's got a baby." And then, "She's dead."

"The baby?"

"Her. The mother. The baby's breathing."

Its entire body throbs. Instead of clutching the mother, it hangs backwards and holds on with its mouth, and I'm about to comment on the strangeness of this when I realize it's attached to one of her nipples. I peer at the mother, who I think must be alive if she has milk. No, she's dead, all right. The eyes are like apple seeds, lifeless. Her mouth is pulled back and I am unnerved to see teeth . . . all this time I thought there were only claws to worry about. "What hap-pened?"

"She's not bleeding." He shines the light back at the colony. "Maybe she had a heart attack."

"They knew," I say. "They knew something bad was going to happen."

He brings the beam down again. The baby squeaks. He says we've got to get it to his house right away and start feeding it with an eye dropper before it dehydrates. "Here," handing me the flashlight. He picks up the mother and tries to tug the baby free. It grabs the mother's fur with its hind claws.

"You're shining the light in its face," he growls, wrench-ing sideways, out of the beam.

"Sorry." Never have I heard such an angry tone from him. I contemplate the circle of wall where the beam is now aimed, but when he gasps I swing the light back down. The baby is in his right hand, detached from the mother.

"I killed it," he says softly, astonished.

"No."

"I killed it. I pulled it too hard. I broke its neck." He gapes at the tiny body.

"Are you sure?"

He straightens and walks over to our spot and sits, holding out his hands, each with its bat, as if anticipating some magic, or punishment. And then he starts to cry, a sound like choking.

"It got hurt from the fall," I say, alarmed. "The way it was biting her, I think its neck was already broken." I sit next to him. "It's out of its misery," I say. This was my mother's pronouncement whenever she squashed a bug or whenever a pet of mine died, and although I always thought, "What misery?" I did feel a slight, if uncertain, comfort.

"Anyhow"—I switch off the light—"it would have needed its mother."

Not that I'm certain of this, either.

Abel sets the bodies down, between his feet. He has stopped crying. "I should have just left it on her. I should have brought them home together."

"You didn't know."

"I *should* have known." He picks up the flashlight and shines it at the roof. The bats hang like ripe fruit. You almost expect the whole bunch to start dropping.

He sighs and switches the light off.

"It was only a bat," I say.

"It knew how to fly," he says. "It knew how to navigate

by sonar." He starts switching the flashlight on and off. "If I hadn't touched them," he says, "maybe the baby would have let go of her after a while and another mother would have come down and rescued it."

"Do they do that?"

"If you leave things alone, that's better. There are scientists who think that. They think you should never interfere."

He sounds so intelligent and lost. I say, "When I called you stupid. Before. I was just angry. You're not stupid at all."

He looks toward the mouth of the cave. "It's stopped raining."

"Are we going to bury them?"

"I guess." He releases a shaky breath that goes straight to my heart. He says that if I wait here he'll get the trowel.

As soon as he's gone I switch on the flashlight and study the corpses. Fan out one of the mother's wings. It's like cooked chicken skin. "Poor thing," I say, trying to summon more pity than I feel because I want to be as grief-stricken as he is.

Because I am furious with love. I am in love with him.

CHAPTER TWENTY-SEVEN

Sixteen days after my return from Vancouver, I miscarry. It's three a.m. The alarm under my pillow has just gone off to wake me for my middle-of-the-night tea drink, and as I pull myself to a sitting position I feel the wetness between my legs. Four days ago, just in case, I began wearing sanitary napkins, but I've already bled through to the sheet. The cramps—is it possible?—are gone.

For what remains of the night, I sit at my desk and bleed. Every half-hour or so, after changing napkins, I investigate the soiled one for evidence of rudimentary life. What do I expect to find? A half-formed foot? An eyeball? There are promising clots. I sit back down at the desk and catch up on my math homework. My mind is lucid, the absence of pain as sharp as a recovered sense.

At eight o'clock I dress for school and eat breakfast, but as soon as my father leaves the house I return to my desk and do more homework until Mrs. Carver arrives. When I tell her the news she rushes to get a juice glass and has me hold it between my legs so that she can collect a sample. In the kitchen she adds water to the blood and then drains off the diluted portion and we both look at what's left. She points to a yellow blob. "Placenta."

It's over. Still, I bleed heavily for three days. During this time I continue to go to school. I feel an urge to pay close attention, I take reams of notes. At home I inventory my wardrobe. All the clothes of my mother's that I can't see myself wearing again—anything too fussy or pastel coloured—I return to her closet. I work fast. I *walk* fast. The time-bomb click of my heels going down the halls at school is an unexpected gratification.

On Friday night, with the bleeding almost over, the cramps return, as Mrs. Carver said they might. She said I wasn't to worry, though, it would only be my womb shrinking.

The pain wakes me about an hour after I've fallen asleep. Next door I hear my father rattling his newspaper. I picture him holding a baby in his arms, his awkwardness and joy. My throat constricts.

"I killed it," I think, awed. "I killed my own baby."

I cry weakly, hampered by not wanting him to hear and because I have no right to this grief, which seems to be convulsing straight from my womb. How can Abel not feel something? How is it possible that his baby and I have been caught up in a bloody fight to the death and he hasn't even felt the twinge that would drive him to pick up the phone?

I go to my desk and turn on the lamp. Pull down my underpants. From an exercise book I rip out a page and wipe one end of it between my legs.

The smear is like a banner. No, it's like a rag! *A rag of dark red.*

I wait a few minutes, waving the page and blowing on it, then I pull up my underpants, sit down, and where the now-dried smear is I write the word "Romance." There's no need to refer to Rimbaud's poem—from reading Abel's letter a hundred times I know it down to the exclamation marks. In flowing, coiling letters intended to parody his calligraphic script, I write:

I

When you are eighteen you aren't really suspicious.
—One fine day, you've had enough of waiting and
    morning sickness,
And the Bear Pit Café with its crappy lanterns!
—You go walking beneath the green neon signs of the
    promenade.

The neon signs smell bad on lousy afternoons in
    September!
The air is so hard sometimes, you open your eyelids;
The alleyway, full of noises,—the lying bastard not far
    away,—
Carries odours of pot, and odours of booze . . .

II

Then you see a very long rag
Of dark-red, framed by a loud slut,
Pierced by a local rock star, who is running away
From soft little babies, small, perfectly dead . . .

I read it over and start to laugh . . . a breathless, trembling, unnatural sound. I cover my mouth with my hands. I glance toward the mirror on the closet door and see a skinny, hunched-over person, eyes big as bowling balls, naked except for oversized underpants. Have I lost my mind? I don't care. I grab the pen again and at the bottom of the

page scrawl: "I WAS PREGNANT! I FLEW ALL THE WAY
OUT TO TELL YOU AND CAUGHT YOU NECKING
WITH THAT SLUT!! SO I HAD AN ABORTION!!" I draw
an arrow to the smear. "HERE'S WHAT'S LEFT OF THE
BABY!!"

I put the page in an envelope, address it and go back to
bed. Despite the cramps, I sleep.

I mail the letter the next day. A week later the phone calls
start, two and three a night for five nights straight. My
father, instructed to say, "She doesn't want to speak to you
ever again," then slam down the receiver, listens and makes
sympathetic noises, says, "I'll tell her, son, but she still
won't come to the phone," and, "Maybe you should give
her some time to sort herself out, some breathing space, I
hate to think what all these calls must be costing."

"Hang up!" I hiss, frantic in case Abel mentions the
abortion.

He doesn't, although his concern for my health begins to
strike my father as odd. "In bed?" my father says. "No, no,
she's up and around." To me, he says, "I know he's the one
who broke it off, but he couldn't be more worried about
you. He couldn't be sorrier."

"He's too late."

"Well, he's in the slough of despond by the sounds of it.
And you'll probably bite my head off for saying so, but you
don't seem to be all that happy and gay yourself."

"Happy?" I say, uncomprehending. "Gay?"

A week later the letters start arriving. I cry to see my name
on the envelope in his handwriting. I weaken. I don't open
the envelope though. I burn it in the metal wastepaper bas-

ket. Watching the flames, for those five or six seconds, I let myself wonder about the contents: the poem or drawing, the plea, the explanation. "He doesn't love me," I say, so that I won't be tempted to put the fire out.

Sometimes it goes out on its own. "He doesn't love me," I say and light another match.

CHAPTER TWENTY-EIGHT

I graduate from high school with a seventy-six percent average. The year before, my average was ninety-three, but that was back when I still cared. Seventy-six strikes me as improbably high, considering how I never once raised my hand during class and how completely unprepared I was for the final exams. As long as I passed, I kept telling myself, that was all that mattered. I had no plans for going on to university. In fact, I'd already landed a full-time job at a second-hand bookstore downtown.

I write my last exam on a Monday morning in June. That same day, at four o'clock, I start work at BOOKS! BOOKS! BOOKS! My hours are from four until ten, Monday to Saturday. By the end of the first day I know all there is to know, which is next to nothing. By the end of the first week, I feel as if I've been there for years. I feel secure and unpressured. Hours go by when I don't think of Abel at all.

There is only one other employee, Don Shaw, who is also the manager. He is in his mid-forties, about my height. He's a bachelor, he never married. He has small clever eyes, narrow shoulders and wide hips. His hair is beige and dense, like sod. One day a mentally ill man comes into the store and calmly starts taking books from the shelves and throwing them on the floor, and when Don Shaw says, "I think you had better leave," the man says in an aristocratic English accent, "I think you had better buy yourself a new hair-piece," then strolls out. Afterwards Don Shaw sees me glancing at his hair and he leans toward me and says, slyly, "Pull. Go ahead."

He's always inviting me to touch him, feel how icy his hands are, feel how the hard tubular lump on his forearm moves around under the skin like a loose battery. He also has *things* he wants me to touch, such as the leather uphol-stery on his hundred-year-old divan. He lives only a few minutes away in a low-rise apartment building adjoining a laundromat. The vibration from the washing machines tilts his pictures, the steam from the dryers pours through his heating vents and bakes the plaster. He says, "It's like living in the belly of a beast."

He says, based on nothing, "You'd love it."

He craves warmth. He wears thick-ribbed corduroy pants, grey or brown, and drab sweater-vests from some bygone era. On the most sweltering days, the shirt under the vest might be short-sleeved, but not necessarily. He looks like what he is: a failed man of letters. During his shift, which is ten in the morning until I show up, he reads text-books from the philosophy section. At night he devotes himself to writing poems he calls Exhalations. I ask if he has been published. He seems not to hear. And then he says, "When you refuse to rupture the flow of your thought with line breaks and punctuation, you find that even the most enthusiastic editors, who once compared you to Joyce and Wallace Stevens, stop returning your phone calls."

A muscle twitches in his cheek. He could say more, but won't. He hoards his injuries. He is bitterly amused by his own thoughts. When I arrive at the store he smiles to him-self as if to suggest he knows exactly why I'm late or early or right on time, and for a moment I wonder if it isn't true that my small, careful life isn't actually reckless and silly.

"Madame Kirk," he says.

"Don Shaw," I say.

Our greeting ritual.

Even talking about him to other people I say Don Shaw, both names. Don on its own is too informal. And Mr. Shaw, if I called him that he'd think I was being sarcastic.

The name of the man who owns the place is Ernie Wat-son. Him we call the Fire Chief, owing to the fact that our paycheques arrive (via special delivery mail) in Halifax Fire Department envelopes. For the five years that Don Shaw has worked at BOOKS! BOOKS! BOOKS! he has never once spoken to the Fire Chief let alone met him. Any money left over in the safe at the end of the week goes into a numbered bank account; the utility bills are handled long distance. Occasionally there's a problem that can't be overlooked (the toilet flooding, the lock on the front door jamming . . . both occur during my first week) and then we have to phone a panicky old woman named Beryl. "Oh dear oh dear oh dear oh dear," she says rapidly, as if it were one long word. She sends her husband, Buddy, who has tearful eyes and the loveliest hands, narrow and white; while you're explaining what's wrong he holds them up in the manner of a surgeon waiting for his gloves.

Don Shaw has no doubt that the Fire Chief bought the store *because* of the frayed wiring and the towers of yellowing books in the basement, the ancient oil furnace down there, that he's just biding his time until, without any outright foul play on his part, this tinderbox burns to the ground and he can collect a multi-million-dollar insurance settlement.

"So if it happens," I say, "it'll be in the winter when the furnace is on."

Don Shaw gets my drift. "By which time," he says, "our Madame Kirk will have gone on to bigger and better things."

I applied for this job because the ad in the newspaper said "easy-going atmosphere" and I thought I might have a few free minutes, here and there, to study shorthand. I was overly pessimistic. Here and there I have hours at a stretch. Hardly anybody comes in, and those who do sit on boxes of recently arrived books (no sense unpacking them when the shelves are already crammed) and read for hours at a time, we don't care. How the store works is, we buy used books at ten percent of the cover price, any kind of book, university textbook, government manual, pornography, the only criterion being reasonable intactness. Hardly anybody shows up with just a boxful; the stuff arrives by the carload—some dead pharmacist's reference library, or a housewife's complete Harlequin Romance collection. "You'll buy it *all?*" the person says, wide-eyed at such luck. Yes, we'll buy it all. Then we'll sell it at fifty percent of the cover price. But since, in fact, we *won't* sell it, since we take in ten times more stock than we get rid of, the system is mad. Furthermore, as Don Shaw admitted during my interview, the Fire Chief has no way of keeping track of all this inventory. We could be stealing half of it for resale to some other second-hand bookstore.

"You don't have to be smart to work here," he said. "You don't have to be charming and full of pep. You just have to be trustworthy." He scanned me up and down, a relay between my breasts and mouth, as if in these features lay the clues to my integrity. When he stopped to meet my eye, his expression was shrewd and bereaved. I thought I must remind him of some old flame. He said, "How trustworthy is Louise Kirk?"

"Extremely," I answered. "Perfectly."

It's true, I am. A year earlier, before the party and Vancouver and the placenta in a juice glass (a sight I wished I'd been spared), I probably would have helped myself to the odd paperback novel, because why not? I lived by no overriding principles. What governed my behaviour was how hopeful or hopeless I felt on any given day. I'd have stolen the paperbacks on days when my horizons seemed to have shrunk to the next moment. I'd have felt myself entitled.

Now, with my horizons as narrow as they've ever been, I feel entitled to very little. I *want* very little, only to earn some money while teaching myself how to type and take shorthand, and to go out occasionally, to go out on a date. Without Abel, I'm nobody, I have nothing, I'm resigned to that. All I have is the oxlike instinct that shoves you toward the next moment. If I'm not going to jump off a cliff, and I guess I'm not, then I may as well try to make my life bearable. I can't imagine ever again being wildly happy, but maybe I can be happy *enough*.

I can at least try to stay out of trouble, and with that in mind I go the Hassle-free Clinic in Yorkville and get myself a prescription for birth control pills. Another secret to be kept from my father. Although, that same day, I confess to him why it is I haven't heard back from any universities: I never mailed in any applications.

He is crestfallen. I am surprised to discover what big plans he'd had for me. Lawyer. Professor. Biologist. Diplomat.

I say, "Diplomat! Are you kidding? I'm the most undiplomatic person you know."

He throws around his arms. "You could see the world! Meet fascinating, exciting, cultivated people. Learn new languages. New ways of life!"

I say, "I want to learn how to type."

I have a movie in my head of my near future. It's very detailed, in the beginning anyway, influenced by the layout and atmosphere of my father's office and by Aunt Verna's stories of her years working downtown for the president of a large brokerage firm. The opening scene has me taking dictation. My boss is in his forties. He is a good-natured, portly man, not the brains of the company, but in no danger of losing his job. It's winter, the end of the day, the streetlights have just come on. In the windows of the building next door you can see secretaries putting the covers over their typewriters. In the office where we are, there's a cozy feeling, a winding down of efficiency. My boss loosens his tie. I uncross my legs. I wear a tweed skirt and white tailored blouse. I close my notebook and say, "I'll type these up first thing in the morning."

He waves his hand. "No hurry."

On the way back to my desk, I pass the desks of other secretaries. We say goodnight to each other. A few of us regularly eat lunch together at the snack bar of a department store. Grilled-cheese or clubhouse sandwiches, apple pie à la mode. Afterwards we stop at the cosmetics counter and slash our wrists with lipstick and say, "Is that too red?" "What do you think?" Occasionally one of us breaks down and buys a tube. To buy almost anything aside from food and nylons is to splurge.

I take the subway home. I am an expert at the origami folding that keeps the pages of my newspaper out of other people's faces. I read "Dear Abby" and do the crossword. Near my stop there's a fruit stand, and every evening I buy a fresh navel orange for tomorrow's breakfast. The walk to my place is about ten minutes, not long. I live on the top floor of a Victorian house, two rooms plus a bathroom with a clawfoot tub. There is a cat—grey, fat, shy. There is an asparagus fern on top of the refrigerator. A two-burner stove. For supper I scramble eggs or heat up a can of spaghetti and meatballs. The kitchen table is an old wooden drop-leaf pushed into a corner.

Suddenly, in this movie, it's summer. I have changed out of my office clothes and into white shorts and a blue-and-white-striped T-shirt. I wash the dishes listening to classical music on the radio, then I make a cup of coffee and take it out onto the fire escape. The view is of the roofs of other such houses and of treetops and stars coming out.

One night the new guy in the second-floor apartment also happens to be on the fire escape. We start talking, and he invites me down for a glass of wine. He's a medical or engineering student, or he's studying for the bar. He's about five foot nine, nice looking, not too handsome, not too straight but not a hippy, either. Blond or sandy-haired.

Maybe he wears wire-framed glasses. His friends are few and close. His interests lie outside of the visual arts and music and science. So he's not a medical student, then. A law student, that's better. The kind of person who takes sides, who fights for what he believes in.

You see what I'm driving at. He isn't Abel. He can't be anything like Abel, and most of the time he doesn't even exist. I finish my coffee and go back inside and sit in a wing-back chair and read a Jane Austen novel, or it could be that I'm already at Dickens. (I'm working my way through the great literary works in alphabetical order according to author.) The odd time that I *do* keep things going with the guy from downstairs, that I accept his invitation and let the night advance until we're kissing, the movie always flaps off the reel.

If this is loyalty to Abel, I'm tired of it. I admit that I love him. My love is a fact, like the law of gravity. But it doesn't change anything. What am I being loyal to? What is there left to betray?

All I want is to go out on dates with nice young men any-one would approve of. Maybe I want to sleep with them. I'm so lonely sometimes. Sometimes at the store I have such a desperate, pent-up feeling I wonder if I'm turning into Don Shaw. I try to concentrate on my shorthand exer-cises but I keep glancing up at the window and willing every half-decent-looking guy under thirty to come through the door. I lower my standards to include the short, the squat. And then one of these guys does come in and he heads straight for the pornography section. Predictably enough. The store is in the middle of a block of pawnbrokers and plumbing-supply outlets. Two buildings down is a hard-drinking bar called the Morgan, and when I leave at ten o'clock there are always a couple of middle-aged men swaying on the sidewalk. They wear cheap suit jackets. An inordinate number have full heads of hair, neatly combed. Some have ducktails. Every so often I get one of these guys in the store, and either he's just a friendly drunk or he starts pestering me and crashing into the shelves, and I have to grab the broom and herd him out. It's not as frightening as it sounds. It can be funny in a pathetic way. There's one guy (an exception in that he's completely bald), he calls me Slim, and after I throw him out and lock the door he pounds on the glass yelling, "Slim! I love you! Hey, Slim, let's get married!" and the only thing that upsets me about this is, I know how he feels. I know that urgency.

CHAPTER TWENTY-NINE

By the middle of July I find myself questioning how much time I spend on buses and subways going to and from work. Although my plan was to wait until the spring before looking for an apartment downtown, I start wondering if I shouldn't find a place a lot sooner than that.

Also in the middle of July, perhaps because I can't think of leaving home—leaving my father—without thinking of what my mother did, I start having dreams about her. The sweetest, saddest dreams. She's dead but has come back to life to pick up something, a blouse or a pair of shoes, and before she goes away again we sit at the kitchen table, just the two of us. She's the age she was when she left: thirty-three. I'm the age I am now. She's always dressed oddly—in a majorette's outfit, a hula skirt. One time she has on Mrs. Dingwall's baggy red pants. She is serene. Her eyes seem crushed, they're like chips of ice. I think she may be blind. I ask her how she died and why she left but can never get an answer, or I can't hear it. Sometimes I cry, and she strokes my hair. In one version, I'm curled up in her lap. The dream is just awash in love, mine for her, hers for me.

When I wake up, it takes me a few minutes to remember that she isn't dead, or isn't as far as I know. I wonder about the love in the dream. One morning it strikes me that I may be summoning feelings from infancy, and at breakfast I ask my father, "What was Mom like when I was a baby?"

He looks up from the newspaper. "A baby?"

"Was she happy?"

"Happy?" The question seems to terrorize him.

"Did she like being a mother?"

"Of course. Of course, she did."

"Well, she wasn't crazy about other people's babies. I remember when Gord and Ward Dingwall were born, she wouldn't even look in the carriage."

"They weren't hers. They weren't her flesh and blood."

"So—" I'm suddenly shy. "So, she was happy back *then,* anyway."

"She was never what you'd call carefree or contented, she was never the cheerful type. I suppose it would be more accurate to say she had a sense of purpose. Looking after a baby, *her* baby, that was an important, worthwhile job. She took it very seriously. There was a right and wrong way to do everything. The diaper had to be folded just so, just so." He frowns, obviously remembering his many failed attempts.

"I'll bet she changed it every ten seconds."

He sets down his coffee cup. "You were an occasion," he says. "You were an occasion she rose to."

An occasion she rose to. The phrase stay in my mind for days. What does it mean? I think I know, and then I don't. It begins to take on a venerableness, as if I'd read it on a plaque. By the end of the week I believe I've been offered a clue to my destiny. In dreams about my mother (during this time I have several more) I still feel her love, and still wonder about it when I wake up, but now I also feel her ambition.

You might think, as a consequence, I'd reconsider going to university. That never once occurs to me. In fact, I find myself even more convinced that making humble plans is the right thing. I have a destiny. No matter what I do, it will arrive. Now that I have cleared the way, it can *start* arriving.

Believing this, I start to calm down, generally. At the same time I grow watchful. Any incident may be the one from which this second stage of my life takes its direction. A handsome guy walks by outside the store window, and instead of becoming tense and predatory, I fall into a languorous study of him as a possibility. Either he'll come through the door or he won't. Either we are ordained to meet or we aren't.

I don't discount the effect of the weather on my state of mind. Since the first of August we've had ninety-degree temperatures and afternoons pounding with thunder and then, just as I'm leaving for work, there's a brief downpour that only makes the air more humid. The least activity—removing a book from the shelf—becomes a marathon. I am bound to be less keyed up and yet the heat can't account for my conviction that my life is about to change. I keep thinking of that sweltering August down in the ravine when there were thunderstorms every day and they seemed so portentous, when what finally happened was, I fell out of love with Mrs. Richter and in love with Abel. Not that I now expect to fall out of love with *him,* that won't be it. I might love somebody else, though. A little.

During the mornings and early afternoons I practise typing on my father's old Remington in the wind from a pair of powerful electric fans that I place at opposite corners of the study. Here, too, I am aware of being both more relaxed and more alert to my surroundings. I seem to anticipate the ringing of the phone, but I never answer it. I get up, open the door and strain to hear Mrs. Carver's "Hello?" What if it's Abel? Sometimes I'm certain it is, I have a premonition. I cling to the door frame until I realize it's only Mrs. Carver's daughter, or her friend Mrs. Sawchuk, and then I sink to the floor and tell myself that this feeling, this punch in the ribs, is relief.

Around noon my father sometimes calls to see how I am. When we're through chatting, he has me put Mrs. Carver back on the line. Now that I'm no longer home in the evenings she stays to eat supper with him. I only recently learned this, although my father claims to have told me weeks ago. I'm tempted to eavesdrop on the extension, but they'd probably catch me because there's an echo when both phones are off the hook, so I hang up and tiptoe down the hall to gather what I can from Mrs. Carver's intermittent noises of sympathy and interest. Often she laughs, a dry coughing sound rarely heard otherwise. One day she comes out with this complete and astonishing sentence: "I wouldn't turn down a glass of sherry."

"What do you talk about?" I ask my father that night.

"Oh, what's going on at the office. All the shenanigans, the gossip. She seems to get a kick out of that kind of thing."

"Are you . . . would you ever take her out?"

"Take her out?"

"On a date."

"A date?"

"She's only three years older than you."

He looks dumbfounded. "I'm still a married man."

"Not really."

"In the eyes of the law, your mother and I are still man and wife. And Mrs. Carver, she's . . . she's . . ."

I wait.

"Well, she's a decent, respectable, proper—"

"All right, all right. So, will she stay on, then? After I move out?"

A pause. He doesn't like to talk about my moving out. "I haven't thought about it. I suppose she will. For a while."

"I hope so. I don't want to have to worry about you."

"You know . . ." He looks off. "She's smarter than I ever gave her credit for. Uniquely informed. Learned, really."

"What do you mean?"

"All that medical esoterica, those folk remedies of hers. They're not just Irish, they're from around the world. China, Turkey. She has me drinking a tea."

I go rigid.

"For my arthritis. An ancient Turkish brew. Some old woman in a delicatessen on Bloor Street sells her the ingredients. Under an oath of secrecy, all very clandestine." He flexes his fingers. "Tastes like the devil, but darned if it doesn't seem to be doing the trick."

Upon reflection, I decide I don't have to worry about Mrs. Carver telling him. Why would she? There's nothing to be gained by it, and she, of all people, is hardly likely to let anything slip. Besides, from how she has been acting, you'd never guess there was an abortion between us. She never refers to it, I never get any unusually anxious looks. Apparently she has a gift for putting unpleasantness behind her.

If so, lucky her. And lucky me, for not having to worry about *her* worrying. All the same, there *is* an abortion between us, a squalid light. There are moments when everything about her—the bargain-basement clothes, the cheap hair dye, the whispering, the teas and superstitions, even the back-to-normal behaviour, implying, as this does, an over-familiarity with matters bloody—is a reminder. I know how unfair I'm being. I can't help myself. When I arrive home from work, I am bewildered to think I still live in this house, with these people. Sometimes I open the door to the front-hall closet just for the sake of depressing myself with the sight of all my mother's hats. I hear her voice—not the tender one of my dreams but the sardonic one of my memories—saying, "Crap! Throw them out!"

I start reading the classified ads and making appointments to look at unfurnished flats. Usually I know within two seconds of the landlord's opening the front door that I'm wasting my time. Still, I climb the stairs into realms of heat I can't believe are safe for humans. Cracked plaster, a crying baby somewhere, peeling wallpaper, a room under the eaves only a five-year-old could stand up straight in—what the ad meant by "cozy." The whole place painted a high-gloss, institutional cream means "newly decorated." "Bright" means not pitch dark. I'd been avoiding basements, but lured by the phrase "high and dry," I end up standing in one, hunched under a pipe whose steady drip the landlord tries to pass off as condensation.

According to Don Shaw I'm never going to find any-thing, not in my price range, not where I'm looking. He keeps telling me about apartments for rent in this neigh-bourhood. "You'd love living around here," he says.

I laugh.

"Oh," he says. "The heartless laugh of the young girl."

One day a furnished place comes up for rent in his build-ing. "It would be perfect for you," he says. "Quiet, right at the back. All you'll ever hear is the sparrows in the maple tree."

I tell him to forget it.

"Everything within walking distance," he goes on. "Streetcar stop out front, laundromat downstairs, grocery store on the corner."

"Hookers on the corner."

"That's right. Hookers keeping the sex addicts occupied so that pretty girls like Madame Kirk can walk around unmolested."

Pretty. Except for Abel nobody has ever called me pretty. I feel myself blushing. Don Shaw smiles to himself.

That night, as I'm closing up, there he is, walking through the door.

"Don Shaw," I say, surprised.

"Madame Kirk."

"Did you forget something?"

"I did not." He smiles at his shoes, which are shined. His hair is also shiny, he's used some sort of oil and combed it straight back. And he's wearing cologne—Old Spice. I can smell it from here.

With a touch of unease I say, "What's the occasion?"

He looks up. Pats his hair. "Oh . . . I, uh, I met a friend, an old friend, for dinner."

I don't believe him. More than once he has described himself as a recluse. I turn and crouch to open the safe, which is recessed into the wall.

He says, "I was on my way home and thought that, since I was passing by, I'd drop in and make you an offer."

My heart launches into a dull pounding. I put the money pouch in the safe, shut the door, spin the combination.

"You are obviously disinclined to view the apartment on your own," he says, "and so I'm here to offer myself as your escort."

I straighten. Still with my back to him, I open the ledger and write down the afternoon's take: seventeen dollars.

"Well?" he says.

I turn around. "Right now?"

He dangles a key. "The current tenant is out of town."

"And you just happen to have the key."

"I'm the superintendent."

"You *are?*"

"I told you that."

No, he didn't. It doesn't matter. I retrieve my purse from under the counter. "I don't know. I'm really tired."

"It won't take long."

"But I'll miss the ten-fifteen bus."

"The buses run until two a.m."

I sigh. I wonder at my lack of forcefulness.

"Live dangerously," he says.

It's still hot out. On the steps of the Morgan four men, my bald admirer among them, argue over something they keep trying to grab from each other. A deck of cards or a pack of cigarettes. "Slim!" my admirer yells. He stumbles over. His head is a sphere. "I love you!" he yells.

"Go on, get back," Don Shaw says, waving a hand, but the head rides like the moon alongside my right shoulder. At the intersection, it falls away. I look around. He is spooling backwards into traffic. "Marry me!" he yells.

We turn left onto a block of darkened thrift shops and second-hand furniture stores. A store called Bargain Shoes displaying nothing but frilly organza dresses for little girls. Then an empty lot, blue chicory flowers mysteriously vibrant in the gloom. We don't speak. He steps over the legs of a woman lying in a doorway and muttering to herself. I am shocked that it's a woman and that he seemed hardly to notice her. I glance at him. His expression is strained. His slicked-back hair makes it look as though he's wearing a futuristic helmet.

At the corner we pass two girls in miniskirts and heavy make-up, they're about my age, maybe prostitutes, maybe just a couple of bored girls escaping hot apartments. We pass a coffee shop, light as day inside, only one customer, a wizened version of Brigitte Bardot: the pout, the teased blond hair under a red polka-dot scarf. She sits at the window, smoking.

The building next door is where we stop. It's an old, haphazard brick mansion painted iron red. A laundromat consumes half of the ground floor. "This is it," Don Shaw says. "Willow House."

There is no irony in his tone. There are willows in the yard. I look up at the higher stories and try to spot the charm I must be missing. A couple of turrets, yes, but they're wrapped in brown shingles, and most of the woodwork is lost under aluminum siding.

"Well, what do you think?" he asks.

I see no sense in humouring him. "It's ugly."

"Ugly." He tries to hold on to his smile. "That's not the word that leaps to *my* mind. But if, to you, living history is ugly, if an accretion of eras is ugly, then . . ."

"Then," I say, "it's ugly." I gesture at three possible front doors. "Which one?"

The middle one. Inside, in the large foyer, a dim naked bulb hangs by a cord. Directly underneath, two wooden chairs face each other. "What's this?" I say. "The interrogation room?"

He picks the chairs up and sets them against the wall. "The kids move them around."

"What kids?"

"A brother and sister in apartment three. Good kids, just nowhere to play." He indicates the staircase.

"Go ahead," I say.

I don't want him looking at my rear end. When he starts climbing, I try not to look at his: the womanly girth of his hips. The stairs are the original hardwood, pale and worn to a velvety texture, sagging in the middle, a first indication, in this house, of its ghosts. I ask how many tenants there are.

"Ten. Six apartments. One on the first floor, mine. Three on the second, two on the third. Yours is on the second at the back."

"*Mine?*"

"The apartment that uh, that, uh—"

"That's for rent," I finish.

He can't get the key to turn. "Come on," he mutters.

Once we're in, he loosens up, flicking on the overhead light. "Eight-foot ceilings. All the original mouldings. New linoleum." He turns in a circle. "You get a cross breeze with the two windows."

Maybe so, but it must be a hundred degrees in here. And the linoleum has a fake-brick pattern, and there's just this one tiny room, apparently, since everything is in view: a single bed, a kitchen alcove, a brown-corduroy chesterfield, a card table and four chairs.

"Is there a bathroom?" I ask.

"Bathroom!" He strides over to what I took for a closet door and throws it open. "Toilet. Sink. Bathtub. Shower."

"A plumbing extravaganza."

He slides me a combative smile. "I believe I told you it was snug."

"Snug. That's not the word that leaps to *my* mind."

"I see." Nodding at his shoes.

"So—" I move toward the door. "Now I suppose we go down to your place and you show me your etchings."

I say this out of impatience for whatever experience I'm meant to have this evening, but also because I'm discovering that when I hurt him, and then pity him, he becomes almost attractive.

The muscle twitches in his cheek.

"You can offer me something to drink," I say.

As soon as he opens the door to his apartment, I feel the humidity.

"Oh," I say. "It's big."

It's lovely. Who would have thought? Floor-to-ceiling wooden bookshelves, a worn Oriental carpet, antique furniture, not refinished (I notice stain marks on the coffee table, battered chair legs) but tasteful. When he turns on a lamp I see his desk and, next to it, an upright piano. "You have a piano," I say, and feel a sudden, breathless grief. I could be standing in the Richters' living room in Greenwoods.

"I don't play," he says. "Do you?"

I look at him. His laughable hair. I detect the throb underfoot from the laundromat machines. "No. I had a boyfriend who played. Really well." I drop into a maroon armchair. "It's like a steam bath in here."

He hurries across the room and raises the venetian blinds. A fan is revealed. He switches it on.

"Your books must be ruined," I say.

"I'm not a collector. I buy books for what's in them. I only hold on to these because I have the shelves."

He goes into the kitchen. From the chair I glimpse a clean white tile floor and blue cupboards. He moves around quietly. When he emerges it's with a tumbler of ice water in one hand and two wine glasses and a corkscrew in the other. The bottle is under his arm.

I press the tumbler to my cheek, my forehead. He sits across from me on the divan and starts uncorking the wine.

"I'll touch it in a second," I say as he fills our glasses.

He looks up quickly.

"The divan. You're always telling me I should touch it. So here I am. Ready to touch."

He purses his lips, unsure of how to take this, and yet

game, and why wouldn't he be? I'm where he's been trying to get me for two months. I'm frail and fainting, alluding to seduction. Seeing his confidence rise, however, my interest drops, and so I inspect him for something to be ... not aroused by, that's out of the question, something to be moved by.

His eyes, I decide, the intelligence and suffering not entirely extinguished by all that craftiness. I need more, though. I survey the apartment. The desk is a rolltop. Nothing on it except for a leather-bound binder stuffed with papers.

I set down the tumbler and pick up my wine. "To poetry," I say.

He pauses a moment before raising his glass.

"Will you read me something?" I ask. "Of yours?"

He takes a drink. "No." Quietly. "I don't think I will."

I get up and sit next to him.

Our thighs touch. On the back of my knees I can feel the softness of the leather. "It's like skin." I run my hand over it.

His face is empty.

I reach across his chest and turn off the lamp.

He trembles. Or it's the vibration from the washing machines. I kiss him. His breath smells faintly of mushrooms, a relief from the overpowering briskness of the cologne. I shut my eyes. His lips are as soft as the divan. His desperation, though I sense it twisting inside him, stays contained. He puts down his glass and brings his arm around my shoulders. I let myself sink back. I sink into the kiss but not so deeply that I forget it's Don Shaw's mouth, it's Don Shaw's fingers unbuttoning my blouse.

We make love there on the divan. As if I were a sleeping child he kisses my forehead, my throat. Lingering, gentle kisses meant to relax me. But they're not working. I shift my inner gaze to his, and that's better. The trick is to imagine what *he* feels, to see it all from his point of view. I am only a girl, too young and pretty to be here. I am a gift. Nobody would believe it.

He comes in a sudden, single spasm. I open my eyes to his grimacing face. Almost frightened, I roll out from under him, onto the floor. He collapses. I get up and grab my clothes. My stomach is slick with his sweat. I step in front of the fan but before I'm dry I start dressing.

"What's your hurry?" he gasps.

"I'd better go. My dad will start worrying."

"Why don't you phone him?"

I button up my skirt. "Where's my purse?"

He sits up and switches on the lamp. "Hey," he says.

I glance over . . . at a chubby, middle-aged man with oily, beige hair sticking out in horns.

"Stay," he says. "Just for a few more minutes. You haven't even drunk your wine."

"I can't. I'm sorry."

He reaches for his shirt. "I'll walk you to the bus stop."

"No!" I spin around.

He goes still.

"I'll be okay." I spot my purse beside the maroon chair and I rush over and pick it up. I feel as though a crime has been committed, some harmless prank, lighting matches, and now the house is on fire.

"Well." He nods at the floor.

I can't afford to start pitying him again. "I'll see you tomorrow," I say.

He doesn't look up. "I take it you won't be renting the apartment."

"No."

More nodding.

"I'll see you tomorrow," I say again.

I want to convince him. Not to offer false hope but because it irks me to think that he has already resigned himself to something I wasn't certain of until this moment.

CHAPTER THIRTY

Before settling down to hard drinking, Abel turns the dead-bolt. If you keep knocking, and he's still conscious, he may slide out one of his ready-made notes. Either CALL YOU LATER (How? His phone has been disconnected), or THANKS, JUST LEAVE IT (whatever you're shouting you've brought: the bag of groceries, the milk that will go sour in his overheated hallway) or STILL ALIVE! (the exclamation mark for *your* sake, to applaud a circumstance he himself finds merely interesting). It used to be he would occasionally talk to you through the door, but after all the vomiting and damage to his throat his voice is too soft, and, anyway, all he ever said was along the lines of call you later, or just leave it. That he was still alive, you gathered.

He didn't write the notes himself. He had Joyce, a waitress from his piano-bar days, do it. Three lots of fifty each. During the Depression, Joyce won a national penmanship contest, and when you pick the note up off the floor and there's her lovely flowing script and the faint pencil line she drew to keep the words straight, you feel that at least you've been dismissed with some ceremony, as if by a butler. He keeps each lot in a different pocket of his army greatcoat, but he gets them mixed up anyway, he gives you the THANKS, JUST LEAVE IT note when you've arrived empty handed. Sometimes the STILL ALIVE! note is already waiting for you. I tell him he can't make such a sweeping claim, that he should at least write in the time: STILL ALIVE! AT 4:30 or 6:00 or whenever. And so he tries. He finds the pen. With a wobbling hand he adds the numbers, and you stand there wondering, is that a nine or a seven, a three or an eight?

If he isn't drinking hard—and he can go for two days restricting himself to what he calls therapeutic hits—the door is usually ajar. People walk right in. Old friends from the piano bar. Cindy, the beautiful manicurist from across the hall, taking a break between clients. Archie, the superintendent, beer in hand. There being nowhere to sit, Archie leans against the refrigerator and tells jokes in a grim, rapid-fire manner. Abel, lounging on the bed, nods as if to jazz. Cindy laughs, but at things in general, to promote optimism. Upon entering the apartment she announces herself cheerfully with, "I've had it up to here," or, "Don't even ask," referring, supposedly, to her failing business. Her smile veers on the hysterical, which is why I think her high spirits are for show, for his sake.

I come by every day now, on my way to work and then, if I can, on my way home. His parents come after supper, making the hour-and-a-half trip from Waterloo where Mr. Richter, now in semi-retirement, teaches chemistry. Even *they* don't always get in. At least three mornings a week I arrive to find a bag of groceries and Tupperware containers of cooked food still out in the hall. Mrs. Richter brings flowers from her garden—daisies, black-eyed Susans, tea roses—bundling the stems in a wet rag and, over that, plastic wrap. Once, the rag was torn from the orange-and-red skirt she had on the first time I saw her.

I know he wants me there in the mornings, but it's always a relief when I'm not shut out by the deadbolt. The second relief is the sound of his raspy breathing. I go to the bed. He sleeps on his back, the book he was reading before he dropped off—*Blake's Complete Poems* or Yeats's *Selected Poetry*—often still opened on his chest. I think, "One day I might be looking at a corpse." I try to imagine it, but the rush of dread this produces seems too familiar to be anything other than the outskirts of a feeling there's no preparing myself for.

I put away any groceries. If his mother brought flowers, I throw out the old bouquet and arrange the new one in his only drinking glass. The cats cry at my feet, I don't know why, their bowls are full, they recoil when I try to pat them. He goes on sleeping. It isn't until I throw back the covers that he opens his eyes. "Louise," he says as if we've been parted for years. I help him to his feet. He tells me what he was dreaming about: another planet, its mauve atmosphere and plates of light, a glass airplane hangar filled with swallowtail butterflies the size of zeppelins. He often dreams we're making love. So do I. In my dreams we are children again. In his, our bodies are surreal. I have three breasts or I'm covered in nipples. He has hands like tree branches, infinitely fingered, he has a penis that extends out of telescopic sleeves.

"Far out," I say.

"It was," he says, ignoring the sarcasm. "It was beautiful."

While he sways and trembles, I open the cigar box. Usually there's a cigarette inside, already rolled. I light it and insert it between his lips, wincing along with him at his first inhalation, which he admits scalds his throat. He looks to make sure the ashtray is nearby; he wouldn't want to spill ashes on his clean carpet. His mother has told me (in a tone of hopefulness, taking it as a positive sign) that his blackouts never last more than a few hours. So it must be during the intervals that he puts himself and the apartment back together. Still, I glance around for damage—splinters of glass, whisky splashed on the wall. I scan his face and arms for bruises. One morning, catching me at this, he says, "I drink in the bathtub."

"You have a *bath?*"

"I don't run the water."

I light his cigarette.

"I know when I'm going to black out," he says.

"How?"

"I hear wailing."

"Like somebody crying?"

"Like a siren. Far off."

"A blackout siren," I say.

He smiles as if this were a staggering witticism. "Louise," he says.

"I've got to get going," I say, irritated. "I'm late."

His candour terrifies me. Only a couple of weeks ago, he would never have raised the subject of his drinking, not to me. I've been lecturing him all year to face the truth and fight back, but this seems to be facing the truth only for the sake of proving that there's nothing alarming about it, nothing you can't casually dismiss.

One morning I open the door to find him scrubbing the carpet. The sleeves of his pyjama top are rolled up, and for the first time in months I see the shocking thinness of his forearms.

"What happened?" I say. The water in the bucket is pink. "Oh, God, did you hemorrhage?"

He continues scrubbing with both hands, one to steady the other. He's using a nail brush. "Just a bit of blood."

"I'll drive you to the hospital."

"I'm all right. I took my blood pressure."

"Abel, please. For my sake."

"I'm okay. I feel fine now."

"Well, then let me finish this."

"It just needs rinsing." He goes to the bed and sits.

I empty and refill the bucket, then find a dishcloth. "Wait!" I say when I hear him fumbling for a cigarette. I hurry over to light it.

"You're so fierce," he says. "You're like a mongoose."

He means this as a compliment. I go back to the bucket and kneel down and start dabbing at the stain. "Doesn't it hurt?" I say.

"What?"

"Everything. Vomiting."

"My throat hurts sometimes."

"I'm sure smoking helps." I wring out the dishcloth. "How bad does it get?"

"Not too bad."

Which I take to mean *really* bad. "How do you stand it? By drinking?"

"I tell myself there's a portion of pain in the world, a daily portion, and it has to go somewhere. When I'm in pain, somebody else isn't. A child dying of bone cancer in New Jersey. A man being tortured in Kampala. For the space of time that my throat burns, their pain lifts."

"Do you believe that?"

"I don't know."

"You're a masochist." I carry the bucket to the sink, dump out the water. "Would you drink some orange juice?" I ask this without hope.

But he cocks his head, intrigued. "Orange juice. Why not? The juice of an orange."

His glass has flowers in it. I find a plastic measuring cup and use that.

"Orange juice in a measuring cup," he says happily. I hold the cup to his mouth. He turns his head. "I'll drink it later. Thanks."

I set the cup on the table, between the flowers and ashtray, and look at my watch. Eight-thirty. I'm going to be late for work. It doesn't matter, my boss is on holiday. I sit on the floor with my back against the bed, my shoulder against his calf. Outside the window, which is up by the ceiling, two pigeons strut back and forth. A truck rattles by.

"I could stay here forever," he says.

I pat his foot.

But he doesn't mean here with me, in this moment. "At the teetering point," he goes on. "Knowing any second I could fall off the edge. The paradox is, if I knew I *had* forever, even a good chance of another six months, in my mind I'd be somewhere else."

"You *could* have another six months," I say helplessly. "More."

"When you're just about to take off, you look at everything for the last time, as if you could hold on to it somehow."

"Stop it. You're scaring me."

"Everything is exactly what it is. Everything is . . ."

"What?" I say finally.

"Itself. Everything is itself."

He sounds so captivated. There's no retrieving him. I say, "I don't even know what you're talking about."

"The pigeons," he says. "They're not trees or cats or measuring cups. They're pigeons. They moan, they make their flimsy nests, lay their white eggs. They aren't right or wrong or important or unimportant or anyone's name for them. Out of oblivion came these nameless *things*."

"And then came a name for them."

"The snake in paradise. You say to yourself 'pigeon' and the pigeon before your eyes is corrupted by everything you know about pigeons. You see your *idea* of a pigeon."

"Because you can't help it. Because out of oblivion came a mouth. And vocal cords. And a brain."

"And then one day the names drop away. They don't matter. They don't tell you anything."

"What is *this?*" I take hold of his foot.

"My foot."

I've missed his point. He isn't disputing that things *have* names. "Your *cold bony* foot," I say, letting it go. I twist around to look up at him. "Try harder. Okay? Be strong. Why can't you be strong?"

"I'm not very good for you, am I?"

"You're horrible for me."

"I'm sorry."

"Don't be sorry. Be infuriated."

"Be like you."

"That's right. Be like me. Be exactly like me!"

CHAPTER THIRTY-ONE

Although I suspect Don Shaw knows it is over between us, everything is, including my job, I want to make sure he has no excuse for phoning me at home, so after rushing out of his apartment I head for the store.

I leave the lights off. (I can see clearly enough in the pulsing glow from the plumbing-supply store across the street, its eternally dripping neon tap.) I go to the counter, find a piece of paper and a pen and sit on the stool. Between my legs I'm still wet. The spicy smell of his cologne is on my clothes. I think of the way he looked when he came, that deathly grimace, and it seems so funny and horrible. How could he have been surprised that I ran out? I feel guilty but also a little used, more than justified. Overall I have an efficient, virtuous feeling, as if I'd cleaned out a closet.

What should I write? How about a rendition of my mother's goodbye note? "I have gone, I am not coming back, Buddy knows how to work the adding machine." Or, "The truth shall make you free." Just that. Let him, who thinks he knows me so well, wonder.

In the end, I write: "Dear Don Shaw. I've decided to take your advice and 'Live Dangerously.' Sorry about leaving you in the lurch. Here's my paycheque back as partial compensation. Goodbye and good luck. Best wishes, Madame Kirk. P.S. Last night was beautiful."

The P.S. to compensate for the "best wishes." Not even as a formality can I bring myself to write "love." By "beautiful" I mean the night we walked through—the chicory flowers, the woman in the coffee shop. Of course, he'll think I mean the sex. That's all right.

I fold the note and put it on top of the ledger. Outside, after I've locked the door, I drop the keys through the mail slot. The jangle of them hitting the floor gives me a moment's pause in which I see myself living with Don Shaw, married to him, stuck at home with our chubby, sod-haired children. Could I bear it? Probably, somehow. All my futures, including these first meagre samplings, must be bearable, it seems to me, if I can picture them.

In the middle of September, I find a place to live. A studio apartment on the top floor of a three-floor building and in a corner at the front, so there are windows on two sides. It's not much bigger than the place Don Shaw tried to foist on me but it's in a far better neighbourhood and close to a subway stop. It has more character, too: dark wainscotting; one of those old, round-shouldered refrigerators from the fifties. And a bed that drops from the wall when you open a pair of double doors. "A Murphy bed!" exclaims my father upon seeing it. He says its creator, William L. Murphy, also invented the grip in the hairpin, a comment that draws a scornful huff from Mrs. Carver, and I remember that her dead husband, the genius whose every idea got stolen out from under him, invented the electric curling iron.

The huff is telling. She used to be so nervous around my father, dashing out of rooms he ambled into, clutching her heart when he exclaimed. Whether he realizes it or not, they are starting to act like a married couple, and if that leads them backwards into romance, I won't mind. I'm already being mistaken for her daughter. On the day of the move, my landlord refers to her and my father as "your parents," and I let the assumption ride. For the rest of the afternoon I find myself looking at her, this energetic little woman who is helping lug boxes into the elevator, and I think, as if I were the landlord, that you can see where I got my dark eyes from.

Anyway, thank God my father has someone at home. Though he watched me pack, my actual departure stuns him. Though I told him I had rented a U-Haul trailer to transport my dresser, desk, chair and the glass tea table from the basement, when he sees the trailer parked in the driveway, he says, "Now what do you suppose that's doing there?" Only the Murphy bed perks him up. Otherwise he sighs and observes that I'm leaving the nest, striking out on my own, sallying forth into the big world. Twice he gets out his wallet and starts peeling off bills, and I push his hand away, telling him I'm fine, I have plenty of money. I have a job!

Not yet, I don't. But I applied at a brokerage firm the Friday before and felt I made a good impression on the personnel manager, Miss Penn, a glum woman who, for most of the interview, sat turned toward the window, gazing out. That I barely passed the shorthand test was apparently not a concern. "Oh, well," she said, dropping my transcription into the garbage pail. Also she spoke witheringly of my two competitors: a university graduate with "a chip on her shoulder the size of that typewriter" and a "love child" with "hair out to here and dirty fingernails." Still, I didn't think much of my chances until, in answer to the question "Why do you want this job?" I came out with, "My aunt, who was like a mother to me, she worked in a brokerage firm" (*Was* this the reason? I wondered as I spoke), and Miss Penn, smiling wanly in profile, said, "Yeah, I had an aunt like that."

She phones Thursday with the news. I'm to start on Monday. I use the time to practise taking dictation from newsreaders on the radio and to let down the Scotch-taped-up hems of my mother's skirts and dresses, which I emptied out of her closet while my father looked on without comment (the most telling sign, so far, of a turn in his romantic affections). The man I am to work for, Mr. Fraser, is a senior partner whose secretary of thirty-seven years died after a long battle with cancer. I have some apprehension about filling her shoes but don't think too much about it until Sunday night when I'm in bed and then I try to picture myself on the job and can't get past turning on the typewriter. How many copies of a letter are you supposed to make? Do you use carbon paper or the photocopying machine? What is a stock, exactly? What kind of *thing?* And what's the difference between a stock and a bond? Between a stenographer and a secretary, for that matter? I writhe around and the Murphy bed bounces on its thin metal legs and I start to worry that it's going to flip back into the wall and crush me.

My illuminated bedside clock says ten to one. Ten to ten out West. I hate it that Abel is still so much with me that I half live on Vancouver time. I'll be eating breakfast and think of him asleep. Around noon I'll imagine him loping off to school or, now that it's summer, sitting at the piano in his pyjamas, picking out some moody piece. I can't stop doing this. It's a form of obsessive, psychic voyeurism. No, it's more active than that, more depraved, it's me trying to control him through long-distance hypnosis. I veto sex and girls but not melancholy. The melancholy I exaggerate.

I get up and go into the kitchen to make myself a cup of warm milk and honey. Warily, keeping well back (the only other time I used the stove I singed my hair), I turn on a burner. Flames fly up. I turn it down, but that just turns it right off. I turn it on again, and now there's only hissing. I try another burner. More hissing. The pilot light, wherever that is, must be out. I turn everything off, including the kitchen light, leave the milk in the pot and go sit at my desk, on my only chair. The church clock across the street tolls the hour. I picture Abel sprawled on his chesterfield and listening to a record, something dismal and intellectual. Eric Satie. A phone rings next door. Five, six, seven rings before it stops. I look at my own phone. I chose a black model because white or pink—the alternatives—seemed too frivolous for the possible instrument of my undoing. It would be so easy to call him. Nobody to overhear, no incriminating Vancouver number turning up on my father's bill.

I lift the receiver. In drifts the Angel of Love. I dial zero and immediately the operator comes on, startling me. I answer her questions, act as though I really intend to make the call (I'll hang up as soon as she puts me through), but at the other end, instead of ringing, somebody starts talking.

"Pardon?" I say.

"Your party must have moved," the operator says.

"Moved?"

"Changed residences." She repeats the name and number I gave. "Is that right?"

"Yes, but—"

"If you hold one moment I can find out if they left a forwarding number."

In the pause, I fight for breath. I envision their abandoned ranch-style Vancouver house, the blank curtainless windows.

"It's a local number," the operator says. She starts to reel it off.

"No," I say. "That's all right."

"Don't you—?"

I hang up. Frozen, I wait for her to call back. When that danger seems over, I stand and go the window.

He's here, in Toronto. And all these months I've been monitoring his life in Vancouver. I feel foolish, outmanoeuvred. Why hasn't he tried to see me? Oh, I know why. If he called, if my father gave him my new number and I picked up the phone and it was him, would I even let him talk? Maybe. But he doesn't know that.

Just as well.

I stay at the window, looking at the empty intersection. The streetlights go on changing. A cat crosses against the red. I count the seconds allotted each colour; I have nothing better to do. I am alone, cut off, living in an apartment whose bed, oven and phone can't be trusted. In a few hours I will start a job from which I'll almost certainly be fired. I'll wear a pleated yellow skirt and matching bolero jacket that went out of fashion twenty years ago.

Does he ever think about me? Does he look at the sky and think, "Louise is seeing the same sky"? *Then you see a very tiny rag of dark blue, framed by a small branch, pierced by an unlucky star.*

I go to the front-hall closet and take down my jewellery box from the top shelf. I have no jewellery, I don't wear it. What I keep in here are the two letters he sent me before I went out to Vancouver. I don't know why I've saved them. I haven't looked at them in almost a year.

I read them both through, expecting to feel something different this time but getting caught up in the same old irritation and perplexity. Why *these* poems? And why tell me that beauty is truth, truth beauty, and that the truth shall make me free? The truth, when I stumbled upon it, made me suicidal.

Then I get to the drawings. The sea anemone. I never really appreciated it before, but it's quite beautiful, so intricate. Well, he's talented, I never said he wasn't. The other drawing is the one of him and me dressed in monks' robes: "Abelard and Hell-Louise," as he's written underneath.

"No, we aren't," I think. "We're not them." Abelard and Héloïse's love was indestructible, and everything they suffered came from outside that love. With Abel and me, the assault came from within. From him.

"He doesn't love me," I think. It's a thought I've had so many times I hardly hear it any more as a statement of fact. It has become a kind of mantra, what I say to remind myself never again to get my hopes up.

I return the letters to the box, put the box away, then pull my blanket and pillow onto the floor. I lie on my back, looking up at ribs of light fanning in through the blinds onto the ceiling. I'm not worried any more. I'm not even irritated. I suppose I ought to feel lost, or depressed, and maybe I do underneath. All I'm aware of feeling, though, is a tender curiosity about the person I've become, a recaptured calmness that vindicates this room and this night but isn't influenced by them. It begins with me. I can feel it leaving my body in waves, like a signal.

CHAPTER THIRTY-TWO

In the schoolyard Abel and I go on acting as if we don't know each other, though I never let him out of my sight. He stays by the fence and is generally ignored, except when he catches the attention of Jerry Kochonowski, he of the square head, blond brush cut and walleye. Last year Jerry would yell, "Hey, Kraut! How many Jews did your Nazi father kill?" Now it's "Hey, Nazi! Killed any Jews lately?" or, "Show us your swastika!" His friends seem tired of this game but none of them speaks up. Jerry is a bully from a family of bullies, older brothers in and out of jail, a father who hits him with a board.

"Bashes me right across the noggin," he brags, unwittingly offering an explanation for how he came to have that eye.

Nobody, probably least of all Jerry, expects Abel to answer the taunts. I don't say anything either, hard as that is. It would only make things worse, a girl of my lowly status coming to his defence, although what keeps me quiet is not wanting Maureen Hellier to know that he matters to me. Of all people, she's the one who tells Jerry to leave him alone, and she's so sure of herself, so impervious to ridicule, that Jerry will occasionally back down. When he doesn't, she reports him to the teacher on yard duty. She and her girl-friends then troop over to Abel—there's no escaping them—and start going on about how awful Jerry is and how adopted children are just like other children and they bet Abel's real parents are Canadian but even if they aren't, that's okay, lots of people have German relatives. "Rudeness is why there are wars," Maureen invariably announces. Later, when Abel and I meet, I try to get him to admit that she's a stupid know-it-all. He pretends to be suddenly interested in some insect or leaf. If we're in his kitchen he goes into the living room and starts playing the piano.

I slide onto the bench next to him. The Angel of Love is there, too, leaking light along the keys. Usually he plays something by Bach, who is his favourite composer, and mine now, as well. I like how crisp and mysterious the music sounds; it reminds me of the ravine, lying under the pine trees and the sun coming down in splinters through the needles.

I can't believe that anyone could play better than he does, but I never tell him because then he'll make me listen to a record of the same piece and try to get me to hear the difference. It isn't the flattery he minds, it's the laxity of perception, the inaccuracy. When I call a frog a toad, or a damselfly a dragonfly, he is just as anxious to straighten me out. When I spot Jerry across the ravine and say, "There's fathead!" he still corrects me, but indirectly; he says, "Blond boy at four o'clock," as if this neutral way of putting it were only a confirmation.

With the shorter days and colder weather and with the snow already deep by mid-November, we see less and less of Jerry, or of anyone, in the ravine. We ourselves still go down after school, although not as often. Abel prefers what he calls night prowls, and once, maybe twice a week I sneak out to join him, provided no bad weather has been forecast. It isn't easy. I've got to smuggle my snowsuit, hat, scarf, mitts and boots into my bedroom, stay awake until midnight and then climb out the window without alerting my father.

In the summer when we did this, there were crickets chirping, maybe someone's dog barking. In the winter, there is no sound that doesn't come from us. The unavoidable whistling my leggings make as I walk shears through a world in suspended animation. We keep our flashlights off until we're in the ravine, and then we start searching for animal tracks. Along ridges and down by the river, we sometimes come upon the neat, straight tracks of a red fox. The same tracks, sloppy and meandering, mean it's a dog. Prints like little human feet mean skunk. We look for abandoned birds' nests and visit the ones we found before. In the spirea bushes there's a sparrow's nest threaded with blue fishing line and with what we think is the red string you tear off a Band-Aid wrapper. Nearby, dangling from a branch and threatening to fall but always still there, is an oriole's nest in the shape of a Dutch boy's shoe.

At around two o'clock we start heading back. More often than not, as we enter the subdivision, we hear his mother calling.

"Where does she think you go to?" I asked the first time we heard her.

He said he didn't know.

"Doesn't she say, 'Where were you?'"

"She's just glad to find me. I always let her find me."

"And she's not mad?"

"She'd probably be out for a walk anyway. She's an insomniac."

"What's that?"

"A person who can't sleep."

"But doesn't she worry that *you're* not getting enough sleep?"

"I'm an insomniac, too."

Under my window he makes a step of his linked hands and I climb up onto the ledge. He waits until I'm inside, then sets off in the direction his mother is calling. I always feel a little desolate then. He never looks more unconquerable or more completely himself than he does from the back, at night, walking away.

By early June it seems that Abel has made it through another school year in one piece. He doesn't act relieved, however; he doesn't talk about the near brush with death. He talks about the success of his strategy, as if Jerry Kochonowski were only an element in a successful experiment.

"I completely ignored him," he says. "I played dead. When you play dead, it dulls a predator's killer instinct."

Or sharpens it.

One day I have a dentist appointment after school and so I don't make it to the ravine until four-thirty. Abel said he'd be in the sumach grove but he's not there. I use the crow call, the loudest and most urgent in our repertoire. No answer. I run around cawing. I go to the cave, back to the grove, down to the river. I climb up to the ledge and look inside my old fort. I keep on climbing to the top. From here

I can see the river and the sludge factory. Men are beginning to leave for the day. Maybe Al knows something. Al, the manager, who gave us a bag of green mints once and had such a wrinkled, mischievous face that I could no longer think of him as a spy. I start hurrying down. I am at the ledge when I spot a boy racing across the Camp Wana-wingo clearing. Not Abel, a blond boy.

Jerry Kochonowski. By himself.

I stumble the rest of the way down. I run screaming, "Abel!" It doesn't matter who hears. My legs feel like tree stumps. The bridge is too far away. I run straight into the water, which is only knee deep at this point but so putrid I've never stuck a finger in it before.

He appears from behind a bush. His shirt is off and he's holding it above his right eye. "It's okay," he says, coming to the bank. "I'm okay."

"What happened?" I slog out of the water. "What did he do?"

"Threw a piece of brick."

"Let me see."

He takes away the shirt, and there's a saw-toothed gash.

I cover my mouth with my hands.

"It's starting to coagulate," he says.

I don't know what that means, but it sounds bad. "Come on," I say, "let's go to the factory before they close. They might have bandages or something."

"I don't need bandages. I just need to keep applying pressure."

"We'd better go home and call a doctor."

"I've got to sit down." He drops onto the sand.

I drop beside him. "I saw him running away. I knew he'd hurt you. I—" My voice catches.

"It's okay. I'm okay."

"But what happened?"

"I was looking for that bullfrog we saw yesterday. I heard rustling in the bushes over there and thought it was you—"

"I wouldn't rustle," I say desperately.

"I went over to see and it was Jerry crouched down, trying to hide, so I thought I'd better get away fast and I started to run but he yelled 'Help!' so I ran back and he threw the brick and took off."

"That stupid fathead. I hate him. I hate him. We have to call the police."

"No."

"Why not?"

"It's all over now." He takes the shirt from his face. "How does it look?"

"Awful. Oh, your shirt's all bloody." I am wearing a pale blue cotton jacket over my blouse and I pull it off and give it to him.

"Are you sure? The blood might not come out."

"Then I'll burn it."

He folds the jacket into a square. "Don't cry, okay?"

"Didn't you hear me calling?"

"I blacked out."

"Blacked out?" I jump to my feet. "I'm going to the factory right now!"

"No." He reaches for my hand and draws me down. My hand in his silences me. He says, "Before you came I was doing mental exercises. Counting backwards from a hundred by intervals of seven. I'm pretty sure I don't have brain damage. Do I sound normal?"

"He tried to kill you."

"We're not going to tell anyone, okay?"

"What about your parents?"

"I'll say I tripped and fell on a rock. A jagged rock."

"You're going to let him get away with it?"

"He won't do it again."

"How do you know?"

"I just do. Promise you won't tell anyone."

Sobs punch at my throat. His expression is confusingly sympathetic, as if I were the bleeding one. When I can speak I say, "Only if he leaves you alone from now on."

"Don't worry."

He lies back. So do I. He turns his head toward me, keeping the jacket in place with his elbow. We are still holding hands. He says, "You'd better wash your feet and legs when you get home. You'd better wash your shoes, too."

"I will."

"Don't cry."

"What if I cry because I love you?"

He blinks. But he doesn't look away. He's thinking, considering the question. "Do you?"

I kiss him on the mouth. He shuts his eyes. I kiss him harder. He lets go of my hand and brings that arm around me and we roll to face each other. We push at each other's lips and bodies. I can't get near enough to the feeling this produces. When we stop, the coat has fallen from his forehead. The gash, which I'd almost forgotten about, gives me a start.

"Is it still bleeding?" he asks.

"A little. It's swelling."

He repositions the coat. "I might need stitches after all."

"We'd better go, then."

"In a minute."

"Doesn't it hurt?"

"Not too much."

He is staring at me. His face seems years younger. I say, "You love me, too."

He nods.

"You love me very, very much."

He nods.

We kiss all the time. We will be collecting stones, picking wild strawberries, and a look will pass between us, as if we've both just heard a strange noise, and wherever we happen to be, we'll start searching for a private place. We don't speak; there are no preliminaries. As soon as we lie down, we're kissing.

We have progressed to opening our mouths. We touch tongues, suck on each other's bottom lips. I have a rough idea about sexual intercourse but I can't imagine doing anything more sexual than this. When it's over, before we stand up, I might tell him I love him and he'll say, "Okay." So then I'll say, "You love me," and he'll redden and say, "Yes." We never talk about the kissing.

Or about the scar. He refuses to. It is a sideways Z, which I suspect secretly pleases him, as it could be the mark of Zorro. Nine stitches were required. We stuck to our lie, but his father seemed to know that if there was a rock, it was thrown.

He said, "You didn't break the fall with your hands?" and Abel slid his hands into his pockets and shook his head.

"Where exactly was this rock?" Mr. Richter asked then.

Again Abel hesitated, so I said, "Where they're building the new house, on Spruce Court," and Mr. Richter looked at me, a stern and unconvinced but not unkindly look. Mrs. Richter, who would have walked by that house many times and seen the piles of excavated stones, cried, "Abel, what if Louise had fallen into the pit?"

"Louise is careful," Abel murmured.

"Louise is good," Mrs. Richter cried, hugging me, "to let you ruin her jacket."

I am not careful. I am not good. I am vengeful is what I am.

I have thought, since Abel died, that by always being furious on his behalf I allowed him to take the high road. Or else I gave him no other choice. In my company, he would never admit that somebody was even exasperating let alone obnoxious or mean. But then why should he, when I could be counted on to say the worst? Unlike him, I required an accounting. I understood perfectly the eye-for-an-eye argument. The turn-the-other-cheek argument struck me as wrong in an almost physical sense, a threat to natural order and balance.

I find it maddening, then, when I see Jerry in the ravine, unpunished and unafraid, fishing off the bridge or setting campfires he never properly puts out, which means we have to pour water on them later. These days he is usually by himself, his gang having mysteriously dropped away, and I say to Abel, why don't we capture him and tie him up in the cave? Make him swallow ground glass? Shove twigs under his fingernails? In the ravine, Abel and I no longer bother putting any distance between ourselves, but when I start going on like this, he tries to move out of listening range. Or he tries to make a deal. "Let's set a deadline," he'll say. "In one week you never talk about Jerry ever again."

"Or what?" I'll say.

"Or you pass the deadline." As if this were dire, and "deadline" itself has a forbidding enough ring that I am temporarily silenced.

And then a real, comprehensible deadline comes along. He tells me that on July twenty-first he and his parents are going to Vancouver for three weeks to visit Mr. Richter's brother, Uncle Helmut, who's trying to get them to move out there.

"*Are* you going to move out there?"

"I don't know." He shrugs. "Maybe."

So there it is: a line, like death to me.

On the morning that they leave, it rains. I help Mrs. Carver prepare a stew by chopping carrots and celery into the pill-size pieces she requires. After that, I watch a movie on television about a composer who dies young, bleeding all over his piano in the last scene. I cry silently as the composer's girlfriend, George, cries. By the time the movie is over, the rain has stopped. I decide I may as well head down to the ravine.

I go into the cave and just sit, my mind empty of thought. Behind me, where the bats sleep, is a steady ticking sound. Water dripping. Deadlines passing. Eventually I move out onto the ledge and consider getting Abel's gardening gloves and cutting back more nettles to enlarge our lookout post.

But I only stand there, watching the path. And not five minutes go by before I see Jerry Kochonowski wending his way up.

I seem to wake from a spell. I creep into the cave and grab a spear. Creep out. He has stopped and is looking all around, though not up at me. The tenseness leaves my chest. He goes over to a pile of rocks and sits. A calm feeling comes over me, a simple understanding of what needs to be done. I move to the other side of the ledge. Holding the spear up and aimed, I start climbing down. A step, then a pause to see if he heard, then a step. I am right behind him before he turns around.

"Oh," he says, standing. "Hi."

His face is flushed, his bad eye veering off as if to a conspirator. Instinctively I glance that way.

"Do you have any water?" he says. "I'm dying of thirst."

I draw back my arm.

He glances at the spear. "What's that?"

I hurl it at his chest.

"Hey!"

I get him in the shoulder. The spear dangles, then falls out.

"What did you do that for?" he says.

He's not even bleeding. I scan the rocks. I snatch one up and throw it as hard as I can. He tries to dodge but it hits him above the ear and he stumbles. *Now* there's blood. He doesn't seem to realize. His good eye has a look of witless, struggling confusion. The savagery is in his other eye. I pick up the spear. He looks at me and then at the pile of rocks. Then he turns and staggers down the hill.

CHAPTER THIRTY-THREE

I wake up rigid, jaw clenched, the names MacLellan, Fraser and Eliot running through my mind. Who are they? I think, bewildered. Friends of my father's? Famous explorers? Then it comes to me. Today is my first day of work.

I take a shower, fix my hair, put on my yellow pleated skirt and matching bolero jacket. But I am only observing the formalities. I now understand why condemned prisoners eat a last meal: you just do what comes next. It's simple enough. Out on the street I join the mass of office workers draining into the subway. I let myself be shuffled onto a packed car. I grab a pole. It's stifling in here but everyone seems cool and unruffled. The men read newspapers, the women paperback books. There is a dignified atmosphere. The train makes sudden puzzling stops, creeps forward, screeches, thrusts ahead. As one, pretending not to notice, we lurch and sway.

Half of the train empties at the King station. Hundreds of us walking fast in a single direction. I find it bracing while it lasts, like singing the national anthem. Back up on the street, we fan out into columns, mine heading west toward a new black office tower. I enter the revolving door on the strength of someone else's push. Enter the elevator and fix on the ascending numbers: the reverse countdown to my humiliation. At thirty-seven, I step onto a dove-grey carpet that holds the footprints of earlier arrivals. The brokerage firm takes up the entire floor, and two others besides. This foyer, with its four elevators, is their lobby.

"Louise Kirk?"

It's the receptionist. She seems far away and lonely down there at the end.

"Yes?"

She smiles and holds up a finger. "Good morning. MacLellan, Fraser and Eliot." I go over to her. On her large presidential desk, aside from the phone, a pen and a pink message pad, there is only a tubular glass vase holding a single purple orchid. Behind her, attached to the wall, is a box of cubbyholes that looks like those birdhouses you see on farms.

"One moment," she says, "I'll check if he's come in yet." She rolls her eyes as if at the comical gall of people who phone before nine o'clock. She has short blond hair layered like petals, like a petalled bathing cap. She's very pretty. "Good morning, Mr. Gage," she says. "Should I put Mr. Webster through?" Her coral nail polish matches her lipstick and blouse. On the fourth finger of her left hand is a stripe of white skin where a ring was. "Hi there"—speaking to me now—"I'm Debbie Luke."

"Hi."

"Pat, you know, the personnel manager, Pat Penn, she called a few minutes ago to say she won't be coming in today. She's got a migraine. Poor thing, she gets at least one a week. More when the weather's like this. Kind of muggy like it is? She has to lie perfectly still with the cold cloth, the ear plugs, the black eye patches, the whole bit. It must be just awful."

All this said in a thrilled, confidential manner, looking up at me and quickly away and therefore giving the impression that there is far more to the story than she can tell, a surprising, even romantic, complication. I start to speak but she lifts her hand. "Good morning. MacLellan, Fraser and Eliot."

I wonder what I'm meant to do. Miss Penn instructed me to report to her office first thing. Maybe I can go home. My stomach tightens. If I go now, it'll be a jailbreak. I won't come back.

"I'm afraid he's out of the country until next Tuesday. Could I take a message for his secretary?" There follows a silence during which she writes on her pad while casting me a series of furtive looks that describe what she's hearing: something perplexing, now exasperating, now reasonable. "Okay," she says when the call is over. She swivels to poke the message into a cubbyhole. "We just have to hold tight"—swivelling back—"until one of the other girls shows up to take you to Mr. Fraser's office. It's way at the other end. He's already here. He's here every day at seven. He's old, you know, a widower, up at the crack of dawn. I don't want to call him to come and get you, it's such a long walk, and he's all bent over. But what a sweetheart." She turns as the door behind her opens. "You'll just love him. Oh. Speak of the devil. Good morning, Mr. Fraser."

"Good morning, Debbie." A deep voice, full and resounding, like a stage actor's. He glances at me. "I'm expecting a young lady. . . ." Another glance.

Debbie, bursting, as if at the reunion of long-lost relations, nods in my direction.

"Ah!" the man says. "Louise Kirk?"

"Yes," I say. "Hello."

He regards me frankly, taking his time. He is tall, still a tall man though stooped to a degree that obliges him to tilt his neck back just to see forward. His face is long; his frank look may be partly the result of his chin jutting out. A bald head splattered in liver spots the colour of peanut butter. Eyes the same shade. That expression he has, of both terrible sadness and a private, indestructible joy, is one I've noticed before in old men.

He comes toward me, smiling. "Pleased to have you on board."

We shake hands. "I'm pleased to be here," I say, trying to sound upbeat, like Debbie. I hate it that I will disappoint him and we will both be embarrassed by all this initial goodwill.

Sometimes I'm lucky. Of all the possible bosses in this city I end up with Mr. Fraser, who—it immediately becomes obvious—needs a secretary only to keep up appearances, which, of course, is perfect, considering that until I learn a few things I'm a secretary in appearance only.

There is very little for either of us to do. In this way, oddly, the job resembles my last one, except that at the bookstore our uselessness was spoken of and ridiculed, whereas here, the situation goes unmentioned (at least it does between Mr. Fraser and me) although not unacknowledged. That we come to work for the sake of inventing businesslike activities with which to fill our days is nothing we can keep from each other. And yet I don't feel wasted or unnecessary. I feel as though I am involved in the preservation of certain lofty but no longer fashionable virtues. Civility and contemplation.

That first morning, at least a half-hour is consumed by his acquainting me with the contents of my desk. Betty's old desk. It's an oak antique, sticky here and there from something spilled. Mr. Fraser and I examine the paper drawer first, its three trays, one for letterhead, one for plain bond, one for the yellow tissue you use to make copies. "I prefer white," he says of the tissue. "But the fellow who does the ordering tells me it's no longer available." I close that drawer. "They don't make it any more," he says. I open the top drawer. "Stapler, pencil sharpener," he says, launching into an inventory. "Glue, Scotch tape, paperclips, thumbtacks." His deep voice and thoughtful delivery lend each item a fleeting stature. He points a wavering finger at the cardboard thumbtack box. "Is that right? Thumbtacks?"

I open the box. "Yes."

"Now what the Sam Hill did she use thumbtacks for? What's in that green box there?"

I open it.

"Now what do you suppose those are?"

"They look like those plastic tabs you put on file folders."

He clasps his hands, pleased. "That's it."

I am seated at the desk. He stands beside me, bent forward at an angle that would be alarming if he weren't so naturally stooped. He presses his tie against his chest to keep it out of the way. It is navy with maroon dots. Very tasteful. His navy pinstripe suit is too large and I wonder if he has recently lost weight, if perhaps Betty's death took a toll. He is unprepared for the personal items we find in the bottom drawer, though they aren't much, just a nail file, a pair of reading glasses, a tube of lip balm, a jar of rosewater hand lotion and a white comb. "Ah," he says. He strokes his tie. "You see, I should have emptied this out."

"I don't mind."

I go to shut the drawer but he says, "No, you'll be wanting to put your own things in here," and he reaches in and fumbles around, trying to pick up the nail file, but he can't get a finger under it, so he picks up the glasses. I take out the rest and hand it to him and he thanks me and puts it all in his jacket pockets.

"Now, then," standing straighter. He frowns. He seems to have forgotten something. He turns to face the filing cabinets.

"You sure have a lot of filing cabinets," I prompt.

He perks up. "Twelve in all. Forty-eight drawers."

They are grey metal, far from new. Four are in his office; the rest have been lined up out here in the alcove to form a wall against the vacant corridor. We're in an outpost, and there is no escaping a feeling of banishment, but perhaps it is an invited banishment, a compromise, because nowhere else on our long trek from the reception desk did I see any furniture like this, not just the cabinets and my desk but everything: his great hulk of a desk, the wrought-iron coat rack, a magnificent marble-topped credenza, the glass-doored bookcases in his office and the oil paintings he has in there, four or five from the quick glance I got, all of sailing ships.

He waves toward the filing cabinets and says, "One drawer for every year I've been in the brokerage business."

"Forty-eight years," I say. I can't even imagine living that long.

"June the sixth, nineteen twenty-one, that's the day I hung out my shingle. It's just a coincidence, though, the drawers being the same as the years. I mean to say, we file alphabetically by client name. Do you want to take a look?" He asks this doubtfully.

"Sure."

We go to the nearest cabinet, the uppermost drawer, whose label reads "Nyman – O'Farrel."

"Should be two *l*'s in O'Farrell," he says, peering. He pulls the drawer open with effort, a grim ferocity jumping to his face. "Runners need greasing," he says. Inside, the files are jammed and disorderly, papers sticking out of folders, name tabs falling off. He closes it and tugs opens the one beneath and it's just as chaotic. "I suppose they could do with some tidying up," he says.

"Get rid of all the inactive ones," I offer, surprising myself. I didn't realize I knew about inactive files.

"Well, now," Mr. Fraser says, "if we go that route, we'll empty them out. Ninety percent of these people are no longer in the land of the living."

"Oh."

He smiles. His lips are as thin as string, quite red. His smile is amused but sympathetic, and the thought comes to me that he requested a secretary who was inexperienced and uncertain, although he wouldn't have been so explicit. "Who will put up with me," he might have said.

The following weeks are a lulling, protected time reminiscent of the dreamlike days after an illness when the worst is over but you're still in bed. At work the phone rarely rings, few people drop by. Mr. Fraser himself leaves me alone once he has established that for the next several hours I will be reasonably occupied. On my desk, when I arrive at nine o'clock, there are always several letters waiting to be typed. He has written them out on lined foolscap in a slightly shaky but legible hand and included the date and the person's address, though I could easily have found the address on his Rolodex.

"My thoughts flow more freely from the pen," he told me the first morning, and I wondered if he'd heard I wasn't very good at taking dictation. After a few days I wondered if he'd meant it as joke, his thoughts flowing more freely, because one letter is hardly different from the next. "Apologies for having been out of touch lately," he starts out, "but as you may know Betty passed away in July, losing her long hard battle with cancer, and I am only now getting back into the swing of things." Then he asks after the man's family— he trusts that the wife is well, that the children and grandchildren are keeping out of trouble. Which brings him to his own child, Jonathan: "Jonathan's wife, Hazel, gave birth to another son on June twenty-ninth. I'm arranging for the whole kit and caboodle to fly in from Halifax over Christmas." As a P.S. he encloses an article cut out of the *Financial Post* or *The Globe and Mail*. "In case you missed it," he says. Or, "Thought this might be of interest."

When I bring him the typed versions, he reads them over slowly, more than once. In the end he makes one or two arbitrary changes: "I'm arranging" might become "I'm making arrangements," or the other way around; "be of interest" can turn into "be of some interest" or "pique your interest."

"Sorry," he says, giving the letters back.

"That's all right," I say. And it is. I'm glad of the opportunity to practise my typing.

We can stretch this out, the typing and changes and retyping, until Hank Bell arrives, pushing the mail cart. Hank is a spectral man. Blond, very pale, of indeterminate age, always smiling, always humming mournful tunes. He drops on my desk an impressively large bundle, but it's mostly annual reports and newsletters. I open everything, pile it neatly and take it into Mr. Fraser's office. Now it's ten-thirty, time for me to put our china cups and saucers on the tarnished silver tray and walk the length of the corridor to the executive kitchen where nobody ever is but where fresh coffee awaits in a stainless-steel pot. There are packaged cookies as well: fig newtons and shortbreads. I take one of each for each of us.

Back in Mr. Fraser's office I set down his cup and he hands me two client files, two new ones every day, from which I am to remove any correspondence pertaining to the Ontario Securities Commission. For about a week I almost believe there is some kind of investigation to be conducted, but as the correspondence mounts in a tray on his desk, I let that notion drop. I am touched by his meting out of the files. I feel that he isn't so much prolonging the work as limiting the amount of time I spend on any one unnecessary activity, taking care that I don't get too bored. It may be he also hopes to acquaint me with the business, because you can't read so many letters without picking up a few things, such as that a stock is a certificate, not, as I had imagined, a metallic bar or a plaque. You can't read so many letters, written over so many decades, without learning about his family, either. Presumably he means for me to know that his wife's name was Pam and that she died five years ago of a heart attack. That Jonathan is a chartered accountant. That there was another, older son, Eric, who was killed in a car accident on January thirty-first, 1960, which, coincidentally, is the same day my mother disappeared.

I usually finish the files at around twelve-thirty, twelve forty-five. At five to one Debbie phones to ask if I'm ready, and I meet her at the reception and we take our sandwiches to the underground mall where we each buy a carton of juice, then find a bench to sit on. Mondays, Wednesdays and Fridays we are joined by Lorna Lawton, a snide chain-smoking girl who works in the retail sales department and whose lunch hour changes on Tuesdays and Thursdays for a reason so infuriating to her she can't seem to speak of it. We talk about the other employees, or Debbie does. She is indiscreet and conspiratorial and charitable. Lorna is hateful, blowing smoke and muttering "that bitch" and "that bastard." Sweet, humming Hank from the mail room is "that moron." Mr. Fraser she is a little easier on, in my presence anyway; him she calls, with something approaching tolerance, "the hunchback."

I wonder why Debbie is friendly with someone like Lorna, but then I also wonder why she took so immediately to me. The very first day, as I was leaving to go home, she said, "I have to tell you, you're not at all what I was expecting."

"How do you mean?" I asked fearfully, thinking she meant unqualified, but she said, "Oh, you know, young, on the ball."

The second day, introducing me to Lorna, she said, "Louise is nobody's fool," and again I had no idea what she was talking about let alone how, after scarcely more than an hour in my presence, she could make such a claim. It reminded me a bit of Don Shaw, the groundless presumptions, except that with Debbie I get the feeling she thinks I am smarter and better than I am, as opposed to darker and sexier. She flatters me excessively and maybe insincerely and yet I sense no harm in her. Quite the opposite. She says she loves my hair. I tell her she's crazy, my hair is horrible, it's lank. She smiles as if we both know better. She says she wishes she had my figure, and urges me to try on clothes I can't afford. This is after we've eaten, when there's still time to window shop. Lorna, who is also skinny and lank haired, tags along, snarling. I take for granted that I'm included in her list of enemies, although back in the office she always walks me to my alcove while resuming some earlier rant. At my desk she seems affronted when I sit down, she acts rudely dismissed.

"See you later," I say to her back.

I work on shorthand exercises. At two-thirty Mr. Fraser returns from the Baron, a steakhouse where he has eaten lunch since the end of the Second World War. As he hangs his hat on the coat rack he asks how I'm doing, is everything working out? I suspect that the question comes at this time of day because he's had a drink and is loosened up.

I tell him I'm fine.

He says he's glad to hear it. His woebegone, radiant eyes are a little tired by now, a little slow to take me in.

In the afternoons I photocopy any articles he circled

from the morning papers. Then I go through his A–F Rolodex and type up fresh cards and throw out the old ones, unless there's a red *D* written beside the name, standing for Deceased. These cards, which represent not even ten percent of the total (apparently the system stopped being updated decades ago), are to be removed and placed on his desk. What does he do with them? Tucks them away somewhere, I suspect.

At four-thirty I water Betty's African violets and rinse out the cups and saucers in the executive washroom. At five I poke my head into Mr. Fraser's office to say goodnight. Often he is reading from a volume of his twenty-four-volume set of the Encyclopedia Britannica. "Oh, Louise," he says, as if returning from a dream. "Goodnight, my dear. And thank you."

Evenings.

My father has been by to stabilize the Murphy bed (a matter of tightening screws) and to show me how to work the stove. I now turn on the burners with aplomb. For a couple of nights I listened to classical music on the radio, as in my old fantasy, but against a backdrop of violins and harpsichords the apartment took on a spinsterish aspect, so I switched to the FM rock station. Dinner is scrambled eggs or spaghetti. On Wednesday or Thursday—half a week away from Mrs. Carver's Sunday roast and the leftovers I brought back to make sandwiches with—I treat myself to meat: a fried pork chop or a Salisbury steak cooked under the broiler. I eat sitting at my desk. After stacking the dishes in the sink (to be washed as needed), I rinse out my pantyhose and hang them, like a girl in a French movie, over the shower rod. Then I brew a pot of tea and drag the chair to the kitchen window so that I can look at the five-storey apartment building across the drive.

I have assigned the residents occupations and names. The place where the windows are always open, even when it's raining, where the long grey curtains stream out and hang against the brick and nobody is ever home, the guy there—it must be a guy—is a bartender, maybe a cab driver, named Ed. The middle-aged, big-breasted, red-haired woman who vacuums in a see-through negligée and whose windowsills are lined with books, she is Madame Broulé, a high-school French teacher. Directly beneath her is Glenn, the lowly government clerk brooding over his glory days as a varsity football star; this from a silver cup on his sill (it looks like a trophy) but also from how he always seems to be sitting at his kitchen table, smoking cigarettes in the gloom, a big man wearing a tie and sports jacket and smoking for as long as I watch.

When the teapot is empty I drag the chair back to the desk and spend an hour or so working on my office wardrobe, making small, updating alterations to cuffs and collars. Then I iron whatever outfit I plan to wear tomorrow. At nine-thirty I get into my pyjamas, pull the bed out of the wall and lie down to read Jane Austen. By ten-thirty I'm asleep.

Saturday nights aren't so manageable. I get agitated, I feel I should be out at a movie or a restaurant. Except I don't want to go alone, and who could I call to go with me? Debbie plays contract bridge Saturday nights (as well as Tuesday, Thursday and Sunday nights, one of the reasons, she admits, her dentist husband left her for a divorcée ten years his senior, but Debbie didn't care because he was so depressed all the time, crying on the toilet, wishing he was a glass blower or wood worker and yet terrified of being poor). That somebody with the opposite of a poker face could be a card sharp seems unlikely, but apparently Debbie is well known in bridge circles. She thinks I could be a card sharp, too. "You've got a quick mind," she says. "You've got the competitive spirit." I do? She has said I'm always welcome to kibitz, which means watch her play. Maybe one night I will. Not on a Saturday night, though; I can't imagine just sitting quietly, hour after hour, on a Saturday night.

Who else is there? Alice Keystone. A few weeks after I moved in, Alice phoned to tell me she'd got a part-time job selling religious children's books door-to-door. She hinted at wanting to drop by one evening, but I pictured her in that teacup-patterned dress she used to wear and it made me feel panicky, as if I could be pulled back to high school and the misery of last year, and I put her off, I said, "It's so hectic at work, I just come home and eat something and fall into bed." I promised to phone her when "things let up."

There's Lorna. Who spends her Friday and Saturday nights drinking at a bar called the Pigskin, where motorcycle-gang types try to pull her onto their laps, but "if you tell them to go fuck themselves they back off." The bartender is a friend of hers, that's why she goes, he gives her free drinks and lets her pee in the lane outside the kitchen door so she can avoid the disgusting toilets. "You should drop by," she has said more than once.

There's Abel.

Sometimes I change into black jeans and a black sweater and go out and buy cigarettes at the corner milk store, then walk around the block smoking and coughing and feeling nauseated and intriguing. One night I ride the subway and try to cheer myself up by seeing everybody through Abel's eyes. It's hard at first, but I get the knack. You have to tell yourself that there's a saving grace, it's there somewhere. Forget the big ears, concentrate on the shiny hair, the luscious lips. Don't see fat, see robust, see an intelligent face. The smelly drunk snoring in the corner, what's he got going for him? A Roman profile, red socks—a debonair touch—although maybe they're the only pair he owns.

Eventually my mood lifts enough that I don't mind going back to my empty apartment. I get off at Yonge Street and transfer to the northbound platform. I imagine Abel somewhere in the city, on a street or even on another subway platform, wafting along on this same feeling of brotherly love.

And then a crazy-looking man hurries down the platform and stops right beside me, so close that our shoulders touch. I step aside. He holds up to his ear a transistor radio, which is blaring static. He switches the radio off and says into the speaker, "Headquarters, come in, come in." I move farther away. He follows. He turns the radio on again and listens to more static, then turns it off and says, "Suspect approximately five foot five, light brown hair, slight build." He brings back the static. "Roger," he says decisively and comes up to me and puts a hand on my shoulder.

I jerk free. "Don't."

"I'm afraid I have to bring you in for questioning, Miss."

"Leave me alone, please."

He fumbles with the radio, not so adept now, catching fragments of music. Flustered, he switches it on and off. I walk quickly down the platform. "Suspect resisting arrest," he says, hurrying after me.

He reaches out a hand, and I lurch to one side, banging my thigh against the arm of a bench.

"Shit," I say.

"Let me help you, Miss."

I swing around. "Go fuck yourself!"

He swallows. The other people on the platform ignore us. Do they think we're having a lovers' quarrel? He rushes away, muttering at the radio. I am close to tears. "Go fuck yourself," I think. It sounds so vicious. Maybe it's true that motorcycle-gang members back off to hear it coming out of the mouth of a woman. We skinny, lank-haired, angry young women, our awful power.

Later, around midnight, sitting at my desk, I open the phone book to the *R*'s. Richardson, Richmond. Richter.

Karl. 241 Grenadier Road.

So they live out by High Park. I lie on my bed with the knowledge in me like a serum. My leg, where I hit it on the bench, throbs. I fall asleep wearing my black clothes.

The next day, Sunday, I take the eastbound subway to the end of the line. Out on the street I sit on a bench and wait for my father. It's late October, cold and windy, dead leaves rattling down the sidewalk. I carry my dirty laundry in a white plastic basket. My father pulls up in Mrs. Carver's wreck of a car, he says his own wouldn't start. As we're driving north I watch a glove-shaped cloud creep across the sky. Mrs. Carver is at the house, cooking dinner. She's always there now but never overnight, if the two of them are to be believed. I think they are. We eat roast pork, sweet potatoes, green beans, a lemon meringue pie for dessert. My father drives me back downtown. Somehow the bag of leftovers ends up under my clean clothes, at the bottom of the hamper. I don't realize until the next morning. I don't realize that the dress I wear to work still gives off a smell of pork even though I've sprayed it with perfume. Troy Warren tells me this a couple of years later. He says, "I fell for you anyway."

CHAPTER THIRTY-FOUR

Because of all the unlikely incidents that lead up to Troy and me running into each other—which we do literally: he hits me with his car—you could say that either we were fated to meet (his sentiment) or (mine) we met despite fate.

He tells me he almost never acts impulsively, and yet that morning, he makes a sudden decision to drive to his old girlfriend's house on the off chance that his watch is still in the alley where she threw it the week before. (His clean shirts and changes of underwear, also thrown out the window, he managed to retrieve at the time.) We've had rain since then; even if the watch is there it'll probably be ruined, and even if it's there and not ruined, she won't have left for work yet and might catch him prowling around. Nevertheless, he goes, only to lose his nerve once he pulls up in front of her house. Another urge strikes him then: to drive past the apartment building he lived in when he first came to Toronto four years ago. A quarter of an hour later, driving up Yonge Street, he passes a donut shop and gets a craving for a chocolate eclair. Which is how he happens to be turning right onto Wellesley at nine-twenty in the morning.

My day begins badly. The hot water runs out while I'm taking a shower, and then, on the subway, I fall asleep. By the time I open my eyes I've missed my stop by so many stations that the train has gone to the end of the line and is

now travelling north again. I get off and race across to the
other platform. Five minutes go by, ten. Finally an
announcement comes over the PA that the southbound line
is experiencing electrical problems, so I go up onto the
street and start walking. It's almost Halloween, there are
pumpkins and skeletons in store windows. Despite my
hurry I stop at one window that has a pumpkin carved to be
a beauty: cat's eyes, slits for long eyelashes, two tiny triangu-
lar nostrils and a rosebud mouth holding a cigarette. It
reminds me of my mother . . . the eyes, the cigarette. "Don't
open until ten," a voice behind me says, and a legless man
on a trolley wheels himself closer and extends a can of pen-
cils. I choose one, pay for two, then start walking again,
twirling the pencil like a baton, reminded now of Abel lac-
ing a twig through his fingers. I'm crossing a street when the
pencil flies out of my hand and falls straight down into the
nickel-sized hole of a sewer grate, such a perfectly aimed
shot that I stop, and a car turning right hits me.

I stumble sideways, unhurt. The driver leaps out. "Are
you all right, Miss?"

"I'm fine. It was just a bump."

"Are you sure?" He is looking in horror at my leg, the
huge purple bruise I got Saturday night evading the guy
with the transistor radio.

"Oh, I already had that."

"Well, thank God. I mean, thank God you're not hurt. I
didn't even see you."

He has a southern accent. Collar-length blond hair as fine
and straight as mine. I like how he's dressed, in a brown

leather jacket, white shirt and blue jeans. He offers to drive me wherever I'm going. His car is an old red convertible, and partly because I've never before ridden in a convertible, I accept.

"Troy Warren," he says then. He smiles and holds out his hand.

I hold out mine. "Louise Kirk."

"Louise Kirk." We shake. "Well," he says, "pleased to make your acquaintance, and thanks for being so gracious."

The traffic is slow-moving. He asks what I do and when I tell him, he says, "Ah," and tries to look impressed.

"Yes," I say. "A lowly secretary with even more lowly ambitions."

He glances at me, smiling. He has a nice face, a quizzical cast to his constantly changing expressions, as though you are meant to take him with a grain of salt. Not that he seems insincere; he seems, if anything, like somebody trying to cover up for too much sincerity. I can imagine saying to Debbie, "He's handsome in an unconventional way." I find myself telling him about Debbie and about Mr. Fraser and Lorna and then about my apartment and the people I watch every evening in the building across the lane. I fit it all in within seven blocks. He eggs me on with just the right questions and reactions. We are stopped in front of my office building before it occurs to me to ask him what he does.

"I have a record store."

"Really?"

"Just a small one. No big deal."

"But it's yours? You own it?"

"It's mine."

"That's a big deal." I try to guess his age. Under thirty. "What's it called?"

"Warren Records."

"After Warren Beatty?" I joke.

"After Warren Peace."

I laugh.

"You're pretty cheerful," he says, "for someone who just got hit by a car."

"You know, I think I've seen it. On Bloor, right?"

"Drop by sometime."

"I don't have a record player."

"You don't?"

"Uh-uh."

"And why should you, after all, a girl with your lowly ambitions?"

We smile at each other. The car behind us honks, and I say we're blocking traffic and he says would I have dinner with him some evening and I say, "I'm free tonight," and he asks me for my address and arranges to pick me up around seven.

At lunch, with Lorna and Debbie, I say, "He's got these neat grey eyes, really sweet and kind of . . . I don't know . . . ardent."

"Ah," Debbie breathes. "Ardent."

"What does that mean?" Lorna says.

"Warm."

"Why didn't you just say that?"

"I feel like I could tell him anything."

Lorna snorts. "Do yourself a favour. Don't."

But I do. We aren't in the restaurant half an hour before I admit that I had sex with the last man I worked for. He has already told me about his old girlfriend throwing his shirts and boxer shorts and antique watch from a third-floor window because he turned down her proposal of marriage. Is he upset? About the breakup, no, he's relieved, he saw it coming. He isn't happy about having hurt her, of course. She was his first friend when he came from North Carolina. She found him a place to live and a job teaching music theory at a night school.

I ask him what instrument he plays. If it's piano, I may as well get up and go home.

"Oh," he says, "I'm not a musician. I took a few music-theory courses at college. My students all knew more than I did."

I reach for my wine.

The waiter poured out a glass for each of us, although I ordered a Coke. It's an Italian restaurant, red-and-white-checkered tablecloths, candles in chubby, wicker-covered wine bottles, the waiter old and slow and possibly short-sighted. I say to Troy, "How does he know I'm not under-age?"

"Are you?"

"By two years."

"That's about where I put you."

"How old are you?"

"Twenty-four."

"So you're into corrupting young girls?"

"Is that what I'm doing?"

His smile may not be heart-stopping but it's irresistible. I say, "I guess we'll find out." I raise my glass. I feel flirtatious and confident, like a southern belle. "Tell me all about yourself," I say. "Do you have brothers and sisters? Is North Carolina where you grew up?"

It is. Near Fayetteville, on a prosperous tobacco farm. No brothers, two younger sisters still living at home. His mother, who is ten years older than his father, is lovely and tender-hearted but eccentric—"something of a scatterbrain." When he was a boy she would go around gathering up his favourite clothes and toys, his treasured books, and then drop them off on the front steps of the poor and occasionally even at middle-class homes, so that the housewives, who knew where the boxes had come from, were obliged to cart them all back and suffer through one of her embraces, another of her peculiarities being to take people in her arms and hold them for embarrassing lengths of time. The father was worse: a wooden-legged man who told wooden-legged jokes and then turned stony and murderous if you laughed too loud. He had lost the leg in the Second World War, and that made him a hero. A few years later he shot to death a tramp he surprised carrying a lead pipe out of the cellar (no charges laid, not against a veteran claiming self-defence), and that made him a hero you took care never to cross. No one knew this better than Troy, so for the most part he and his father got along even to the extent of exchanging civilities before the father strapped him on the back of his legs, five strikes to each calf and hard enough to raise welts.

"Are you ready, son?"

"Yes, sir."

"It'll be over with before you know it."

"Thank you, sir."

What had Troy done? Oh, shown up a few minutes late for supper, played a record too loud. Then came college and coffee houses and protest songs and returning home with new ways of looking at things but keeping silent for the sake of keeping the peace and, frankly, to protect his allowance and tuition. The showdown took place after college, when his father decided that before Troy started putting his business degree to use, he should enlist in the Marines. Troy was stunned. True, his father supported the war in Vietnam, but many times he'd said that the actual fighting was better left to boys with low IQs and no prospects, which Troy took to mean, "Not you, son." Now what? Troy didn't know, he couldn't think, so he just blurted out the truth: "Sir, I can't do that. I am a pacifist." His father, after a long moment, left the room, came back with his shotgun, pointed it at Troy's head and said, "Son, what you are is a coward, I always knew it. I'm giving you five minutes to get out of my sight. That's five counts of sixty, starting now. One, two, three . . ." Barely time for Troy to grab his wallet and a bag of clothes and run. Out on the front lawn his mother caught up with him and wrapped him in her inescapable embrace, while his father, gun aimed, stood on the porch and counted out the last of the five minutes: "Forty-eight, forty-nine . . ." Would he have pulled the trigger? Apparently his mother thought so because at fifty-three she undraped herself and backed away. Two days later Troy was in Canada, convinced that had he remained in the States, his days as a civilian would have been numbered.

I can't match that for a life, or for a delivery, either—he made it all sound hilarious—but I give it a go with stories of my mother, her cleaning mania and pyromania (burning my sweater) and then her disappearance. I tell him how my father thought she'd run off with some lady's man. "I never thought that," I say. "I figured she just wanted to be free."

"Maybe," Troy says. "And maybe she just couldn't bear the competition of a beautiful daughter."

I feel my face heat up. "Oh, that wasn't it. I was no threat to anybody, least of all her. Believe you me."

"No, I don't think I will believe you."

"One day I'll show you a picture of her."

He reacts slightly, a brief fixity of expression, and I realize I've just said that I expect us to go on seeing each other.

By ten-thirty we're at his apartment. He rents the entire second floor of a refurbished turn-of-the-century building, right on Bloor Street and only a block west of his store. On the third floor is a model-train club, men walking around until all hours fabricating miniature level-crossing gates and those tiny broccoli-like trees, one of which Troy has on his kitchen table from the time they invited him up. It was eerie, he says, not just how extensive and intricate the rail lines were but the serious, quiet atmosphere, as though something of great consequence was going on.

"How do you know it wasn't?" I say.

I am wandering from room to room, glass of Kahlúa in hand, and he is following and apologizing for the unwashed dishes, the clothes draped over chairs. "Don't worry," I say, "I'm no fan of immaculateness." I can't believe how much space he has. Three huge bedrooms, kitchen the size of a

living room, bathroom the size of a kitchen. Two of the
bedrooms are given over to boxes of records, overflow
from the store. His personal collection takes up an entire
wall of bookcases in the living room.

"Are they in any order?" I ask.

"An inscrutable order. The store is where all my ordering
talent goes."

"Where did you get the money, anyway, to buy a store?"

"I borrowed it. I'm drowning in debt."

"This furniture didn't come cheap either, I'll bet." I look
around approvingly at all the blond wood and creamy
leather. "Is it new?"

"Fairly new."

"Is it for sitting on?"

"You're welcome to do whatever you want on it."

I drop onto the chesterfield. "Are the records for listening to?"

"What would you like to hear?"

"Put on something you like. What kind of music do you
like?"

"All kinds. Classical, country, bluegrass, jazz, musicals . . ."

"Musicals?"

"What's funny about that?"

"Like *Oklahoma!?*"

"You bet."

"Do you have that?"

It takes a while but he finds the record and puts it on as I
help myself to more Kahlúa. He sits across from me, holding his beer in both hands. "Too loud," he says and gets up
to turn the volume down. I look at the back of him. Square

shoulders, not as wide as Abel's, and he's not as tall or as lean, either, but that's fine, that's good. He returns to his chair. I drain my glass, and refill it.

"How do you know if a musician is drunk?" I say.

"Is this a joke?"

"He can't get by the first bar."

"That's pretty bad."

I tell him about *A Thousand and One Side-Splitters,* which I still occasionally leaf through. "The funniest part," I say, "is how it's organized. Alphabetically by theme. Alcoholics, Cooking, Taxes. But then they're all cross-referenced. So under Alcoholics, it says, See Clergy, Lawyers. Under Sex—" I start laughing. "Oh, God, under Sex it says, See Epileptics."

"It doesn't."

"It does! Under Epileptics, it says, See—" I am laughing too hard to go on.

He laughs. "What?"

"Clergy!"

"What does it say under Clergy?"

"See Alcoholics, Dwarfs, Egg Farmers—"

"Egg Farmers?"

"Cows, Pregnancy. Oh, God. Oh, God." I drain my glass and set it down harder than I mean to on the coffee table. I want to say, "Why don't you sit here beside me?" but what comes out is, "I had an abortion," and a shudder of grief goes through me such as I have not felt in a year.

Thus the night deteriorates. Periodically he tries to withdraw the Kahlúa bottle, but I clutch it to my chest. "Don't worry," I say. "This isn't like me. I'm never like this." The drunker and more weepy I get, the more urgency I feel about making him understand who Abel is and why I loved him. *Loved.* I am as careful about using that word in the past tense as I am about holding on to the Kahlúa bottle. Even when I throw up, I won't let it go. I bring it home, though by then it's empty. He delivers me into my apartment, strips me down to my underwear and puts me to bed. I have no memory of anything beyond staring at the holes in his kitchen-sink drain and thinking how uniform they are, how heartless.

I expect never to hear from him again, but the next afternoon he phones me at work and asks how I'm feeling.

"Horrible," I say. I tell him I'm sorry, I don't know what got into me.

"Well," he says, "we could always give it another try."

"You're asking me out again?"

"I believe I am."

"Are you crazy?"

"Crazy enough, I guess."

On Saturday night, on his big squeaking bed, we have sex. I am anxious to make amends. He is adoring and languid, he won't let me hurry things. We go on for hours, with breaks to drink pineapple juice out of yellow plastic glasses and to eat Jiffy-popped popcorn and canned peach slices. Sometime after midnight I hear a train whistle from upstairs and realize I've dozed off. We both have. I get up on one elbow and touch my finger to his mouth. He doesn't stir. It's a fleshy, generous mouth. His whole face has a soft, generous look, a bit thrown together, the nose listing to the side, one ear sticking out more than the other. But it's as if that's the point, as if his face were made to serve its expression, which, even in sleep, is droll and welcoming.

I wonder if I love him. I don't see how I couldn't.

CHAPTER THIRTY-FIVE

Abel and I have both reached the stage where we talk about his death matter-of-factly, but that can only be because we have no idea what we're talking about. As he himself once said, your own death is never more than a rumour. Every time I open the front door and listen for his breathing, I don't really expect not to hear it. The not hearing is unimaginable, infinitely deferred. He is still in his own apartment, he drinks, blacks out, revives himself, washes the floor. You can't go from that to death. There are phases, emergencies. There are miracles.

One day I find that I have also reached the stage where I can bring myself to ask why he never said he loved me. Why he could never say the words.

"I said them," he whispers.

"Once. You said, 'I love you too much,' as if it were a curse."

"You always knew how I felt."

"I thought I knew when you were with me. But when we weren't together, I had no way of knowing how you felt."

"The same."

"You can't even say it now. You can't say, 'I love you, Louise.'"

"I love you, Louise."

"In a court of law you could claim that you were merely

repeating what I'd just said, merely considering the idea."

"I love you, Louise."

It's Saturday, late morning. He's still in bed (though he assures me he'll get up soon, "everything's fine") so I have taken off my clothes and gotten under the blanket to lie with him. "Have you lost your voice?" I ask. He won't answer directly; he says, "I feel like whispering today." His breath is sweet. Maybe he has switched to drinking liqueurs, or maybe it's because his lips have stopped bleeding. His face is nearly translucent; you can see the finer veins as if, at this late date, what was hidden may as well start showing itself. Overall, he's beginning to resemble a delicate child.

I tell him this, and he says, "I used to think that if living in the world was natural and good, then living should rejuvenate you. I couldn't understand why we didn't start out old and decrepit and end up young and perfect."

"That was before you realized that old and decrepit *is* perfect."

He nods.

"Because everything is perfect."

"That's right."

"I'm not agreeing with you. I'm quoting you."

"You're merely considering the idea."

"How do you choose between things, then? Why buy this and not that? Why be with this person and not that one?"

"It's natural to be drawn to certain things and people more than to others."

"So what's wrong with being drawn to one above all others?"

"It isn't wrong."

I give his hand a small squeeze. "So why couldn't you love me above all others?"

"I love you above all others I love."

"You mean, if all your girlfriends were all drowning and you could only save one, it'd be me?"

He smiles. "You're a good swimmer."

I have to smile back. "I'd save you. I'd sacrifice anybody for you."

"When I'm out of the way, that will change."

"It won't. You'll take my love with you."

"Don't let that happen. Keep it for yourself."

"What if I can't? What if you take it anyway?"

He rolls onto his back and looks up at the ceiling. "I'm not taking anything. I'm travelling light."

CHAPTER THIRTY-SIX

With Troy, I am the one loved unconditionally. I can go around with dirty hair, be boring and bad tempered. If I make an effort—and most of the time I try to—it's for the luxury of giving pleasure to someone I don't need to make any effort for. I still think about Abel off and on, and then there's a hollowness in my chest, but after a while it is only the Abel feeling, supplanting all the other feelings I ever had for him, even love. That's what I say, and believe. Talking about him with Troy, I take on a wry tone, not intentionally, it just creeps into my voice. Troy is such a sympathetic listener and so sure of himself that the worst he'll say of Abel is, "He sounds complicated." One time he said that he thought the two of them could have been friends.

"Of course you could have," I said. "Everybody's his friend. The town drunk is his friend. The local rapist is his friend."

"Well, there you are," said Troy, taking no offence.

And so he continually wins me.

He has a double-jointed right arm he can rotate at the shoulder, and he pretends to twist it off, it's mine if I'll be his bride. "Marriage is a dying institution," I say. How about moving in with him, then? "Out of wedlock?" I say, feigning shock. He knows I'm not ready, he doesn't push. Besides, we see each other at least four nights a week. He cooks me supper—Shake 'n Bake chicken, or chili con carne—and then we watch TV or listen to records or go to a movie. We make love all over his apartment, on rows of boxes, on every Danish-modern chair. Thursday nights he stays late at the store, which gives me a chance to catch up on my laundry and reading. Friday nights he meets a group of fellow draft dodgers at a Hungarian restaurant where the talk around the table is the anti-war movement and an underground literary magazine called *Rant* that they all seem to write for and that he partly finances, since he's the only one with a steady job. Sometimes I drop by to listen to the passionate conversation, which I find far more comprehensible than any of their published poems and articles. On the weekends, Troy and I drive around in his car, maybe take a walk in the Beaches or out on Toronto Island. I still go to Greenwoods most Sunday afternoons, and a couple of times a month he joins me. My father and Mrs. Carver can't praise him enough, nor he them. "Affable," my father says in a tone of wonder. "The word for Troy is affable." (Obviously he thought I'd end up with some hostile misfit.) And yet for all his affability and humour, Troy has no close friends, I'm not sure why. The draft dodgers find him a little too straight, I suspect. Aside from them, there's only a belligerent record collector named Sammy, who browbeats us into smoking hash with him in the back room of the store. When it's just Troy and me, by ourselves, we never smoke pot and we drink only the occasional beer or glass of wine. Troy says he wants to experience me with a clear head, he wants nothing in the way of his senses.

I say, "Me, too."

Not quite the truth. What I want is for him to be nothing like Abel.

Which isn't quite true either, since they are both sweet tempered and intelligent. It's in the specifics that I can't bear similarities. As a child Troy collected insects, and on our walks, if he identifies a beetle or a butterfly, I turn away. For the same reason, I won't listen to Bach piano music, not with him. Troy's theory is that the more he seems to resemble Abel, the more risk there is, in my mind, of his fooling around on me. When he says this, however, even when he reassures me without mentioning Abel's name, all that does is remind me of what's really going on. I can't bear the resemblances because I can't bear the discrepancies, how Troy comes up short: the collector of dead insects versus the venerator of live ones, the music lover versus the musician. The person with a hundred acquaintances and no close friends versus the person whose every acquaintance is a close friend. All so unjust and depressing. As an antidote I immediately launch into a mental cataloguing of Troy's virtues, starting off with his devotion to me, his loyalty, and often that's as far as I have to go before he steps out of Abel's shadow and is himself. His good, deserving self.

Four years pass. When I think "four years" I have a sense of time unaccounted for and ungraspable as in a dream that takes only a minute to tell although it seemed to last all night. "The years slip by," old people say. I now know what they mean: nothing much changes. Troy and I stay together. I keep working for Mr. Fraser, the two of us main-taining, just barely, the ruse of productivity. Twice I have plodded through the files, reading, organizing, trying to distinguish living clients from dead ones. I was considering going through them again and typing up fresh labels when Mr. Fraser summoned me into his office and asked had I ever seen the movie *Days of Wine and Roses?* I told him no.

"With Lee Remick and Jack, uh . . . Jack . . ."

"I never saw it."

"Jack . . . You know who I mean. Talks fast. Twitches his head around."

"Jack Lemmon?"

"That's it. Jack Lemmon. Now, then. There's a girl, the Lee Remick character, smart as a whip. Secretary in a big, fancy firm, advertising, if I'm not mistaken. But the fellow that hired her can't keep her busy enough, so what she does is, she sits at her desk reading an encyclopedia of world literature, one volume at a time. Not the literature itself, mind you." His look sharpened. "What author are you at?"

I've told him how I'm working my way through the great novels in alphabetical order according to author. "George Eliot," I said. *"Silas Marner."*

"E. M. Forster coming up. There's a writer for you."

"I've got to get through William Faulkner and F. Scott Fitzgerald first."

"A Passage to India. Room with a View." He seemed to lose his train of thought.

"Lee Remick reads the encyclopedia," I prompted.

"That's right. You see, she never went to university. The way she figures it, by the time she has worked her way through to the end of the last volume she'll have a bachelor's degree in English literature under her belt."

"Without the certificate."

"Nothing but a piece of paper."

"You could say the same of a stock certificate."

"Don't get smart with me, young lady. The knowledge is the important thing, doesn't matter a whit how you come by it. Now, then. Novels are all well and good, you know my feelings on that score, but people see a girl reading a novel at her desk and they think she's dillydallying. An encyclopedia, on the other hand—a girl reading an encyclopedia, how do you know she isn't researching something or other?"

He pulled himself to his feet and shuffled, all bent over, to his bookcase and removed the first volume of his set of the Encyclopedia Britannica. Clutching it in both hands, he came back and dropped it on the desk. His look was very intent. "Now, then. You read your way through all twenty-four volumes and, by golly, there's a Ph.D. in general knowledge, right there."

Eight months later, I'm at the end of volume three, which puts me among the *Br*'s: Brahms, Braille, Brain. Because I'm taking this seriously, trying to memorize key facts, progress is sluggish. And yet even at my most bored I never consider quitting or applying for another job within the company. How could I desert Mr. Fraser? Not that anyone aside from Lorna ever suggests I should. The draft dodgers think I have it made. As a secretary I'm nothing to them, but as a secretary who does nothing, I'm a subversive, and now that I'm spending my afternoons reading the encyclopedia—at my boss's insistence, no less—I'm a star. A performer. "Ask me about any subject that starts with A or B," I say, "up to Boswell."

"Ares!" they shout. "Attila the Hun!" "Bismarck!"

Draft dodgers with warmongers on the brain.

I sometimes wonder if I'm living the life I've been waiting for or the one I'm making do with. Is a person meant to be content? I can't believe I've entered a lasting state of mind. And the truth is, it does wear thin. Toward the end of every August, I start to feel anxious, which I realize is partly a hangover from when I used to get so upset about going back to school, but it's more than that, it's an accumulation of guilt and confusion over not moving in with Troy, resisting his patient, jokey pleas. Suddenly I'm restless for I don't know what . . . something wild, a swerve from the straight and narrow.

In this mood Lorna becomes a kindred spirit. She says, "One day I swear I'm going to throw my typewriter out the window," and instead of ignoring her, as I normally would, I say, "The windows here are unbreakable."

"Okay," she says, "down the stairs."

"Can you imagine?" I say, because I *can*. You pick up your typewriter, lug it to the stairwell, you peer down those thirty-seven flights to make sure the coast is clear and then you . . . just . . . let go.

I dream about having sex with Abel. When I wake up, before I gain full consciousness, I'm aware of the Angel of Love flickering in the corner by my dresser. "Go away," I think weakly.

Call him, she urges. Call him.

She's hard to resist. The first year that I was going through this anxious period, I looked up the Richters' phone number again. On the verge of dialling I grabbed the newspaper and flipped through to the Classifieds. A new apartment, that's what I needed. Something bigger, quieter.

I take it back, then, about nothing having changed in four years. Where I live has changed three times. And yet—I suppose because my furniture always comes with me—I never seem to experience any real upheaval. That is to say, upheaval is the point: fixable, household upheaval created to distract me from myself. As to where I end up, that hardly matters, I'm so rarely at home. Still, on the day of the move I always get vague, unreasonable expectations of greater fulfillment. Which are soon enough dashed. The first place I rented, a one-bedroom flat in an old Victorian mansion, had a prostitute living in the attic, clients always lurking on the porch, pounding on my door if they found hers locked. The second place had poisoned mice that staggered upstairs from the restaurant below and crawled into my shoes. A year later I was back in an old mansion, on the second floor this time, looking out onto a blue spruce tree that a cat burglar climbed so he could break into my living room and steal the record player and speakers Troy had given me as a house-warming gift. A house-warming gift! Though I never told Troy about my moving plans until after I'd signed the lease, he always took the news valiantly, more so each time, since with every move I migrated several blocks closer to his apartment.

"Pure coincidence," I said the third time.

"Pure, unconscious desire," he said.

CHAPTER THIRTY-SEVEN

"Abel, you know what I don't understand?"

"What?"

"If everything and everybody is perfect, why do you drink?"

A pause and then, "Everything is perfect in itself."

"Whether you drink or not."

"Right."

"But more perfect for *you* when you drink."

Another pause.

"We don't have to talk about this if you don't want to."

"Maybe that's it."

"What is?"

"That it's more perfect."

"But *is* it?"

"Louise, I don't know what you want me to say."

"What you feel. The truth."

"I'm not escaping, I don't feel that. I'm not *looking* for perfection."

"Are you looking for *anything?*"

"Sure."

"What?"

"Whatever's there."

"You mean, whatever you see."

"Right."

"I'm just trying to understand."

"I know."

"You don't make it easy."

"I know."

"That's okay. Nobody's perfect."

A few days later, Saturday afternoon, I fall asleep on the chesterfield and have a dream about Tim Todd. We're sitting under a weeping willow. There are things he wants to show me but he's hesitating, afraid I'll be dismissive. These things are in a brown paper bag, so they can't be fish, at least not live ones. In any case I'd prefer not to know. Finally he says, "Well, do you want to take a look?" and there is such wistfulness and despair in his voice that I almost relent.

"Some other time," I say.

I wake up on the verge of tears. "Tim Todd," I think, wondering if I cared about him more than I ever realized. No, this is belated guilt, it's regret over having hurt him. Which is not to say that, under similar circumstances, I wouldn't hurt him again.

And then something else occurs to me—about why Abel drinks—and I get up and go to the window, uncertain whether I've had this thought before. I suspect I have but that I let it go. Probably I was still hoping that the reason lay outside of him, in the form of an awful memory, say, or an abstract philosophy, and that he could repudiate it if he really wanted to.

I guess I've used up all of my faith because suddenly it seems obvious that he drinks out of sheer helplessness. If life means doing harm, making decisions, choosing one person over another, then he's not cut out for it. And doing nothing isn't the answer; that's just making a decision by default. Better to *be* nothing than to do nothing.

Is that how he sees it? He knows how much his death will hurt us, so he must be under the impression that by staying alive he'll eventually hurt us even more. Maybe we should pretend we've stopped caring what he does. Say, "We've given up on you, Abel. You don't matter." Well, that would gratify him, our falling in line with what he has been telling us for months. How do we get around that? How do we persuade him that he's entitled to cause pain and, what's more, that he has a responsibility to *bear* the pain he causes?

If only I could say, "You're worthy of your own life," and make him believe me. Too late. Too late. He seems completely enraptured now by the idea of no longer existing. I think he imagines the space he'll vacate, the actual physical space, and there we'll be, his parents and I, waving our hands around trying to find him, but at least we won't come up against any resistance. There won't be anything to collide with, only air.

CHAPTER THIRTY-EIGHT

On a Friday night in August of 1973, Mr. Fraser dies. I find out when I arrive for work on Monday. Debbie is sobbing into her hands, while Lorna, from the other side of the desk, tries to man the phones. It's Lorna who tells me. Her sympathetic tone is almost as shocking as the news. She says that Mr. MacLellan wants me to go straight to his office.

Mr. MacLellan is the president. "Please," he says, indicating a chair, then handing me a box of Kleenex, though my eyes are dry. He perches on the corner of his desk. "You've heard."

"Just now."

"If it's any comfort, he went peacefully."

"How do you know?" I don't mean to be insolent, I just wonder how he can say that, if Mr. Fraser died alone.

He touches the knot of his tie. Maroon, with gold flecks. He is tall and suave, somewhere in his late fifties, salt-and-pepper hair, the sort of man who could never be anything less than a president. "He was found in bed," he says. "Saturday morning by the cleaning lady. It appears that he died in his sleep. Heart failure, most likely, but we don't yet know."

He says that the funeral will be held Wednesday afternoon. Until then, and afterwards for as long as I want, I can take a leave of absence. In the meantime, Personnel will find me something suitable at the same salary. I hardly listen. I am still thinking of Mr. Fraser in bed, fighting for breath.

"I'm the executor of the will," Mr. MacLellan goes on, "which was revised only last month. I can tell you that you are a beneficiary."

I look up.

"Mr. Fraser thought very highly of you. He has left you fifteen thousand dollars and his twenty-four-volume set of the Encyclopedia Britannica."

I don't cry until the funeral, and then I cry so much that the daughter-in-law keeps glancing around. It was meeting the grandsons for the first time, it was how much the oldest resembled Mr. Fraser, the same brown eyes, the same quick smile suggesting immediate comprehension, and the poignancy and mystery of that, as if Mr. Fraser were somehow conscious in the boy. At the reception, which is held in Mr. MacLellan's mansion, Pat Penn of Personnel asks in her listless way when I'll be coming back to the office, and the prospect of resurrecting myself as a secretary to some other vice-president is suddenly unthinkable.

"I'm not," I say. "I'm not coming back."

"Well," she says, unfazed, "let me know your new phone number."

Because, of course, she assumes, as do I, that because it's August I'll be moving soon. I haven't found an apartment yet, or even given my notice, but I've started reconstructing the flattened boxes from my last move.

A few hours later, over at Troy's place, I wonder if I

spoke too hastily. I say, "It's not as if I need the money. But I need to work. I need to do something."

"I could always use you in the store," he says.

"You could?"

"Why not? You know music. You're easy on the eye."

"I'm charming. I'm friendly."

"We can work on that."

"Maybe I should break down and live with you, too," I say, in a burst of infatuation. "Maybe we should spend every waking minute within shouting distance. I could have *both* spare rooms, right? My own private bedroom and living room?"

"Whatever you want," he says carefully.

"Oh, well, I'll think about it."

"Will you?"

"I guess. I don't know. I'll see how I feel tomorrow."

I feel worse. I wake up late and with a headache. "Mr. Fraser is dead," I think. I can't believe it. He was so old and weathered, like a tree or rock. He had earned his right to be here, more than I've earned mine. I think of the times I've felt sorry for myself and am ashamed. There he was, returning home every evening to an empty apartment, his days numbered, his dead wife and dead son waiting at the end of his thoughts. I imagine him eating supper alone, a linen napkin, good silverware. Rolling up his sleeves to wash the dishes. What did he do then? I suppose he read the newspaper or maybe a hardcover novel or a book about sailing ships. He must have gone to bed at a decent hour, considering what an early riser he was. I imagine him, in blue cotton pyjamas, setting his alarm clock, which would have been an old-fashioned wind-up kind. Did he set it the night he died? He once told me that on Saturday mornings he visited somebody in a retirement home, an aunt or cousin on his wife's side (I remember being struck by his loyalty to such a distant relation). Oh, it's wrenching to think of him setting the alarm, allowing himself the modest assumption that he would need waking up.

I look at my own clock. A quarter to eleven. I decide I should probably go into the office to clean out my desk, get that over with. An hour later, just as I'm just about to leave, the phone rings. It's my father, calling from his office. He asks how I am, how the funeral went, and then says he'd like to drop by.

"Now?"

"If you're not busy, not on your way out somewhere."

"What's the matter?"

"Just some news."

"Bad news. I can tell by your voice."

"Don't worry. Listen, I'll pick us up some lunch, a couple of egg-salad sandwiches, how's that?"

His office isn't far, he arrives within half an hour. "On the move again," he says, noticing the boxes.

"Tell me."

"Let's go into the kitchen."

He puts the bag of food on the table, then sits and takes a folded piece of paper from his inside jacket pocket. "This arrived yesterday," he says, handing it to me.

It's a handwritten letter. "Winnipeg," I say, reading the return address. The rest I read to myself:

Dear Mr. Kirk:

As Helen Grace Kirk's common-law husband, it is my sad duty to inform you that she passed away on July nineteenth of lung cancer. She went quickly and didn't suffer unduly. The reason I didn't notify you about the funeral is that it was a small affair, at Grace's request.

We never had much in the way of possessions, but Grace said she wanted your daughter, Louise, to have the wedding rings you gave her so that Louise would have something to remember her by. She also wanted Louise to have the ashes to scatter where she sees fit. I'm sending these along by special delivery mail. I hope this isn't too much of a shock. She said you were always good to her and that Louise had a fine sense of humour.

Yours truly,
Wendell Wells

"Lung cancer," I say.

"Are you all right?"

"Well, it *is* a shock, isn't it? Wendell Wells." I rub my temples—the headache's coming back.

"He's a gardener."

"How do you know that?"

"I tracked down his number and gave him a call."

"When?"

"This morning. Just before I called you." He retrieves the letter and returns it to his pocket.

"And you got hold of him?"

"Oh, yes."

I only now notice that his eyes are red-rimmed. "That must have been hard."

"It wasn't too bad, easier than I expected. He was very civil, said he was glad to hear from me. He was in pretty rough shape, though. Broke down a couple of times. It seems he and your mother met five years ago at the place where they both worked. Some rich big-wig banker's country estate. She was the housekeeper."

"Housekeeper!"

"Apparently she ran the place. She'd have been good at it, making sure everything was ship-shape, spic and span. Before that, she moved around quite bit, so she told him. Worked all over the Prairies."

"As a housekeeper?"

"As a cocktail waitress."

"Cocktail waitress! How could she have been a cocktail waitress? She hated hearing people slurp their drinks. She must have lost her mind."

"Wendell—" he makes a helpless gesture, acknowledging the unlikelihood of the first-name basis, "he said her mind was as sharp as a tack, right up until the end. He had no idea that she'd been married or even what her real name was, but in the last few days she decided to make a clean breast of it. He had thought she was a spinster named Grace White."

"White. After her teeth. After her skin." I take the sandwiches out of the bag. "So. Dead at forty-five."

"Forty-six in November," he says quietly.

I start eating one of the sandwiches. I wasn't hungry before, but now I'm famished. "Does Grandma Hahn know?"

"Wendell says he tried to get hold of her but couldn't find her. It's possible she died a few years back. No records turned up, though."

"Boy, the women in that family sure know how to make themselves scarce."

"*You're* a woman in that family, may I remind you." He picks up a sandwich. "I'm glad about the rings. I'm happy about that."

" 'To remember her by.' Well, I remember the *rings*."

"It's the right thing that they come to you."

"What am *I* supposed to do with them?"

"You could have them reset."

"I don't wear jewellery. And what about the rest of her things? I guess Wendell, the gardener of few possessions, is holding on to them."

He sets the sandwich back down. "You're still angry. Still hurt."

"I'm not *still* angry and hurt. I'm *suddenly* angry and hurt. 'Louise had a fine sense of humour.' Is that all she told him? Is that all she remembered?"

"It may be all *he* remembered from the many things she said."

"Scatter the ashes where I see fit. Where would that be? In the path of an Eaton's delivery truck?"

"Well." He looks crushed.

"Oh, I'm sorry. I'm sorry." I reach across the table and put my hand over his. "It's just all so crazy. I can't believe it."

"It's hard to believe, all right. A bolt from the blue."

The ashes and rings arrive in Greenwoods the following

Wednesday afternoon. He offers to drop them by the apartment but I say they can wait until Sunday when Troy and I come for dinner. After hanging up from that call, I phone Troy at the store and say, "I'm inquiring about the two rooms in the sunny downtown flat. Are they still available?"

"As far as I know, yes, they are."

"I'm in a position to pay an exorbitant rent."

"The rent is ridiculously low, as it happens."

"Will the landlord paint one room canary yellow and the other amber?"

"Both yellow, you mean?"

"Different shades of yellow."

"I believe that can be arranged."

"Tell him he has a deal."

A pause, while he rings up a sale, and then, "Have you changed your mind yet?"

"Not yet."

"What made you decide?"

"I don't know. My mother's ashes arrived."

"Louise . . ."

"I want to move in with you. I *do*."

"Are you sure?"

"Yes, I'm sure. I'm sure."

We start clearing the rooms of boxes that evening. On Saturday morning we buy the paint. "Yellow for stimulation," I say. "Yellow for cheerfulness." That's not why. Yellow for luck. Because I'm *not* sure.

CHAPTER THIRTY-NINE

We are driving home from Greenwoods. The rings are in an envelope in my purse, the ashes in a white china urn I hold on my lap. It is both smaller than I thought it would be—about the size of a rose vase—and heavier. It is appropriately slim and curvaceous. Handing it over to me, my father said, "I was thinking, when you feel ready to do the scattering, we might make a more formal ceremony of it. Invite Aunt Verna to visit for a few days . . ."

"Don't drag Aunt Verna all the way here for that. Invite her when somebody gets married or has a baby."

Everyone—my father, Mrs. Carver, Troy—perked up. Whose marriage? Whose baby? (I had already surprised my father and Mrs. Carver with the news that Troy and I were moving in together.) But I was only offering the prospect of future developments in exchange for refusing to even consider a scattering ceremony. It was all I could do to *take* the ashes.

"Well, it's for you to decide," my father said, with a glance at Mrs. Carver, whose idea it probably was. Some gesture of appeasement toward my mother's spirit.

In the car I hold the urn by what feels like its hips and try to recall if my mother ever said where she'd like to be scattered. The only time I can remember ashes coming into the conversation was when she told Mrs. Bently some story she'd heard, and found hilarious, about a woman discovering that her dead husband had been unfaithful to her and so she used his ashes as cat litter. I tell this to Troy, who shakes his head. "Where *will* you scatter them?" he asks.

"I don't know. I don't have a cat."

"Hey, that's your mother you're talking about."

"Who was the least sentimental of women."

For the rest of the ride home we don't talk. I can guess from his pensive expression that he's mulling over what I said about marriage and babies. When he pulls up in front of my apartment he offers to help me pack dishes, since it's only nine-thirty, but I'm afraid he'll launch into a discussion of our future, and I tell him I just want to go to bed.

"Don't forget to call your landlord," he says. To give my notice, he means. As I'm walking away, he calls out, "Pick you up around nine," and I remember that he's taking tomorrow off so we can start painting the rooms.

Upstairs, sitting on my bed, I try the rings on. A perfect fit. My hands are her hands, without the manicured nails and cigarette. It's weird though, wearing her rings, it's too personal, like trying on her underwear (something I never did). I return the rings to the envelope and put them in the top drawer of my dresser. The urn I carry into the kitchen and set down on the table. After looking at it for a minute, trying to see it as a centrepiece, I stick it in the fridge, out of sight. Except what if I forget it when I move? I take it back out and prise up the cork-lined stopper. The smell is the smell of ash from any fire. I pour out a bit onto the kitchen table. Grey powdery chunks. I rub the powder between my fingers, expecting to feel . . . I don't know, a rush of sadness or repulsion, but I can't make the leap from what is essentially dirt, to her. I go into the living room and sit at my desk. Ash is all down the front of my sweater, which used to be her sweater. "So she *has* come back for her clothes," I think, not cynically, not bothering to wipe the ash away.

I open the phone book to look up my landlord's number. His last name is Salter. I leaf through as far as the *R*'s, then slow down. Ralston. Richie.

Richter, Karl. 241 Grenadier Road. Above that: Richter, Abelard. 249 Ontario Street.

My heart starts pounding. I put my hand on the phone. I lift the receiver. If the Angel of Love is here, she's keeping her distance. I dial the first number, a nine. The subsiding clicks sound explosively loud. I press the receiver against my shoulder while I dial the rest, then bring it back up to my head in a kind of horrified trance, as though it were a gun.

He answers on the second ring. "Hello?" His unmistakeable hoarse voice.

"It's me. Louise."

There is shouting and laughter in the background. "Hello?" he says again.

I clear my throat. "It's Louise."

"Louise?"

"How are you?"

A pause, and then, "Fine. I'm fine. How are *you?*"

"Oh, I'm . . . I'm okay, I guess. I just wanted to see you how you were." Now, on a piano, somebody is playing *Chopsticks*. "Do you have company?"

"Just the usual uproar."

"Is there another phone? I can hardly hear you."

"Where are you calling from?"

"My place. My apartment."

"Where's that?"

Obviously he never looked up *my* name in the phone book. "Spadina and Dupont."

"Would you like to meet somewhere near there?"

"What, now?"

"Or I could come to your place."

"Right now, you mean?"

"Unless you'd like me to call you back later, when it's a little quieter around here."

"No. It's okay. You can come here."

I give him the address. After hanging up, I go on clutching the receiver for several minutes. Then I run into the bathroom and brush my teeth and put on some lipstick. I figure it will take him about three-quarters of an hour if he comes by streetcar and subway, but he arrives within twenty minutes. He has ridden a bike and brought it up the stairs. A bizarre, rusty, high-seated, wide-handled contraption.

"Where'd you get that?" I say. The first thing I say.

"In the basement of the house where I'm living." He wheels it in and leans it against the wall.

I can hardly look at him. His eyes. His hair, still long. He's wearing a green T-shirt. Blue jeans. He's taller but maybe not, maybe it's only that I'm used to Troy.

In the bike's wicker carrier is a large bottle of rum. "It's already mixed," he says. He notices the boxes. "Do you have any glasses?"

"Somewhere." I find the box marked "Good Dishes" and unwrap two wine goblets. He fills them to the top.

"I don't have any ice," I say. "I mean, my freezer is one big block of ice."

"This is fine."

He looks around, at the leaded-glass windows and built-in bookshelves, the brass light fixtures. Through his eyes, I'm suddenly impressed by what a great place it is.

"Why are you leaving?" he says.

"I'm not. I've changed my mind." Just this second I have.

"That's good." He smiles. It dazzles me. I sit on a box of books.

He sits on the box across from me. "So," he says, and I look at him, and the roar of everything we know about each other and have done to each other seems to pass between us.

"Oh, Abel—" My voice breaks. I put my drink on the floor.

He puts his on a box. He reaches for my hand. The thrill races up my arm into my chest. I can't speak for a minute, and then I say, "That letter I sent you . . ."

He lets out his breath.

"It was so cruel," I say.

"No."

"Yes, it was. It was vicious."

"I didn't read it that way."

"You didn't?"

He shakes his head. He studies my fingertips.

"It must have hurt you, though."

"I was hurt for you. For what you felt you . . . had to do."

"I saw you with that girl."

"You really flew out, then?"

"How do you think I knew about her? I spied on your house, all one morning, in the park across the street. I followed you downtown. I heard you play the piano in that bar. The Bear Pit."

"Why didn't you come up to me?"

"Why did you stop phoning me?"

He bites his lip.

"Well," I say, "when I finally worked up enough nerve to come up to you, I found you kissing that girl. Who was she, anyway?"

He shrugs. "A girl."

"Did you love her?"

He gives his head such a noncommittal shake that he may only be shaking off the question.

"I don't know," I say, agitated. I draw my hand away. "Maybe I'd have had an abortion no matter what you did. Maybe I didn't want a baby."

He looks at me and then down. I look at his face. His full, crisply defined lips, his cleft chin, which is so familiar and dear to me, like his mother's kitchen in Greenwoods, or the ravine. I pick up his hand again and bring it to my lips. I move it down my neck, down to my breasts.

We make love on the floor, among the boxes. I start crying, and we go into the bedroom, and this time the lovemaking is more deliberate, almost formal, restrained by our mutual amazement. "Do you have a girlfriend?" I say afterwards, believing that, now, I can bear to know.

But he says he doesn't.

I turn to face him. "Is there a girl who's under the impression that she's your girlfriend?"

A small smile. "No."

"I love you, Abel."

I dream that Troy's father is stomping around the Hungarian restaurant, shooting draft dodgers in the legs. I open my eyes. It's morning. Somebody is knocking at the front door.

"Louise? It's me!"

I yank at the sheet, which is bunched under Abel's legs. He opens his eyes. I jump out of bed and grab my bathrobe from the chair. I am groping to find a sleeve when Troy appears in the doorway.

He looks me. At Abel.

Abel pulls a corner of the sheet over himself.

"Sorry to intrude," Troy says with a tight smile. He walks away. I wait for a slam. It doesn't come. Only the faint click of the lock catching.

"Who was that?" Abel says.

"A friend. He was going to help me pack. Oh, God, I should have phoned him." I hear how natural I sound: embarrassed, but not extremely. Just a little guilty. It's as if I've tapped into some emergency reservoir of cunning.

"Maybe you should go after him."

A car door shuts. An engine starts up. "Too late," I say.

An hour later I am scrambling the four eggs that I found at the back of my fridge. Abel is examining the ashes, a small pile of which are still on the kitchen table from when I showed them to him last night.

He says, "The unbelievable complexity that was your mother reduced to this," and I am suddenly struck by the miracle of his being here, in my kitchen, without his shirt on. All I had to do was phone. All I had to do was stop resisting.

I go to put the plates on the table, but he makes me hold off until he has brushed every last speck back into the urn. Watching him, weak with love, my hands start to tremble, and I set the plates back on the counter. "If she were here," I say, "she'd just wipe them up with the dishcloth."

"If she were here confronting her own ashes," he says. "Wouldn't that be something?"

He leaves right after breakfast. He's having coffee with some filmmaker friend and then he's playing piano for another friend's dance rehearsal. Later, around five o'clock, I'm meeting him at a bar, where we'll have dinner together.

It isn't until I hear the front door of the house close that I allow myself to think of Troy. I sink into a kitchen chair as the awfulness of what happened settles over me. The way he just stood there. *Sorry to intrude.* I cover my mouth with my hands and start to cry.

I've got to talk to him right away, explain everything, how I never planned any of it. I, of all people, *I* know how it feels to be betrayed. Why would I want to put him through that? I didn't want to. I wanted to love him.

I take a taxi to his apartment. Although I have a key, I knock. No answer. I knock again, then let myself in.

"Troy?" I peek into the bedroom. It's as if I'm playing the part he played a couple of hours earlier. But in this version, the bed's empty.

I look everywhere, just in case. In case what? I don't know. I check the bathroom, kitchen, the two spare rooms.

My heart drops to see that he has lain down newspapers in preparation for a day of painting.

"Oh, Troy," I say. "Where are you?"

I go back to the kitchen and look out the window, and there's his car, parked in the lane. I phone the store. Ginny, his sales clerk, answers. "Yep, he's here," she says cheerfully. "Should I put you through?"

"No, it's all right, it's not important."

I hang up, stunned. He's okay. He's at work, behaving normally. Still, I've got to talk to him. "You're better off without me," I'll say. "I never wanted to hurt you. I'm so grateful to you." Nothing I can think of won't sound like something I got from an old movie. But it's all true, and if it goes unsaid, then what do I leave him with?

When I arrive at the store, Ginny, who is serving a customer, points to the back. I squeeze past boxes of records lining the aisle. In the doorway I stop. He's at his desk, rifling through a pile of receipts. He seems smaller, older. His ears poke out of his hair.

He glances up.

"Hi," I say, and my eyes fill.

He looks down. "What are you doing here?"

"I went by your apartment. I thought you'd be there."

"Was that Abel?"

"Yes. He . . ." I was going to say "He phoned me," but I haven't the heart to lie. Or to tell the truth, either.

He picks up a pen and appears to study it. "Are you going to see him again?"

"I'm sorry." I step past the threshold. "I'm so, so sorry. I—"

"How long has it been going on?"

"Just last night." I fish a Kleenex out of my purse and dab my eyes.

"That was the first time?"

"The first time I've even talked to him, since—"

"Would you have told me if I hadn't caught you?"

"Of course I would have."

He balances the pen across his coffee mug. "So you want to be with him?"

I can't bring myself to answer.

"In other words, you do. And I take it he feels the same way."

"Yes," I whisper.

"You're sure of that, now?"

I don't say anything.

"Jesus." He bows his head.

"Troy . . ." I touch his shoulder.

He seizes my hand. "Don't do it." He looks up at me. His eyes are red-rimmed. "Please. Please. Don't do it."

"I'm sorry." I start to cry.

The phone rings. He drops my hand and grabs the receiver. Slams it down. He picks it up again and dials a few numbers. He shuts his eyes.

"I never wanted to hurt you," I say.

"Jesus," he says furiously. He hits the side of his head with the receiver. "Jesus." Hits himself again, harder. "Jesus."

"Stop that!" I grab the receiver and place it in the cradle.

His shoulders slump.

I kneel beside him and take hold of his arm. "We don't have to stop seeing each other. We can still—"

He lets out a bitter laugh. "Don't say it."

"What?"

"We cannot still be friends. I don't want to be your friend." He stares at the phone. "I just want . . ." He withdraws his arm from my grasp. His sleeve brushes a receipt, which falls onto his lap. He picks it up and sets it in the file tray. "I just want you to go," he says quietly.

I stand. "Should I call you later?"

He shakes his head.

"Tomorrow, then?"

He looks up. There's a distance to his expression, an inattentiveness, as if I have distracted him from a grief that has nothing to do with me. "Louise," he says, "you are free. I release you." He picks up the receiver and starts dialling.

CHAPTER FORTY

From looking up their number in the phone book I already know that Abel and his parents moved back to Toronto in 1969. He tells me it was the end of June. He had just graduated. In September, around the time I began working for Mr. Fraser, he entered the University of Toronto. He started out taking courses in general humanities before deciding to major in English literature. Three years later, as opposed to the usual four, he graduated with an honours B.A.

"I always thought you'd end up studying music or science," I say.

"That was all I knew," he says, "music and science."

He lived with his parents during those years. Monday and Tuesday nights, to earn pocket money, he played jazz piano in the bar of a seedy downtown hotel called the Sherwood. It was like being paid to practise, he said, since nobody really listened. At least that's how it was in the beginning. Within a couple of months the regulars were his friends, and for them he played fifties rock-and-roll. The manager wanted to hire him full time, but Abel resisted until he had his degree, and then, with no other job prospects on the horizon, he started working six nights a week.

He rented a room in a nearby house. Most of the other tenants were people from the bar. After only a couple of weeks he took over collecting the rent for the whole place, something to do with the landlord threatening evictions. When he tells me this I say, "Oh, no," because I have a feeling that, to him, a rent collector is somebody who lets people pay what they can and then makes up the shortfall himself. He admits as much but says, "It works out. I cover someone's rent, he covers my drinks."

I could never live in that house, put up with the clamour and intrusion, friends of friends arriving and heading straight for the fridge or strolling into the bathroom to urinate while you're crouched in the tub. Dogs barking, cats spraying the walls, and in the middle of the night somebody banging on the piano. *His* piano. How does he stand it?

By relishing it, that's how. In the mornings he cheerfully vacuums the mutual hallways and picks up the endless litter of beer and liquor bottles. Mr. Clean he's called by the other tenants, who all have nicknames for each other, like a bunch of boys in a tree house. There's His Honour (a sixty-year-old judge with a chronic gambling habit), Mop (a skinny, frizzy-haired former typesetter who lost his left hand trying to repair a lawn mower), Happy (a morose would-be playwright), Mr. Fix-it (the house handyman, a former jockey), Cleats (a would-be tap dancer) and Jimbo (a big, happy guy . . . I don't know what he does).

They have names for each other's rooms, as well. Abel's impeccable room is the Shrine. It's right at the top of the house and has a large picture window looking out onto a mature horse chestnut tree. He says that if he owned a decent camera, he'd set it on a tripod in front of the window and every morning at the same time snap a picture, and then, when he had a year's worth of pictures, all of them dated, he'd mount them at eye level in a ring around the room.

"Would you take them when you leave?" I ask.

"They wouldn't work anywhere else. The point is, you look out the window on any given day one year down the road—September fifteenth, nineteen-eighty, say—and you see that the chestnuts are still green. Then you look at the picture that was taken on September fifteenth five or six years ago—however long it's been—and you see that back then the chestnuts had already turned brown. Then and now . . . you live in both at once."

"What a great idea," I say happily, although it's not the idea I'm happy about. It's that he didn't bristle at the suggestion of moving out of here eventually. He didn't say, "Leave? Why would I leave?"

He is obviously so settled in, especially in this room, which is very much like his room in Greenwoods: the same shade of olive-green on the walls, the same bookcases, the desk and easel. And his four-poster bed with its dark green chenille spread. For me, lying on that bed is the fulfillment of a childhood fantasy. I often lie on it and read when he's working at the bar. I wedge his chair under the door handle to keep people from barging in, then choose a couple of poetry books, because that's mostly what there is. He shelves the books in order of height, tall ones top left, short ones bottom right, so a search for any particular title or author requires the investigation of many spines, some of them seductive enough that I usually get waylaid. (He swears his ordering system is purely for visual effect, but I think he set it up, unconsciously or not, in order to interfere with the tyranny of a predetermined choice.)

This comes later, though, this solitary reading. For the first couple of weeks I try to be with him every minute. Most days he rides his bike to various rundown bars and I tag along on one of the derelict bikes always to be found in the front hall. Awaiting us will be a person with some big plan to start a publishing house devoted solely to books of rhyming poetry, or to open a vegetarian restaurant pet store with glass-topped tables that double as terrariums. One guy—Abel calls him the best photographer in Canada—wants to make a twelve-hour documentary about the minute-to-minute existence of some insect.

"A spider might be better," Abel says.

"What kind of spider?" the guy asks.

"Female black widow."

"Can they be found locally?"

I snort.

"You'd have to go further south," Abel says, as if it were a reasonable question. "Florida or Kansas."

"I'll need a travel budget," the guy says.

How does Abel know these people? From school, from bars. Some are grey haired, some are younger than we are, some seem to have mental problems, some are obviously brilliant. All are male, I'm relieved to discover (except for a terrifyingly intense woman who plays bagpipe jazz and who wants Abel to make a record with her, but because she is plain and at least thirty, I don't consider her a threat). The one thing they have in common is their earnestness. They apply for government grants. They haul out diagrams and resumés, take notes. At first, Abel just listens, but after two or three beers he starts doling out ideas. These people

depend on him heavily, you can tell. I've never seen supposedly heterosexual men look at another man with such
hunger.

It's the same at the hotel bar. Except there, half of the
adoring fans are women, and instead of picking his brain
they light his cigarettes, buy his drinks. Most are middle-
aged boozy types. A few are pretty, though, my age or a bit
older. Rough, sexy girls with husky voices. Has Abel slept
with any of them? He refuses to answer directly, which I
take for yes and which obliges me to be at the bar every
night to make sure I'm the one he leaves with.

By closing time he's drunk. Not slurring drunk but wist-
ful, a soft, suffused look on his face. We walk the three short
blocks to his house. Going to my apartment is out of the
question. There are never any taxis around, and I won't let
him get on a bike, not in his condition. He staggers a little. I
have restricted myself to one draft beer; I'm sober. I'm
tired, though, and if I've been at the bar for more than a
couple of hours, I'm coughing from the cigarette smoke.
Still, I take a few puffs of the joint he lights. Marijuana gives
me energy, and it'll be hours yet before we sleep. This walk
alone takes a good twenty minutes. While everyone who
started out with us disappears in the distance, we gaze at the
stars and contemplate shadows on the sidewalk. If we hear
a cricket, we have to pinpoint its location. All stray cats
must be hailed and won over. "O, masters of profundity!"
Abel calls to them, quoting Neruda. "Secret police of the
neighbourhoods!"

At the house, in the enormous kitchen with its homemade barnboard table, its purple walls and its curling-up,

starlight-patterned linoleum floor tiles that one of the dogs is steadily eating, a tile or two a week, he fixes us something to eat. Sandwiches or fried leftovers. Whoever is still up and wanting conversation gets it. So there goes another hour. Then we wash and dry the dishes, ours and a dozen other people's. Finally it's time to go to his room. First, though, he pours himself a large rum and Coke. "Can I make you one?" he always asks and I always say no, it'll give me a headache. He never suffers from hangovers. I find this commendable. His appetite for liquor and drugs I see as life-embracing and poetic.

At around five o'clock we finally fall asleep. At seven, the judge gets up and wakes me with his coughing. Abel is comatose until his alarm goes off at nine, and then he hops out of bed, refreshed. I try to doze a while longer, but it's next to impossible. Doors are slamming, the vacuum's roaring.

Four hours may be enough sleep for him, but I need twice that much, and within a couple weeks I'm so exhausted I can barely finish a sentence. He buys me iron pills. He urges me to take naps. "You don't have to come to the bar every night," he says. Yes I do, but maybe I don't have to be there for the entire five hours. I start showing up around midnight. I eat supper at the house, ride one of the bikes to my apartment, sleep, shower, ride back downtown, read in his room, then walk to the bar to bring him home unmolested.

The only night we stay over at my place is Sunday, his night off. Sunday mornings we walk in High Park, then go to his parents' house for lunch. His mother hugs the breath out of me. On my first visit she wept. So did I, glad that Abel could witness how much like a daughter I am in this household. She looks like an old lady, with her white hair, but she still wears it long and wound around her head. She still dresses flamboyantly and still wanders the streets at all hours, though in silence now, presumably.

Late Sunday afternoon I take the subway out to Greenwoods. I don't ask him to come. My father and Mrs. Carver are reeling from my breakup with Troy; it's better that I go on my own. When I return to my apartment, and there's his bike in the hallway, the magnitude of my relief is another kind of weight. When will I start taking it for granted that he'll show up? Usually he's sitting at the kitchen table, a glass of rum and Coke by his hand, a volume of the Encyclopedia Britannica opened in front of him. He looks up, his mind still caught by whatever he was reading and finding fascinating and won't forget. If he were me, he'd be way past the *B*'s by now.

One night he says that the fifteen-thousand-dollar inheritance may have been Mr. Fraser's way of buying me time. "He gives you the encyclopedias, he gives you a couple of years' wages. Maybe he was trying to tell you that just because he's gone doesn't mean you're out of a job."

And maybe Abel is trying to tell me that I'm wasting my days, following him from meeting to meeting. I know I am. And yet it frightens me to think of us being apart for too many hours. If only he'd swear never to betray me again. But I can't bring myself to ask it of him. It's one thing to say, "Have you slept with her?" and pretend to be only teasing and curious. To say, "Promise never to sleep with her" . . . there's no rescuing that. I'd sound like the clinging, terrified despot I am.

As a compromise, I start lugging the encyclopedia around with me, the third volume with its endless *Br*'s. While he has his meetings, I sit at another table and read. I find it hard to concentrate, though. I'm accustomed to the cave quiet of Mr. Fraser's alcove, and even if I weren't I can't not listen when Abel talks. In an entire afternoon I'll be lucky to get through a single entry. I begin to feel anxious.

And then, in the middle of October, I am told something that gives me release. It comes from Howie, the retired jockey everybody calls Mr. Fix-it but I call Howie, out of respect. I like him more than I do any of the other tenants, mostly because, apart from Abel, he's the only one who doesn't strike me as being deluded or self-destructive. His riding career ended when a horse fell on him and shattered his knee, and now he works as a groomer at the Woodbine racetrack. Here in the house, he repairs leaky taps and falling-off door hinges, and if anyone asks where something is, he knows. "Third drawer down," he says in his clipped voice. He is chivalrous, fanatically so. He jumps up to open doors and to pull back my chair. He scolds the other men for using language he thinks I might find offensive. "We have a lady present," he says.

It's a Tuesday morning. Abel is doing his laundry down in the basement. I'm in the kitchen with Howie, who has Tuesdays off. At one end of the table I read a three-day-old newspaper and drink coffee; at the other he eats his bacon and eggs. He's a quiet, diligent eater. I almost forget he's there, and then he says, "I hope you don't consider me too forward if I tell you what a fine couple I think you and Abel make."

"Gee, thanks, Howie," I say, touched.

He is frowning. "About time he found the right girl."

"We've known each other a long time."

He doesn't seem to hear. "Some of the girls he used to bring around," he says, "they couldn't hold a candle to you."

My heart quickens. "Girls from the bar?"

"Oh, they're likeable. I've got nothing against them personally. Only they don't have your kind of class. You're more Abel's type, the intellectual type."

"Well," I say, "I hate to admit it, but I worry about those girls. The way they flirt with him. You've seen them. He's a pretty easy target when he's had enough to drink."

"You have nothing to worry about. Abel knows what's what. That girl Bonnie? The redhead? The other night, you weren't there, she goes to sit on his lap and he says, 'I'm taken, Bonnie,' and she says, 'Not right now, you're not.' And you know what he says to that?"

"What?"

"He says, 'Now and forever.'"

"Really?"

" 'Now and forever,' those were his words. 'Now and forever.' He was dead serious. You have nothing to worry about. You take it from me."

And so I do take it from him. I decide to trust his instincts over my own. I remind myself that he knows where everything is in this house, and such is my craving for reassurance it seems possible that he may also know—through the same uncanny avenues open to Mrs. Carver—how everybody *feels* in this house.

I spend that day with Abel, since it's already past eleven o'clock. The next morning I get up when he does, have breakfast with him, then go back to my apartment and sit at my kitchen table and read the encyclopedia, and that's what I do every weekday from then on. My hours aren't exactly office hours—I start late, I take plenty of breaks—still, I'm accomplishing something. Of course, I don't expect this to be a profession. I don't even expect to make it to the end of the *C*'s. My dream is to work with Abel on one of his projects, if any of them ever gets off the ground. I tell him I'm willing to invest some of my inheritance in the one he chooses and to pay the entire rent on a two-bedroom apartment that would allow him to have an office or studio space at home. Constantly I'm trying to sell him on the idea of our living together. Only *not in that house.*

He says, "Everybody here loves you."

"And I love them," I lie. "But I'd feel like Snow White living with the seven dwarfs and their seventy pals."

"I've signed a lease," he reminds me.

Which he could break if he wanted to. Well, I can wait. I can scheme.

CHAPTER FORTY-ONE

A couple of weeks before Christmas the judge buys a fourteen-foot-high spruce tree for the living room, whose ceiling is twelve feet high. "I could've told you it was twelve foot," says Howie, and he saws off the top, producing a second, little tree he mounts on a plank and gives to Abel for his room. That night, after coming back from the bar, Abel and I decorate it. I make aluminum-foil balls. He makes an angel out of cigarette papers and a Q-tip. On her tiny cotton-swab head he glues strands of my hair.

"She looks like a lunatic," I say.

"All the best angels do," he says.

A couple of nights later there's a party to decorate the big tree. It turns out that the judge owns boxes and boxes of antique ornaments. He says that when each of his three marriages fell apart, these boxes were all he walked away with. In exchange, his wives got cars and houses, Limoges china, Waterford crystal.

"But I came out the winner," he declares, holding a blue glass bird to the light.

About fifty people show up, and for a change some of them arrive bearing alcohol and food. The tap dancer, who is now studying opera, treats us to an inflamed version of "O, Holy Night." Abel plays the piano. Somebody hands out carol sheets and we all sing with great gusto. I am happy. I am drunk on the crème de menthe an elderly woman wearing sparkly red slacks keeps pouring into my glass.

My hangover the next morning is a sore throat and cough by the time I'm ready to go home. Abel takes my temperature and says I have a mild fever. He phones for a taxi. "Don't bother dragging yourself to the bar," he says. "I'll come by your place first thing in the morning."

Outside my apartment, Norman, the guy who wants to make the documentary about an insect, is waiting for me. Last week I slipped him two hundred dollars and asked him to pick up a camera that I could give to Abel for Christmas. He found one and has it with him: a refurbished Nikon he claims is worth at least five hundred dollars. "A steal at a hundred and seventy-five," he says.

I let him keep the change, simply to get rid of him faster. For the rest of the day I sleep, waking up once around dinnertime to eat an orange. When I wake up again it's three o'clock in the morning. My sore throat and cough are gone. I'm light-headed, though, wound up, as if I'd drunk a glass of champagne. I get dressed and call a taxi. If I'm not going to sleep any more tonight, I may as well lie awake next to Abel. At the last minute I decide to bring the camera so that we have something under our little tree. Where's the wrapping paper? I can't find it. I empty the purple velvet Seagram's bag I keep my pennies in and use that.

The house is unlocked, as it usually is. In the front hall the sleeping dogs lift their muzzles. "It's only me," I whisper. Buster, the Pekinese, barks once. Lights are on everywhere, but it's quiet.

I climb the stairs.

There's a line of light under Abel's door. He must be reading. Or he fell asleep reading.

I go in.

The woman, curled against his back, opens her eyes. She sits up, pulling the sheet over her breasts. It's the jazz bagpipe player. We stare at each other. I feel as though hands are cupping and uncupping my ears. She punches Abel's shoulder and he wakes and pushes the hair away from his face. "Hey," he says, drunkenly. "Louise."

I approach the bed.

"When did you get here?" he says.

I hit him across the head with the Seagram's bag. He lifts his arms to protect himself. I hit him again. I'm yelling now. "Bastard! Bastard!" The woman runs to the wall. I throw the bag at the tree, which topples over. "Merry Christmas!" I scream.

Out in the hall I stagger. I slip on the stairs. Howie appears. His lean and worried face. "Louise?" He hurries over. I get to my feet and shove past him. Doors open. "What's going on?" bellows the judge. I hear Abel now, calling, thudding down the stairs. I hurry up. The front door won't open.

"Louise." He's right behind me. He touches my arm.

I swing around. "I hate you!" I punch his chest. "I hate you!"

He sways backwards.

"You're sick!" I scream. "You're evil! I hate you!"

The taxi I arrived in is still out front. I bang on the driver's window. At home, on the mat in front of the kitchen sink, I collapse. The phone rings. The sun rises. I go to the bathroom and wash my face.

I feel as if I've been pulled back into a pit of loneliness, and everybody I've ever known is down here. Don Shaw. Troy, poor Troy. Tim Todd . . . did Tim ever get out? Mr. Fraser never did, this is where he died. My father and Mrs. Carver got out but it took them both a long time.

All the lonely people, all of them so much braver than I am. Alice, selling books door-to-door, Debbie with her bridge championships, Aunt Verna lugging her steamer trunk up from Texas. Even my mother, after she left us. Whatever else might be said about my mother, it took guts to traipse around the Prairies looking for work, never once breaking down and asking if she could come home.

Maybe *I* should leave. Jump on a bus and go wherever it takes me. Change my name.

CHAPTER FORTY-TWO

I don't go anywhere. I stay at home and cry. I eat cereal and peanut-butter sandwiches and watch TV with the sound turned down because crying gives me headaches. Every few hours, from eight in the morning until midnight, the phone rings. On the third day I take the receiver off the hook. Not long afterwards there's a knock on my door.

"Anybody home?"

It's my father. I let him in and he hands me a bag of shortbread cookies.

"Mrs. Carver baked a batch yesterday. Thought I'd drop some by." He's peering at me. "Are you all right?"

"I think I'm coming down with something."

He feels my forehead, looks at my tongue and swollen eyes and says that I don't have a temperature, which means it's probably a cold. Am I drinking plenty of orange juice? Do I have enough soup on hand? Yes, I lie, but he goes out anyway and comes back with two bags of groceries. So now I'm stockpiled for more days of crying.

The next morning, around ten-thirty, I'm woken up by another knock.

"Louise? It's me."

I lie very still, as if he could hear me move.

"Are you there?" He knocks again, four light taps. "I hate it that I hurt you. I hate to think of you . . ." Silence, and then, "If you're there, say something. Tell me to go away, but just say something."

A long silence. Will he use his key?

I hear him descend the stairs and then the faint thud as the front door shuts.

Later, on my way to the bathroom, I notice a piece of paper on the hallway floor. It laps against the baseboard beyond the shoals of unopened mail that one of my neighbours has been slipping under the door. I pick it up.

Here's your key. Call me if you can. Abel.

The key is just inside, as if for a few seconds he gave himself the option of sliding it back out. I use my foot to nudge it further in. The paper I let fall.

Three days later I step on another piece of paper. This one is face up; I can see what it says without even bending.

If you call me at the house and the line's busy, you can always leave a message at the bar. I'll come right over as soon as I get it. Abel.

No *Dear Louise*. No *Love Abel*. I pick it up and take it into the kitchen, and under his signature I write, "I'll never trust you again. I never want to see you again."

The mailbox isn't far, only half a block away. I drop in the envelope with a sense that I'm killing the Angel of Love. But when I turn around I find I'm breathing for what seems like the first time in a week.

I spend the holidays at home with my father and Mrs. Carver. Usually, over Christmas, Mrs. Carver goes to Kingston to be with her daughter, but this year Stella and her husband are visiting his family in Calgary, so Mrs. Carver is staying with us. Not overnight, however. Nothing can persuade her to take my old bed, and as for sleeping in my father's study, no, no, no—"That's *his* room"—as if great scientific experiments were being conducted in there.

I don't tell her about Abel. It's too complicated and humiliating. Besides, she had no idea I was even seeing him again. I only say—because I can't hide how miserable I feel—that I was going out with somebody and we broke up. She wrings her hands. I know that she'll tell my father and that the two of them will take care of me now, and they do. I sleep in until eleven, and when I go out into the kitchen she pours me a glass of freshly squeezed orange juice. All day she brings me cups of tea while I lie around reading and dozing. My father, who has the week off, buys a giant jigsaw puzzle called Autumn Splendour and we work on it together at the dining-room table. Sometimes the three of us play a version of charades where it's everybody against everybody else. I tend to win but that's only because I'm so good at deciphering Mrs. Carver's gestures that when it's her turn to act out a phrase I can tell what she's thinking almost as soon as she lifts her hand.

I still cry in the bathroom and at night in bed. I don't wail, though, the way I did at my apartment. Everything here is muted and gentle, as in an English manor. I could live like this forever, I think: the indulged daughter, the fragile spinster. It really seems possible, right up until New Year's Day when my father and I are taking down the decorations and I find myself clutching a hank of drooping tinsel and staring at it with bleak astonishment as if it represented the sum total of everything I had. I sit on the edge of the chesterfield. "I need to get a job," I say.

My father is standing on a chair to reach the angel. He

twists around, and I expect him to say, "There's no hurry, you've got your inheritance, you can stay here as long as you like," or even, "Now might be the time to think about going to university," but what he says is, "It helps to keep busy, keep yourself occupied."

He even has a suggestion. A retired banker, somebody he met through work, has decided to write a history of his Welsh ancestors and is looking for a typist.

"Oh, I've done that," I moan.

"Done what?"

"Worked for an old man."

"Well, of course, he's not young, but you wouldn't know it to look at him. He's one of those energetic types. Full of pep, always on the go. He still keeps an office downtown. I was there last week. He employs a full-time bookkeeper, a very friendly young woman, in her early thirties or there-abouts, very personable. I believe she worked with him at the bank, but either she can't type or she's too busy."

"I can't type *fast*."

"I'm sure accuracy is the thing. Proper spelling and punc-tuation. You might find it interesting, learning about Welsh history. Anyway, it would be something to tide you over until you figure out what you want to do."

"I suppose," I say, only now appreciating what a worry I must be to him sometimes.

A week later I go to see about the job, and all I have to do is say that I'm Saw Kirk's daughter to get myself hired. My feelings are mixed. True, there's nothing elderly or frail about Mr. Roberts. He has a full head of reddish-blond hair, he stands straight and bounces on his toes, he's hearty, he's loud, he says "By God!" a lot, and after only a few minutes he's calling me Kirk as if we've been working alongside each other for years.

Still, I worry about sinking into the twilight life I settled for the last time Abel broke my heart. Here I am again with a nice, semi-retired boss and a job that won't ask very much of me. Fine if you're looking for safety, and back then I was. I thought that my suffering obliged me to drift along until I met up with my fate, which I could never bring myself to fully imagine but which always included Abel, even if it was only as a temptation.

But—as I remind myself—that isn't the case this time. No matter how far down my life I look, I can't see him; there's nothing to flare up any more. The damage is done, it's in my bones, like a limp, and I'm going to have to stop raging about it. Well, I have stopped, almost. Up until a few days ago I kept telling myself, with decreasing faith, "He's sick, he's evil." What I've come around to thinking—and it's just as depressing—is that he simply can't refuse certain people. Howie's story about him fending off that red-headed girl is probably true enough. He can withstand flirting. It's helplessness he collapses under. I'll bet the woman I caught him in bed with did the propositioning, and because she was older, and he was drunk, he didn't know how to turn her down. Right at that moment, confronted with the prospect of humiliating her, he let me fade.

The bookkeeper is a tall, lean woman with a wide seductive face and dark blond hair she wears loose to her shoulders.

"Kirk!" says Mr. Roberts, introducing us. "Slung!"

"*Suzanne,*" she says, rolling her eyes at him, offering her hand—in a jangle of bracelets—to me.

"Louise," I say. Her hand is warm.

She doesn't really work for him, she works for herself; he's just one of her clients, most of whom are likewise retired executives. Instead of talking to her on the phone, they prefer to drop by in person. They go into her office and shut the door. I hear them in there, laughing. Occasionally they show up when she's out somewhere. "Should I wait?" they ask me. They are lost, slumped with disappointment. "When will she be back?" But I can never say for sure. Her hours are irregular because she's also an actress and often has to rush off to an audition. Mr. Roberts keeps irregular hours as well. Where he goes, he never makes clear. To meetings, I presume, until Suzanne tells me he plays poker at an illegal gambling club. "Oh, he's a bad, bad boy," she says, smiling.

There are days when neither of them comes back, and I'm left to answer the phone and to try to decipher Mr. Roberts's handwriting. It's in the evenings that he turns his attention to the family history, working here in the office until all hours, which means that every morning I arrive to find a stack of scrawled notes on my desk. Nothing of a personal nature yet, just general information about Pembrokeshire, Wales, in the mid-1700s: local industry, diet, religion, customs, that sort of thing. So now I know about corn dollies and byres and whinberries and that a cat born in May brings rats to the house and that, back then, if a husband was "impotent, a leper or had fetid breath" his wife could take half of his possessions and kick him out of the house.

Interesting work, as my father predicted. Well, interesting enough to keep my mind off Abel, at least while I'm typing. Still, if it weren't for Suzanne I'd probably call in sick some mornings. When I wake up, the thought of seeing her is what gets me out of bed, and if for some reason she doesn't show up that day, I'm as crushed as any of her clients. She is like a delivery of flowers, always a mild thrill when she comes out of her office and drops onto the reception chesterfield to light a cigarette and chat. The way she kicks off her shoes, crosses her dancer's legs, leans back and shakes her hair seems both unselfconscious and contrived. Staged, in other words, but also entirely true to her nature.

"Well," I say to get her started, "how did the audition go?" and cheerfully, ruefully, she'll say how she knew she didn't have a hope, they wanted an ingenue type this time (a couple of days ago it was a schoolmarm type, before that it was a wholesome type), but what the heck, she gave it a shot. If there hasn't been an audition, I'll ask about Howard and Roy, her two "gentlemen admirers." Not "boyfriends," because they're both pushing sixty, but not lovers, either; she won't have sex with married men. She allows hand holding, though, and lingering hugs. "Lucky them," I say. No, she says, she's the lucky one, and it has nothing to do with being extravagantly wined and dined. It's the mature conversation, the wisdom and perspective. She hopes one day to fall in love with a widower who doesn't worship his dead wife and who wants to start a new family. She says—

and I can't tell if she's serious—"A distinguished older man down on his hands and knees with a bunch of little kids crawling all over him, that's my girlish dream."

It turns out that Mr. Roberts is a former gentleman admirer, something I find out after I catch him sliding his hand around her waist as he's leaving the office. She says, "That's exactly what ended it. All that pawing me in public. And he was always trying to get me to go to bed with him, but I wasn't interested, even though he was divorced by then. This was, what? Five, six years ago now." She starts bouncing on her toes. "Slung!" she yells. "We've already crossed the line! There's a line, and we've crossed it!"

I laugh. She has him exactly. "What did he mean by that?"

"Oh, that once you've kissed a woman on the lips, there's no turning back."

"You kissed Mr. Roberts on the lips?"

"We'd been drinking. Slung!" She begins aggressively unbuttoning her blouse. "I'm going to take off my clothes. Now, you can stay or you can leave, but by God, I'm taking off my clothes!"

I laugh so hard I start to choke. I start to cry. (Shades of my first date with Troy.) She brings me a box of Kleenex and pats my shoulder. "Do you like Chinese food?" she says.

In her white Volkswagen we drive to a restaurant down on Dundas Street. "I love this place," she says after we've both ordered the four-dollar chicken-ball special. "But for the longest time I avoided it because it's where I met the man who broke my heart. He passed himself off as a lonely widower, and then one day, there he was on the front page of the *Financial Post* with his arm around 'Margaret, his charming wife of twenty-five years.' "

"That must have been hard," I say.

"It was. And now—" she opens her hands, "it isn't."

My turn. I know that's why she told me her story, so that I'll feel free to tell her mine. But I can't. The thought of Abel is still such a weight, and I'm afraid I'll start crying again. I notice some men at another table casting her glances. "You could have anybody you wanted," I say.

"So could you."

"Oh, come on."

She rests her chin on her palm. "What do you usually do after work?"

"Go home. Read."

"You don't go out?"

"Not very often."

"Why not?"

I shrug. She looks at me a little longer, then changes the subject to her great-aunt Olive, who lived somewhere along Dundas Street during the Depression. "She was an elevator operator at Eaton's. All her working life confined to a box and a ten-line script: 'Third floor, ladies' apparel. Fourth floor, men's overcoats.' She loved it, though. She never married because back then you couldn't marry and keep your job. She used to say, 'You never know who's going to step through those doors.' "

Three nights later we go out again. To a movie this time, *Alice Doesn't Live Here Any More*, which is about a woman deciding to start a new life as a lounge singer after her husband dies.

"She's already ahead of the game," I say afterwards. "She has an inborn talent. Like you."

"There are about fifty directors in this city who would beg to differ."

"Your imitation of Mr. Roberts, that was perfect. You're an actress. You know you are. You have a stimulating profession." I think of her laughing retired clients and add, "*Two* stimulating professions." I sigh.

She pats my arm. "I take it," she says, "that the great Welsh saga isn't making your heart beat faster."

"Oh, it's okay. It's just . . . well, working in that office isn't like working as an elevator operator. I *know* who's going to step through those doors."

"So what would rather be doing?"

"Working in some *bustling* office, I suppose."

On my lunch hour I start reading the classified ads, but all the jobs I'd qualify for sound like dreary slave labour. For about five minutes I wonder if I should go to university. To study what, though? And I'd be older than everybody else, and I was never very good at sitting still for a lecture. I'm toying with the idea of being a cocktail waitress (if my mother did it, I guess I could give it a try) when Suzanne tells me about a woman she knows—a child psychologist with a hectic practice—who's looking for a receptionist-secretary.

"What's she like?" I ask.

"A cross between Joan Fontaine and Ingrid Bergman. Soft and motherly but very elegant. Mid-forties. Divorced from a callow plastic surgeon named Blake."

"Do you think she'd hire me?"

"Why not? Can you take shorthand?"

"If the person talks very slowly."

"She talks slowly. Come to think of it, she talks *very* slowly."

I get the job and start two weeks later, with the blessing of Mr. Roberts, whose pregnant granddaughter has decided she'd like to be his typist. It's late April, robins hopping around on lawns, yellow forsythia flowers burning through the morning fog. As I walk from the St. George subway station to the office, which is on the ground floor of a Victorian house near the University of Toronto, I have the brisk, wide-awake feeling that I used to detect, and envy, in the steps of other secretaries. Maybe it's because I'm more than a secretary. From the very first morning I was comforting frightened mothers—"I'm sure Dr. McIver sees this kind of thing all the time," "Kids bounce back sooner than you think"—and taking weepy children on my lap. That day I didn't leave until seven o'clock. The next day it was after eight. Katherine—she said to call her that when it's just the two of us—told me I could go home as soon as the last patient was in her office, but I didn't feel right abandoning my post while the mother or father or babysitter was still out in the waiting room. I used the time to read through case histories and try to acquaint myself with all the amazingly various, heartsickening behaviours of unhappy children.

After six months Katherine gives me a good raise and I decide to find another apartment. I'm prone to changing residences in the fall, but the reason has more to do with

Abel, whose ghost hasn't vacated my bedroom yet. If I sleep in there (as opposed to in the living room), whether it's on the bed or on the floor, I'm almost guaranteed to dream about him making love to another woman. "I don't know what to do," I say one day to Katherine, and she's the one who says that the solution may be simply to find somewhere else to live.

I first told her about Abel one sweltering July evening over take-out pizza. It had been an especially long day, we had our feet up on her desk, the fan blowing full-force into our faces, and we were talking about Nicole, an eight-year-old who kept taping her mouth shut and was threatening to *sew* it shut. I felt that the mother was somehow to blame because of her strange nonchalance, not to mention her failure to hide the masking tape. Katherine said that of course the mother came into the picture (she steers clear of words such as *blame*) but that the very concerned, very charming father was no doubt part of it as well. The conversation then turned to charming men in general, to philanderers, and then to the conduct of Katherine's charming, philandering ex-husband, how one time, at a dinner party they were giving, he followed another man's wife right into the washroom. To make sure there were clean towels, he afterwards claimed.

"I'm sure he half believed it," Katherine said. "As he was following her in, I'm sure he was saying to himself, 'I'd better check about the towels.' That way, he could say to *me*—" she smiled, "and he always did, it was the same story every time—that the sex just happened, he had no idea how."

This struck me as so infuriatingly like what Abel would

have said, had I let him speak, that I launched into my story. But in comparison to what she'd put up with—the calculated innocence, the *cruelty*—Abel's betrayal, as I heard myself describing it, sounded almost benign. "He never meant to hurt me," I said. "I know that."

"Maybe not," Katherine said. "All the same, you were right to end it. You acted bravely."

I took this to mean that she wished she'd kicked her husband out sooner.

She is a gently ironic woman with large grey eyes. There is a dreaminess about her that makes you think she isn't even listening until she says something so unequivocal or reasonable (such as, "Why don't you find somewhere else to live?") that your entire way of thinking is suddenly untangled.

I am hoping to get a two-bedroom flat, but through yet another friend of Suzanne's I end up with an entire two-bedroom frame bungalow. The owners, a retired couple named Stan and Ann Canary, have bought a mobile home in Florida and want to hold on to the house as an investment. There's a rose garden, a sun porch, a turret from which you can see the lake, and two semi-feral cats that come and go. On the day I sign the lease, the cats are lolling on the lawn, Suzanne is flirting with Stan Canary, and it occurs to me that the cramp in my throat is from happiness. "I'm happy," I think, as though it were a trick—like balancing on a wire—that I've unexpectedly pulled off. I'm wobbly, I haven't quite got the knack, but it'll come.

It comes and goes, like the cats, whom I name Stan and Ann. It slips through the crack in my heart. I can be doing nothing, looking out my bedroom window at a squirrel clutching its chest in the manner of Mrs. Carver, and there it is: that surge in the blood.

The following spring my father and Mrs. Carver announce their engagement. "Now that you seem settled," my father says, and I say, "Don't tell me *I've* been holding you up!"

"No, no," he says. "We just didn't want to go jumping the gun."

"The way you always do." I kiss him. I'm happy.

The wedding takes place on a warm September morning at Old City Hall, with me, Stella and Stella's husband, Joe, in attendance. Mrs. Carver wears a mauve linen sheath that I helped her pick out. Her bouquet is purple and white orchids. Afterwards, under a rented white tent in my back yard, there's a reception for fifty people, including Suzanne, Katherine, Mr. Roberts and Alice Keystone, whom I haven't seen or spoken to in years but who phoned only a week ago to announce that *she* had just got engaged, to a dog trainer, and because she said, "Oh, I used to just adore Mrs. Carver" (apparently the two of them met a few times, although I have no memory of it), I invited her.

She arrives bearing a large, zeppelin-shaped bundle under each arm. One bundle is wrapped in baby-blue tissue paper, the other in pink, and before I realize that they're wedding gifts—blue for the groom, pink for the bride—I think that, whatever they are, they are meant to match her dress, which has a pattern of blue and pink watering cans.

"They're bolsters," she whispers. "You know, to support your back when you read in bed. I remember your father was always such an avid reader. My mother made them, I only did the 'His' and 'Hers' stitching."

"What a great idea," I say. I laugh because it *is* a great idea, and who else would have thought of it? And because there she is, in her dress, with her flaming cheeks. "I've missed you," I say, also truthfully.

Later, after everyone has gone and I'm sitting in the sun porch eating the last of the wedding cake, I feel an odd wistfulness. It takes me a while to figure out that the feeling is connected to Alice, her engagement. I wish her well, I'm in no hurry to get engaged myself, God knows. But we were fellow outcasts in high school, and now she has somebody to love, and I don't.

Which must mean I *want* somebody to love. But do I? I've grown used to self-sufficiency. I know that loneliness will glide over you like a ghost if you keep still and quiet.

And yet, if I were to meet a man. . . .

There's a man who occasionally comes into the office to pick up his nephew, Peter, and give him a drive home. Peter stutters, except, I've noticed, when he's talking to his uncle Matthew. I've overhead enough between the two of them to know that Matthew lives by himself and coaches Peter's baseball team. He looks to be in his early-to-mid-thirties. Short and with a round, pleasant face. I caught him staring at me once.

He comes into the office the following Friday. Just as he and Peter are about to leave, I ask if he's looking forward to the weekend.

"I sure am," he says. "How about you?"

"I don't have anything planned."

"She could come watch my baseball game," says Peter.

So that's our first date: me watching him coach Peter's baseball team in a tournament. He could hardly have contrived anything to put himself in a more attractive light: the hearty, reassuring leader of young boys. Who is no less hearty or reassuring when they lose.

On our second date, at a French restaurant, I learn that he's an accountant who "came this close" to being married once. "It wasn't meant to be," he says easily. I am warmed by his optimism and by how his eyes soften when we talk about Peter, and yet, by dessert, it's clear that there won't be a third date. "I can't believe it," he says after I admit that Peter's tournament was not only the first game of baseball I'd ever sat through but the first game of sports, period. He says, "You mean to tell me you never rooted for your high-school football team?" He sounds truly puzzled. What *I* find unbelievable is that the only books he owns are *Ask a Handyman* and *The World Almanac of Natural Disasters*.

The next morning I say to Katherine, "It wasn't a complete fiasco. At least I could feel myself *hoping* to be won over."

"Maybe it's still too early," she says.

"You mean, I'm not over Abel? No, I'm over him, I think."

"Do you still love him?"

"I'll always love him. I don't expect to see him again, I don't even want to see him again. And I don't think he's the only man I'll ever love, either. But I don't just *love* him, the way you love an old friend. There's more to it than that."

As I'm speaking I imagine holding my hand a few inches

above a boulder. It's twilight, summer, growing cool. The boulder gives off the heat of the day. My love for Abel is like the heat between the boulder and the falling night. That feeling, or that place.

CHAPTER FORTY-THREE

Eleven months later, out of the blue, I get a call from Mr. Richter. I can tell something is wrong by his hello. I think it's Mrs. Richter, that she has died.

It's Abel. Last night, alone in his apartment, he started vomiting blood. By the time the ambulance arrived he was going into shock. He is stable now.

"I know that the two of you have lost touch with each other," Mr. Richter says, "but his mother thinks a visit from you would do him good."

As soon as I enter the hospital room, Mrs. Richter bursts into tears. Mr. Richter helps her to her feet and the three of us go out into the corridor.

"How is he?" I ask. I only got a glimpse.

"Sleeping," Mr. Richter says. He thanks me for coming. Mrs. Richter clings to my arm. We walk a little way down the corridor and then Mr. Richter gets straight to the point. He says that Abel has cirrhosis of the liver. "Because Abel is so young," he says, "the doctors think that his liver must have been damaged to begin with." He speaks gently, as if he were the presiding physician. "Anyway, the cirrhosis itself isn't the problem right now. It's the ulcers he has developed in his stomach, which the drinking makes worse. Sometimes they rupture, and that is what happened last night."

"He could have died," Mrs. Richter sobs.

She is too distraught to return to the room. "Why don't you sit with him, Louise?" says Mr. Richter. "We will go to the cafeteria."

The chair Mrs. Richter vacated is still warm. I thought he would be yellow and drawn but he looks wonderful with his white face and long wavy hair, his serene expression. I take his hand. It's cold. He opens his eyes. "Louise," he says, and the hardness in me, what remained of it after the phone call, the clot of resistance that got me here dry eyed, just evaporates.

CHAPTER FORTY-FOUR

In some ways, the year of trying to save him is much easier than the years of trying to forget him and the months of trying to hold on to him. Those times I was alone. All I had for a lure was myself. Whereas everybody he knows wants to save him, and the lure, this time, is the whole world.

At first, he doesn't oppose us. He checks himself into the Marwood Clinic. Despite relapsing, he continues to go to twice-weekly meetings for another three months. The reason he stops going is not clear, something to do with his counsellor quitting. "If he would only come home," Mrs. Richter says, "we could watch over him." Which is exactly why he won't go home. He stays on in the basement apartment where he has been living ever since the rooming house sold in the spring of 1975. At around the same time, the piano bar at the hotel closed down, and that's when he started driving a taxi. Does he ever drive drunk? I ask him this while he's still in the hospital; I think it's a question that needs to be asked. He says no, and I find I believe him. For one thing, I realize that he wouldn't risk anybody else's life. What he likes about the job, he says, is that he can set his own hours and travel all over the city, meeting new people, hearing their stories. He's thinking of writing some of the stories down. He sounds hopeful.

But then he always sounds hopeful. When he quits driving, and then when he starts spending almost all day in bed, he claims to be catching up on his reading, learning to meditate. "Everything is fine," he says up until the day he dies.

On my birthday I stop in to see him before going out to dinner with Suzanne. He has a gift for me. Some small thing he has wrapped, without tape, in a page torn from one of his books.

"A rock," I say, feeling it. I unwrap it, and it *is* a rock. "Just what I always wanted."

"It's a meteorite," he says.

I look at it more closely. It's black and rust coloured. Glossy.

"A piece of the solar system," he says.

I reach for his hand and kiss it. "Where did you get it?"

"I bought it."

"Really?" I didn't think he had the strength to go any farther than across the street to the liquor store.

"Years ago," he says.

I look at the torn-out page. It's Rimbaud's "Romance." All four stanzas. "At last," I say.

" 'You're in love,' " he says, quoting from it. " 'Your sonnets make her laugh. All your friends disappear.' "

And then he coughs and a jet of blood lands on my lap.

"Oh, God." I jump up. "Oh, God."

"Sorry." He wipes his mouth with a handkerchief.

The blood slides down my skirt. "Let's go the hospital," I say.

"I'll clean it up," he says, coming to his feet.

"For God's sake, Abel! This is an emergency!"

He stands there looking at the floor, waiting for me to calm down. "*I'll* clean it," I say and head for the bathroom.

When I come back out, he's on his hands and knees, dabbing a sponge at a spot on the carpet. I sit on the bed. Every few seconds he separates the fibres with his fingers, then gets back to dabbing. He bites his lip. His arms shake. I should probably take over except I've fallen into a kind of stupor where I seem to be watching him as though he were a stranger in a movie. Who is he? Why is he so thin and pale?

He glances up. "It's better to get it out right away," he says, and a feeling of pure, ungrasping compassion comes over me for this skeletal human being who is still trying so hard to protect everyone from himself. Not from his claims; he never made those. From his detachment. It occurs to me that the distance I seem to be holding him at right now is the one he has always maintained between himself and the rest of the world. How else do you preserve the illusion that the people you love are perfect? Or that you can bear to let them go?

"I'm sorry," I say. Sorry for the way things are, naturally, but as I speak I'm wondering, why is it that, between us, I got all the anger? I can't believe I sent him that letter.

He stops dabbing and gives me a tender look. "I'm fine now," he says. "Everything's fine."

I nod.

"You'll be fine, too."

"I know."

I leave at about nine o'clock. Some time over the next three hours he takes off his clothes, gets a blanket, a bottle of whisky and a bottle of tranquilizers and goes to the roof of his apartment building. It's a clear night. Lots of stars. He drinks the whisky and swallows the pills, then lies on the blanket.

He is found a little after midnight by Archie, the super-intendent, who wondered why the door to the transformer, which is the same door leading to the roof, was ajar.

CHAPTER FORTY-FIVE

"Always on May eleventh the weather is beautiful," Mrs. Richter declares.

"Is that true?" Mr. Richter says, sounding astonished. He drives below the speed limit, sitting very straight.

"Always," she says firmly. "Always on Abel's birthday."

We are on our way to the ravine to scatter his ashes. The funeral was so crowded that at least a hundred people had to stay out on the church lawn, but today there are only the three of us. Mrs. Richter holds the box, not an urn but a carved wooden box. I have the three green plastic bowls that I bought yesterday at Zellers: green, his favourite colour, plastic because the glass ones were too heavy. We have rolled the windows down, it's so warm . . . already, at only nine o'clock in the morning. Spring has come early this year, the forsythia blossoms finished, the big hardwood trees in leaf. Abel used to keep charts of when the leaves of certain trees opened. This year I have found myself keeping a mental note. Horse chestnuts: April fifteenth. Maple saplings: April sixteenth. Oaks: April twenty-ninth.

At the top of the ravine, there's a small paved lot, empty at this hour. We set the bowls on the hood of the car and Mrs. Richter pours out the ashes.

"So," says Mr. Richter, who has never been here before. "The famous ravine."

But not the ravine it was. A six-lane highway now cuts through it about a quarter of a mile to the east of the river, roughly following the river's course. The sludge factory is gone. Camp Wanawingo has been turned into a grassy area that the city supplies with picnic benches and garbage pails. This walk down, however, is much the same, with the wooded slopes rising up steep as walls. On the eastern slope the white bloodroot flowers are like little jagged cups. A brown butterfly flickers above them.

"Look!" Mrs. Richter cries. "What kind is that?"

"A mourning cloak," Mr. Richter says.

"Ah," she says.

We stop and watch it. Are they thinking it's Abel, or a sign from Abel? I say, "If you want, you could start here."

"Yes," Mrs. Richter says, smiling at me, "let's get started." She goes over to the flowers and throws a handful of ash as if she were broadcasting seed. Mr. Richter goes to the other slope. He looks at it a moment, then selects a silver birch and carefully distributes a bracelet of ash around the trunk. I wait; I want to save mine for the cave. Because I knew I'd be climbing, I've worn running shoes and blue jeans. Mr. Richter wears a black suit. Mrs. Richter is all in red and orange—red skirt, orange shawl, a red bandanna around her head. You'd think she was on her way to a carnival, and it's true that her mood seems gay. She hums and sways her hips, moving down the path.

I point out where the sumach grove is, having told them in the car that it was one of his favourite spots. Then I head for the cave. "Take your time," Mr. Richter calls after me. "We'll meet you back at the car."

I've brought a Swiss Army knife, but the nettles have died back and I climb up easily. How many years has it been? Fourteen. Fifteen. Bars of sunlight spread across the ledge and into the cave's mouth. I let myself imagine that they're a sign from the Angel of Love, who, not unexpectedly, hasn't appeared since before Abel died. I take a step inside. Without even looking up I know that the bats are gone. I go farther in. The spears are gone, too.

I start scattering the ashes. What do I feel? A heaviness of heart. I had hoped to feel something more, to have a revelation, but the things that occur to me have occurred to me a hundred times before. His excruciating sensitivity to the physical world. His rapturous dreams. His guilt and anguish over the death of the baby bat. His dread of interfering and of choosing. But why did he have these feelings in the first place? Why was he who he was?

I go back out onto the ledge and turn the bowl over, letting the wind take what's left. I look for the Richters. After a moment I see them heading toward the river. I'd better go down, they might lose their way. They seem to get confused a lot lately. It doesn't strike me as a sign of age, though. They're like children, expressing amazement at the most casual news, stopping to stare, as if everything they've gone through has made the world more scenic.

The three of us eat an early lunch at the Greenwoods shopping centre. Over coffee Mrs. Richter asks where my mother's ashes are, and I am forced to admit that I haven't scattered them yet.

"Oh, Louise," she says, "it's time."

Back home, after they drop me off, I go down to the basement and retrieve the urn from behind a bunch of old paint cans and bring it upstairs. I suppose I could just throw the ashes in my rose garden. But they're red roses and I think she liked only white. I can't remember.

I carry the urn outside and look around the lawn and this I *do* remember: her arguing with my father that it would be better to have stone courtyards, you don't have to mow stones. I start walking up to Queen Street, toward the stores. Melba's Fashions, Lila's Beauty Salon. But when I get there I wonder what I could have been thinking. I can't just throw the ashes on the sidewalk for everyone to tramp on, and nobody's going to let me scatter them *inside* the stores.

I head east along Queen. I enter Kew Gardens. It's still a gorgeous day, more like late June. I walk past people lying on blankets, past the purple and yellow petunia beds, the tennis courts. None of this would have appealed to her. I reach the crowded boardwalk. She hated crowds. What about the beach? We never went to the beach. I imagine her looking at the sand and seeing only dirt, looking at the sunbathers and seeing only fat. I go to the shore and consider the blue lake, the blue sky, white seagulls lounging on air currents. What would her objection to this have been? Oh, the water's polluted, the seagulls are vicious.

My vision blurs with unshed tears. Abel we could have scattered anywhere. So why don't I just scatter *her* anywhere?

I can't. Somehow I can't.

Back at my house the door is open. I forgot to lock it. I go into the living room and push aside the things on my mantelpiece—books, a stone Buddha, the meteorite—and set the urn in the middle. It really is lovely; she probably picked it out herself. Of course she picked it out. She wouldn't have risked the chance of being put in anything vulgar.

And she wouldn't have wanted to be on a mantelpiece, either. Out in public.

I pick the urn up again and go out to the sun porch and put it on a shelf between some vases and clay pots. There, that's better. Whenever I'm out here—watching the sun go down, looking at my roses—I'll see it, I'll think, "My mother." I won't forget her, that's for sure.

Not that I would have anyway. Not that we forget.

ACKNOWLEDGEMENTS

For their generous counsel I am indebted to:

The experts—Dr. Rick Davis in Guelph, Dr. Donner Dewdney in Des Moines and Dennis James at the Centre for Addiction and Mental Health in Toronto;

The friends and family—Christopher Dewdney, Beth Kirkwood, Marni Jackson, Anne Mackenzie and Brian Fawcett;

The agents—Jackie Kaiser and Nicole Winstanley;

The editors—Iris Tupholme at HarperCollins Canada, who is my support, and Sara Bershtel at Metropolitan Books in New York, who is my beacon.